# *Jason Cody*

# *Wheel on the Nile*

**By J Cruz**

*For*

*Max*

*JCz*

*27/09/2021*

Published in August 2021

ISBN 978-1-9164780-1-5

Published by Poseidon Publishing

Poseidon Publishing


PoseidonEpub@gmail.com

**Dear Reader,**

The following story is a fictional account based at the time of the attacks of 9/11 on the U.S.A. The characters in this story are fictional creations and hold no relation to anyone living or dead. The story which follows was pulled from my dreams and imagination.

Thank you and I hope you enjoy reading it.

**J Cruz**

# *One*

The dry and barren lands of Egypt are divided into East and West by the waters of the Nile as it runs its serpentine course to the Mediterranean Ocean. A ship plies those waters racing ahead of eight larger pursuing ships. The ancient paddle steamer the SS Karim runs at full speed as the larger cruise boats pursue it. Armed militia line the railings of the pursuing ships and fighters run along the banks of the Nile. Jason Cody runs across the sun deck of the Karim, keeping low. He stops at the circular sun deck bar and finds Forester coaching Abu on ammunition supply. A voice cuts across the noise of the preparations.

"Jason! Jason!" Cody turns as Sara Peters runs to him. "Jason, I'm sorry!"

"Sorry? About what," Jason asks.

"Jason, I'm sorry. I saw your sister's number on your phone and I asked Mister Kohlemete to call but the lines to the States are jammed. Are you sure she was in the North Tower?" Jason looks away, hearing his sister's screams in his head. His heart catches in his chest as a shadow crosses his face. Jason looks Sara in the eyes and says.

"Yes, thank you! But you shouldn't have done that. Kohlemete should be calling for Military support. We need them to get through this."

"Jason, Kohlemete says they're not coming. As soon as he mentions the Karim, they hang up. Jason, we're on our own!" Jason looks into Sara's eyes, seeing the fear there, he cups her head in his hands and says.

"Sara, I promise you we will get through this, all of us. I won't let anything happen to you or the others." Tears fall from Sara's cheeks as she mouths, *'I love you.'*


"Sara, you need to get to safety. Please." Sara steps back but stays silent amid the heat of the day and the noise of the preparations. She holds Jason with the pain in her eyes and the tears that fall from them. A stray bullet strikes the deck near Jason's foot, bringing the two out of their trance.

"Jason!"

"Sara, get below. Go now!"

"Please be safe!"

"I will," Jason promises and runs the distance to the forward position he picked out earlier. As he approaches, he cannot see Kopi or the rifle he'd asked for. He stops, looking around the sun deck at the passengers and crew. He sees them looking to him for guidance, for strength, for leadership. The excitement of the preparations has been replaced with a fear thick in the air. Jason can see it in their eyes. The fear is thick. It's as if the hot air of Egypt is a tangible thing trying to strangle him. He finds it difficult to breathe. Jason stands tall trying to be strong for all but his palms sweat and his stomach is in knots. He thinks.

*'Days ago I was a Junior Agent still wet behind the ears, waiting to be assigned to South America. Look at the mess I've made of things. Powers, you said I was the best you ever trained, that I was ready for this assignment. I hope to god you were right!'*

**Eight Months Earlier.**

**Quantico, FBI Training Facility, Virginia, USA, 10:24 February 12, 2001**

3

Megan Powers adjusts the gun belt over her hips so it accentuates her figure. She checks herself in the mirror, hanging in her locker and says.

"Let's see, hair in place, except for the one silver wisp. Lipstick and mascara are looking good, killer chocolate eyes, perfect. Game face on!" She closes her locker and walks from the staff lounge. She pins her ID to her shirt and dusts off her instructor's badge as she goes. Megan is rounding the corner, heading for the Armory, when she spots a familiar face.

"Junior Agent Jason Cody, how are you?"

"Fine Powers how are you?" Jason smiles at the surprise meeting.

"I've been better but I hear you're about to become part of the Bureau's dirty little secret?" Cody stops walking and looks Megan Powers in the eye. He feels his chest constrict and takes a breath to calm himself saying.

"I'm not supposed to talk about that. How did you know?"

"Jason, all of the instructors know. How do you think Assistant Director Roberts chose you? He didn't pull your name out of a hat, you know. I wrote a very nice recommendation for you." Jason breaths out and smiles, saying.

"Oh? And what's that going to cost me?" Megan stops and gives Cody the once over.

"I'd say your body but you know that's against 'Regs' but, I have to say, yum! Six-foot-two, dark curly hair and those hazel-brown eyes that never stop asking, if I was going to get sacked for having fun, you would definitely be my second choice."

"Second?"

"Have you seen Xavier Rodriguez? That boy's built like a Sherman Tank and those thighs! Oh my god! Definitely my first choice." Cody laughs.

"You really know how to hurt a guy Powers. Well, maybe the next batch of recruits will have the guy who's worth it?"

"Next batch? Cody, haven't you heard? Recruitment's been canceled. No new field agents until the Bureau can find the funds." Jason creases his brow as they walk towards the Armory.

"What will you do?"

"Reassigned somewhere, I guess."

"I'm sorry."

"Ah, don't worry. I'll tough it out until the funding comes through. They can't get rid of me that easily." Megan says, looking concerned. She turns to Cody. "When do you leave?"

"Wednesday, thought I'd get some practice fire in."

"What, you planning on killing someone out there?"

"No! I just..."

"Jason, don't bother. I've never trained a student more prepared for foreign assignment than you. Save those bullets for when you need them. Oh, and one more thing, come on in." Jason steps back.

"In the Armory? I thought no one was to go in there but you?"

"Jason, you're about to be assigned to Cairo, Egypt, where the FBI is not supposed to have Agents or offices. You are no one. Now, get in here!" Megan opens the outer door and an inner storeroom. She flips on the lights and rips open a box.

"Here. These were supposed to be distributed to all Agents in the field last year but they canceled the project." Megan opens a plain white box and hands it to Cody. "It looks like the standard-issue mobile phone but it has some extra features. Most importantly, a GPS Mapping and Tracking System. It's designed to provide maps and directions for cities around the world."

"Why cancel it?"

"Support. The maps need constant updating and the Bureau doesn't have the money but it might come in handy."

"Megan thanks but I don't want to get you in trouble."

"No trouble Cody. Now, get out of here. Go find yourself a little cutie and have some fun!" Jason nods, smiling and turns to go.

"Hey, Cody!" Jason turns back. "While you're out there, save the world for me." Jason grins broadly.

"Will do Powers." Megan watches him as he walks away and says.

"God knows, someone needs to."

## Venice, Florida, USA, Huffman Aviation 10:43 March 04, 2001

It's a hot and humid day in Venice. The few passing clouds are providing little shelter from the sun. Two Middle Eastern men, Mohamed Atta and Marwan Al-Sheh step out of their Ford Mustang in front of Huffman Aviation School. Atta straightens his Armani shirt and jeans. Atta pushes back black hair and scratches his two day old beard. Atta leads the way into the air-conditioned office. The owner appears from the back office wearing a dark blue Huffman Aviation shirt and cap.

"Your lessons started at nine o'clock this morning. I've had your instructors waiting for you for the past two hours. So what the hell? If you two can't be on time, do us the courtesy of phoning at least. Mohamed Atta stops and looks at Marwan.

"We are sorry but we were held up. It won't happen again."

"Good, because if you are late again, don't bother coming back. You two say you're serious about training to be commercial pilots. Well I suggest you start acting like it. Now let's save as much of the day as we can."


### Washington DC, FBI Headquarters 08:56 August 06, 2001

Sunlight filters through thick plates of bulletproof glass into Neal Roberts's office. Roberts sits with his shirt sleeves rolled up, leaning over his desk. At fifty-two, he has been in the Bureau longer than most. His twenty-four long years of service has got him to where he is. It has also turned his once black hair gray at the temples. Permanent worry lines form around his mouth and between his eyebrows. It's been a long time since he made the move to administration and then to the Assistant Director's chair.

Neal waits for the call as he looks over reports. It's the same call every morning at nine. The call came from Arkansas during the previous administration. This summer, they come from Crawford, Texas. After three years of budget cuts under the Democrats, Roberts hopes they might have a chance. 'At least this administration is pro-security.' He thinks.

He glances at the clock on his desk, nine-o-seven. Neal shifts in his seat, knowing the later the call, the worse the news will be. His eyes fall on the picture of his wife and daughter. He smiles and wishes he could see them more. The job has always come first with him. Perhaps he can take them out this weekend for a picnic, somewhere remote, no phones, no pagers, only the three of them for a whole weekend. Perhaps?

The light on his phone glows red. Neal punches the button and lifts the receiver before it rings.

"Yes Sir."

"Roberts, I need all reports and information the Mole had access to gathered, collated and ready to transport. I want everything confined to a secure site. No one is to have access except myself, you and the god damn interrogators!" There is a pause and Roberts becomes concerned. Never has he heard the Director lose it like this.

"Sir," Neal pauses. "It sounds like it was pretty rough in there." He says, cringing at his own words.

"You don't know the half of it!" The Director says. Roberts can hear the forced control in the Director's voice.

"Neal, this Mole thing has changed everything for us. As far as Congress is concerned, everything we do is wrong. The President says we should have tried and executed the bastard. I'm not sure I disagree with him. When I think of the damage he has done. On top of that, everything we have for the President is old news. Good god, I can't believe the only thing we could come up with is a new theory on Al Capone."

The Director pauses.

"What about the intel on the Al Qaeda members taking pilot training," Neal asks.

"Shelve it! CIA had it first. At least they gave their report on it before I did." *'No room for second place.'* Roberts thinks but says.

"So you want us to gather everything the mole had access to or worked on. Is that right, sir?"

"Yes, and I want our best people on damage control."

"Sir?"

"You know the rumor about combining the two intelligence agencies."

"Yes sir?" Roberts says, his brow creasing further.

"Well, it's just passed the rumor stage. The President's aide showed me a draft copy of a bill to be introduced later this year. The FBI and CIA will be combined into one agency, with the CIA running the show. Neal this is no longer about national security. This is survival!"

"Right, we put an 'eyes only' security classification on all mole-related documents," Roberts says.

"I want a total lock-down on all information to and from Hanssen." The Director adds.

"Can we do that? I thought the Justice Department was handling arrangements."

"Justice knows what a hot potato this is and are happy not to be involved. We'll be handling all interrogations. We give the CIA only what pertains to them. That goes for the

Pentagon and the White House, that way it appears to be impartial."

"Congress will scream bloody murder if we don't let them in on the interrogations."

"That's where you come in Neal. I'm sorry but you're the only one I can trust to handle this thing right. You know how it is."

*'Yeah! Shit rolls downhill.'* Roberts thinks but says.

"Yes sir, I do."

"Neal, I don't have to tell you how important this is. I'm relying on you. We can't afford any slip-ups. One wrong memo and the Bureau could be history. I'll do everything I can at this end. It's your job to put the best face on what comes out of the interrogations."

"I understand sir."

"Good! I won't be back until the President returns."

"Understood sir." The Director hangs up.


Roberts stares at the receiver in his hand for a full ten seconds before placing it back in its cradle. He props his elbows on his desk, massaging his temples with both hands. Neal doesn't have a headache yet but can feel one on its way. *'So much for the weekend,'* he thinks, as he reaches for the half-empty bottle of aspirin in his top drawer.

*'Why me.'* Neal thinks as he pops two tablets in his mouth. He knew being Assistant Director wasn't going to be easy. This is another situation where he questions accepting the job. The last time had been the bombing of the USS Cole. What a media circus that had been. The problem is, this is set to make the Cole look like a training exercise. He buzzes His secretary Jean and asks her to get MacDonald ASAP. He realizes he is being short with her but lets it stand. The sooner things get rolling, the better. He places his head in his hands, thinking about the mole, Robert Hanssen.

Twenty years of spying for the Russians and until the CIA turned him, the Bureau had no idea. At least that's the way the media is playing it. In fact, they'd been narrowing it down for months. It was only by chance the CIA got there first. A knock at the door brings him back to the present. Roberts buzzes the door lock.

"Come in, Nathan." Nathan Mac Donald pushes in and takes the chair opposite. Like Neal, his dress is a study in mediocrity, gray suit, white shirt and tie. Bureau agents pride themselves on attracting as little attention as possible. In Washington DC, a city of suits, a small army of agents could cross the Mall without a second glance. Nathan is only a year Neal's junior but his energy and quick movements belong to a much younger man. Although lately, he's been losing the battle of the bulge. As a result, his stomach strains at his trousers and his jacket remains unbuttoned. His thick brown hair is laced with disorganized gray streaks.

Nathan looks across the desk. When Neal doesn't speak, he takes the lead.

"What's up?" Neal takes a breath and says.

"We have full control of the mole interrogations." Though welcome news, it inwardly sounds alarm bells. The overtime alone will be enormous. Nathan mentally makes a note to cancel all engagements outside of work and sleep for the next three months. So much for the holiday in Barbados.

Neal continues. "This is to be *'Eyes Only'* security. That means the Director, myself, you and the interrogators."

"What about secretarial staff?"

"Hand-pick those with the highest security. Interview each one. Make sure about loyalties. I want zero leaks on this. No digital copies.

"Taped transcripts?"

"Nothing! Hard copies only. If it won't go through a shredder, we don't use it. CIA, Pentagon, White House, all get copies of only the information pertaining to them."

"They'll want their people in on the interrogations." Mac Donald says.

"No! Is the answer to all requests."

"What about the report on Al-Qaeda members taking pilot training? They were reported training in Commercial planes." Mac Donald asks. Roberts creases his brow and stares at the desk.

"Shelve it. It's old news." Mac Donald frowns.

"Let me see if I can find a couple of junior agents to hand it to. Maybe Miller and Jones? You know, for the experience."

"Fine. As long as it doesn't take anyone off Hanssen."


**El-Minya Egypt, 16:23 August 29, 2001**

The afternoon sun creeps across the azure sky as the market of El-Minya, awakens from its mid-day slumber. Amber and gold colors reflect from the mud-brick buildings. A light breeze moves over the rooftops but does little to cool the air between the stalls while the shoppers move in lazy chaos along the dirt road.

The crowd respectfully parts for a man in black robes and turban. He appears an apparition in the waves of rising heat. With a long gray beard and dark features, he walks towards a carpet shop. Seeing the Man-in-Black, the proprietor of the shop slips into the back. A bearded gentleman in white emerges to greet the Man-in-Black. He signals a coffee seller across the road. Two boys run across and assemble a makeshift café table in a patch of shade. Having greeted each other warmly, the two gentlemen are seated on boxes between the carpet seller's and a pot maker's shop. Strong coffee and chrysanthemum tea appear with a large nickel kettle of hot water.

An hour later, the men rise. The boys clear the cups, crates and large kettle. The proprietor of the carpet shop pays the eldest boy. He runs back to his father, the money locked in his hand. The passers-by have begun to dwindle. The coffee seller stacks his crates and packs away his stall. He moves the cups and kettles into his house on a narrow alley. Inside, the mother and girls do the washing up while the father takes the large kettle into a back storeroom.

Carefully he unscrews the bottom revealing a secret compartment. He takes out a tape recorder packed in rags. The eldest son, standing at the door, receives the tape and leaves.

In the dusty alley outside, the son is accosted by a Beggar. The son backs away in fear. The Beggar stinks of sewage and sweat. His eyes, two black beads in a sun-browned face. The teen turns to go but a dirty hand shoots out, catching his wrist. The son cries out as he struggles. His father hearing the cries, runs to the door. He sees his son being accosted by the filthy man. The father kicks the Beggar violently. Finally, the dirty man releases the son, who races away. The father continues screaming and ranting at the Beggar. He does not see but feels the knife cut into his abdomen. The Beggar steps deftly away as the corpse drops where it stood. The Beggar whistles to unseen comrades then runs after the son. The family emerge from the house but are pushed back inside by armed men.

A young boy is hiding behind sacks of grain and stores. He has been resting in the storeroom, his secret place. He's seen his father remove the tape and give it to his brother. Now the sound of gunmen in the family house tells him to hide. He pulls back into the sacks of grain and coffee. The gunmen enter the room but see only the pile of stores. One fires into the sacks but the boy remains still. They return to

17

the main room of the house where the family cowers under Russian made rifles. The boy peaks out from his hiding place wide-eyed but cannot see. He can only hear the pleading of his mother and her screams, as each brother or sister are murdered. Outside the neighbors hear the muffled screams, as the sounds of death tinge the evening sky red. While the sun god Ra, drops behind the hills of El-Minya.

### Cairo Egypt, Old Cairo Hotel 01:58 September 3, 2001

*Jason Cody stands on the observation deck of the World Trade Center. He steps down to the bottom set of seats and leans out over the railing looking down along the smooth sides of the building. He sees the metal edging running down the building. They appear to merge further and further away. His eyes are drawn down, pulled down the building. His mind reels as vertigo grips him. Shifting his eyes to the horizon, he grips the railings*

*In the distance, an object catches his eye. A jet banking against the cloud streaked sky. It appears motionless as if suspended by strings. He can see the vapor trails off the tips of the wings and the tail section with the AA symbol. The sun glints off the wing as it turns. He can see the line of windows and the passengers in their seats...*

Jason Cody sits up in bed, covered in sweat. He looks at his phone as it vibrates on the side table. Cody groans, two o'clock in the morning and it's time to get going. He shuts off the alarm, showers and dresses quickly. Twenty-six years old and already in line to be a full Field Agent, only one last training mission to complete. He combs his dark hair in the mirror. In fifteen minutes, he is out the door of his hotel room, slipping down the back stairs.

Walking along the road, Jason feels his phone vibrating in his pocket. He glances at the screen, smiles and answers.

"So why is my beautiful little sister calling me at two in the morning?"

"No, is it? I'm so sorry I forgot to check again!" Jennifer says.

"Don't worry Sis. I was up anyway. So what's happening in the big apple?" Jason asks.

"Oh, not much just wanted to give you the news. I ... what do you mean you're up, you're not sleeping again? You're not having more dreams, are you?"

Cody turns right and says.

"Nothing of the kind I have a story to cover."

"Oh!" Jen says, knowing the code.

"Yeah, I'll tell you all about it later. So what's this news that almost woke me in the middle of the night?"

"Oh, I got it the M.M.C. job. I won't be in the main offices but hey, I'm doing it. Got the job and living the dream in the Big Apple. Oh, and I'll be working at the World Trade Center!" Jason misses a step and stumbles.

"Oh, hey. That's great." An old green compact pulls up. Banged and rusting it has seen better days. The door opens as it stops. Jason creases his brow as he says.

"Hey sis, my rides' turned up. I gotta go but I am so proud of you. I'll treat you to a night out when I get back. Love you, Jen. Gotta go. Bye!"

"Bye big brother," Jennifer says, sitting on her bed. She presses the disconnect key on the phone and holds it to her heart. She turns her hazel eyes to the window looking to the East. Something doesn't feel right but she can't fathom what it might be, other than her big brother being on another mission. Jen's heart pounds in her ears as she looks out.

"I miss you, my stupid big brother. Wish you were here. Please be safe!"

## Old Cairo, Egypt 02:37 September 3, 2001

The half-moon throws a dim light from a cloudless sky. Blue-gray details of the houses lining the road come to life, as Jason's eyes grow accustomed to the dark. On the rooftop of a deserted house opposite the safe-house, Junior Agent Jason Cody waits. He checks the alley below him on his left and the road between his position and the safe-house.

"Okay Mark, the coast is clear," Cody says, speaking to his lapel.

"Now stay alert. This is routine but you never know." Mark reminds him.

"Got it boss," Cody responds.


From his position on the rooftop, Cody looks out on the length of road running directly towards him. It turns to his left in front of the corner safe-house and runs away towards central Cairo. The roof Jason is on is a perfect position for observation. He can see anyone approaching on the road and the alley alongside the house.

Cody crouches behind a low wall surrounding the roof terrace. Old mud-brick construction crumbles at his touch, as a hot breeze blows over the rooftops. It dries his perspiration before it shows on his shirt. He wears typical tourist garb, Khaki shirt and trousers. With his shoulder bag, he looks the part and could be lost in a crowd of tourists.

The smell of the land and dying cooking fires comes to Cody on the breeze. Only two other ways onto the road exist. On his left is the alley running alongside the house where he sits and there is another alley which enters from his right, twenty-five yards up the road ahead. Jason watches as Mark Rider enters the corner safe-house. A few minutes later, he sees the informant appear from his left and enter. Except for the single door, there is no other entrance.

"Heads up Mark, he is entering the building."

Jason settles down to the waiting. *'Just another surveillance job.'* He thinks. *'Like the last one and the one before that.'* He looks over the road and checks the receiver, green lights across the panel and the tape is recording. He has finished a year of specialized training with distinction. Tonight he will complete his final field training. After this he will be assigned to South America, Brazil hopefully. He's trained for the assignment and is fluent in Spanish and Portuguese. He also familiar with some of the indigenous dialects. With any luck, he could move up quickly. He scans the road before him and pulls out his earpiece. Just another surveillance job. The same routine he was doing before being accepted for overseas assignment.

The meeting is dragging on longer than Cody expected. Usually, these things are over in five minutes. He wonders what the holdup is. Jason's attention is drawn to a dark figure entering the road from the alley ahead. He watches a hunched figure as it makes its way towards Jason's position. The figure stops opposite the corner safe-house. Jason watches it settle into the recess of a doorway and prepare for a night's sleep. As Cody looks, a cold chill runs down his spine and the hairs on the back of his neck stand up.

The overwhelming feeling something is wrong pulls at his mind. He checks the receiver and tape are working then pushes the earpiece into his ear. He can hear Mark's voice speaking rapidly in Egyptian. The informant's voice sounds scared and keeps demanding the money in English. Jason pulls out the infra-red scope. He focuses on the figure crouched in the doorway, the conversation in his ear. A cold sweat runs down his back. The image is fuzzy green but he can clearly make out the eyes. The Beggar's eyes are locked on the safe-house. In his ear, Jason can hear the informant yell something. It sounds like *'wheel.'*

Jason ducks below the wall, speaking softly into his lapel.

"Mark, possible trouble, be alert..." The sound of an explosion through his earpiece stops him mid-sentence. He pops his head up above the wall and scans the street below, nothing. Through the earpiece, he hears machine gunfire and the sound of Mark's Beretta. Jason doesn't think he acts. His reflexes have taken over as he vaults down the stairs.

Cody stops himself as he reaches the door, sweat covering his brow. Taking a breath, he makes quick checks of the alley, clear. He checks the street, nothing. *'Wait! The Beggar.'* He pulls his head back into the alley a moment before the wall in front of him explodes. . He hears the sound of a bullet whizzing inches from his face. Cody's Beretta appears in his hand. Jason turns, firing two shots in the Beggar's direction, as the Beggar disappears into the far alley.

Jason sprints across the road. He puts the safe-house between himself and the alley where the Beggar disappeared. He turns, kicks in the door and jumps to the right, his back to the wall. The door explodes from within. Bullets and splinters fly into the street. Silence follows. The splintered door creaks eerily on its hinges. Jason can hear footsteps retreating. He pushes open the door with one hand while staying pressed against the wall. Nothing. He bursts into the room gun raised. Empty. He moves to the opposite side of the room and peeks through a doorway into a short hallway. Slipping into the hall, he moves towards the back of the house. As he does, the sound of voices grow louder. A single door stands on the right, a carpet hanging opposite. Jason faces the door, raises his gun and kicks.

Bad move! In the far wall of the small room, a hole has been blown out. Two men are trying to push through the hole at the same time. When the door slams open, the same two men attempt to swing their guns around to shoot. The Beretta goes into rapid-fire. Six shell casings eject in the air before the men can free their weapons. Jason back peddles as he fires, looking for the wall behind him. Instead of finding the wall, he falls backwards through the hanging carpet. Cody rolls left out of the line of fire as bullets shred the old carpet. Springing up, he pastes himself against the near-wall for shelter, covering his face against the dust.

The dust clears. Cody hears the cursing of retreating gunmen. He looks at the room around him. Table and chairs upturned, the body of a man stretched out on the floor in front of the entry. Another body in front of Jason against the far wall, it's Mark.

"Mark! Mark!" He whispers urgently. No sound comes from the still form. Sounds of yelling from the other room bring him back. He again presses himself against the wall. His Beretta aimed at the carpet covered doorway.

The sounds subside, degenerating into shouts and curses. Jason pushes aside the carpet, checking the hallway. He finds it and the room across empty. The only evidence of the gunmen is an irregular hole blown out of the thick mud-brick wall. Bloodstains covering the broken wall, testify to his accuracy. Cody returns to the room hidden by the hanging carpet. He moves to Mark's side and gently turns him from the floor. Blood drips thick and sticky from Mark's chest. An expression of pain crosses Jason's face as he looks over the remains of his friend and mentor.

Mark's body oozes blood as Jason pulls him onto his back. He stops. The horror of the moment strikes him. The smell of the blood. The sweat and heat of the room all congeal and go to Jason's stomach. His head swoons. Jason feels his own conscience slipping away and puts a hand out, catching Mark's outstretched hand. Jason grasps the hand and Mark's hand grips back.

Cody catches his breath. Mark's chest is making small movements. Jason places his fingers on his neck, looking for a pulse. There is a thread of a heartbeat.

"Mark, Mark, can you hear me." Mark coughs, his chest going into spasm, blood spurting from his lips. He controls the coughing to speak. Cody moves in close listening.

"Get away. Tape."

"What tape?" Mark pulls his hand free from Cody's grip and points to the second man lying in the room.

"Get tape. Attack on US Soil Go." The effort has been too much for Mark. He dies, his hand outstretched, pointing at the body of the informant.

Cody rechecks his pulse. Mark Rider is dead. Jason moves to the body he tripped over as he stepped back through the carpet. What Cody thought was a man he sees is only a boy. Seventeen or eighteen with dark curly hair. He is dressed in a dirty white shirt and trousers soaked in blood. Cody makes a quick search of the body going through his pockets and under him but he finds no tape.

The heat is rising in the small room. The stench of blood and sweat makes Jason's head swim. His first instinct is to get out of there. Cody stands to do so but the memory of Mark's words stops him. *'Remember, if anything goes wrong, get the gear and get out before the authorities turn up.'* Cody turns half expecting to see Mark giving one of his lectures. When he looks, his breathing is easier, a cool breeze has entered the hot little room. Mark lies on the floor, his hand pointing at the informant his eyes looking directly at Jason. The voice is too real to be his imagination. Jason looks into Mark's eyes and sees life and Mark looks back. Cody shakes himself and the feeling goes. When he looks again, he sees Mark as he actually lies. His hand outstretched pointing at the informant but his face is turned blindly to the ceiling.

A sense of urgency grips Jason. He is compelled to follow Mark's last order from the grave. Cody pulls at Mark's shirt and removes the wire he'd attached earlier. He reaches around to Mark's back and pulls out his holster but is unable to find his handgun. He searches the hallway and the room where the gunmen entered, no sign of it. Probably carried off by one of the shooters. Cody sweeps the floor with his feet, erasing his footprints. He backs his way out of the house, collecting his brass as he goes. Jason sprints across the road and returns to the roof. He grabs the equipment and quietly slips down to the door. As he approaches the front door, Jason hears the sound of a car stopping.

Jason cracks open the door and peers out through the alley entrance. Across the road, blue flashing lights blind him momentarily. He squints against the glare and sees two Cairo Police getting out of their car. One notices the splintered door hanging off its hinges. They pull their guns and enter the house where Mark's body lay. Cody waits a moment. When he is sure it is clear, he slips into the alley and walks away.

### Old Cairo Hotel, Cairo, Egypt 04:18 September 3, 2001

Jason's shaky hand works the key to his room. The Old Cairo Hotel was once a five-star establishment but time and decay have made it a passable two-star. He enters the room and stands stock still, unsure what to do. His chest is tight and he struggles for air. He focuses on the floor, forcing a deep breath. It comes out ragged. His stomach churns. Jason drops his bag and runs to the toilet. Five minutes later, Jason sits on the floor of the bathroom in a sweat, trying to focus on what's happened. He remembers the blood on the broken wall and his stomach makes another complaint.

A few minutes later, Cody steps out of the bathroom and breaths deeply. With the oxygen comes clarity. Cody knows what must be done, Mark's words still echoing in his ears. *'Cover your tracks.'* He heads for the bath. Stepping into the tub, Jason strips off his clothes, checking himself for wounds. He clears the tub of his discards and starts the shower. He embraces the cold water hoping it will wash away more than dirt and blood. After several minutes of scrubbing, Jason emerges feeling clean only in the physical sense.

Roughly rubbing himself down with a clean towel, he picks up the phone and dials.

"Hello." The voice at the other end answers sleepily.

"Alistair, it's Jason. We have a situation." The line carries static for a moment, the voice returns.

"Jason, what's happened?" Alistair McAllen's English accent comes across loud and clear.

"Ambush, Mark is dead, the informant as well."

"Are you all right?"

"Yes." Jason stops, his chest beginning to constrict again. He forces a calming breath and continues. "Yes, I think so. There was a lot of blood but I've cleaned up. It's just my things I need to deal with." Alistair asks.

"Where are you?"

"My hotel."

"Jason, listen carefully. I want you to wait twenty-five minutes. Gather everything and place it in a sheet from your bed. Make a bundle and leave it outside your door for laundry pick up."

"What about the equipment?"

"Everything Jason. Then I want you to get some sleep. I need you sharp in the morning."

"Sleep! Alistair, you must be joking!"

"Then I want you to make a sequential report of what happened tonight, every detail. I will be running you through it tomorrow. We are going to handle this as an attack on a lone agent. Remember Mark Rider acted alone, you were asleep all night and know nothing about it. It's four-thirty-five. I want the laundry out at five. Have you got that."

"Yes, five o'clock."

"Listen to me dear boy. I know this is difficult but we have got to handle this properly. Remember you were in all night and know nothing. I will see you in the morning." The sound of the receiver settling back in its cradle ends further objections. Jason checks the time and gathers his things, holding back his Beretta and bag. At five precisely, he places the bundle outside his room.

From the end of the hallway, a boy emerges from an alcove and snatches up the bundle. He disappears into the exit stairwell. He runs from the back of the hotel to an open bed truck sat idling. He hefts the bundle to waiting hands and runs off into the dark, while the truck speeds away in the opposite direction. A bent and twisted Beggar watches the truck go and curses the night.

# *Two*

Jason has been unable to close his eyes or even think of sleeping. His mind dwells on the image of Mark Rider. Mark, his body broken and bloody. After an hour of frustration, he gives up and goes for an early breakfast.

Cody drinks his coffee slowly and reads the paper. He tries to put the previous night out of his mind, focusing on the headlines of the day. He notices a large group is descending on the dining room and decides it's time to go. Jason checks his watch, six-thirty, too early. Still, he can make notes while he waits for McAllen. He walks to the lobby and requests a taxi.

The taxi speeds along the Porto Said Road, as Jason thinks about the night before. It feels like a bad dream in the bright sunlight of Cairo. They pass over the Giza Bridge and the taxi deposits him on Sudan Street across from the National Research Center. It is six-fifty-four in the morning. Jason decides it's too early to go up. He takes a walk to focus his mind. As he rounds the far corner, he runs into McAllen walking in the opposite direction.

"Aren't you going the wrong way." Alistair McAllen doesn't break stride or make eye contact as he passes. Jason, taken by surprise, has to turn and run to keep pace.

"I thought you'd be in bed Commander."

"I don't think either of us got much sleep after your phone call." Jason looks away feeling a new wave of guilt.

They enter the Isis Building where the unofficial FBI offices are on the seventeenth floor. As they ride the elevator McAllen comments.

"There is no getting around it Jason. An incident like this might be what it takes to shut us down." Cody's mind rolls over the problems they face. An incident like this could sideline him for future foreign assignments. Then there is the current political climate back in Washington.

If word gets out, there would be no end of questions. Congress would demand to know what FBI agents are doing in Egypt when there are no official offices. Cody can hear the good Senators demanding explanations, when the only reason is the preservation of American interests. With the CIA refusing to share intel. The FBI has been forced to place agents around the world.

The new Republican administration is pro-security. However, with the mess out in Wako Texas, the President has a hard time convincing even his supporters.

"I wouldn't worry about what the rest of the world is going to do Jason. The real question is what are you and I going to do." Jason looks at the Commander in his white linen suit. He marvels at how McAllen can read him like a book, while his blue eyes and silver hair give nothing away.

The burnished steel doors open and the elevator deposits them in the lobby on the seventeenth floor. The lobby is decorated in white marble and burgundy carpet. A teak reception counter curves outward from an inset in the far wall. They walk past the empty counter. The building staff are not on duty yet. At the end of the hall, they reach their office.

Inside the FBI offices could not be more different. Each time he enters, Jason feels he's been teleported to a London office. The floor is carpeted in deep green wool with a Victorian pattern sewn in. The walls of the office are lined in sturdy teak paneling. Chairs, desks, side tables and lamps are finely crafted. Most of the furniture has been specially ordered from the Orient. The only things out of place are the rows of metal filing cabinets lining the walls.

Alistair walks to his office. It has views of the city in one direction and the great pyramid in the other. Jason looks at the Great Pyramid. He wonders how many deaths it has stood silent witness to.

"I'm afraid there's no time for enjoying the view Jason, we have serious work to do."

Jason and Commander McAllen spend the morning going over the events of the previous night. The Commander allows him to run through the details as he remembers it. Then McAllen runs him through it again and again. Each time Jason tells it, he becomes a little more detached. After an hour of retelling the story. McAllen asks about details, Jason had mentioned but did not realize the significance of.

Piece by piece, McAllen reconstructs the previous night. Asking questions from different perspectives. Inquiring about the faces of the gunmen, allowing Jason to realize he has seen them and could recognize at least one. By nine o'clock, Jason's head hurts but the Commander does not let up.

"You say the heat got to you. What do you mean by that?"

"I don't know. I thought I was hallucinating for a moment. Then it stopped."

"What stopped Jason. What did you see or hear that made you think you were hallucinating?" Jason pauses and takes a breath. His mind does not want to go there. He does not want to see Mark's body shot full of holes. Jason focuses his mind and he is there. Mark's eyes looking at him, pleading with him. His hand pointing at the dead informant, his words distant and unclear. Commander McAllen studies Jason as he watches the young agent remembering the incident.

Jason turns away, composing himself but McAllen is not letting him off that easy.

"What is it Jason, what do you remember?"

"It's nothing it must have been the heat."

"What must have been the heat." The Commander insists.

"It is nothing." Jason pauses as he forms his reply. "For a moment, I thought I saw Mark looking at me. I could hear him in my head but only for an instant." The Commander leans in his blue eyes, intent.

"What did you hear in your head, Jason?"

"He told me to go. He told me to get out before the police got there." Jason looks at the desk avoiding the Commander's eyes.

McAllen holds the young man under his gaze for a moment deciding if he had been told everything. He has not but McAllen chooses to let it go.

"Now. The two gunmen are trying to swing around to fire at you from the hole in the far wall. You can see one man clearly. The one you said was fatter than the other."

"Yes."

"The man you shot has slumped against him and is pinning the big man's gun arm."

"Yes."

"The big man frees his arm, how?"

"The thinner man falls back into the far room and off the big man's arm."

"Does he fall, or is he pushed?" Cody concentrates on the question, seeing the incident one moment at a time.

"No, there is a hand on the thin man's shoulder. It is pulling him back into the room."

"What are you doing." The Commander asks.

"I'm still firing but my last shot goes wide. I am taking aim while I step back out of the room."

"Can you see past the man who is aiming at you? Don't look at the gun look past it. Tell me what you see."

"It's black."

"Is there no light? How can you see."

"There is light but the black is moving. It's a black robe."

"Can you see a face?"

"The arm is pointing through the hole at me. I think a Man-in-Black robes is telling the gunman to shoot."

"Who? Who is telling the gunman? Can you see his face?"

"A Man-in-Black is bending down to get a look at me. The gunman is spinning round to fire. I can see the beard of the Man-in-Black. The machine-gun has begun to fire. The bullets are tearing up the wall. I'm throwing myself back to find the wall behind me." Cody sits up with a start breathing fast.

"What is it?"

"I fell back over the informant." Cody regains control of his breathing and relaxes in his chair. The Commander sits back with a look of disappointment stroking his beard.


McAllen observes Cody for a moment, then runs a hand through his hair saying.

"Well, we've been working non-stop all morning. Why don't we get a cup of tea and a bite before we continue." Jason relaxes at the suggestion and gets up to stretch his tired back. He drops his arms, turning for the door when suddenly, he is back in the safe house.

*The heat is causing the dust to swirl before his eyes, the air feels thick and heavy. Jason turns slowly taking in the small hot room. The carpet moves back and Mark Rider enters.*

*'Tell him Jason. Tell Alistair what I said. Remember, 'Get tape. Attack on US soil. Go.' Tell Him!'*

"Jason! Jason, are you all right?" Alistair asks.

"Get tape. Attack on US soil. Go."

"What? Jason, what are you saying?"

"I just remembered. Mark's last words. 'Get tape. attack on US soil. Go!'"

"When did he say this?"

"They were his last words. He pointed at the informant and said those words. How could I forget?"

"Well you've remembered now and hopefully, it's not too late."

There is a knock at the door. Alistair locks his case in his lower desk drawer, pulls up the bottom of his center drawer and conceals the tape recorder. Jason watches. With a nod from the Commander, he disappears down the hall. When Cody returns, he has the Head of Egyptian National security in tow.

Major Haraddi, standing nearly as tall as Cody's six-foot-two, embodies all of the pomp of the Egyptian military. His sharply pressed uniform carries more bars, medals and insignia's than even the Egyptian President. It is rumored that he has to remove half of them when in the President's presence. It is further rumored this is not done willingly.

"Good morning Commander McAllen." Haraddi puffs out his chest as he speaks.

"Good morning Major Haraddi. To what do we owe this honor?" McAllen says, smile in place. Cody smirks behind the Major's back.

The cynical reply makes Major Haraddi cautious. He is a man who is accustomed to being in control. Though he will not admit it, this is the reason he avoids the Americans. Yes, he is head of Egyptian Security but Commander McAllen has intelligence from the world over. Egypt's most carefully guarded secrets continually appear in the Commander's files.

"Commander McAllen, I regret to inform you I am here in an official capacity."

"Official capacity, what do you mean?" The Commander shoots a warning glance at Cody. The Major sees it and looks the young man over before speaking again.

"I regret to inform you we have found Mister Rider early this morning in old Cairo. I'm afraid he is dead."

The Commander sits back in his chair and slumps.

"How? What happened?"

"It happened in the early hours of this morning in an empty house. He and another man were killed by automatic weapons fire. I'm afraid that's all we know at this time." Haraddi tries to put some feeling into this last statement. "If you please, Commander. I would appreciate it if you and Agent Cody could accompany me to the site. I would appreciate any help you could give us on this matter."

"Yes, yes, of course. We will accompany you." Alistair McAllen takes his white linen jacket and hat from the coat tree. "What am I thinking. Agent Cody, you must stay here and contact Washington. Inform them of what the Major has told us and make arrangements for Mark's..." He chokes a little. "..for the body to be flown back to Washington."

"I must insist that you both accompany me, Agent Cody as well."

"Why?" Commander McAllen turns to Haraddi. "Agent Cody has only been with us a few months and he will be moving on to other assignments in another few weeks. I need him to stay and liaison with Washington. Agent Cody cannot help you, Major."


Major Haraddi bristles at being denied a chance to directly question Cody but there is time, there is always time. If he was not sure before, he now knows the FBI is not innocent in last night's events. He stares accusingly at Cody.

"I am sorry Major Haraddi. The Commander is now the senior member of the team and I must respect his wishes." Cody smiles in response to the Major's accusing stare.

"Of course you must Agent Cody. I trust you can avail yourself for questions later in the day."

"Yes, of course, Major. Anything I can do to help," Jason says with all honesty. As Cody speaks, he catches a sidelong glance from McAllen and a nod that says, *'well done.'*

**Old Cairo 10:32 September 3, 2001**

Commander McAllen follows Major Haraddi's explanation of the events. They have spent the better part of an hour examining the scene.

"You see Commander, it could not have been a robbery as you suggest. What robbers in Cairo use automatic weapons? None, I think." The Major smiles.

"I have to agree with you Major. It is not like the local thugs but that leaves us both in a very uncomfortable position. The American people get upset when one of their own is killed by, what did you call them, Fundamentalist Extremists. I am afraid I have to be careful how this is handled with Washington. I would think the same applies for you." McAllen's eyes narrow as he speaks and he casually pulls back the carpet glancing at the closed door across the hall. The door is new and out of keeping with the age of the house.

"Yes, I see what you mean." The Major replies as he grapples with the new problem. How does he handle having an American FBI agent who is not supposed to be in Egypt, shot and killed? McAllen releases the carpet of the small windowless room.

"Was this the only room with any evidence of a struggle?" The Commander asks again.

"Yes, yes the only room." The Major replies. While the Major is lost in thought, McAllen takes advantage of the moment. Alistair steps out of the small hot room pushing aside the carpet.

"Then I'll be on my way. I don't want to hinder your investigation. You will let us know as soon as you have any leads." The carpet falls back in his wake, momentarily obscuring his actions. McAllen opens the newly hung door across the hall and steps inside. "Oh sorry, I must have got turned around." He turns to leave finding Major Haraddi at his side.

The Major glares at the lone man in the room, firmly closing the door as the Commander leaves.

"I'll let you know what my superiors in Washington say once I have spoken to them. Perhaps you and I can discuss our final reports before we submit them. If we agree, we can keep the political waters calm." The Commander calls back to Haraddi. He is walking with his usual long strides forcing Major Haraddi to hurry to keep up.

"That would be most gracious of you, Commander. I will put all of our resources on this. I think we should have some results in the next few days."

"Excellent. Can I suggest until we hear otherwise we treat this as a tourist mugging." McAllen stops and makes eye contact with Haraddi. "That will give those in charge a plausible story to report. What do you think?"

"Yes, yes my thinking exactly."

"Good! You will let me know when you have more information." McAllen picks up the pace again.

"Yes, of course," Haraddi says.

Haraddi watches McAllen's back as he walks across the road. He has not offered McAllen a ride back to his office, nor does he care to. As far as he is concerned, this incident is wholly the Bureaus fault. He knows Agent Rider kept this house and used it for meetings. He knows a lot more about the unofficial FBI business than he lets on.

The Commander walks quickly across the road into the shaded alleyway. He stops out of sight, closing his eyes. Concentrating, Alistair recalls the room behind the new door. He relaxes and allows himself to see the room with all its details. The walls are painted mud brick, old and neglected with large gouges along one side. The far wall the same with a large wardrobe against it. The wardrobe looks out of place but why? The floor newly swept, a policeman sweeping it with a straw brush in hand.

McAllen concentrates on the floor in front of the man. The floor is swept but what about behind him? Alistair focuses, looking closely at the feet of the man and the floor behind. Scrape marks on the floor. The wardrobe has recently been moved. The hole in the wall Agent Cody spoke of must be behind the wardrobe. McAllen catalogs the information for future use. He thinks of his friend Mark Rider lying shot and bleeding in the small airless room as he hails a taxi. It is a long ride and Alistair allows himself the time to grieve for his friend.

When Commander McAllen returns, Jason senses a stark change in him. The man is the same but the soft edges have disappeared. He is focused and ready.

"I have contacted Washington as you asked. They send their deepest regrets and say they will make arrangements for the return of his body." Cody pauses watching the Commander's face but it gives no comment. He continues.

"They have asked if you will be okay to oversee things until a new Head of Office can be assigned. Commander, I thought you would be taking over." Cody asks.

"No, no your government and I have an agreement that goes back many years. I work in an advisory capacity only. That way if I give them poor information. They can say it was from an outside source. It works for me, as well. You see, I can also advise the Egyptian and other governments without creating problems politically. I don't think your government would want a possible double agent in charge of one of their offices."

"Double agent? I can't believe you could be..."

"Never believe Jason. You must always suspect in this business. Look at the FBI mole Hanssen. I'm sure his co-workers never suspected he was a double agent." The

Commander leans forward making his point with a letter opener Cody previously considered harmless.

"That is what made Hanssen the perfect spy. I work for more than one government. Therefore I have the ability to divide my loyalties. I ask you, how else would you define a double agent if not an agent with divided loyalties?" The Commander can see concern and confusion in Cody.

"Remember, when you play this game, you play for keeps. If trusting people is something you do automatically, then don't. You trust the wrong person. You end up dead."

The Commander relaxes a bit and sits back in his chair.

"Now then, we have work to do and I need your help. We must get to Mark's body before the autopsy is performed. Mark did not go there to hear some informant's ravings. He was after a tape. A tape important enough to kill for. We need that tape!" Cody creases his forehead and clears his throat.

"Commander, Washington wants us to sit tight until the new head of office arrives. They said to work up our reports and be ready."

Commander McAllen leans forward and makes his point, letter opener in hand.

"You can sit here all you want Agent Cody but Mark Rider was my friend. I believe what he was working on, to be of international importance. The fact he was my friend means I will do everything I can to catch his killer. Do you want to stay here and worry over your report, or are you going to help me catch Mark's killer?" Cody raises a finger to speak but McAllen cuts him off. "Good. I'm going to need your help. We need to examine the body for clues. Mark was far too good an agent not to leave something behind." The Commander says as he collects his things. Cody grabs his hat and bag.

"I'll do the talking and try to distract them while you inspect the body."

"Me! Why not you inspect the body. " Cody says, his throat tightening.

"Because dear boy, I am the idea man. Political analysis is a mental game and is what I am good at. Also, Mark was my friend and I wouldn't want to be the one to do that to him."

"What! Do what to him?"

"Never mind. I'll fill you in on the way."

## Cairo Morgue, 12:47 September 3, 2001

Cody pulls Mark's body onto its back. He has investigated places no one should have the right to and the bile is rising in his throat. Nothing, either it wasn't here, or the Egyptian police already have the tape. The coolness of the morgue is the only consolation but it doesn't stop him wanting to regurgitate his breakfast. The morgue attendant and McAllen reappear as he is washing up.

"Have you found anything of interest Mister Cody?" The attendant's smirk tells Jason he knows the answer.

"Nothing remarkable." He responds.

"I told you our friend here misses nothing, Jason. This is all a waste of time as far as I can see. As I told you Mister Zawahri, my young friend here is a by the book sort of man. He is forever telling me what forms I need to be filling. I've tried to tell him all of this will be taken care of by yourself."

"That is correct, Mister Cody. We will make a thorough examination of the body and report any findings directly to you."

This is the plan McAllen suggested. A variation on good cop bad cop.

"No offense but you must understand, I have to do my job and I have my superiors to answer to."

"Ah, in that we are the same Mister Cody and I hope you are now satisfied there is nothing to be found." The little man smiles as he zips up the body bag.

"Yes, I am satisfied with this body but what about the other," Cody asks.

"The other? Oh yes, there is one other, now let me see." Zawahri closes the drawer and moves four drawers down. He pulls the drawer open and unzips the bag.

"Mister Zawahri, I believe the other we spoke of was a young man." Zawahri looks down on the body of a woman in her thirties.

"Are you sure, Commander?"

"Yes, quite sure."

"I am sorry but this is the only other body in the morgue at this time." Zawahri smiles and shrugs an apology.

"Are you certain Mister Zawahri. Major Haraddi is certain both bodies were brought here." The Commander says.

"Well, it is easily checked if you gentlemen will accompany me. Zawahri stretches his arms out as if he is herding goats but Cody has had enough.

Jason grabs the latch of the freezer drawer next to Mark's and pulls.

"Please don't bother Mister Zawahri, it's much easier to have a look." The drawer rolls out to a bump stop and a black body bag bumps with it.

"You see much easier," Cody announces. Zawahri tries to look astonished but his irritation shows through as the Commander rolls his eyes to the ceiling. Zawahri moves forward and makes a show of examining the tag.

"I don't believe this is your man Mister Cody." Cody is not to be stopped. He pulls open the zipper and exposes the body.

"This must be him." He announces.

"Are you sure Mister Cody," Zawahri says, thoroughly vexed.

"Well unless you get a lot of people with so many bullet holes I would venture to say this is he."

"This body has not been examined, it has not been identified. As you can imagine, the identification may take some time." Zawahri indicates the man's mutilated face. Cody leans forward, placing his hand on the gurney. Without realizing, he touches the dead man's arm.

At the touch, the room goes dark.

*Cody is standing in the small hot room. Mark is turning towards him, pointing towards the informant. Mark's lips are moving.*

*'Tape, get the tape and go!' Cody sees Mark's arm pointing at the young man. He is not pointing in general but at his head. The heat of the small room is suffocating him. The room spins. He is going to pass out. Jason pulls his hand from the body, the vision blurs.*

Cody drops down, hugging his knees. His head below the edge of the drawer. He looks for air, air without the smell of death on it. He breathes deeply a few times. Jason stands to the concerned looks of McAllen and the attendant.

"Are you all right?" McAllen says, stepping in to offer a hand.

"Yeah, I'm fine. Just need some air." Cody says.

"Please, we can go back to my office. You can sit in the air-conditioning. I guarantee you will feel better. The midday sun penetrates even this far below ground."

"Yes, I think that's an excellent idea let's get away from all of this." McAllen agrees. The attendant closes up the body bag and the three men return towards the offices. They are near the office when Cody stops.

"I forgot my bag. I'll be right back." Zawahri turns to accompany him but McAllen heads him off.

"Don't be long, we've got a meeting in half an hour."

"I'll just be a minute."


Cody races back to the morgue. Grabs a disposable glove and forceps from the instrument tray, pulls out the informant's drawer and unzips the bag exposing the informant's head. In the distance, he can hear McAllen and Zawahri arguing. Jason will have to be fast. He pulls a penlight from his pocket, holding it in his teeth, he peers down the dead man's throat. New smells of death rise from the corpse. Jason pulls back and takes a breath. He steels himself and looks. Nothing.

Jason can't believe it. It should be here. Every fiber of his being tells him it is here. He shakes off the shock, his reason returning. Using the tongs, he pulls up the tongue, to better see down the throat. There, he sees the edge of something white deep in the throat. He holds the tongue down with one hand and feels his way into the throat. He guides the tongs over the object. Got it! The tongs clamp down firmly on the object. He pulls, it's stuck. He pulls again but the cartridge is stuck.

Cody can hear McAllen and Zawahri getting closer. In desperation, Jason grabs the jaw He pulls it down towards the chest. Cody feels the object move up the throat. Jason repeats the movement. McAllen's voice is around the corner. He makes one last desperate pull and the tongs come out with a jerk.

"I thoroughly object to your distrust of myself and my associate Zawahri. I am going to make a personal complaint to your President at our next meeting." McAllen raises his voice half to make his point and half to warn Cody. Zawahri pauses for a moment, then says.

"Bah! I will outlive twenty presidents. Who else could they get to do this god-forsaken work? Now, where is he?" Zawahri turns and marches towards the morgue with

McAllen complaining close at his heels. At that moment, Cody pops around the corner.

"Sorry to be so long but I had trouble finding it." Cody smiles his excuse and pushes past the thoroughly irritated attendant.

"Your obsession with that old bag is going to cost us diplomatic relations one of these days young man." McAllen smiles but Zawahri is not amused.

In the taxi on the return journey, McAllen asks.

"So Jason, I hope we didn't go through that for nothing." Cody pulls out the tape wrapped in the rubber glove and smiles.

"Put that away boy," McAllen whispers, firmly pushing his hand down. "Remember the walls of Egypt don't only have ears they have eyes as well." Jason slips the glove and tape into his bag, glancing at the rear view mirror. The driver is staring, trying to see what is going on in the back seat. McAllen and Cody make eye contact and ride the rest of the way in silence.

# *Three*

Jason returns from lunch and finds the Commander at work on the tape. They have spent the last hour trying to decipher its contents.

"Any luck?" Jason says as he hangs his hat and bag. He gets no reply. He sticks his head into McAllen's office and finds him, head down, listening with a set of headphones. Jason enters and knocks hard on McAllen's desk. The vibration makes the Commander jump.

"Are you trying to give me a heart attack," McAllen yells over the volume of the tape. Jason leans forward and pulls the headphones off of one side and says.

"Sorry, just trying to say hello."

"Well, you've got a lot to learn about tact, I would say." The Commander pulls the headphones away and sighs.

"Any progress." Cody inquires.

"Not much, I'm afraid. There is too much noise on this thing. I can't make out the details. I got a few more scraps but nothing of substance."

Commander McAllen rubs his eyes, the strain of the task reflected in his face. Cody has never seen him looking so tired.

"Anything I can do to help." Jason inquires.

"Yes." The Commander pulls himself up in the chair.

"I've sent a copy off to Washington by dispatch. Give our contacts a call and confirm the package was logged onto military transport. Then get Washington on the phone and talk to the audio lab. See if they have got anywhere with the digital copy we uploaded. Then I want you to run down to the travel agent."

"You going somewhere." Jason cocks one eyebrow.

"What? No, no, I've discovered the meaning of the words the informant was yelling just before he was killed."

"Wheel on the Nile? You mean it's a clue?"

"Well, I don't know if it's a clue but it does mean something. In the past, it was wheels, not wheel." Cody returns a blank look.

"In the past, there were a number of wheels on the Nile. They were the steam-driven boats which carried people and goods on the Nile."

"You mean the old paddle-wheel steamers?"

"Exactly. The locals called them 'Wheels' due to the large wheels that propelled them."

"So 'Wheel' would indicate only one of the steamboats is the right boat."

"Very good, and there is only one boat from the era left. The SS Karim, originally built in England and formerly owned by King Fuad, up until his death. It was inherited by King Farouk and it remained his property until the revolution of 1952. Then it was used by Presidents Nassar and Sadat during their reigns. The Karim was decommissioned and is now the flagship of Nile Tours Ltd.."

"Amazing."

"Thank you."

"And you got all of that from your files." Jason indicates the wall of filing cabinets filled to overflowing. McAllen shifts in his seat and looks at his desk.

"No, I got all of that from a brochure I picked up." Jason suppresses a smile.

"But I found out what 'Wheel on the Nile' means from one of my contacts in the city." McAllen huffs.

"So now we know this, why do you want me to go to the travel agency."

"Because I need to know when the Karim sails and what are its ports of call," McAllen says with an exasperated look.

"Got it."

Jason smiles and slips out. He pulls the door closed to his office. Picking up the phone, Cody dials the Washington FBI number. He waits through the static until a voice comes on the line.

"Dispatch and communications." A female voice says.

"This is Agent Jason Cody."

"Please hold the line, Agent Cody." A moment later. "Your line is not secure Agent Cody. Would you like to call again at a more convenient time?"

"That won't be necessary. I would like to confirm the logging in of an embassy dispatch bound for Washington Headquarters."

"Checking."

"I have no report of any dispatches logged in from Cairo."

"Are you sure?"

"Yes Sir, I've checked all logs and ..." The voice pauses. "Sir my screen shows a call being made to your mobile on a secure line." Cody thanks her just as his mobile starts ringing.

"Jason Cody here."

"Agent Cody, are you in the office?"

"Yes, I..."

"Take a walk. I'll call you back in thirty minutes." The caller hangs up.


Jason thinks, trying to place the voice. Unable to make the connection, he calls the FBI's audio labs and discovers the digital copy has been degraded by interference during the upload. The lab people are trying to determine the cause. Jason pops back into McAllen's office and reports the news from the audio lab and the missing tape.

"Do you think it could have been the courier," Jason asks.

"The courier is a trusted man. We have used him hundreds of times with far more important matters. No, I fear there may be foul play in this." McAllen narrows his eyebrows. "I'll find out what happened to the courier. I need you to hand-carry this copy to dispatch at the embassy and see it gets there without fail." McAllen pulls a tape from his desk drawer, handing it to Jason. "Here, and don't lose sight of it."

## Cairo, US Embassy 15:39 September 3, 2001

Jason flashes his ID to the guard at the US. Embassy gates as his phone rings. Pulling out his mobile, he wanders into the embassy gardens.

"Cody here."

"Agent Cody, are you alone?" The voice sounds familiar.

"Yes. Who is speaking."

"This is Neal Roberts in Washington."

"Mister Roberts sir, I didn't recognize your voice."

"Listen, Agent Cody, I need a favor." Jason knows a favor and an order are the same thing in Assistant Director Roberts' vocabulary.

"Name it sir. I have never had the chance to thank you for putting in the word on my transfer, sir." Roberts pauses.

"Agent Cody we have been seeing a great deal of Al-Qaeda chatter in the Middle East over the last few months and it's increasing. Most of the activity is centered in Egypt and Afghanistan. We are picking up a concentration of activity in the Cairo and El-Minya areas. We received your report of Agent Rider's death. We believe he was on to a major operation. This is why I've contacted you."

Jason concentrates on the phone and Roberts's voice. The rest of the Cairo falls into the background, becoming a blur of images and noise.

"How can I help sir," Jason asks.

"I need you to be our eyes and ears in Egypt. We are going to need detailed daily reports of all information. We want to know specifically what Rider was working on and why he was killed."

"What about Mark's reports? Is there anything in those that give us an indication?"

"No, I'm afraid Mark Rider was one of the last surviving dinosaurs in our business. Paperwork and reports were not his strong point."

"Sir may I suggest Commander McAllen. He would be the person to ask what Mark was working on. I know he and Mark conferred closely on intel passing through the office."

"We have spoken to McAllen but for some reason, Mark chose not to include him. In fact, the last communication we have was dated a week earlier. In it he says. '..have discovered a possible Al-Qaeda, government link. Will keep HQ informed. Have not divulged to number-two at this time..'. Why he chose not to include McAllen, we don't know."

"Jason we need one of our own on this. Someone responsible to the US Government, not a free agent." It's a new voice on the line which Cody recognizes.

"Yes sir Mister Mac Donald, I didn't know you were there sir."

"Jason, I put you out there on Assistant Director Roberts recommendation. He said you were a bright kid, a waste of good resources doing surveillance. It's time to prove I made the right decision. As of now, you are a full field operative with full security clearance and access to all related files. I suggest you study up. I'll make all reports available to you."

"Cody, I want you in Cairo. Keep an eye on McAllen until backup arrives. School's out Agent Cody, it's time to go to work." Roberts says.


Cody stops. He tries to focus on the words but something is intruding on his conscious. Jason wanders close to the tall wrought iron fence surrounding the embassy. He feels eyes boring into him. He scans the street opposite, looking for the source.

"If you need anything, let us know and Cody, be careful. I don't want to lose anyone else. Good luck!" McDonald says.

"Thank you sir!" Jason says as he studies the opposite side of the road. Nothing. He makes a mental note to watch his back and walks to the Embassy entrance.

Across the road crouching low in an alley, a dark figure in rags watches Cody enter the Embassy. The Beggar carefully folds away the highly sensitive microphone he has been listening with, securing it in an inner pocket.

## Washington DC, FBI Headquarters 11:39 September 3, 2001

Roberts and McDonald sit opposite each other, a speaker phone between them. Neal Roberts is beginning to feel his age. His stiff collar contrasts with the deep creases in his face. Too many times, he has been forced to send men and women to their deaths. Over the years, those decisions have stamped themselves on his face where other men wear laugh lines. In front of the desk sits Nathan McDonald. He and Roberts are friends from Vietnam. When Roberts told him he was going to join the FBI, Nathan said *'where do I sign up.'*

Neal and Nathan look at the intelligence reports scattered around Neal's desk.

"He's young to be given this kind of responsibility," McDonald says.

"He's the only one we have out there," Neal responds, looking through Jason's file. "What's this about Cody's parents being killed?" He asks. McDonald responds.

"From what we've been able to determine, an official close to the President at the time, let slip some comments which offended the Saudis. Agent Cody's parents' deaths were the Saudis response. The Official was sacked and Jason and his sister received a full compensation package until they turned twenty-one." Neal looks at Nathan and shakes his head.

"Sometimes, I don't know why we put up with that sort of crap. It's a complete waste." McDonald nods and says.

"What about the replacement for Rider. Can't she do the field assignment?"

"She might if we could find her. Our messages have not been returned and she's not been seen for the past two days. The last they heard she was in Saudi. Also, there's the question of commitment under fire."

"What do you mean?" Neal Roberts picks up the personnel file on Taara Sefi and opens the folder. He points to the psyche-analysis. Nathan reads aloud.

"Taara Sefi – first-generation Afghani born in the US. Excellent recruit for information gathering. Should not be exposed to direct fire situations as personal beliefs may interfere. Devout follower of Islam."

McDonald raises his eyebrows.

"Unless you have a seasoned field operative stashed away somewhere I don't know about?" Roberts lets the question hang. McDonald shakes his head, saying.

"With the last three budget cuts..."

"Well, we can't wait for Congress to debate National Security before we take action." Roberts lets out a breath and massages one of his temples.

"Every major security organization is sending us intel on some plot by Al-Qaeda." He indicates one of the memos on his desk.

"Look at this. British Government MI-6 branch, intel indicating a strong possibility of a terrorist plot against a major US institution." He quotes. Neal Roberts sits back and rubs his temples with both hands for a moment, then leans forward saying.

"We need someone who is on our side out there. Someone who is one hundred percent reliable. Someone who won't question orders or let personal beliefs get in the way. We need Agent Cody."

### Cairo 17:07 September 3, 2001

Cody steps out of the air-conditioning of the Thomas Cook Travel Agents and into the afternoon heat. The setting sun highlights the Cairo skyline. Jason adjusts his hat. The sidewalk is packed with coach loads of tourists moving slowly. The hawkers are out in force, unwilling to let the tourists leave without suitable curios.

Jason tries to look beyond the buses lining the curb for a cab when something catches his eye. A dark ragged shape crouching low, appearing and disappearing between the passing tourists. Jason walks towards the Beggar. Each time he catches sight of it, it's too far away. Cody walks faster, forcing the Beggar to make a move. He pushes aside a hawker showing him postcards. The Beggar is moving at speed through the crowd. Jason can see he appears to be crippled. Cody presses the advantage. He is gaining on the

Beggar, about to reach him when a large tourist blocks his way.

"Excuse me!" Jason says as he squeezes past, only to find the Beggar has disappeared. He looks around but there is no sign.

"I saw him, young man! I saw where he went. He stol' your wallet didn't he." An elderly American shouts as he pushes excitedly out of a coach parked at the curb. "They're all a bunch of fakers anyway. That fellow just stood up and ran down the alley behind the stall there. Just as fast as one of those Olympic runners. He just..." Cody doesn't stay to hear the rest. He pushes past the objecting stall owner. The alley runs a narrow winding course away from the road. He rounds a sharp bend and comes face to face with an attractive young woman about his own age. Cody runs up on her, nearly knocking her down. She flattens herself against the wall in time to avoid his charge.

"Excuse me, sorry." He says. Swerving to avoid her, he knocks a large sports bag out of her hands. He glances back and sees her staring after him with dark eyes. Something about her makes him want to stop but there is no time. He continues running for another minute until the path comes to an abrupt end.

Several small doors are set into the walls but all are locked. Cody backtracks along the footpath. At the road, there is no sign of the Beggar or the girl. Jason cannot understand where the Beggar has gone. Exiting the alley, he spots the American who pointed out the alley. Jason turns away, not wanting to be drawn into conversation. Moving through the crowd, Cody drinks heavily from his water bottle. He gathers his thoughts and waves down a taxi. The heat of the day is past its worst but still unbearable as only September in Egypt can be. *'Only mad dogs and tourists,'* Jason thinks as he slides into the air-conditioned cab.

Red high-heeled sandals, red-painted toes, red hip-huger bell bottoms and a bare middle, Sadi admires herself for a moment. She smiles at her tanned body and bejeweled navel under a creamy white low cut blouse. Standing in front of the mirror, she pushes back her black hair. The only clue she was not all woman is the extra strength in her arms and light beard growth. However, Sadi has dealt with these things. Experience has taught her how to relax her muscles so they do not look masculine. The stubble on her chin is easily hidden under a veil.

What had been a deformity at birth has turned out to be a vital asset in life. Sadi's father left home after seeing the child the doctors said was both boy and girl. His mother raised her as a boy but nature did not allow the illusion to last. Sadi did not see his father again until she was in her teens. Her father had been her first kill, her first successful assassination. Dressed as a girl, Sadi easily penetrated her father's bedchamber. Completely fooling him into believing Sadi was a young girl, not the son he abandoned. As he was at his most excited, she slit his throat.

Sadi thinks back on the moment as she adjusts her veil. She knows the eyes of the shopkeeper have followed her from the time she entered. She doesn't mind. In some ways, she enjoys being able to fool them. They do not suspect their desire will be their death. Sadi thinks of her father and how good it had felt to drive her knife into the pig.

He had rejected Sadi and told the village she was a freak. Spawn of the devil had infected his wife's womb. He rejected him publicly as his son. He made sure Sadi's mother suffered for delivering a freak into the world. In the end, it was Sadi who made him suffer. Cutting off his manhood and feeding it to him. His father's blood had been warm and felt good as it had bathed her body.

The memory of the night makes her smile and look for the young American Agent she's been following. She sees the young man getting into a taxi. *'Probably returning to his office. No need to follow him now, his time will come.'* She thinks. Sadi admires her firm young breasts in the mirror. She thinks back to her youth when she hated them. When they began growing, the other boys laughed at her when they swam, while the older boys tried to rape her. She paid them back. Her unusual birth had also given her incredible strength. They all were made to suffer. Now, they are good for nothing but crawling on their bellies and begging in the streets.

Sadi glances at the Agent in the cab before it pulls away. *'I'll bet you won't be able to resist me. I'll bet you die with a smile on your lips.'* Sadi smiles at the thought, picks up her sports bag and waves down a taxi. Tonight she will finalize three months of planning. For three months she has made herself a regular visitor to the palace. She has become accepted by the guards. Yesterday she met her mark. A man who controls the military of Egypt. A man who stands loyal to the President. A man who must be removed if the plan is to go ahead. Conveniently, he is a man who has a passion for young women. Sadi reaches into her bag and strokes the gun. It is too bad she has to use the weapon.

Too bad she cannot slit the man's throat and watch as he dies.

## Cairo, FBI Offices 17:47 September 3, 2001

Cody arrives back at the office to find McAllen digging through one of Mark's carved wooden file drawers. He berates himself for not having thought of doing the same earlier. There is no way of knowing if the Commander has removed anything. The thought stops him. He realizes the conversation with Neal Roberts has made him suspicious of everyone, including McAllen. What had McDonald said *'..we need one of our own working on this. Someone responsible to the US Government, not a free agent.'*

The words sound louder in his head than on the phone. Cody drifts into Rider's office and watches while McAllen riffles the file drawers and folders.

"Find anything interesting." It comes out more accusing than casual. McAllen's head comes up at the words. His eyes focus on Jason, appraising him.

"Good, I was wondering when you were going to wake up." The Commander smiles slyly.

"I don't know what you mean."

"Of course you do boy. Your antenna are up and your eyes are sharper, your blood is rushing. You're beginning to feel the paranoia that follows a man in this job. The very fact you get paranoid is not a bad thing, no. The paranoia is what keeps you alive but you have to have a special kind of paranoia. A precise, honed and focused paranoia is what you need. That's the feeling you're beginning to experience but you haven't been at it long enough. To live with it, without it ruling you. That's the real art of the game." The Commander says as he looks over the file in his hand.

"Not letting your opponent know what you're thinking or feeling." He returns his gaze to Cody.

"But for now, why don't you get your hands out of your pockets and help with these files."

"What are we looking for?" Cody asks as he pulls his hands to his sides.

"About three weeks ago, Mark and I had a long discussion about the internal integrity of the Egyptian Government."

"In terms of what?" McAllen raises a hand holding back Jason's questions.

"As you know, the current government is the most democratic Egypt has had in its long history. Which means the current president and his supporters are under constant scrutiny from certain factions in the population. I refer to the fundamentalists who wish to return to the traditions of Islam." The Commander says.

"As it stands, the only reason the Fundamentalists have not been able to overthrow the Government is the President has surrounded himself with loyal people. People who are passionate about reform."

"What about the people. Won't they make a stink if things were to change?" McAllen's look becomes one of exasperation.

Alistair appraises Cody again. He realizes Jason's time in Egypt has been spent learning the tricks of the agency, not the intricacies of Egyptian Politics. McAllen rephrases.

"The majority of people really don't care what happens in government. In some ways, the Egyptian people have become like the peoples of developed countries. As long as they can prosper and have the few luxuries they desire, one government is as good as another. The real danger lies there, in ambivalence."

"What do you mean?" McAllen smiles and motions for Jason to sit in a chair near Mark's desk.

"It should be obvious. If you cannot rely on the will of the people to stop the fundamentalist movement, the only thing preventing change are the politicians. In the early years, the politicians were dead set against going back to the ways of fundamentalism. The New Constitution broke new ground in Egypt. It also enraged the foundations of Fundamentalist Islam. Suddenly the people of Egypt had rights you and I take for granted. They had the vote, both men and women. They had the right to practice other religions, to break with traditional dress. All of these things were made possible and all of these things would be undone should the Fundamentalist element be allowed back into power."

"What does this have to do with what you and Mark were discussing," Jason asks.

"What we were discussing was the very possibility of that happening. That is exactly the sort of thing we do here. We examine the political fabric of the region looking for flaws. We invent scenarios of how those flaws could be used to meet a political end. Then if those ends are not in the interest of your Government, we inform the appropriate parties and point out where they are vulnerable."

"Isn't that taking sides in what has nothing to do with the United States?"

"Of course we take sides. That's the whole point of it. To make it worse, the sides can change daily. One day we support the Egyptian President and the next he makes a policy change and our support goes to his opponent. Every day the politics of the nations change a little. Every day our position is altered by those changes. One day our support goes to Jerusalem the next the Jewish state threatens to start a war in the Middle East. Who do we support then, eh? Not the Palestinians. Rocks and suicide bombers are not going to stop a war. No, we support Libya. Why? Because Libya has an army, the Jewish state respects. Part of Jerusalem was once part of Libya and they want it back. Stir up old border conflicts, throw in some threatening words and suddenly, all is quiet again. That is the kind of thing we do. We maintain the status quo, sometimes and sometimes we help to change it."

McAllen becomes aware of the file in his hand as he finishes. "Ah, this is hopeless. I don't see how Neal could find anything in these files. None of the papers has anything to do with one another." McAllen rubs his hair back and stares around the room. "There has to be a key to this mess but what it is, I'll be damned if I know." McAllen turns to Cody. "Mark Rider was a brilliant man in his own right. He didn't have the same capacity for remembering things I've been gifted with. However, he always commented he had a filing system second to none. Now I understand what he meant. He has taken all of his sensitive papers and scattered them throughout his files, mixing them with routine reports and personal papers. He could put his hand on file in a matter of seconds. I know, I've seen him do it. For someone other than himself to find it is near impossible."

"He probably thought should anything happen to him, all of this would go back to Washington and reorganized by a team. He was just doing his job." Jason says, shrugging at his comment.

"I believe you are right. Unfortunately, we don't have a team or the time. I have this morning gone through all but one of these filing cabinets. I've been trying to find a paper Mark and I worked over while looking at a possible Fundamentalists take over. So far, I've found nothing."

McAllen rises and stuffs the file in his hand back into the open file drawer. "I'm going to continue with the files, why don't you look around the room, the whole office for that matter. Try to find hiding places Mark might have."

"Have you checked the desk?" Jason inquires.

"Yes, the first place I looked. Have another go if you like."

Jason sits down at the desk pulling out a drawer or two, he finds the usual papers and pens but it doesn't feel right, too easy. He takes a good look around Mark's office. Shelves filled with books on Egypt extended along the wall to Jason's left and the wall opposite where he sits. The wall to his right is the bank of filing cabinets McAllen has been going through. Scattered around the walls are photographs of various archaeological digs. In the corner behind the desk, there is a display cabinet.

"What about these pots and clay statues he collected."

"Oh those, souvenirs of his time on the digs. He, like so many westerners, became fascinated with the history of the place. He used to spend his holidays assisting any team that would have him. Over the years, he has managed to acquire a few pieces."

McAllen turns as he speaks and notices Cody has the door open.

"Be careful with those. Some are quite fragile." He comments.

"I will be. By the way, Mark left a note for you." McAllen looks around.

"A note. For me? Let me see that." McAllen takes the note and reads. *'Alistair stop snooping around my office.'* McAllen makes a face. "Mark never was a very trusting sort." Cody smiles. "Well don't smile too big. I doubt you will find anything else in there," McAllen says. Jason's smile drops as he replaces the clay vessel.

Over the next hour, the two men search Rider's office. In the end, the room is in shambles. The desk chair has been turned over and filling cabinets pulled away from the wall. Still, the office will not give up its secrets. McAllen walks around the room tapping the floorboards. Jason sits still in the center of the room, frustrated. He is beginning to think there is nothing to find, or McAllen has already found it.

"You do realize the floor is glued down. If you do find a loose board, the only thing under it will be concrete."

The Commander stops and frowns at Jason.

"Well if you have a better idea, then let's hear it." Frustrated and tired, the Commander rights the desk chair and sits down.

"I have known this man for over ten years and now I realize how little I knew about him. Mark was a real master at playing the game. You would do well to emulate him."

Jason moves around until the desk supports his back. He closes his eyes. Opening them again, he finds himself staring at a low bookshelf running along the back wall. It looks to be made of solid wood and in good condition, except for one section in the center. The top edge of the shelf is worn as though someone is in the habit of sitting on it.

Jason gets up and attempts to sit there. However, a replica of the Rosetta Stone on the shelf makes sitting impossible.

"What are you doing now." The Commander asks.

"The other offices don't have these bookcases. Were they here when you took over the offices?" Jason asks.

"No everything in this office Mark had made to measure." McAllen sits up at his own words.

"Including those bookcases! Hand rubbed teak crafted in Burma." Cody examines the bookshelf and notes the front edge of the shelf is not solid wood. He grabs the front of the shelf and pulls. It feels solid.

"These shelves are very thick. Are they solid?"

"That's what Mark said but I see what you mean. They look as if something could be inside." Cody feels under the shelf. He finds an indentation in the board.

"There's something here. Wait a minute." He pushes the indentation and it springs back like a release but nothing happens. He feels around the opposite side and finds a second button. Pressing both, the facing of the shelf pops out. It comes away smoothly.

"What have you found," McAllen asks. Cody hands the facing to McAllen to examine and peers in. Inside a wide wooden drawer can be seen with two pull strings Attached. Cody carefully pulls it out to find the drawer is actually a wooden box containing a beautifully preserved cuneiform tablet. "Why that sly devil." McAllen remarks.

Cody goes to each of the shelves removing the facings and contents. When he's finished, there are several antiquities and passports in different names. Cody also finds twenty thousand US Dollars in cash and several papers on the structure of the Egyptian Government. The latter of these, Commander McAllen and Jason examine at Mark's desk.


"Here." McAllen shows Jason an old piece of a brown paper bag. Between the grease marks are Mark's notes and a diagram of the Egyptian Governmental structure.

"We could have got this from the government," Cody comments.

"Not this information you couldn't. Look closer." The Commander points to symbols under the names of the government officials.

"These symbols are Mark's way of indicating the affiliation of the individual official. You see, the alpha indicates loyalty to the president, the omega undecided and gamma for those with sympathy towards the fundamentalists. These marks in the black ink are those Mark and I made when we first arrived at this hypothesis. Since then he has made several changes, the symbols in blue."

"What are these red symbols?" Cody points to a Theta symbol below the name of Ahmed Mohamed Hammed Ali, a Sub-Commander of the Air Defense Forces.

"The red symbols are the whole point?" McAllen says. "The red marks are those individuals with confirmed links to Al-Qaeda. Hmm, Mark must have found out a good deal."

"Why do you say that?"

"Well, when we first made this diagram there were maybe five officials with known affiliations but now..." McAllen says. The point is not lost on Cody. The page becomes alive with red symbols. They seemed to rise above the paper and burn with an unearthly fire.

"It's a house of cards." Cody breathes.

"Yes," McAllen says gravely. Cody cannot pull his eyes away from the page.

"The control of the entire Egyptian Government is held by the power of these top few officials," McAllen remarks.

"If someone were to remove these officials, the military and government would topple. In every key position, there is an agent of Al-Qaeda at its head or second in command. One busy night of assassinations would put Al-Qaeda in charge. With the might of the Egyptian Army, Bin Laden could unite the Arab world. I may be wrong but I believe finding those responsible for this, will not only prevent a coup but will bring us to Mark's killers as well."

McAllen's face wears a grave expression. Cody looks at the page on the desk the red symbols looming large.

"If the Egyptian Government is so precariously balanced, why hasn't it toppled? What about Parliament, don't they have any influence." Jason asks, pulling his eyes from the page. Alistair sighs and says.

"Parliament is incidental. Passing a few laws will not stop a military takeover. The power is in the Presidency and the military. It hasn't happened due to the disorganized nature of the Fundamentalist movement. The motive behind the movement is the same as any rebel force. The only purpose is to exalt the leader of the campaign. In short, for him to achieve power."

McAllen pauses. "The problem with the fundamentalists is each one wants to achieve that same power. That's what's kept them fighting amongst themselves. That's how we've controlled them so far. We've promoted the internal conflicts and it's worked."

"Now there is one leader," Remarks Cody.

"Yes, Bin Laden. Who would have thought a spoiled little rich boy could cause so much trouble. If his parents had given him James Bond novels instead of the Koran, he would most likely be trying to do our job."

"What's this," Cody asks, pulling another page from the pile on Mark's desk.

"That is the piece of the puzzle I was looking for. We have tracked an increase in terrorist communication in Egypt. We think it's the annual meeting of the Muslim Brotherhood. It's happened this way for the last three years in early September but we cannot place it with any event or movement of any of their people."

"What about the movement of a thing," Cody says as he pulls out a brochure advertising King Faud's Nile Steamer the SS Karim. He points to a section circled in red advertising the annual voyage from Aswan to Cairo.

"Does the itinerary of the Karim work with the movement of the Fundamentalist leaders?"

"It certainly appears Mark thought so," McAllen remarks. Cody asks.

"Are there other..."

"None at this time of year, since the tourist shootings a few years ago, the government has imposed a ban on tourism through the Fundamentalist territories. There are only six boats a year, making the trip from Aswan to Cairo. The leader could be posing as a tourist." McAllen says as he places the brochure next to a page of Mark's notes. The previous year's itinerary matches the spats of increased chatter.

"When did you say the next sailing is," McAllen asks.

"In two days," Jason replies.

"Then I think we should be ready to move at a moment's notice." Jason looks at McAllen but says nothing.

### The Old Cairo Hotel, Cairo 22:48 3, September 2001

Jason sits in his hotel room copying the documents they found and preparing his report for Washington. He's downloaded a large package of information from the FBI's secure Web site. Most of the information concerns Commander McAllen. He's had past dealings with the FBI, CIA and European Governments, several Middle Eastern concerns and the Russian S.A.S.

Looking at his long resume of international government and business contacts, it's no wonder Washington wants someone they can trust. Jason takes a deep breath looking up. He will have to stay sharp. *McAllen comes across as the trustworthy friend of Mark Rider but 'for all I know, it could have been McAllen, who set up the hit,'* he thinks.

"No! Don't let your imagination run away with you, Cody." He says out loud. "Not even you knew where he was to meet the informant." Jason stands suddenly, trying to shake the feeling of paranoia. He paces the room, stopping to look out the window.

Jason feels a tingling at the back of his neck as he stares into the night. It's the same feeling he had the night Mark was killed. The same feeling when he'd seen the Beggar. Cody feels something evil is happening out there and there is nothing he can do to stop it.

## The Presidential Palace, Cairo 02:43 September 4, 2001

A dark figure slides silently from shadow to shadow along the inner courtyard of the old palace. The slim figure moves from one hiding place to the next, avoiding the eyes of the guards on patrol. The figure dips into a planter near the side gate. Sadi removes a large sports bag she concealed earlier. Creeping to the gate, she notes the guard has found her gift of wine and dozes lightly under the effects of the drug she added.

Sadi creeps to the guard and deftly plucks away his keys. She slowly and painstakingly turns the lock in the gate, making no noise. She lightly replaces the keys on the guard's belt. She has mistaken the guard as being drugged, when in fact the wine bottle sits untouched. He's put it aside, waiting for the end of his shift to enjoy its contents. As Sadi replaces the keys, the light tug on his belt rouses him from his light sleep. He cracks open one eye and sees the form of a young woman slipping silently through a gate he knows to have been locked. Jumping to his feet, he raises the alarm and dashes into the road. He looks but sees no one.

Soldiers pour from doors hidden near the gate. The guard relays what he's seen. Within minutes the soldiers cover every inch of the adjacent streets. Two are stationed at every crossroads. There can be no movement on the road without their knowledge. In a recessed doorway of an old house, the black eyes of the Beggar watch the patrols as she adjusts the black rags around her. Sadi knows they will find nothing as she fastens the black rags in place, making her transformation complete.

**The Old Cairo Hotel, Cairo 04:27 September 4, 2001**

*Jason Cody stands on the observation deck of the World Trade Center. He steps down to the bottom set of seats and leans out over the railing looking down along the smooth sides of the building. He sees the metal edging running down the building. They appear to merge further and further away. His eyes are drawn down, pulled down the building. His mind reels as vertigo grips him. Shifting his eyes to the horizon, he grips the railings.*

*In the distance, an object catches his eye. A jet banking against the cloud streaked sky. It appears motionless as if suspended by strings. He can see the vapor trails off the tips of the wings and the tail section with the AA symbol. The sun glints off the wing as it turns. He can see the line of windows and the passengers in their seats. Before the wing, a movement grabs his attention. In one of the windows, someone is waving. Jason sees a little blond girl smiling and waving. He lifts his hand to return the wave...*

The phone rings an insistent tone. Cody pulls his head from under the pillow and peers bleary-eyed through the darkness. His shirt is drenched and the images of the dream dance before his eyes. Fumbling in the dark, he finds the hotel phone and lifts the receiver from its cradle. He relaxes back on the bed with the receiver next to his ear.

"Cody, are you their boy?" It is Alistair's voice. The urgency of it pulls him from the edge of another dream.

"Commander, what is it?"

"No time to talk Jason. You must get out of the hotel. Now!"

"Why what's happened?"

"Egyptian National Security forces are on their way to arrest you."

"Arrest me. Why?"

"Someone has killed the Egyptian Military Commander at the Palace tonight. The Speaker for the Shura Council and his bodyguards were on the scene. They made a ruling. In addition to rounding up the usual suspects, they announced all agents of foreign governments are to be arrested. My contact distinctly heard your name and saw Major Haraddi sign the order."

"Why?"

"Why indeed? I think Mark's intelligence is closer to the truth than he realized. This rounding up of the intelligence community is their way of getting rid of outside interference."

"No prying eyes?" Cody speculates.

"Exactly," McAllen says.

"What about you?"

"Don't worry about me. I'm on retainer with the President. Not even Major Haraddi would have the balls to arrest me."

"Shouldn't I go along with what they want? If I run, it makes me look guilty."

"If you stay, it could be weeks, even months before you see the light of day again. By then, whatever they are planning will be done and you would emerge to a changed Egypt."

"If they let me out, you mean."

"Precisely! Now stop wasting time and get packing. I'll have a car waiting for you out back in ten minutes. It will take you to the airport and have you on your way to Aswan before Haraddi's men have time to get their boots on."

"Airport, where am I going?"

"Well, you can't stay in Cairo, can you? You did say someone should investigate the leads we found. So I can only assume you took it upon yourself."

"Is that what you're going to tell Haraddi," Jason asks as he pulls on his trousers.

"No, that's what I am going to tell Washington." Jason stops.

"Washington!"

"Yes but don't worry, I won't get you in trouble. Besides, I'm sure you'll be filling Washington in with your reports."

Jason looks around the room. He doesn't know what to do or where to turn.

"My reports!" McAllen hears the panic in Jason's voice. He pauses and speaks slowly.

"Jason, what if you decide to stay? Allow yourself to be captured. Knowing what you know, could you say you would be best serving America or Egypt? I don't think you can. I believe there are times when it's necessary to step outside the box, the rules, orders. Step over whatever restraints prevent you from doing what is right. Jason if you don't take action now, it will be too late. The very fact they are rounding up the intelligence community means they are ready to make their move. You have a chance to make a difference, Jason. You won't get a second." Jason takes a deep breath, grips the receiver tight and says.

"What time does that fight leave?"

## Cairo, FBI Offices 08:39 September 4, 2001

Major Haraddi stands to his full height, an obstinate pillar in the center of Commander McAllen's office. His military uniform is creased neatly and fully adorned with medals and ribbons.

"I will ask you again Commander McAllen, where is Agent Cody." He juts out his chin smoothing the wrinkles of his neck. His eyes dark and serious, study McAllen.

"I will tell you again, Major Haraddi, I do not know." Commander McAllen's calm exterior is wearing thin.

"Furthermore, Major Haraddi I am not the person in charge here as you well know. I am a consultant working with the late Mister Rider and now with Mister Cody." The Major bristles at the statement, stepping forward, a fighter about to strike. His thick dark hair slides down on his forehead only to be flicked back by a quick hand. His olive complexion deepens with his anger.

McAllen sits fast, not giving in to the physical threat. The Commander is a seasoned contender in confrontation. He knows when to hold. Haraddi stops short of McAllen's desk, keeping his temper in check. He will not be the one to lose control.

"Commander this is a grave matter. I must know where Agent Jason Cody is."

"As far as Mister Cody is concerned, I can only repeat, I do not know. You keep saying this is serious but you have not said anything more. You must understand I can't just drag an American citizen into this office at your whim Major. I need to know why."

"If you do not tell me where I can find Agent Cody, I will be forced to have him picked up on the charge of murder." Major Haraddi is at an end to his patience.

"Murder, by what foolishness would you consider Jason Cody, a murderer? That is the most ridiculous thing I've ever heard." Commander McAllen says. "Major, have you taken leave of your senses."

"Out of my mind am I. Let me tell you, your Agent Cody has registered a 9mm Beretta as his personal sidearm. This is allowed by my government."

"What of it?"

"A 9mm weapon was used to kill the General of Military Command last night." Major Haraddi smirks as he delivers his coup-de-gra. He does not like these Americans being in his country. To him, they represent the American Government's hold over Egypt.

"The General of Military Command, you say?" Commander McAllen quickly assimilates the information. Major Haraddi accepts the assassination was unknown to the Commander.

"Surely Major, because a certain caliber weapon was used does not mean that Agent Cody was involved..."

"Perhaps not but I am here to ascertain whether or not Agent Cody's weapon was the murder weapon." Major Haraddi is close to his limit, his rising frustration causing his ears to go red.

"Does the Major always suspect the allies of his government when there is a murder?" The voice is female. Both men turn to see a young Arab woman standing in the door to Commander McAllen's office.

She appears a modern Arab woman wearing designer trousers and a light colored blouse. A bright blue scarf wraps around her neck, covering her head. Raven black hair and olive skin contrast her hazel blue eyes, which hold Haraddi in their gaze. At five-foot-four, this lady keeps her strengths well hidden.

Major Haraddi stops and swallows hard. Her eyes sweep over the details the men and the room, noticing everything but appearing to see nothing. Commander McAllen smiles and nods his approval to the young lady who smiles back.

"Do I know you?" The Major asks.

"No, you and I have not had the pleasure. I am Agent Taara Sefi. I have asked you a question, Major. You will answer it please." As the Major speaks, Taara lets her eyes wander over the room again. Not to the floor as would be expected, inviting Major Haraddi's anger. Seeing her inattention Haraddi's anger flares and his words pour out.

"It is known Western Governments often manipulate the political affairs of Egypt."

"Through assassination?"

"Through all means." Haraddi stammers regaining control, too late.

"These are the bedtime stories for the children of Hamas. I would hate to think the head of Egyptian security is a Fundamentalist sympathizer." It is a dangerous play but Taara does not have the time for another government official getting in her way.

"Of course, we could scarcely think that of you, Major Haraddi, knowing your record for bravery under fire." As she compliments the man, she steps forward and shakes his hand as an equal. The compliment and reminder of Haraddi's action during the attack on the tour bus in Cairo catches him off guard. He finds himself acknowledging the deed and shaking her hand.

"I apologize if my words have brought offense but I am new to Egypt. I am the temporary Section Chief for the FBI in Egypt. I am sorry if we have started off on the wrong foot. However, you will understand I must look after my people."

"Of course, Misses?"

"Miss Sefi if you please. Perhaps you can tell me why you would like to see Agent Cody, Major Haraddi?" Taara asks, smiling and stepping into the room. She sets down a large case she has brought.

"Miss Sefi, you have heard why I would like to see Agent Cody. His weapon must be tested to determine if it was the one that killed our General of Military Command." The Major says, again in control.

"When I visited the President this morning, I was told it was a young woman who was seen leaving the Palace, not a man. Perhaps you would like to test my weapon instead." Taara pulls out her Heckler and Koch 9mm and holds it before herself, examining it. Major Haraddi steps forward to retrieve the weapon but Agent Sefi slips it back into her bag, producing her passport and airline ticket instead.

"However, if you check the arrival time on my plane ticket, you will see I did not arrive until six this morning." She hands Major Haraddi the documents and waits. She is careful not to challenge. Her hands held lightly at her side but her eyes never leave her passport. Haraddi seeing the display of respect, takes his time examining the ticket.

"As you say, this indicates that you arrived at six-o'-three this morning. However, we have yet to determine if you were on the flight."

"I am certain the customs agent will remember so lovely a lady at that early hour," McAllen says. Major Haraddi looks at the Commander and notes the smile of satisfaction on his face.

"No matter, I have orders to arrest all agents of foreign governments. Miss Sefi, you will accompany me to the Cairo security center."

"I know of your orders Major Haraddi, as I told you I came directly from your President's office. He told me I was not in your country and I would be exempt from the order. He also gave me this." She pulls out a folded paper from her handbag and presents it to Major Haraddi.

After making sure it is genuine, the Major practically throws the letter back at Tarra.

"You may be able to fool the President but I am not so easily fooled. You will be watched, I can assure you."

"I thank you for your concern for our safety Major."

Haraddi bristles at the comment and turns to McAllen.

"You, on the other hand, were in Cairo at the time of the assassination Commander. You will accompany me to the Security center." He orders.

"Oh, I couldn't possibly do that."

"What?"

"You see, I have several rather important reports to complete for your President. You do know I am held on retainer with your President."

"Yes but..."

"Well, he did say the reports I am working on are urgent. I wouldn't want to be the one to tell him I can't finish them because I've been detained. You know how he gets.

Besides, I don't own a gun and I certainly would not be mistaken for a young woman."

Haraddi's eyes bulge.

"Major Haraddi, I will gladly have Agent Cody report to you the moment we locate him," Taara says evenly. The Major calms himself, takes a breath and in his best manners, replies.

"Thank you, Miss Sefi. I will wait twelve hours for Mister Cody to present himself then I must issue a warrant for his arrest. Good day."

Commander McAllen locks the front door and returns to his office to find Agent Sefi pulling a device from its case.

"What gifts have you brought Agent Sefi." The Commander asks.

"No gifts Commander, only work and please call me Taara."

"It would be my pleasure. What is it then?"

"An audio distortion device we captured it from a Saudi based Al-Qaeda training camp last winter. They use it for distorting their voices when making propaganda tapes. We have found it very useful for filtering audio surveillance. It helps to suppress the background noise and clarify the speaker's voice. The message I received said you have a tape you are having trouble with and I thought this might help."

"I see you have foreseen our every need and please call me Alistair." The Commander smiles, Taara returns his smile, asking.

"Alistair?"

"Yes, Taara."

"Where is Agent Cody?"

"Ah!"

# *Four*

**Aswan, The Old Cataract Hotel 10:49 September 4, 2001**

Jason tips the porter as his bags are being deposited in his room.

"This is more like it." He says aloud. It was two hours before the small plane touched down in Aswan. Another thirty minutes on bumpy roads before he arrived at the Old Cataract Hotel on the banks of the Nile. Jason can see from his window a path leading down to the water's edge where the SS Karim is moored. On arrival, he booked a cabin on the steamboat and was told it would board tomorrow morning at nine.

Jason takes in the room, no plastic imitations in this hotel. The bedside tables, chairs and writing desk, all appear to be antique. A bowl of fresh fruit sits with a welcome card in the entry. "I think this room is bigger than my apartment back in DC," Jason says to no one.

Cody spends the morning catching up on needed sleep, emerging for lunch showered and rested. In truth, he has no idea what he should be doing. He does not speak the language or have any contacts. He knows this is the worst part of the game, the waiting. When he was spending hours listening in crowded surveillance vans, he always thought it must be better, pursuing leads and tracking down the criminals. Now he realizes waiting in a van is no better than waiting in an empty restaurant.

He returns to his room and spends the remainder of the afternoon, writing up what he has discovered. Jason stands and walks to the window. The sun is setting over the far bank and the Nile waters have changed color reflecting the gold and blues of the sky. In the shadows, he can see the porters loading supplies onto the SS Karim. They do not hurry. Time has no meaning here and tomorrow will see the task finished.

A beeping from Jason's phone brings his attention back to the room.

"Hello."

"Jason it's Alistair, how are you?"

"I'm fine Commander. Is everything all right there?"

"Yes, of course. You did get our message at the desk." Jason plays along.

"Yes I did, is there a problem," Jason asks.

"No, no problem. However, since you are there, I thought you might do me a favor."

"Of course, name it," Jason says.

"In the Aswan old market, there is a carpet maker who goes by the name of Pasha. It's an old joke. He calls himself Pasha, or King of carpets. Anyway, he was making a carpet for Mark and I thought I would like to have it." The Commander sounds conversational but Jason knows this is more than a social call.

"Yes, of course, I'll be happy to get it for you. How do I find Pasha." The Commander explains his shop sports a banner in English proclaiming him to be the King of Carpets.

## Aswan Old Market 17:33 September 4, 2001

Jason picks his way through the crowded market. He finds the local people much more polite than those in Cairo. Once you say no thank you, the matter is settled. A few shop owners make outlandish offers of trips to Tahiti or a free Cadillac if you look in their shop but all is in good fun.

As Cody walks down the row of shops, the aromas he is sure he will forever associate with Egypt fill his senses. The spices in the shops, the coffee and teas made fresh on the street. The smell of the handmade carpets envelops him as he stands in front of a small shop overflowing onto the dirt road. Carpets are piled in every available space. From the rafters, clothes hang on chains with garments in colorful embroidery. Over the shop hangs a banner proclaiming Pasha the King of Carpets with a large yellow crown.

Jason enters the shop and finds a small boy watching the wares as he works on embroidery.

"Can I help you?" He asks in perfect English. Jason has long ago stopped trying to figure out how the locals can tell he speaks English.

"Yes I am looking for Pasha May I see him," Jason asks politely. The boy looks him over and asks.

"What do you want with my father?" Jason smiles at the question. This shop, like others in Egypt, is the accumulated energies of generation after generation.

Jason looks down at the next generation of 'Pasha' in training.

"It's not for myself, I inquire. The Commander has asked..."

"Oh the Commander, he is a very good customer. Please wait here." The boy disappears into the back of the shop. A moment later, an older boy emerges and asks.

"How Can I help you?"

"I'm making a trip down the Nile and Commander McAllen has asked me to pick up a carpet for him. He told me to speak with Pasha," Cody observes the boy as he speaks.

"Yes, the Commander did make an order some time ago but he told us it would not be picked up until later in the month. I am afraid that we do not have the carpet at this shop we will have to send for it. You will come back tomorrow."

The boy looks past Cody. He gestures to the street, inviting Cody to leave.

"The Commander requested that I speak with Pasha directly." Cody stands his ground.

"No, Pasha is not here. Your carpet is not here." The boy drops his voice. "If you stay, you will attract unwanted attention. You will come back tomorrow morning and you will see both Pasha and your carpet. You come back at nine o'clock tomorrow morning and you will see him then. Now go. Please! Go." The boy gestures and pushes Cody into the street as he speaks. The younger Pasha retakes his position.

Cody is wary as he makes his way back to the Hotel. As he leaves the narrow lanes of the old market, he feels the knives of many eyes on him.

Jason does not need to look around. He knows who it is and he knows there will be no chance of catching the Beggar in the market. His only chance will be to draw it out into the open. He jogs across the four-lane road back to the Old Cataract Hotel. Cody feels eyes on his back. He steals a quick glance but sees nothing. The Beggar is not keen on following in places where he is easily caught. Cody returns to the hotel making plans for tomorrow.

A figure in black rags hobbles to the edge of the road, crouching near a pile of garbage. Blending with the refuse, she watches Cody enter the Hotel grounds. Sadi in her beggar's rags is careful not to move into the bright lights where she is easily seen. She is satisfied to watch and learn for the time being. When she is sure Cody is in for the night, she turns and makes her way back to the market and the carpet seller's shop.

## Washington DC, FBI Headquarters 08:33 September 4, 2001

Neal Roberts reads over the reports for the second time, then buzzes his secretary Jean.

"I need McDonald!" A few minutes later, the door buzzes and Nathan McDonald steppes into the room.

"What's the problem, Neal," McDonald asks.

"What the hell is going on in Egypt, Nathan? Less than twenty-four hours ago, we sat here and spoke with Agent Cody. Did I or did I not specifically tell him to stay in Cairo. Tell me this is some kind of a joke." He throws the report from Egyptian security across the desk at McDonald.

"No joke Sir," Nathan says as he reads through the one page of broken English.

"The Egyptian Security forces do have a warrant for Agent Cody's arrest and are hunting him as we speak."

"Why?"

"As it says, the head of the Egyptian Military, General Asra Seif Nader, was shot at approximately 02:30 hours. As a precaution, all foreign Agents are being rounded up for questioning."

"That doesn't make any sense. The US. has always maintained a good relationship with Egypt. Why would they turn on us." Roberts asks.

"Sir, if you read the report I received from Agent Sefi and Commander McAllen, I think it will answer your question." Nathan places the report on Roberts's desk facing him. Roberts holds McDonald's eye, placing one hand on the report.

"Summarize."

McDonald clears his throat and says.

"The assassination was carried out at the Presidential Palace last night about 02:30 hours their time. McAllen believes it happened there for several reasons. First, the Egyptian President was to be in the building but changed plans at the last moment. This has raised the possibility the Egyptian Military Commander was the next best target. This has forced the President to agree to the round-up of foreign agents. Secondly and Commander McAllen believes the real reason for the assassination is political.

Under normal circumstances should anything happen to the Egyptian President, the controlling power of the government would shift to the leader of the Shoura Assembly. However, the military control would shift to the Egyptian Military Commander. It's a check and balance system set up by the early Presidents of Egypt. With the frequency of political assassinations in the region, it was thought a split would make a coup more difficult. With the Egyptian Military Commander dead, the chance of a successful coup has increased." Nathan takes a breath and continues.

"Third, the leader of the Egyptian Arab Shoura Assembly, General Sefi Mohammad Abdel Himid and his advisers stepped in and ordered an emergency meeting of the assembly. This morning they drafted a proposal for a military security lockdown of Cairo and the round-up of foreign agents and diplomats."

"So the Egyptian Security forces are rounding up diplomats and their families?"

"No. According to the Commander's sources, no other foreigners have been picked up, arrested or detained. The US. Embassy was sent an official notice, asking personnel not to make movements outside their normal routines. As of the sending of this report, one hour ago, the only attempt to detain anyone has been Agents Cody, Sefi and Commander McAllen."

"Why? What threat to the Shoura Assembly can they possibly be."

"McAllen believes it has to do with the increased Al-Qaeda communications we've been picking up. He believes there may be a political coup planned for the next few weeks."

"How sure are they."

"Not enough to inform the Egyptian President but enough to warrant Agent Cody pursuing the investigation in the field." Nathan McDonald stops and takes a breath while Roberts works the details over in his mind.

*'The mole has taken priority over all other business. There is an overwhelming lack of attention to other areas. Orders from the Director put their best Agents on the mole while everything else waits. Action is needed but if the Director finds out, there will be repercussions.'* Roberts thinks, then says.

"Ken Woods, wasn't he in the think tank on the USS Cole?"

"Yes, I believe so."

"Who worked research with him on that?"

"Primarily Susan Kelly but they're both working on Hanssen, Director's orders."

"I know but our mole is contained. Egypt is not. As of tomorrow, they've both come down with the seven-day flu. Put them down in the basement where the Director won't stumble across them. Make sure they have everything they need. I want a preliminary report as of Wednesday and a full analysis by this time next week."

"That's not a lot of time."

"I know but we no longer have a lot of time. The mole team just handed me this." Roberts passes a folder marked secure documents to Nathan.

"All relevant agencies need to have this information ASAP. I want all field Agents to be informed. No one uses the Intel-Tracking Software. I want full monitors on the system by 06:00. Maybe we can find out who else besides the Russians knows about this."

"I'll make sure Agent Cody knows." McDonald reaches for the door as he speaks but Roberts stops him.

"Do it now and do it yourself. I want Cody's take on this coup business. See if you can sniff out whether we're being led down the garden path on this one."

**Aswan Egypt, 08:27 September 5, 2001**

Cody deposits his bags with reception and settles his bill. He walks out of the hotel with other guests who are doing a last shop before boarding. Jason makes his excuses, slipping away from the group. He crosses the road retracing his steps from the night before.

Jason walks up the dirt road, the heat building with every step. He rounds the corner and hardly recognizes the road. The other shops are set up but the carpet shop has not opened. Approaching, he finds the shop is locked up tight.

Confused and worried, he asks the leather craftier next door but the man does not know. Jason is uncertain what to do. He is about to return when.

"Pssst!" The sound brings his head around but he sees nothing.

"Pssst." Jason looks again and sees a boy peeking out between leather coats at the back of the shop. The boy is gesturing for him to follow.

Jason walks to the rack of coats recognizing the boy he saw yesterday. The boy parts the leather garments, exposing a narrow alley running away from the shop. Cody pushes through the coats. They hurry down the path making a turn left. At the end of a short alley is a door of worm-eaten wood. The boy enters with Jason on his heels.

"Please wait." The boy says and gestures for Jason to sit. He leaves through a red hanging carpet. Jason notices several seats but chooses to stand.

A moment later, the boy returns, leading an elderly woman into the room and sits her down heavily. Her eyes are puffy-red and her cheeks are streaked with tears. She gestures for Jason to sit by her. The small boy disappears for a moment and reappears with another boy who is older but not yet a teenager.

While the other boys are dressed in dirty white clothing, this boy wears a clean white linen shirt hanging over his white trousers. He also wears a bright blue waistcoat embroidered and lined.

The old woman speaks and the new boy steps forward to translate.

"She says Pasha has died. Last night the evil spirit of the night swept in and took her Pasha from her." Jason is shocked and can only say he is sorry for her loss. She nods at his comment and continues. "She says she knew he was dealing with dangerous men but she also knew he took the risk for the family. Now each of his sons will have a shop of their own. Each will be Pasha in time." She pauses wiping away her tears.

"Without the money he received from the selling of whispers, none of this would be possible. The family has grown rich from the whispers but in the end, it took away the only thing she cared about, her Pasha." More tears stream down her face and she catches her breath.

"I do not blame you or the Commander for his death. We have always known there was great risk in what my Pasha was doing. Sadly, his luck has run out." She turns and whispers to the small boy, who stands by.

The boy goes to a small chest in the corner of the room and removes from it a brown paper package tied up with string. Returning he places the package on his mother's lap. She looks down at the package. She fingers the package massaging all sides. The bundle looks to be a garment tied up in paper. Jason sits looking from one boy to the other.

With a sigh, she speaks.

"My husband said this would be his best work and should bring us great fortune." The older boy translates, wrinkling his forehead. The woman continues.

"He told me this would be very valuable and many would be willing to pay a great deal to have it." This is what she has been deciding. She knows something of Pasha's business but does not know what the information is worth.

"I believe he would want,,," She pauses then says. "One-Hundred US Dollars!" She keeps her eyes on the package, not daring to look up at the tall stranger as the older boy translates.


There is a growing silence. Jason can see she is nervous about the price she has set. He glances at the two boys and the old house. Jason reaches into his bag. He secured in it the twenty thousand dollars Commander McAllen sent to him before leaving Cairo. He pulls away two thousand dollars handing it to the old lady. She does not look up but takes the money and pushes the package into Jason's hands. The boys' eyes bulge at the bundle of cash. Jason doesn't want an argument, so he takes the package, thanks the old woman and leaves.

The small boy rushes forward and starts counting the money but the old woman slaps him away. The boys begin speaking rapidly to her and she looks for the first time at the money lying on her lap. She inquires to the older boy who holds up one of the notes and says excitedly.

"One hundred dollars." The old woman quickly counts it. Realizing what the American has done, she grabs the older boy and speaks rapidly to him. He runs to the back of the house and reappears moments later with a bundle in his hands. She pulls off ten of the notes and gestures to the door. The boy tucks the notes away as he flies out the door.

On the far side of the street crouched next to the wall, the Beggar hides. He watched the American enter the alley but now a boy runs out. He has not seen the American leave. He signals a teenage boy. The boy runs to a man drinking tea, who calls to two others. The three men dive into the leather shop while the shopkeeper yells at them. The teenager signals two friends and the three race after the boy.

Jason decided not to return to the market in case it is watched. He walks quickly down the alley shifting past crossroads. Always following his nose, he winds his way between buildings and homes heading for the river. Cody arrives at a crossroads with five possibilities. He cannot decide as three could lead him to the river. He pulls out his phone and switches to the GPS screen. A moment later a map of Aswan appears. It shows him a detailed view of the street systems and indicates his position in the middle of an empty field.

"You are in a field," Says a mechanical voice. He glances at the high mud-brick walls around him.

"Great! You are in a field." Jason repeats mockingly, taking the path ahead.


He sprints away as it narrows to the point only one person can walk. He finds himself turning sideways to squeeze through the path. It twists and opens into a small courtyard with doors and windows on either side. A twenty-foot high cinder-block wall lies directly in front of him.

"Dead end!" Jason curses. He checks around him for an exit but finds none.


Jason pulls a water bottle from his bag and drinks deeply. Cody realizes he is still holding the package from Pasha's widow. He stuffs it into the outside pocket of his bag and returns along the narrow alley. As Jason approaches the crossroads, he hears voices arguing amongst themselves.

Cody slows his pace. Creeping along he comes to a curve in the path. It allows him to glimpse the men at the crossroads. The men argue back and forth before running off. He has a bad feeling about this. He waits for a moment, walks into the crossroads trying to determine where they have gone. He stoops to examine the ground and the recent footprints. It may be a trick of the acoustics or bad luck but Jason does not hear the assailant approach.

One of Jason's pursuers runs into the crossroads. He makes an awkward stop leaning forward over Cody to get his balance. Cody looks up as the man starts yelling for his comrades. Sixteen years of martial arts training and two years of Quantico self-defense clicks in. Jason is mentally detached as he reacts. He stands to his full height of six foot two while his fist shoots up, catching the man under his chin. The assailant lands a good five feet back. Cody looks in disbelief at his fist. All that training and the best he can do is a sucker punch?

Jason hears pounding footfalls driving towards him. He jumps back as a second assailant dives into the crossroads. The distance gives Jason time to react. A quick kick snaps the second assailant's head back. Cody spins out of the way and drops an elbow in the middle of the man's back. He drops on him with all of his weight and feels his spine give as they strike the earth. There is a popping sound and Cody feels the rib snap. He rolls away, ready for the next attack. Nothing, Jason steps away from the two, one lying out cold and the other in pain.

Three men run out of the path behind Cody. He spins around as a large man runs arms wide trying to tackle Cody. Jason strikes open palm, driving the assailant's nose up into his cranium. He is lifted from his feet and collapses in a heap. Cody turns on a man with a knife, who jumps back. A third man chooses that moment to jump Cody from behind. With the man's arms wrapped around him, Cody doesn't have to worry about a knife in the back.

The knifeman makes quick inexperienced slashing movements trying to draw Cody in. Cody circles the man. The attacker on Cody's back tries choking him but Jason's quick movements make holding on difficult. The game goes on for a few seconds but the attacker is impatient. He dives forward, looking to stab his quarry in the chest. Jason's blocking move knocks the knife away. The attacker's forward motion continues and Cody folds the attacker's arm back, dislocating the shoulder and snapping tendons.

Cody spins and breaks the grip of the man on his back, throwing him to the ground. Jason leaps coming down with his foot on the man's pelvis as he lands. The man's back hits the earth at the same moment as Cody hits him. The scream echoes up and down the alley. Cody silences him with a sharp kick to the head.

As Cody steps off the man, he turns looking for the knifeman. Jason sees him next to the wall holding his side. Blood is oozing from a cut on his head. Cody watches as he struggles to his feet, then he runs off screaming. Jason looks for more assailants. Seeing no one, he sprints from the scene.

The path Jason chose runs straight towards the Nile and sets him on the riverfront road. He exits through the back of a tobacco stall. The proprietor sits in silence as Cody passes. He makes his way down the road towards his hotel, stopping at a vendor to buy another bottle of water.

As Jason is drinking, someone hits him from behind. He whirls around to see a youth dancing away and laughing. He smiles and relaxes as a hand slips into his bag. Cody turns and grabs but the second youth is too quick and dances away, holding the package overhead. He throws the parcel to the first youth.

Cody can see the odds are not in his favor. He steps towards the youth who snatched the package and fires a punch at his face. The boy is turning back to look for Cody when the fist lands. Now it's even. Cody goes into a dead run after the teen holding his package. The teen tries to get back to the alleys but Cody is too quick. The teenager is forced to run through traffic crossing the road.

The teen sprint away as Cody struggles to keep up. The teen circles a car and doubles back towards the maze of alleys. Cody knows if the teenager gets into those alleys, he will lose him. In desperation, Jason yells for help.

"Stop, thief!" He yells at the top of his lungs between breaths. "Help! Stop thief!"

It works. Two men push their cameras to their wives and stand with their arms spread wide. Seeing this, a few of the shopkeepers do the same. The youth slows for a moment and Cody accelerates, closing on the boy. The youth sees him closing but sprints away like a gazelle cornered by a lion.

Cody doesn't slow. He has found new reserves and moves closer with every step. The boy stumbles into a taxi and the driver grabs his shirt. He is pulling away but Cody is there and grabs the boy's arm twisting it as he does. The teenager will not give up and holds the Package out away from Cody's reach. There is a sharp pain in Jason's shoulder. He turns to see the third boy with a knife cutting him and grabbing the package as he runs by. The boy in Cody's grasp laughs at his captor. In frustration, Cody's fist finds his smile. Then there is one.

The last teenager is running with impressive speed. This was their plan to give it to this teen. He is by far the fastest runner. Cody takes up the chase but the sun's heat and the exertion have taken its toll. His legs are like lead. He knows it will be some time before he can match the youth's speed. The youth is not taking chances. He streaks towards the tobacco shop where Cody emerged, waving the knife before him as he runs.

The street is in an uproar, the shopkeepers yelling. The walkway has become a spectator stand of onlookers cheering for the youth. Cody knows it's bad. He won't be getting help from the gallery this time. As the boy nears the walkway, there is a movement from the right of him. Behind the cheering crowd, someone is running fast to intercept. The youth is leaning forward. The shopkeeper has moved out of his way. The youth lands his foot on the curb. At the same moment, there is a blur of blue and white connecting with the teenager. The teen drops flat and slides a full three feet face down on the walkway. The figure in blue and white jumps forward, grabs the package and holds it over his head.

The crowd goes wild, clapping and cheering for the young hero. Cody doesn't stop. He sees the danger coming and heads straight for it. The teen he hit at first is up and running towards the young hero but Cody is there. Jason catches the teenager by the throat and hits him. The teen's eyes cloud over and he collapses in a heap.

The boy steps back. Cody recognizes him as the one who translated for Pasha's widow. Jason looks around as he takes the boy by the arm. He and the boy walk quickly across the road into the gardens adjacent to the hotel. Finding a shady spot under a tree, Jason sits the boy down on one of the benches.

Cody glances back across the street. He notices people are milling around the fallen teenager. There is little time before the police will arrive. He turns to the boy and finds he is holding out the package to him. Jason takes it and says.

"Thank you for your help but why did you follow me?"

"Missus Pasha says you have paid too much for the package and asked me to return this money to you." The boy holds out five one hundred dollar bills to Cody and smiles. Cody takes the money and folds it over. He then hands it back to the boy.

"Why don't you keep this? I think you've earned it, don't you?" Cody smiles as he presents it to the boy but the boy wrinkles his small brow and looks down. "What's the matter don't you want it," Cody asks. The boy pulls out another five one hundred dollar notes from a hidden pocket. He looks at the ground as he hands the notes to Cody. Cody straightens the notes and makes a stack. He makes a show of counting the notes. "Is this all of it?" He asks. The boy keeps his head down and nods yes.

"Well," Cody says. "It looks like you and I have come into some money." The boy raises his head and looks at the tall American.

"I think you and I have both worked hard today. What do you say, fifty-fifty?" Cody smiles and the boy brightens up replying. "Sixty-forty!" Cody glances at the scene in front of the tourist stalls and decides it is time to move.

"Let's talk as we walk." He says. The boy is also looking at the crowd milling around the figures on the ground.

"I think you hit him too hard." Says the boy.

"I think we both did." Retorts Jason. The boy looks again.

"Yes, we should be going from here." The boy says.


The two walk towards the Hotel while the boy is negotiating the split of the money. Insisting Cody would not have his package without his help. As they near the entrance to the Hotel, the guard at the gate tries to block the boy's entry. Cody waves him off and the boy offers a few chosen words in Egyptian. As they approach the door, Cody stops the negotiations.

"Look, I say we split it down the middle or nothing."

The boy thinks it over for a moment then consents happy with his share.

"I am Abu." He announces as Cody passes the money over.

"I am Jason Cody." He says, shaking Abu's hand.

"You are an American spy, yes?" The boy asks, returning the handshake. Cody is surprised at the question and asks.

"What makes you think that." The boy's face takes on the appearance of years of experience as he speaks.

"Oh, it is very easy to see you are a spy. Spy's are easy to find. They look like regular tourists but they do not take pictures or buy from the trinket sellers. You should take some pictures if you do not want to be mistaken for a spy Mister Cody." Jason smiles and thinks *'it is true he has not taken one picture the entire time in Aswan.'*

"I think you may be on to something Abu. You're right. I will have to take some pictures but right now I have a boat to catch." Abu creases his forehead and speaks.

"Mister Cody, will you take Abu with you on this boat?" This catches Jason off guard. He does not have time for any extra baggage right now.

"Abu I want to thank you for all of your help but I cannot take you with me. You should return to your mother and help her through this difficult time."


Abu's face creases even more then brightens.

"Oh, you think Missus Pasha is my mother. No Mister Cody, Missus Pasha is my Aunt. My family was killed in El-Minya, I have no family now, only my Aunt." Cody frowns.

"I'm sorry Abu, I didn't know." Abu smiles.

"Of course you did not know I had not told you and don't be sad they all lived good lives." A smile creeps onto Cody's lips as Abu speaks.

"What will you do now," Cody asks.

"I must go with you to Cairo, Mister Cody."

"What, wait, why must you go to Cairo." Cody sees the bundle tied over Abu's shoulder for the first time.

"I must go to Cairo so I can take over my father's business." Cody is relieved and at the same time, confused.

"Does your family live in Cairo," Cody asks.

"Oh no, but my father did business in Cairo." Abu stands proud as he speaks.

"I wish you well but I cannot take you. I'm afraid I have to catch a steamboat and I must be going."

"Oh, you mean a wheel. There is only one wheel on the Nile Mister Cody. I hope that is not your boat." Jason looks in the direction Abu is pointing and sees the SS Karim steaming downriver.

"Damn!" He exclaims and sprints into the hotel.

Abu tries to follow but the doorman prevents his entering. He stands close to the open door. Abu listens, picking up snatches of the conversation. After a few moments, he sees the desk clerk pick up the phone and order a taxi. Abu walks from the Hotel along the long drive and hides behind a shrub. Five minutes later, a yellow taxi drives up.

Hotel porters and the driver strap Cody's bag on the luggage rack, which is a metal basket welded to the back of the old car. Abu notices someone moving around the entrance gate. Looking closer, he sees one of the teenage boys who tried to steal Cody's package. Abu thinks. *'Mister Cody is not out of danger yet,'* and forms a plan.

Abu reties his bundle around his shoulders, so it hangs in front. He pulls from it a short carved stick he'd borrowed from a trinket seller. The taxi is pulling away from the hotel door but must slow down to cross a drainage ditch.

As the Taxi slows, Abu races from his hiding place. Staying low, he grabs the metal luggage rack on the back of the car and pulls himself onto the bumper. He holds tight as the taxi speeds the short distance to the front gate. The vehicle slows while the gate guard raises the crossbar. The guard is busy talking to someone in the guardhouse and does not notice the boy clinging to the back of the car.

The car slows to a stop, waiting for the traffic to clear. Two of the teenage assailants run for the back bumper where Abu is clinging. They reach the luggage rack but Abu is ready for them. He swings the club cracking one boy's knuckles. The other boy curses Abu and yells for help. The sounds of yelling alerts the guard. He sees the boys and gives the taxi driver a warning shout.

Without a glance at the road, the driver hits the accelerator sending the taxi squealing into traffic. Abu hangs on for dear life as the force of the acceleration has

131

him dangling out in mid-air. For a moment he is suspended over the hot road. The sound of honking and squealing brakes catches his attention. Another taxi is barreling down on them. Abu pulls in his legs as the following taxi gives the bumper a nudge. Abu's taxi accelerates while the driver remains oblivious to the commotion he has caused. The taxi races for the train station with Abu clinging to the rear. The sun shines down from its zenith as the cab makes quick work of the journey across Aswan.

Having jumped off at the first opportunity, Abu stands rubbing his bottom. The taxi hit some hard bumps and the springs in the old taxi are nearly gone. He hobbles to the train schedule working the ache out of his bottom. He finds the next train to Kom Ombo, where he heard the SS Karim will stop. He reasons Mister Cody will join the boat there. Looking over the people arriving, Abu spots a lady and makes his move.

A middle-aged lady has waved away two other boys who carry bags for tips. As she is paying her taxi driver, Abu sees his chance. He runs to her bag and lifts it. He moves a few paces off and calls waving back to her.

"Lady, hey lady, come on, or we miss the train!" Abu moves away as quickly as the heavy bag will allow.

"No, put that down at once, young man!" She yells, turning back to the cab driver with money in both hands, she says. "Oh here, take it all." The cabby thanks her, smiling broadly.

The woman hurries, trying to catch up with Abu, as he winds through the crowds.

"Hurry up lady, this way." Abu says and stops in front of a closed ticket window, saying. "Hurry up lady, or you will miss your train." He gestures to the closed ticket window. The woman hustles to where Abu stands with her bag, out of both breath and patience. "What do you think you're doing. I have never, in all of my visits to Egypt, received treatment of this sort. I shall complain to the station master if you do not release my bag at once. I will have nothing more to do with this. Do you hear what I am telling you?" She announces loudly.

" Okay but if you leave now, you will never get your ticket in time to catch the train." Abu gestures to the large crowd of people crushing in on the single open window. The woman looks at the mob and realizes what the boy is saying. There is no way she can purchase her ticket in time and the next train is not due for four hours. She is about to protest to no one in particular when there is a movement at the ticket window.

As if planned, the window slides open with a ticketing agent behind. Instantly, the focus of the mob is on her and the newly opened window. Abu kicks, elbows and uses the lady's bag to stop the men from pushing her out of the way. Clutching her handbag close to her chest, she purchases her ticket. With Abu parting the crowd, they make their way out of the lobby and past security.

On the platform, Abu finds her a bench. He stands next to her, keeping a close eye on her bag.

"So it seems you knew better all along or was it only luck the ticket seller opened?" She inquires.

"Please lady, when you are only this tall." Abu makes a gesture of his height with his free hand. "It is easy to see under the blind covering the window." Abu smiles his most charming and shrugs. Not convinced, the woman turns away in a humph but does not send him away.

Five minutes later, the train arrives and the passengers are allowed off while the platform guards hold back those ready to depart. The crowds of departing passengers alight the train in a mass panic, each passenger trying to gain a seat. The woman who Abu is assisting stays seated. She has purchased a first-class compartment. She waits for the crowd to alight, looking on with disinterest.

As the platform clears, she stands and walks to the first-class cars at the front of the train. Abu is struggling with the lady's bag when he sees Mister Cody ahead of him. He steps behind the woman, hiding behind her skirt. When they arrive at the lady's carriage, Cody has climbed inside.

"Well young man, I have to admit you have been a great help to me." She reaches into her handbag and pulls out ten Egyptian dollars to tip Abu. He accepts the money and pushes the bag towards the train attendant.

The last of the porters and baggage handlers are clearing the platform. Abu races to the front of the train and jumps off the platform. He runs up the tracks a few yards and hides behind a pile of old rails. Peeking around the stack, he watches as the train pulls out. Abu hopes his luck will hold.

The train is passing and Abu spots the train guard at the rear, cudgel in hand. The train picks up speed and the guard moves to the far side. Abu sprints for the train, reaching for the ladder at the side of the baggage car, his fingers close on the bottom rung of the ladder. He gets two hands on the rung. His right hand gains purchase on the second rung and he pulls himself up. Abu climbs fast to the top of the car.

Once on top, he cannot relax. He finds the ladder going down between the cars. Abu hides below the roof line and next to the door. He waits and hopes this trainman is as lazy as most. Peeking through the window, Abu can see the train-guard enter the car. He scrambles up the ladder again and lies flat on the roof. After a few minutes, Abu climbs down and peeks through the window. He sees the trainman making a cup of tea and settling down in a large chair. Abu knows it is unlikely the train-guard will move again before Kom Ombo. He returns to the top of the car and sits with his back to the wind.

In his compartment, Jason's Cell phone beeps.

"Jason, this is Nathan McDonald."

"Yes Sir..."

"Listen closely."

"Sir?" Jason moves to the edge of his seat.

"I have just received a memo which I will relay to you in an e-mail. You know, about the mole. It seems he has been indiscreet with our enforcement tracking software." *'Great! What else do they have the keys to the front door.'* Jason thinks. "I am issuing strict orders for all field agents to stay off of the tracking site. There is a good chance the Russians may have sold it to Bin Laden, which would explain why we haven't been able to find him. I've placed an encrypted package on the web for you. Pick it up ASAP. You need the information now not later. Oh and one other thing you should know, you've become a hot property. We'll talk soon. Stay safe!" Nathan rings off.

Jason puts the phone down slowly, *Hot Property!* He knows the meaning without the code book. Someone has marked him for elimination and he will have to be careful. Although he has a private compartment to Kom Ombo, he feels the need to pull the shade and lock the door. Jason tries to sit back and enjoy the ride but the circumstance does not lend itself to relaxation. The constant jostling of the train sets his nerves on edge.

# *Five*

Cody's taxi drives onto a narrow dirt road racing between houses and the backs of shops. He can see the town of Kom Ombo miles away and is worried about where the driver is taking him. His hand slides into his bag finding his Beretta. The taxi bumps down the narrow road past crumbling mud-brick huts. The road turns and the buildings come to an end. Jason can see the Nile in front of the taxi and the SS Karim sitting at the quay.

It is not the dead-end Jason had feared. The train journey has made him tense. He frowns and thinks. *'It isn't the train journey. It's the message from Neal Roberts.'* Since Jason found out he is a marked man, his nerves have been on edge. He's checking everyone, looking for a trap. Jason takes a deep breath and lets it out slowly. *'Easy Cody, easy,'* Jason thinks. He has always been in control, always self-assured but being a hunted man, he hasn't a clue whether he should be getting in deeper or getting out. He holsters his weapon and flexes the tension from his hand. This spy business is not all he thought it would be.

The taxi slowly bumps down the narrow road, crowded with tourists. Jason sees other cruise boats moored two and three deep in the distance. The taxi pulls to the side and Abu jumps from the rear bumper dashing behind a coach. The driver unloads Cody's bag, which a porter picks up. Cody leads the way along the quay to where the SS Karim has a private berth.

Walking along the Nile, Jason catches snatches of conversation, his senses heightened. There are disagreements between husbands and wives, while others hurry to the cool of the ships. He passes two men admiring a large piece of machinery being loaded. One man is saying to the other, he had worked on the development of one similar. Cody shakes his head. Here in ancient Egypt, they find more interest in a machine than the history beneath their feet.

A small group of tourists follows Cody into the opulent mahogany lobby of the Karim and reception. While he fills out his cabin card, room keys are handed out to his fellow passengers.

"Oh, Mister Cody. I thought you had missed us in Aswan."

"Oh, hello, Missus?"

"Covington. We didn't see you on the boat earlier and thought you had missed it altogether." She says.

"I had to cover a story in Aswan for the independent press."

"Oh, you shouldn't work, this is a holiday! Never mind, you're here now. You must promise to sit with us at lunch. Of course you will that's settled then. I'll save you a seat. See you in ten minutes." She collects her key as Cody completes his check-in.

Cody watches the disappearing keys, only two remain and one of those is pulled out and laid in front of him.

"Is the boat very full?" He asks.

"Oh yes, we are always full for this voyage. Not many boats make the trip from Aswan to Cairo anymore. Not since the shootings three years ago. A very bad business that was, did you know it was teenagers filled with some nonsense from a senile old Cleric, warriors for Islam. It was terrible for business and now we need special permission to make the trip. Here is your key and your cabin is on this deck halfway down on the right. The boy will show you the way."

The concierge speaks to the man carrying Cody's bag. Cody makes a quick search of the room, ignoring the brass and mahogany décor. Satisfying himself it is safe, he unpacks. There is a knock on the door and a young man in uniform presents Jason a letter on a silver tray. The letter outlines the excursions he can make and the meal schedule. The messenger informs him, lunch is being served.

Jason pulls out his laptop. Finding a wall socket, he sets up his computer and cell phone. In minutes he is downloading an encrypted package from the local FBI website while getting ready for lunch. The file finishes downloading when a message pops up. It informs him another file is available to download.

Jason sits at the writing desk, reading over the files. Neal Roberts has sent him a more in-depth report. In it are the death of the Egyptian Military Commander and Egyptian Security seeking him for murder. The final item is a file on the new Egyptian Field Office's Chief of Section. He reads over Taara Sefi's field experience. Jason studies the black and white photo, spotting her headscarf. He scrolls down the page to the section on religion. *'Follower of Islam.'* Cody scrolls back to the photo of his new boss. It shouldn't make a difference but it does. He looks at his clenched fist. It wasn't her. She's too young. Jason runs his hands through his hair, trying to push the memory from his mind but all he can think of is a brick wall.

The memory transports Jason back to the brick wall where the soldiers pushed his parents. His father yelling. His voice filled with anger and outrage, demanding they look at their marriage certificate and diplomatic pass. His mother's voice calm, telling his uncle Jeremy to watch over Jason and Jennifer. Then the first stone falls striking her in the chest and Jason panics.

His father throws himself over his mother but she stands aside and returns a stone of her own, hitting a soldier who had pulled them from the car. The soldier fires a stone back at her but Jason's father is there to take the blow. Now the rocks and stones are falling in earnest. His father is covering his mother with his body but a large rock strikes him in the head. His body sags against her. She looks at his father then turns her eyes to Jason. The stones seem to pause mid-flight.

*'I love you, Jason. I love…'* A stone strikes her in the head she wavers on the edge of consciousness. A storm of rocks and stones flies at his parents, burying them with

their weight. Jason sees only a blur. Greedy hands snatching up rocks and throwing them as fast as they can, mothers, old women, children.

Jason looks around the square for someone to help and for the first time, sees the mounds of rocks ringing the empty lot. It was planned, it was planned all along. Jason's blood burns with hatred, he feels it hot under his skin. He becomes aware of a force like steel against his chest. It's his uncle Jeremy but why is he pressing him so hard, then Jason realizes. It is he who is pressing against his uncle's arm. He looks to where his parents had stood only moments before. Only a pile of stones remains.

Jason feels detached. His parents are not under the pile of stones. No, of course they aren't. They're waiting for him in the car. He feels his uncle lifting him as the soldiers fire in the air stopping the stones. Jason and Jennifer are bundled into the back seat. His uncle yells for the driver to get out of there. Jason sees the soldiers wade into the empty lot as the motor starts. The car begins to pull away. Jason's uncle is saying how sorry he is. Two shots are fired as the car drives off. The sound shakes Jason to the marrow. Jason looks at Taara's photo again and thinks. *'This one needs to prove herself.'* He leans back in his chair and takes a deep breath. He has reports to get out and needs to call the Cairo office. *'No time for lunch. I'll get room service later,'* he thinks.

 

On the quay, Abu watched as Cody entered the boat. He's had no chance of following with the porters and deckhands watching so closely. The porters are loading the last of the supplies before departure. While the guards are distracted in conversation, Abu sees his chance. He changes his vest around so the black lining is out. He holds his bundle low and moves with purpose towards a small stack of boxes to be loaded. As Abu walks across the dirt road, he sees a Man in Black robes talking to a woman and pointing to the SS Karim.

 

Abu ducks behind a shrub. He hears the man say to the woman.

"I want you to go on to Asyut. Keep an eye on him. I don't want him making any more connections. Wherever he lands I, want you there, do you understand?" The woman nods and asks.

 

"What will you do now?" The man stares at the boat for a moment before he answers.

"Nothing, I will continue as planned but I will not use the river." The woman nods in comprehension. Abu has become absorbed in the conversation of the two strangers. He strains to see the faces of the two but the Man-in-Black is walking away. A taxi pulls up and the man gets in. The taxi pulls away and the woman turns her face from the dust. She curses the driver and walks away.

Abu returns his attention to the quay. There are only three bundles left and two men are walking towards them. He must move quickly while the guards are deep in conversation. Abu has no choice. The second man is struggling with two of the bundles and leaves one. Abu walks over and hefts the large bundle onto his shoulder. Staggering under the weight, He follows the last of the porters across the gangway.

Onshore, some of the crew are enjoying their last moments before they report to work. One of the cabin crew, a tall man, walks away from the clearing as the others start for the boat. The tall man begins to urinate. A voice comes from behind speaking in Egyptian.

"Are you working on the Karim," it asks. The man does not turn but answers while he finishes.

"Yes, we will make the journey all the way to Cairo this time. It will be good to see Ca..." He does not get a chance to finish his sentence. A garrote is slipped over his head and holds him suspended off of the ground. His body convulses as he attempts to free himself but the strength of the man holding him is too great. The cord cuts deeply into his neck. The tall man goes limp in the hands of his assailant. A second man steps up and strips the jacket off the dead man, handing it to a third. This man brushes down the jacket before he puts it on. He straightens himself and combs his hair back in the fashion of the dead man while the other two carry away the body. He finishes his grooming and slides a knife up his sleeve.

Onboard the Karim, a man watches from the upper deck as the passengers and crew board. He wears a dirty shirt, trousers and the turban of the coal stokers. His face betrays little but his eyes are sharp and miss nothing. He has seen the boy slip on board. He steps away from the rail, making a mental note to deal with the little rat.

# *Six*

Taara Sefi puts down the phone and finishes making notes. Files and papers cover the desk cascading off and onto the floor. Mark Rider's old office is cluttered with rows upon rows of papers stacked down the center of the room. As Taara is finishing her note, a knock comes at the door.

"Come in." She calls and Commander McAllen enters the room. He steps around the rows of papers on the floor.

"I see you've been busy. Are you working on Mark's filing system?" The Commander asks with a smile.

"Oh, I've cracked it. I'm just arranging the files for transport Back to Washington." Taara says, returning the Commander's smile.

The Commander looks amused and asks.

"How did you manage to break Mark's code if I'm not intruding." Alistair's smile becomes tight.

"It was right in front of us all of the time." She says with an air of triumph.

147

"Where in front of us may I ask?" The Commander's smile slips away.

"There," Taara points to the replica of the Rosetta Stone holding center stage on the far bookshelf. He turns and looks at the replica.

"What has the Rosetta Stone to do with Mark's filling system?" "I reasoned since Mark is part Greek and one of the languages on the Rosetta Stone is Greek, maybe the Greek alphabet is part of it. I located Greek symbols on the drawers."

"Yes we saw those but they didn't seem to relate." The Commander says, speaking over her.

"Not directly, no." She returns. "I also noticed sand script symbols etched into the design of the drawer fronts. Well," She says. "The Greek alphabet seems to be a decoy. However, the Sanskrit symbols were so cleverly worked into the drawer fronts I thought they might be the actual filling code. I found a book on the comparative alphabets of the ancient cultures in Mark's bookshelf. When I opened it, the pages fell open to the Greek alphabet and if you look, there has been detailed underlining of each of the letters of the Greek alphabet. These patterns of underlining are repeated in the section on Sanskrit."

Taara shows the Commander the two sections of the book with the underlined letters. The Commander arches one eyebrow and looks at Taara with renewed interest.

"Well, after that, it was simple. I find the drawer with the appropriate symbol and go through until I find a page with a cuneiform symbol at the top."

"Cuneiform?"

"Oh yes, I couldn't find any other symbols on the pages except cuneiform on the upper right-hand corner. Once I found one, I was able to go through and pull out all of the corresponding pages." She spread her arms out, indicating the collection of files she has arranged on the center of the floor and smiles.

"So what is the pile on the desk then?" The Commander points to the accumulation of pages piled high.

"Oh those, for some reason they don't match with anything in the files. They are personal papers and accounts scattered throughout the drawers." She says as she rearranges her headscarf.

"Well, I don't want to pull you away from all of this but how is your Arabic." The Commander asks, smiling.

"Good, I think. My parents are Afghani and I've been stationed in Saudi for the past three years."

"Good. I have been able to isolate a bit more of the conversation using your filter but I can't make it out. Could you give it a try? Perhaps you can make out what the informant is saying." The two walk to the Commander's office where he has been analyzing the tape. "By the way, was that phone call from our boy." He inquires.

"Yes. Your contact in Aswan has given him a clue. It's Hieroglyphics sewn into a robe." She says as she sits down at the Commander's desk.

"Has he been able to decode it?" The Commander asks.

"No but he will be sending us a copy as soon as he gets to Luxor." She responds. The Commander looks confused.

"Why in Luxor, why not now." He asks.

"Because it is a large garment and he can't very well fax it to us. Agent Cody said he would buy a camera in Luxor and photograph it." Taara frowns as she adds. "Oh, also, your contact Pasha has been killed. I'm sorry." Taara frowns again as she places the headset over her ears, ending the conversation. The Commander creases his brow at her words but says nothing.

## Luxor Egypt, on the SS Karim 08:24 September 6, 2001

Jason Cody has finished his breakfast later than the other passengers. He's discovered most of the passengers are from an English tour group.

"So how does it feel young man." It is Andrew Covington and his wife Mary who sit opposite Cody. Jason looks up from his coffee and smiles. Andrew is tall and slim with white hair. He has the appearance of a man who had been very fit in his younger days. Mister Covington is dressed in a beige colored linen suit with a white shirt open at the collar. Jason feels underdressed in his shorts and a button-down shirt. Missus Covington also wears a light colored linen dress and a scarf around her shoulders, giving her high cheekbones and white hair a stately look.

"What do you mean," Cody asks.

"I mean being the token 'Yank' on this voyage." Covington chuckles at his own joke as his wife touches his hand in a gentle reprimand. She smiles at Jason. Cody returns the smile, unsure of what to say. Missus Covington jumps in covering the awkward moment.

"Are you planning to join us in many of the excursions?" She asks.

"Yes, but I haven't had time to study the itinerary yet." He replies.

"Are you traveling alone?"

"Yes I have been stationed in Cairo with the US. News Service but my time here is up. I'm using some of my vacation to enjoy Egypt." Cody returns to his coffee, hoping not to be drawn into further conversation.

"You know you are not the only single person on board?" Missus Covington says.

"Leave the man alone, Mary. I'm sure he is intelligent enough to figure out who is or is not attached. You don't have to go playing matchmaker with every single person you meet." The couple's voices drop to a whisper as they speak amongst themselves and Cody excuses himself.

After Jason has changed, he returns to the lobby.

"Oh, Mister Cody, are you not joining us for the excursion to the Temple of Karnak? If you are, we will be leaving shortly." Missus Covington asks across the lobby full of tourists.

"No," Jason calls back. "My camera stopped working. I have to go into Luxor to buy another." Missus Covington hurries over to Jason.

"Well that is too bad but if you don't replace it here, there won't be another chance until we reach Cairo." She says, stepping around Mark Harris and his wife Jan.

"Yes, that's what Mister Harradi has told me." Jason agrees.

"It's unfortunate you will be missing the temple but perhaps you can join us later after you make your purchase. Any taxi can take you there." Missus Covington says. Jason thinks for a moment. It's imperative he gets the information to Washington and the Commander as soon as possible. On the other hand, he does not want to appear to be anything other than an average tourist.

"It is the one thing I would say you must see in Luxor. Would you agree Mister Harris?" Missus Covington asks, looking for support from her fellow traveler.


"What? Oh yes, the Temple at Karnak, yes by all means. It is possibly the most awe-inspiring sight in all of Egypt. Then we are off to the Temple at Dendera. Which is the best preserved temple from the period? Yes, I would say it is a must-see!" Mister Harris relates with complete seriousness while his wife provides the smile. The couple Jason learns has been to Egypt no fewer than eight times. Mister Harris considers himself an amateur archaeologist. He enjoys being seen in Khaki colored shirt and trousers, a

153

white scarf around his neck. Missus Harris dresses in the female role of the archaeologist with a matching khaki skirt, blouse and a white sun hat. Jason looks at his watch as the crew announces his taxi has arrived.

"I'll do my best. What time do you leave from Karnak?" They give him the details which he dutifully marks on his excursion brochure.

## Egypt, Temple of Karnak 10:43 September 6, 2001

The heat of the day is building as Jason halfheartedly hunts for his fellow tourists. He wonders through the giant columns and statues of The Temple of Karnak. Finding a shady spot behind one of the columns, he sits down for a rest. He is happy he decided to see it. At no time in his studies could books or photos convey the power and grandeur of the temple. Sitting among the fifty columns, he can only imagine what the temple looked like in its day. He looks up at the blocks of stone above, connecting row upon row of columns. Jason admires the architecture as a stoneworker inches his way around the column. The stone worker sees Jason and moves in closer. In his hand, he carries a sharpened trowel.

"Hello! You made it after all. We were just about to give up on you. What?" Missus Covington stops short of finishing her thought, looking past Jason. Jason sees her eyes wide. He jumps and turns, his hand going instinctively for his Beretta. The stone worker has dropped the hand holding the trowel to his side. He hides it under the folds of his simple garment. His other hand is raised palm up, begging for money. "I don't believe this. Get away you, get away!" Missus Covington yells. Jason does not move but releases the Beretta's restraining strap. Missus Covington makes to chase him off but her husband holds her back. The worker grows bold stepping forward. There is a sudden movement from his left. Gerald Forester has grabbed the man's arm, pulling it into an arm lock. The stoneworker panics and tries to get away. A moment's struggle and the worker has regained his freedom but loses the trowel. Realizing he is unarmed and outnumbered, the stone worker runs off.

"Mister Forester, are you all right." Mister and Missus Covington ask. Gerald conceals the trowel behind his back and assures everyone he is fine.

"I didn't want the situation to get ugly." He reassures them. "Strength in numbers, you know."

"How right you are Mister Forester." Andrew Covington remarks. "These scoundrels are getting bolder at every turn." Jason replaces the Beretta's restraining strap. Missus Covington moves in close to Jason and says.

"Mister Cody I am happy to see you found us but I hope this is not a prelude to the rest of the day?"

## Outskirts of Luxor, Egypt 11:42 September 6, 2001

Jason notes fewer mud houses along the road as the tour coach drives from Luxor. They pass another armed checkpoint at the edge of a village. The armed men at the checkpoint casually hold onto their weapons, more as show than protection. The bus is passing through the edge of the Fundamentalist's territory. In the past coaches have been shot at. The Egyptian Government takes a dim view of this and has Tourist Police escort every tour.

Jason looks out the window as the bus speeds along. The contrast of what he sees is striking. The towns of Egypt are tenuous invaders in a vast desert. They cling to the Nile, Egypt's lifeblood. To his left are a scattering of houses. Jason notes the few houses clustered along the banks of irrigation canals that etch their way across the desert. The tiny channels are turning the sand into fertile land.

"Do you mind if I show you my new toy, Mister Cody?" It is Gerald Forester who leans across the aisle of the coach to speak. Jason looks down and sees he is holding out a digital camera.

"Not at all," Jason replies. It looks like I should have had you with me when I bought my camera. I ended up with one of the new digital ones but no one in the shop told me I would have to charge the battery before I could use it," Jason says.

"You mean you didn't get any pictures of Karnak? Don't worry about it. I've taken enough photos for both of us. I can give you a copy of what I have if you like."

"Yes, thank you. It would be nice to have something to remember it by," Jason replies.

"I took one of you just before we all found each other. I thought you might like to see it."


Forester flips through several shots of the columns until he finds the one he is looking for. Cody sees himself on the screen immediately before Missus Covington greeted him. He is sitting entranced by the rows of columns. At the base of the column behind Jason is the stone worker, trowel in hand. Jason sees the reason Mister Forester is showing him the picture. The laborer is not looking to pick Cody's pocket. He is poised and ready to strike.

"It looks like that man is trying to cut the strap of your bag." It is Clive Peters who speaks.

Clive is sitting behind Jason. He has been peaking around the edge of the seat, interested in the conversation. Forester looks back and smiles at Peters. He is a shy, thin man and Forester cannot imagine him being very successful. Peters has a receding hairline and light colored eyes. He is dressed in shorts and a button-down shirt which looks more American than English.

"They do that you know, pickpockets these days, cut the straps to bags and run off with them. It happens all the time these days. That's some camera you've got there. Good pictures?" Mister Forester looks at Peters and says.

"Yes, excellent pictures, quite small and easy to slip into a pocket." Forester demonstrates this by tucking it away in his shirt pocket.

"I'll get you those copies later today. I can put it on a CD for you." He says, cutting Peters out of the conversation.

"That would be great. This thing is useless without a charge." Jason pulls the new Sony out of his bag and shows it to Forester.

Clive Peters watches the interchange between the two men. After a moment, he sits back and looks to his daughter sitting next to him.

"What was that all about?" Sara Peters inquires.

"Oh, nothing, just boys with their toys. It seems we have a few shutterbugs with us." He says. Sara says nothing but she smiles and her deep brown eyes tells him she understands. Clive appraises his daughter as she sits next to him. Twenty-three and pretty, not beautiful but a good catch for most men. She's worn her long brown hair up for the excursions today. It reminds him of her mother, now ten years gone. Sara is brighter than most. Clive has made sure she attended the best schools while sacrificing the things he wanted. It's been seven years since he's had a vacation and Sara insisted he should go to Egypt. It's a voyage he has always dreamed of. He agreed, providing they both go as a graduation present.

"He's a nice-looking chap, the American. Don't you think?" Clive remarks to his daughter.

"Please father, I hadn't noticed and you should be enjoying the ride, not playing matchmaker." She gently chides but her eyes stray to Jason's profile between the seats. Clive sees this and smiles to himself. *'It won't be long now.'* He thinks and mentally checks he will have enough for a wedding when the time comes. He feels content and a bit sad at the thought of losing Sara to another man. However, that is the way of life. He comforts himself with the thought as the coach rolls on through the dry heat of Egypt.

## Temple of Dendera, Egypt 12:23 September 6, 2001

Cody looks over the ruins, noting where the Tourist Police are. The temple guide makes a slow procession around the temple with his group in tow. Cody realizes a conspiracy that has sprung up amongst the members of the group. He finds himself and Miss Peters have been paired up as if by magic. Whenever the group is to move forward, she appears by his side. If the path narrows, the group hangs back and encourages the two young people to go on together. At first, Jason thought it was only Missus Covington who is behind the plot but soon it becomes apparent Mister Peters and the rest have joined in. They are taking as much amusement in matchmaking as the guide's explanations.

The guide informs his group, they are following the procession of the sacred idols. These were brought out annually and presented to the sun. He shows them a replica of the earliest representation of astrology set in the ceiling above their heads. He makes a point of saying the original is in Paris at the Louvre. They walk on and find themselves on the roof of the temple, where they are encouraged to photograph the site.

After a short time, the group needs to escape from the summer heat. They make their way back down to the coolness of the temple. Sun hats become fans and water bottles come out as people find seats in the shade of the temple. The guide from the boat, Abdel Kedesh, meets them. He tells the group that there are several interesting sections of the temple, which are normally closed to the public. He makes arrangements for the tour to visit a hidden chamber which was not discovered until one-hundred and fifty years after the initial excavation. The majority of the group would rather rest and Jason has no real intention of moving but a discussion begins.

"Well, I really think some of us should go down into the catacombs. Don't you? The guide has obviously paid for us to visit these places. It would be a waste if someone didn't see them." Missus Forester remarks. The debate goes back and forth for a few minutes. In the end, it is decided the two young people should go as there is a tricky entry.

Reluctantly, Jason rises to join Miss Peters for the journey into the dark underworld of the temple.

## Washington DC, FBI Offices 08:04 September 6, 2001

Nathan McDonald weaves his way through the halls of the Washington FBI offices. He steps into Neal's outer office and Jean, who is on the phone, indicates he should go in. As he puts his hand on the doorknob, there was a well-timed buzz of the electric lock releasing it. Nathan looks back at Jean but she is engrossed in other things.

Entering the office, he finds Neal Roberts on the phone and takes a seat. Nathan glances around the room as a matter of habit more than interest. It contains a few pictures of family and one or two with friends on fishing trips. Behind Neal's desk, there are three pictures of Neal with the last three Presidents. Nathan thinks it might be a short run for this one, with the election having been so close.

Neal puts the phone down and turns his full attention to Nathan.

"How is our girl in Egypt doing?" Nathan looks up, not knowing what to say. I don't know, is not an acceptable answer in intelligence circles. He rephrases.

"We haven't heard anything since her last report yesterday. I wasn't prepared to worry. Should I?" Neal looks at a memo on his desk before he hands it to Nathan.

"This just came through from MI-6. It's not new information but the lead is strong and the information appears to be genuine." Nathan reads through the message.

"How good is the source on this," Nathan asks, looking to Neal.

Neal rubs his forehead and replies.

"I've been on the phone all morning trying to pin that down. From what I gather, MI-6 feels the source is believable." Nathan looks hard at Neal, trying to read his compressed features.

"However, you're not sure." Neal sits back and looks to the ceiling. He gathers his thoughts and continues.

"I know MI-6 has beat us repeatedly on intel out of the Middle East. Their intel has proven to be sound, more times than not." Nathan looks up and says.

163

"That's not saying a lot. Our intel could be just as good if we had the time and people to better sift through it." Nathan says.

"We don't have the time or people. This information, therefore, comes from a more reliable source than we can provide." Nathan can see that Neal's mind is made up.

"So what's the plan?"

"We're putting together a general bulletin. We'll tighten all security at domestic and international airports." Nathan looks at the desk.

"You realize a warning like that will be taken with a grain of salt by the airlines. They get those warnings regularly." Neal's face transforms and his frustration shows.

"What should we do? send agents to every airport and screen the passengers. You know our budget constraints." Neal sits back in his chair and closes his eyes, looking for a moment's peace. He looks at Nathan McDonald and says. "We can't release anything more without something solid. We need a lead, something that will better define what, where, when and how. What happened to the suspected Al-Qaeda members taking flying lessons?"

"Agents Miller and Jones picked them up and questioned them. We held them for twenty-four hours but everything checked out. We had to release them." Nathan responds. Neal looks down at the memo and says.

"I don't like it. There has to be something we can do to connect the dots. What are Miller and Jones doing now?"

"They're covering for the Agents working on the Mole."

"Have them pick them up again and this time, hold them. Find a reason, invent a reason but hold them." Nathan gives Neal a moment then asks.

"What does this have to do with Agent Sefi?"

Neal looks Nathan in the eye and says.

"All morning I have been trying to trace this info through British Intelligence. Just now I got off the phone with an operations chief in London. He said the information in the memo was passed to them through their contacts in Egypt. I want you to get on the phone and see what Sefi and McAllen can come up with on this."

"What about Cody."

"Tell him of course but let him follow his own leads. From his last report, he has his hands full." Nathan looks down at the memo lying on the desk and reads it again.

**Information Classified, MI-6 Section, London England**

Sources indicate imminent terrorist attack on US soil within the next two months.

Source of attack known to be Al-Qaeda trained cell members.

Cell members unknown.

Terrorists may have piloting skills, suggests possible hijacking.

**MI-6**

## Egypt, Temple of Dendera 14:06 September 6, 2001

Jason slides the last meter of the slope on the soles of his shoes, then steps carefully into the low passageway. Jason looks along the passage, not seeing Miss Peters, he calls out.

"Miss Peters?"

"I'm here Mister Cody." She responds.

Jason turns to his right and steps down into a taller passage. As he moves the torch, it catches the gold and red pigments on the walls around him. After all of these hundreds of years, they are still brilliant to behold. Jason

166

crouches down to study one of the painted hieroglyphs. He finds it is not painted but inlaid with lapis, ivory and gold.

"That's nothing. Wait until you see this." Cody looks up and sees Miss Peters standing at the end of the passage one hand on her hip, smiling at him. Lit from behind, the silhouette of Sara's body shows through the light material of her blouse and skirt. causing Jason to catch his breath. He cannot take his eyes off of her slender form. He walks towards her wondering if this was one of those moves women instinctively know how to do.

Sara steps aside as he approaches, allowing him to see the walls behind her. The passage Cody has entered is taller than the first. Jason notices the vivid colors of the hieroglyphs covering the walls. Miss Peters begins explaining some of the figures covering the walls. They walk down the passage as she speaks. Sara enlightens Jason to the fact the temple was occupied during the Ptolemaic-Roman period and the walls in this section show both Roman Emperors and Pharaohs. Her explanation becomes more animated as she goes and the colors of the hieroglyphs more vivid with her description.

"Can you imagine what they must have looked like when they were newly finished? They must have been incredible." She concludes. Looking at the figure of the god Horus inlaid with gold and precious gems.

"You seem to know a lot about this, Miss Peters." Sara steps closer to Jason smiling.

"In case I failed to properly introduce myself, Mister Cody, my name is Sara." Caught off guard, Jason stammers slightly.

"Of course, sorry, I'm Jason if you like." She smiles at his embarrassment.

"Oh, I know who you are Mister Cody. Every Woman on the Karim knows your name." Cody blushes his response as he looks into Sara's smiling eyes.

From behind, there is the sound of someone sliding down the stone entrance. Jason turns thankful for the diversion.

"Hello!" No response. He repeats the call again.

"Did you hear someone?" Sara inquires, looking disappointed. There is no response to Jason's calls and he looks back at Sara.

"No, I guess it was just falling sand."

"Well don't worry. Dendera has been standing for thousands of years. I don't think it's going to suddenly trap us like one of your American movies." Sara says, one hand on Jason's forearm.

Sara smiles again and Jason blushes deeper. The heat of mid-day penetrates even into the underground passages and Sara pulls out a Chinese fan and says.

"I don't think we should stay down here too long. The heat is unbearable." Jason asks.

"Are you okay?"

"Oh, yes. I'll be fine." Sara says, smiling.

Cody feels more than hears someone creeping along the corridor behind him.

"Are there any more Hieroglyphs like these?" He asks.

"We can check," Sara says. "Let's walk around and see." Cody follows as they walk around the square of passages containing the hieroglyphs. As they move, Cody can feel the follower creeping along behind. They stay to the main passages ignoring the smaller ones. They arrive at the low entrance passage where they started.

169

"I don't think I can take any more of this heat. I think we should leave." Sara says and Jason agrees.

Going to the entrance, Cody sees the plan of their pursuer. The slope which they slide down they must climb back up. To making it difficult is the slope covered with fine sand and the roof of the exit is so low, you have to crawl out of it. Sara eyes the exit with dismay.

"I may need some help with this." She smiles apologetically.

"Don't worry. You'll do fine." Sara puts her sandal clad foot on a stepping stone and starts scaling the steep sandy incline. Cody pushes against the bottoms of her sandals to give her a foothold as she negotiates the short slope. She must crawl under a low ceiling brace to exit.

Sara stretches her body through the low opening. She is reaching for the base of the stairs when suddenly her support from below is gone. She slips, grabbing the lower step.

"Mister Cody, this is not the time to withdraw your assistance please." She says but Jason is occupied.

The assailant charges into the narrow passage, a knife pointed at Cody's heart. Jason jumps back, flattening himself against the wall but the attacker has the advantage of being small. He can find space in the passage while Cody's large build allows him only room to retreat. The attacker strikes again with his knife, driving Cody down the tight passage. Jason can only hope the attacker will follow him into the larger passage. At that moment, Miss Peters decides to protest Cody's lack of help by kicking her feet and yelling.

"Mister Cody, I would really appreciate it if you would help me out of this." The motion of her kicking attracts the attention of the attacker. He moves towards the helpless girl whose legs struggle on the sandy slope.

The little man chuckles, raising his knife to strike Sara.

"Mister Cody, this is not funny. Would you please help me out of this before I ruin my skirt." She yells at the top of her lungs. The sound of her screams distracts the attacker. Cody dives forward in a full football tackle. With one hand he catches the extended knife hand knocking the blade free. As the two men fly down the narrow passage, Cody grabs the attacker by the neck and pushes his head down. With a powerful thrust, it strikes the stone floor. There is a crack and Cody feels for the first time, another man's life passing through his hands. The attacker goes limp in Cody's grip.

Cody can feel the blood drain away from his own face. He feels faint and is ill. After a brief moment, he struggles to his feet. He returns to where Miss Peters is still struggling and again offers his support. Sara's protesting goes on for the next few minutes while she manages the last few feet of the assent. Jason puts his remaining strength into making the assent himself but the exertion and heat have drained him. He emerges from the outer opening and sees Sara's screams have brought the rest of the group.

He pulls himself up with help from Mister Forester and faces Miss Peters.

"Mister Cody, you will explain yourself." She says while setting herself directly in his path, arms crossed.

"I am truly sorry but the heat. I don't know exactly what happened. I woke up on the floor." Cody tries to straighten and brush off his clothes as Sara's icy stare warms slightly.

"I heard you laugh Mister Cody." She accuses.

"I was ill I am sorry to say. I can assure you that at no time did I laugh." The frankness of his proclamation causes Sara to step back. She feels less sure of what she has heard.

"I think we should all get back to the air conditioning of the coach. This heat has taken the fun out of the adventure. Mister Kedesh can we board the coach and return please." Says Missus Covington.

"Yes, of course. Would all of you please go to the coach and I will gather any stragglers." Kedesh makes to climb down into the passages but Cody kicks the metal grate closed.

"There's no one else down there Mister Kedesh but I think there may be others scattered around the temple." Cody looks at Kedesh, who shrugs and walks off to find the others. Gerald Forester walks next to Cody and looks him over.

"Are you okay?"

"Yes, I'm fine now that I'm out of that pit." Jason looks straight ahead to the coach.

"You look better now but I would put something on that cut of yours."

"Cut?"

"On your forearm." Cody looks down at his arm just above the wrist. The attacker got to him before he knocked the knife from his hand.

"Why don't you go to the back of the coach and lay down I have a first aid kit." Cody looks at Forester but Gerald only smiles away the question.

"Don't worry about the girls. I'll make excuses for you." Forester walks on ahead to join his wife and the others gathering outside the coach.

Showered and refreshed, Cody makes his way out to the general reception area to await the dinner call. He has photographed the garment and placed the photos on the FBI website with messages for both Taara Sefi and Neal Roberts. He has also smoothed things over with Sara. Altogether not too bad an afternoon and the pain in his arm is easing. It will be hard to imagine anything short of dinner being late spoiling his evening.

"Mister Cody." It is the Director of the Karim, Mister Kohlemete. Dark hair combed back with a long mustache he stands five foot eight. He wears a shirt and tie but no jacket.

"Yes," Cody replies, expecting the return of his passport from check-in.

"We have a small problem. I wonder if you would be good enough to help us. Would you please come with me?" Cody finds himself being guided into the small office behind the reception desk. Standing in the center of the room is a larger man both in height and width. He also wears a shirt, tie and black trousers.

"This is Mister Habid, my Assistant Director and I believe you know this young man."

Habid steps to the side revealing a sorry looking young man with his head down. Cody cannot see his face but he knows the bright blue of his vest.

"Abu?" Abu looks up with pain in his eyes. Seeing Cody, he quickly looks down at his hands.

"So you do know him as he claims."

"Yes, we have met but only briefly in Aswan."

"So he is not your valet as he claims."

"No but..."

"Then we will put him off at the next port we have no place for little rats like this one." Now it is Cody's turn to guide Mister Kohlemete. He grasps him by the elbow and guides him from the room. Kohlemete is ruffled but goes along.

"This young man is the son of a man who works closely with my agency. Before I left Aswan, I discovered his parents and family were killed in an accident. I know my agency would not want him to be abandoned. Is there any way we can provide the boy transport to Cairo without causing a scene?"

Mister Kolemete considers the matter.

"There may be room for him with the crew but we are not able to act as ferry transport. The Nile authority would have our license. I don't..."

"Then he is my valet. I simply forgot to mention him on my arrival. I apologize for the mistake and perhaps we could arrange some compensation for the inconvenience." Mister Kohlemete mouths some words of objection but is quickly silenced as Cody pulls out several twenty dollar notes from his pocket and holds them before the Director. A few more notes are added and Abu is guaranteed a bed and food for the remainder of the journey.

"I am sorry to be so much trouble for you, Mister Cody. I..." Cody puts up his hand and cuts the boy off. Passengers are passing by on their way to dinner and the Director and his assistant are still standing by. Cody plays the part of a disgruntled employer saying.

"I think we've had enough of this for one night. We will discuss it tomorrow and not before. Have you eaten?" Abu shakes his head no and looks down to the floor. Cody looks to the Director, who looks to his assistant. Mister Habid sighs and steps beside the boy.

"Okay, let's find you some food and a bed." He says, only slightly more sympathetic. Abu looks up at the large man and nods.

"Abu." Abu looks up to see Jason winking at him. "See you tomorrow." The boy brightens and continues to the lower decks.

## Cairo FBI Offices 16:24 September 6, 2001

The Commander pulls a large set of headphones off and rubs his ears. He removes the cassette from the player and walks it across the hall to Taara Sefi's office.

"How goes the jigsaw puzzle," Alistair asks. Taara looks up from the book she holds.

"Well, we have the pieces if we can just get it to tell us something." She returns her nose to the book. Commander McAllen looks over her shoulder.

"What have you discovered so far?" He asks gently. Taara makes a ducking movement stepping away.

"The main figures are the Gods of old Egypt."

"But?" The Commander anticipates her question.

"These hieroglyphs in the little boxes…"

"Cartouche." Taara looks at McAllen, her eyes questioning. "The little boxes are called cartouche. When they are next to a figure such as these, they provide the name of a Pharaoh. On their own, the figures would be the Gods of ancient Egypt Isis, Osiris, Horus." Commander McAllen points to three of the figures naming them as he goes.

"So what we have here..."

"What we have here is either part of a message or a very expensive souvenir," McAllen says. Taara looks at the arranged pictures and at the book on Hieroglyphics she holds.

"We should make the eff..."

"Oh, I agree we most definitely should." McAllen cuts her off again and Taara shows her annoyance.

"Well since you know these..."

"I was about to propose the very thing. May I see that?" The Commander indicates the book Taara holds.

Taara passes it over to him and he gives it a cursory look. "I think we can do better than this." He drops the book on her desk and selects a text from the bookcase.

"The Pharaohs of Egypt. This should make our job easier. You see, trying to decipher the name on a cartouche by direct translation can be dangerously inaccurate. The style of the hieroglyphs change from one age to the next and often the names were stylized." He smiles at Taara who peers over his shoulder. She opens her mouth to speak but he raises a finger silencing her before she can. "You see, working intelligence in Egypt takes more than a knowledge of the language. It takes time and experience with Egypt herself. You can't just go blundering around and expect to get results. I would think you would know that from your experiences in Saudi Arabia. How long did it take before you were accepted by the people around you?" The Commander looks at Taara who looks away.

"They were just beginning to trust me when I left." She looks into the Commander's eyes, her frustration at the treatment she received coming to the surface.

"I can see it did not sit well with you. You decided if the people wouldn't talk to you, you would have your people do the leg work for you. That was the smartest thing you did." Taara sits on the edge of the desk.

"Yes but we soon learned that what we received was outdated. Everything the informants passed to me was useless."

The Commander moves to her side, sitting on the desk.

"How did you know?" She asks.

"When I saw how you handled Major Haraddi I realized you'd been badly treated before. I guessed you had a rough time of it in Saudi. Unfortunately, our friend Haraddi is more than a bit put out by your behavior. I just learned when Haraddi carried out the President's orders calling off the arrest of foreign agents, he forgot our Agent Cody." Taara looks up at McAllen.

"Is Cody in danger?" McAllen smiles.

"Only in danger of being detained, and I'm beginning to wonder about that."

"What?"

"They want us contained. Why us? Why do they want the US agents contained and no other countries?" Alistair asks out loud.

"Do you think this may be something directed at the US?"

"No. That would be a long shot. It is more likely it involves one of the US. interests in the Middle East."

"You mean Israel."

"Yes, that is the more likely." The Commander pauses in thought before continuing.

"Oh, I also found a piece of information buried on the tape." Taara looks up, surprised.

"You said that the tape had nothing new on it."

"Yes, that's right. The tape we listened to held nothing more. However, when I was about to rewind it, I noticed more tape on the spool. I gave it a little pull and a new section was released."

"Was there anything useful on it?"

The Commander is lost in thought for the moment, then replies.

"Oh, just a name." Taara feels she is pulling teeth.

"What name?"

"Sorry. The name of an informant in Asut." He says.

"When will our boy arrive there." looking up, Taara pulls the information from memory.

"Tomorrow evening." Taara pauses, and then asks.

"Commander?"

"Yes."

"You say someone can't go bumbling around Egypt. Why did you send Cody when you know that to be true?"

The Commander turns to Taara and smiles.

"When you have been in this business as long as I have, you learn a lot about people very quickly. Otherwise, you may not see the next sunrise. I've been watching our Agent Cody and I have learned an interesting fact about him. One which, I don't think he knows himself." Taara sits forward, looking at McAllen with interest. The Commander smiles and says. "I wouldn't worry about Agent Cody. He is one of those rare people who have a natural ability for the job. I don't think we could have a better man out there." McAllen smiles at her and returns to his office. Taara watches McAllen go and wonders what it is he sees when he looks at her. Not for the first time, she feels out of her depth.

# *Seven*

Cody sits at the back corner of the sun deck. He has an excellent view of the shoreline and river. Using casual curiosity, he can keep a wary eye on any approaching boat traffic. Today however, Cody's vigilance gives way to quiet musings. He watches the parade of farms and people pass as the ship travels downstream.

Jason sees a large group of children assembled along the bank. He pulls out his camera, ready to follow Abu's advice. The children are cooling a large water buffalo in the river. One boy steps from the bank onto the animal's back. He walks its length and steps onto its head. Cody clicks away as the boy performs a perfect dive from the head of the beast. He pops up, waving and smiling. Cody returns his wave and smiles.

An insistent beep pulls Jason from the tranquility of the scene. He fishes in his bag for his phone.

"Mister Cody?" A woman's voice inquires.

"Yes, this is Jason Cody." He replies, not recognizing the voice.

"This is Taara Sefi I have taken over for Mister Rider since his accident." Jason unconsciously tenses at the voice of his superior. "I know you are on holiday Mister Cody but we've had a lead on a story and are wondering since you are in the neighborhood?"

"Yes, of course, I'd be happy to cover it for you. Can you give me some details?"

"I think it best if Mister McAllen tells you about it."


McAllen takes the phone.

"Jason, how's the holiday? Hope you can squeeze us into your schedule." McAllen is clearly enjoying the game.

"Of Course I can." Cody smiles at the thought of McAllen's face on the other end of the line.

"Well it's not a big story mind you but it could prove to be crucial." Cody sits up, listening carefully. "There is a man in Asut we need you to have a word with. He's witnessed an event that the local group would rather keep quiet. The tip came from Mister Rider's friend and appears to be reliable."

Cody processes the information. *'Riders friend,'* would indicate they found something on the tape and *'local group'* can only be the Muslim Brotherhood.

"Of course, what can I do?"

"Good boy. We need you to visit this man at his shop in Asut and persuade him to sell the story to us rather than the competition."

"Is there a danger of him going to someone else with the story," Cody asks. After a pause, McAllen's voice comes back.

"He has a history of selling stories to multiple press agencies telling each they have an exclusive. This has made him a bit of a black mark in some reporters' books."


Cody lets the information sink in before he speaks.

"I'll do my best but I am attracting local attention myself. Cody hears a hand go over the mouthpiece. A moment later, McAllen is back.
"I wouldn't worry about your following, get to him first and let the others fall second."

"Will do!"

Cody hangs up and checks his phone. The signal is still good. As they move away from Luxor, the phone signal will become weaker. Egypt has made many advances in recent years but lining the desert with cell phone towers has not been one of them. His best chance of communicating is around the major cities.

Jason pulls out his palm computer and connects to the FBI's website. He finds the file waiting for him. Cody downloads it along with a photo of the informant. He notes the Commander has given him a GPS location on the shop. It should make finding him easier. Jason worries about what the Commander has told him. The informant has been made a black mark. The meaning comes through loud and clear. He has to get to him before he is eliminated, scratched from the game. Cody smiles to himself. Game, he thinks. That's the Commanders term for it. When did he start thinking of it as a game, he wonders? When were fear and revulsion replaced by excitement, even fun?

"Do all Americans require so many gadgets on holiday?" Cody looks up from his thoughts and smiles at Missus Forester.

"No, I'm afraid work has found me even here." He lies and sees Sara Peters and Mary Covington are also headed his way. "Would you three like to join me?" He asks, pushing his technology into his canvas bag.

"It looks like you could use a new bag, Mister Cody. That one is on its way out, you know." Missus Forester smiles sweetly, trying not to embarrass him. Cody smiles broadly at the comment saying.
"I wouldn't know what to do without this one. It's been with me on so many assignments. It's become part of me." Sara interjects.

"What sort of things do you have to carry to be a reporter these days. I thought all you would need is a pencil and paper." She smiles.

Cody decides to oblige rather than create more speculation. He pulls his bag from under his chair and dumps the contents on the wooden table while the three ladies pull up chairs.

"There's not much to it, phone, a computer, a camera and even a pad and pen." Cody holds up the last two items showing he still uses the traditional tools of the trade. Missus Forester looks over the contents and remarks. "That's a computer, that little thing there? I've got makeup compacts bigger. It can't be." Cody opens the computer showing the ladies the small keyboard and screen.

The conversation turns to the excursions and how well preserved the ruins are. Sara is especially amazed.

"I've been to Rome and Athens and yes, they are impressive but compared to what we've seen here, those places are piles of rubble." The other two agree. The conversation turns to the weather and heat. Both Missus Covington and Forester decide it is time to go. Missus Covington rises first, saying her goodbyes.

When she has left, Missus Forester says. "Well, you certainly proved her wrong Mister Cody."

"I don't understand." He says.

"Well, let me just say us girls were talking and having covered the usual topics, we started discussing you. I can tell you, a man traveling alone can be an endless source of conversation and speculation. Sara here, of course, insisted you are what you said, a journalist doing some traveling on your own. I was pushing for you being the son of a rich American who wants you to take over the family business. However, you have other ideas and are here to make your mark in the world."

Cody smiles at the idea. He has never seen joining the FBI as him making his mark in the world. Missus Forester seeing his smile jumps to the conclusion. "I'm right, I'm right."

"Sorry no, I'm just a journalist trying to make my mark in the world." He says, smiling.

"Oh. Oh well, it was fun to think anyway. We girls have to keep one another entertained while you boys are off doing whatever it is you do." Missus forester looks at Sara who adds.

"We could have gone on the rest of the afternoon but suddenly Mary said it was all nonsense. She said she knew you were a spy. Said her husband told her the first night at dinner. We tried to find out how he knew but she wouldn't say." Missus Forester says.

"That's right, said she couldn't. It might jeopardize her husband's position," Sara adds.

Missus Forester remarks. "He must have been in the forces."

"Why do you say that," Cody asks.

"Oh, my Gerald was RAF, you know, Royal Air Force. Since we've arrived, those two have been off together. You know how it is. They can't tell their wives but they can talk to one another for days. It's not fair really." Missus Forester looks down creasing her brow. Sara and Cody have a glimpse of living with someone without being able to share in their life.

"Oh well, it will be good for Gerald to talk about it. He has trouble sleeping sometimes. I know it has to do with some of the things he did in the service." She smiles brightly and announces it is time she too retired. They say their goodbyes and Cody finds that once again, he and Sara are left together. Jason looks into Sara's deep brown eyes and smiles. He thinks, *'at least there isn't someone with a knife this time.'*

Sara returns Jason's smile and says.

"Penny for your thoughts?" Jason smiles and shakes his head.

"It's nothing." She shifts her chair closer saying.

"I'm terribly sorry about all of that it just got so out of hand." She smiles sweetly, glancing down as she talks.

"I don't understand. What got out of hand?"

"Oh, you know Emma, Missus Forester. She decided all of our speculations were fine but when Missus Covington insisted you were a spy, well she had to find out. That's why we all moved over to join you. We had to discover what you carried in your mysterious bag." Sara blushes at her own words.

Cody breaks into a full smile and asks.

"What were all of you looking for in my bag." Sara blushes again.

"Well, Emma insisted your mysterious bag must hold some proof. So we were looking to see if you carried a,,, a gun." Sara says, squirming in her seat. Cody smiles broader, pulling out his bag and placing it in front of Sara.

"Please have a look."

Sara blushes a deep red, which pleases Jason to see. He places his bag back under his chair. With the object gone, Sara recovers saying.

"I must apologize. I can't believe I was party to it." She smiles. Cody thinks he can see her being party to it and many others. His mind flits back to his Beretta, locked safely in his cabin. Sara sees the thoughtful look on his face and misunderstands.

"You're not thinking of this assignment, are you?" She asks.

"Oh, no, not really, I was just wondering when we get to Asyut." He smiles his apology.

"Well, I can answer that for you. Mister Habid says we won't be in Asyut until tomorrow evening. Our guide Mister Kedesh says we should have time for a trip to the local market after dinner. So, Mister Cody that means we have over twenty-four hours until you can get to your interview and my good sir, you need to relax. I've been watching you. I mean, I've noticed you haven't relaxed this whole trip. Well anyway, its time you did. And to start off, I'm going to buy you a drink." Sara smiles.

"I bow to your astute observations but I must insist I buy you a drink to make up for my failure at Dendura," Cody says with a smile. A white-coated waiter stands near the door to the bar. Cody waves him over and asks Sara what she would like from the bar. He orders a gin and tonic for her and for himself.

"Vodka Martini shaken, not stirred." Sara smiles at the joke as the waiter notes the order on his pad.

The waiter walks the short distance down the teak staircase to the main bar and lounge. He stops and bends low, pulling up his pant leg and tightens the straps holding the knife. A few moments later, he returns to the sun deck with a tray of drinks. He serves the woman first, then steps behind the man, serving his drink from the right. He steps to the side of the table presenting the bill, then returns to his station. The sounds of the couple's laughter float across the deck. He smiles wickedly, thinking. *'Not yet! Not yet, but soon.'*

## Asyut, Egypt 17:52 September 7, 2001

Following dinner, the SS Karim docks at Asyut, the first passengers to finish eating emerge from the dining room, discussing whether to take advantage of the evening and visit the market. Jason Cody drifts quietly through central reception as the long metal gangway is lowered to the old wooden pier. He steps out of the ship's external doors and down the gangway to the old wooden dock. Cody crosses the uneven planks and makes his way to the road, which parallels the river. He checks his phone consulting the map.

Studying it, Cody finds the most direct route and plans his approach.

Jason sets off, finding a path between buildings. Walking briskly, he follows the blue dot on his phone's screen. Cody emerges at a crossroads. He makes a left and finds a stalled donkey cart. Jason steps around the cart while a small boy tries to move the stubborn animal.

The concrete buildings give way to mud-brick and Jason enters the older part of the city. Stalls line the street with the merchants' goods piled high. The dirt road climbs as he walks deeper into the market. The heady aromas of the shops float to Jason with the heat of the evening.

Cody finds himself in one of his favorite places, the Egyptian street market. He takes in the confusion of hawkers and buyers, carts and scooters all plying the narrow road. Jason realizes his favorite place is also the most dangerous. It would be easy for an assassin to hide in the crowd.

Jason consults his map as he walks. There should be a road ahead on his left. Cody feels his back begin to tighten and his shoulders rise in a state of readiness. He can feel someone following him. On impulse, Jason turns suddenly and a boy carrying a tray of coffees steps deftly around him. He looks around, scanning the faces but sees nothing. No, there was a brief glimpse, a flash of something dark but only for a moment.

Cody looks again but cannot tell if it was the Beggar. The crowd is too thick. Jason walks on but is twice as vigilant. A few yards on, he finds the side road and gratefully leaves the crowded market. As Cody turns the corner, Abu stops and examines a pot at a pot maker's shop. He pauses, watching as Jason enters a carpet shop. Careful not to be seen, Abu slips around to the side of a spice shop to keep an eye on him.

Coffee and tea arrive with the eldest son of Abdul Mohammad Suleiman, the proprietor of the carpet shop. They sit on the floor and Jason waits patiently for the drinks to be served while he observes his host.

"Please drink." Suleiman gestures for Cody to drink the chrysanthemum tea. Cody drinks the hot beverage and is grateful for how it makes him feel cooler. Suleiman picks up a horsehair fly swatter and works it with precision. He waits while Cody finishes a second sip of tea.

"So what can I do for you and the Commander Mister Cody?" Suleiman asks.

"Perhaps it's what I can do for you, Mister Suleiman." Suleiman snorts at Cody's clumsy entry into negotiation and replies with one of his many responses.
"Unless you are buying me out and making me a rich man, I don't see how." Suleiman's fly swatter shoots out, killing a fly in mid-air. Cody notes he did not look at the fly as he killed it.

Cody decides to be direct.

"Commander McAllen thought you might have some information on a particular Pharaoh." Cody pauses. "Menkaure."

"You mean Mycerinus of course." Suleiman rolls his eyes to the shop's ceiling, observing the flies buzzing around the fluorescent tubes and speaks.

"If it is Mycerinus you want to know about, then I can tell you. He succeeded his father Chepheren about 2532 BC, but his rule was an affront to the gods. The gods, being gods, decided Egypt should suffer for one hundred and fifty years. There you go now you know about Mycerinus. That was free but I don't think you really want to know about Mycerinus. No, I think you want to know about Pasmmetichus the first, now there was a Pharaoh. Did you know that Pasmmeticus was instrumental in restoring the old religion to Egypt? He also raised an army and conquered most of the surrounding lands, including what is now the Jewish state."

Suleiman lets his words hang between them like the dust from his carpets. Cody looks up and says.

"I see what you mean. I was mistaken about my first query. Do you have more information on Pasmmeticus."

Suleiman smiles for the first time. He knows that he has hooked another amateur.

"Yes I have more information but as I told you, the first one is free. For this information, you must pay." Cody doesn't hesitate.

"How much." Suleiman chuckles. Cody can see the bulk of him wiggling as he laughs under his robes of embroidered cotton.

"How much you ask, well that is the thing. You see the information I hold is for you at the right price but I am a man of scruples. Before you arrived, I received a message. Another would also like to buy the information. This man has already offered a very high price. It would be unethical of me to sell it without giving him a chance to bid for it." His chuckle returns, breaking into a laugh. The big man rolls back against his pillows and opens his lungs, swishing the fly swatter to accentuate his pleasure.

Cody knows the tactic. There is no other bidder. Suleiman hopes to start the bidding at a higher level by introducing a third party. It's an old ploy but Cody doesn't have time to waste. Cody decides to call his bluff and ask where the mysterious bidder is hiding. Suleiman insists the man will be here shortly.

"I am afraid the bidding cannot begin until his arrival." The big man says. Jason insists it is all a ploy to raise the price but Suleiman will not be moved. He makes a special effort to reassure Cody he is telling the truth. Suleiman says he would not be in the shop if there were no business to transact. "My son runs the shop now. I only leave the comfort of my air-conditioned home when necessary."

Cody notes Sulieman is sweating profusely and considers that he may be telling the truth.

"How much did this man offer you," Cody asks.

"I will tell you, as he will be here shortly. He has offered me five thousand US. Dollars." Cody decides to take a chance.

"The information is about the al-Gamaa al-Islamiyya is it not." Sulieman stops and looks closely at Cody, reassessing what he might know.

"Yes, it is common knowledge as is the fact he is at this moment moving up and down the Nile making preparations." Cody's head comes up.

"Preparations, what preparations." Suleiman laughs and shakes his finger at Cody.

"If I told you there would be no bargain but I see you are at a slight disadvantage here. I will tell you something to whet your appetite."

Suleiman puts his teacup on the tray.

"This man is not a messenger. He is the leader of the Muslim Brotherhood's militia." He pauses to let the implications sink in. "He has been planning this for over five years and has been instrumental in providing soldiers for Al-Qaeda. The very men who will make the first strike against the West. You are American, yes?" Suleiman's eyes glisten in anticipation of what he already knows.

"Yes," Cody sees no reason to deny it.

"Then, for you, I have special information. I will sell whether or not you win the bidding." Suleiman sits back and thinks. *'I'll sell Egyptian information to the Egyptian and American Information to the American, what could be better?'*

Cody's needs to secure the information Suleiman has.

"Suleiman, you intend for me to bid on this information but what if I refuse to bid. I tell your man I have no interest." Suleiman realizes he has said too much.

"If you do not bid, then I will not sell. Not anything." He tries to sound final but knows his position is not safe. Cody decides to press his position.

"If you do not sell, I will be forced to drag the information out of you." Suleiman shifts in his seat.

"You cannot fool me, sir. Torture is not something you are permitted to do. The authorities will not stand for it." Cody leans forward to make his point.

"You and I both know our governments are on excellent terms. I don't think your President would permit those good relations to be soiled by one informant, spy."

Suleiman is sweating and his hands nervously arrange the tea tray. Cody decides it is time.

"If we can make a deal on the information, I will bid your man up to say, another two thousand." Cody lets the figure hang in the air between them for a moment and then continues. "Of course if I do, I would expect a deal on my information. Say two thousand." Suleiman sees the plan and fires back.

"I can agree to this only if you are successful. If you do not bid the man up, then you owe me the balance of four thousand. Agreed?" Cody considers the deal and says. "If your information is of no use to me, then I pay nothing. Agreed?" Suleiman smiles. He knows what he has and he was planning on selling it to the FBI anyway. This man will save him the trouble of making the trip to Cairo.

"Agreed and I will give you a present for your help in this matter," Suleiman says.

Suleiman pauses, then leans forward and says. "I will give you the name of the man who is the leader of the Muslim Brotherhood's military arm.

"We already know he sits at the right hand of Osama Bin Laden," Cody replies.

"Ah, but that is not the true leader of the brotherhood. Nor is he the man who has planned these attacks on my country and yours." Cody sits up.

"What attacks, when?" He presses. Suleiman holds up his hands as if to hold back the flood of words and says.

"I promise I will tell you when I tell the other bidder. You see, I plan this man should not live to see this evil come to pass." Suleiman's son pushes back the carpet and whispers in his ear.

Suleiman says.

"Ah, this must be him." He rises and walks towards the front of the shop. Cody notices for the first time just how big a man he is. Cody is getting to his feet when Suleiman gives a shout. He turns with incredible speed for a man of his size and takes a running step. Suddenly, he is pushed from the back with incredible force. His chest bulging forward as his body lifts from the floor. Suleiman is hurled towards Cody. Jason responds instinctively. His hands come up catching the man by the shoulders. The result is both men are thrown back against the wall.

Jason feels the impact of the wall against his back. His arms are straining from stopping the big man's forward progress. Suleiman's eyes are bulging at Cody, who catches a breath. Suleiman slowly looks down at the front of his chest. Cody's eyes follow his. Sticking out of his embroidered white robe is a four-inch-long thick black shaft with a wicked hunting point on it. Along the length of the shaft are clumps of tissue from Suleiman. Cody realizes it is only an inch from piercing his own chest. Cody's strength is failing from holding the big man up. He can feel the strength seeping from the man. Suleiman's eyes come up and meet Cody's. He gasps, the pain showing on his face. Cody moves his ear closer as Suleiman is trying to speak.

"Shit." It comes out in a gasp, sweat flowing from the big man. Suleiman looks Cody in the eye, while his left hand seeks a place behind Cody's head. He reaches behind a carpet hanging against the wall knocking aside several tins and books. His hand grasps a white garment and holds it against Cody's chest. With that, the strength leaves his legs and he sinks down. Cody guides him down so he rests on his side. Jason's own strength nearly spent in the effort. As he releases the man, the son who brought the tea earlier pushes Cody aside and bends to his father's face yelling in Egyptian.

Cody stands and looks in the direction the bolt had come from but the assailant is nowhere to be seen. He steps back, catching his breath as the young man holds his father's head close to his ear. Suddenly the son starts yelling at him.

"You have been paid. Why do you stand there? He has paid you! Why don't you kill the pig that has done this?" Cody looks at the boy, confused. The young man points at the garment.

"With that, he has paid you. Now go and kill the devil that has taken my father." Cody looks at the shirt in his hand. It's the same Hieroglyphs as the robe and pushes it into his bag.

Jason goes to the door but pulls back sharply. A black blur shoots across his path, inches from him. He looks in the direction it has come and sees a small man struggling with a large crossbow. Cody doesn't hesitate. Springing from his right foot, he jumps across a stack of rolled carpets. He makes sweeping steeps, springing from foot to foot and covering the short distance in half the time. The archer doesn't have a chance. Cody springs up and kicks. His right foot knocking the man back into a pile of debris, sending the crossbow clattering across the road. Cody closes on the assailant who struggles against an unseen injury. As Cody approaches, the man gasps and collapses.

Cody glances around. He couldn't have been shot. He sees a pool of blood form under the man. Cody lifts him by his shirt. As he does the pile of rubbish moves and Jason sees the reason. The assailant landed on a large piece of corrugated roofing metal buried in the rubble. The piece is cut and mangled, resulting in a wicked saw tooth edge, now embedded in his back. The archer is dead.

Jason makes his way back to the shop and finds the family bending over Suleiman sobbing. The women are screaming at the deceased, shaking him as if to wake him from the dead. The eldest son notices Cody standing at the entry to the shop and stares, his eyes questioning. Cody nods. The boy runs from the shop, pushing past Cody running to the dead assailant.

Cody puts his head down and walks back down the road towards the marketplace. A new sound comes to Jason's and he looks over his shoulder. The son stands over the dead assassin. Using the crossbow, he is beating the body and yelling in triumph. Cody sees the rest of the family running out to join him. Jason turns away and loses himself in the crowded market.

Jason walks through the market, pushing past the shoppers. He turns towards the river and the Karim. As Cody walks, his thoughts run back to his training. He remembers one lecture. The lecturer said less than five percent of agents fired their weapons in the line of duty. He grimaces at the thought. He has taken two lives in the span of a few days. In his heart, he feels justified but there is guilt as well.

Jason walks on, trying to sort out his feelings versus his actions. He did what he had to do. Cody's thoughts become random. He sees the face of his defense instructor. Jason hears his voice. *'Learn to disappear, duck and disappear.'* The thought changes to his Quantico instructor yelling. *'Duck don't' just stand there. Duck!'* The voice becomes real.

"Duck Mister Cody! Duck!"


Cody awakes from his daydream, ducks and rolls forward. Back on his feet, he sees a large bearded man with a saber. The man is recovering, looking for his target. He slashes about, clearing the street between himself and Cody. The swordsman comes at Jason but this time Jason is ready. As the blade comes down, Cody deftly steps aside. Jason left hand guides the blade down in a long arch, the sword passes between them. Cody's right hand sends a stabbing blow to the man's right eye. The swordsman backs away, holding his eye. He slashes wildly as Cody sidesteps the attack.


The saber misses him but catches the strap of his bag, slicing it clean through. No time to reclaim it between swings. Cody leaps, his foot striking the assailant in the head. The assailant stumbles back but recovers quickly and attacks. Cody steps back, catching his foot on a merchant's polished pot. He falls back with a crash. The saber comes down as Cody rolls to the side. It splits a copper pot, which clings to the blade.

Cody kicks the man and sends him into the shop. Jumping to his feet, Jason spins and kicks again. Striking his ribs as the attacker turns. The man falls sideways into the next stall and the road comes alive with shouts and angry cries. In the center of the road Cody sees his bag and he makes for it. A small man in a gray shirt runs out to claim it. As he reaches it, Abu sticks his knife in the back of his thigh. The little man screams and dances away, dropping the bag.

Two more swordsmen appear at the edge of the group as the big man is untangling himself from a rack of scarves. Abu yells.

"This way Mister Cody, this way!" He grabs Cody's bag and runs like the wind straight into the crowd with Cody left standing there. It all happens at once. The two new swordsmen come at him from the left and the big man from the right. All three are intent on running their blades through the American. Cody stands stock still. At the last moment, he springs forward and rolls. From the cursing and clash of steal, he knows they meet where he stood. Jason elbows through the crowd after Abu and finds him waiting near an alley. Seeing Cody, he sprints ahead down a narrow path.

They can hear the attackers closing. Cody looks for a place to stand and fight but Abu makes a right through a small door and disappears. Cody stops facing the door. He looks back at the assailants and sees their numbers have grown to five. Cody bursts through the door. He sees Abu pushing ahead against a large Egyptian woman. Jason runs forward through a room filled with men smoking as Abu clears the hallway of the woman. He runs to the far end of the house, steps up on a chest and slides through a window. Cody seeing the size of the window dives head first through it. He rolls and comes up in a bright courtyard.

Abu is breathing hard and he shakes his head.

"You are too slow Mister Cody. We should have gotten away by now. I have to keep slowing down for you." He scolds. Cody gives him a look. The sound of the swordsmen yelling tells Cody they will be there in a moment. He steps to the side of the window. The first man sticks his head out and Cody's fist strikes him hard across the jaw. There is a crack and the man drops. Cody easily catches his sword. Jason thinks the others may not be eager to stick their heads out. Unfortunately, they have found another way.

"Look out Mister Cody." Abu points to the roof and Cody jumps back as two men drop down swinging their swords. The blades cut the air around him. Cody brings his sword up to parry one blow while he side-steps the other. These men have more skill with the sword than the big man but they contend with one another for position. Cody's three years of fencing training at West Point comes back to him. He makes a quick double step to the left, putting one swordsman in front of him, the other behind. For the moment, Cody has only one assassin to deal with. Jason presses his advantage, slicing rapidly with his own barrage of thrusts and parries. He pushes the assailant into his partner.

The assailant directly in front of Jason loses balance when his partner tries to thrust around him. The distraction is time enough. Cody changes the direction of his blade mid-parry and slices across the man's throat. He feels the bone at the back of his neck as he pulls the blade free. At the same time, the thrust from the man behind catches Cody in the side but this does not stop Jason's progress. He parries the thrust with a downward reverse of his blade and as the dead man falls against his partner, Cody thrusts through the dead man's into the second man. Cody pushes forward and buries the blade to the hilt into the two men.

Jason snatches the sword from the second man's dying hand. Two of the assailants lay before him dead but pulling himself out of the window is another swordsman and the big man has made his way to the roof. Cody sees his chance and runs to the wall under the big man next to the window. He slashes at the man who is still removing himself from the opening and incurs deep wounds on his sword arm. At that moment, the big man finds his courage and jumps down on Cody.

Cody is ready and braces himself, sword extended up. He catches the big man mid-jump just under the ribs and guides the blade up and through his chest. The big man stands staring at the sword point protruding from his chest as Cody takes up the big man's sword. The big man goes white and collapses. Cody leaps to the far side of the body as the swordsman from the window attacks from behind.

The blade misses Cody but rents a new opening in his shirt. Cody whirls around and faces the man. He is wounded and in pain but this one keeps his wits about him. He moves forward with his sword out in front, ready to flick it and cut his opponent. Cody realizes this man's training is superior to his own. Cody back peddles as the assassin advances. Jason finds Abu in the corner, his eyes wide as he watches. Cody pulls open his bag still in the boy's hands and finds the grip of his Beretta.

The gun comes to life in Jason's hand, an extension of his being. He points and fires in one motion. A single bullet leaves the barrel, a single casing springs from the action. Cody sees the man's head snap back as he relaxes his grip on the gun. A small dark hole in the center of the swordsman's head grows red and his eyes glaze over. The support goes out of his legs. He falls, dead before he hits the ground. Abu stands open-mouthed, watching the man change from hate-filled assassin to a corpse. Cody turns to the boy and speaks.

"Don't look. You can't change it. Look away." Abu looks up at the big American, his opinion of him permanently altered.

Cody recovers his bag from the boy and turns to leave the courtyard but Abu stops him.

"This way Mister Cody."

They run to the far corner and exit. Hurrying along a path, they put the dead swordsmen behind them. After a couple of minutes, they slow to a walk. Cody stops and leans back against the wall, applying pressure to the wound in his side. Abu sees this and says.

"You are injured, Mister Cody." Cody stops looking for followers, long enough to investigate the wound. It is not bad. The blade has only sliced the skin. He pulls the water bottle from his bag and splashes his side, cleaning the area.

Abu watches for a moment then disappears up the side path. Cody removes his shirt, using it to clean around the cut. He digs into his bag and finds his first aid kit. Pulling out antiseptic, gauze and bandage, Jason patches himself up. He is taping down the bandage when Abu returns with a multi-pocketed vest.

"Thanks," Cody says, deciding not to ask how he got it. Abu takes away his bloody shirt and buries it under a pile of garbage nearby. Patched and ready, they walk towards the Nile and the SS Karim.

A few minutes further on, the path passes behind the shops of the street market and Jason hears familiar voices.

He squeezes between two stalls and spots several of his fellow travelers. He steps out into the road, approaching the group.

"Hello." He smiles, greeting the Covingtons and Foresters. They are comparing their purchases when he happens upon them. The ladies decide to visit one more spice shop. While the group makes its way down the road, Abu catches up with Jason and pulls him away. Cody announces he is off to a shop and will catch up.

Abu guides Jason into a shop. After a moment of explanation in Egyptian, the old Tailor shows them his workshop at the back. He pulls out a box of shoulder straps and Cody paws through the box, finding one that matches his canvas bag. Abu negotiates the price while the quick fingers of the tailor stitch the strap in place.

Out on the road, Jason shoulders his bag as though nothing has happened. He is standing drinking from his water bottle when the others return. Sara has also found the group and she remarks on Cody's new vest.

"Do all Americans wear those things?" She asks.

"I am afraid my young friend here feels I should look the part of the American tourist." He says apologetically. "It

215

was a gift." He adds. The group smiles at the comment and Missus Forester says.

"I don't think you should go near any American tours Mister Cody. They may mistake you for one of their own." She laughs at her own joke. Cody smiles but Sara is considering the garment seriously.

"Well it does show off your shoulders but I don't think you should wear it like that." She says with a concerned look.

"Well, I won't be wearing it to dinner but it is cooler." Jason returns. The ladies move off in the direction of another trinket shop and Gerald Forester pulls Cody aside.

"She's getting her hooks into you young man. I wouldn't let it go too far if I were you. Holiday romances you know, they're the same as the local wines. Great while you're out here but once you get home, they lose their appeal." He winks at Cody and breaks off. Cody smiles, thinking he is right. He's here to do a job and a relationship would only get in the way.

The ladies return with new purchases and the group makes their way back to the Karim. Cody feeling the adrenaline of his escape offers to buy everyone a nightcap.

The suggestion is met with approval. They set off towards the Nile, leaving the market of Asyut behind.

As their glasses clink the second round, the SS Karim eases smoothly from the landing, pointing its bow in the direction of El-Minya. It moves steadily downstream towards its next stop. The lights of Asyut become a dim memory on the horizon as the group disbands for the night. Cody hurries to his cabin to report before the ship passes the last mobile tower for the next sixty miles.

# *Eight*

Commander McAllen sits at his desk, tapping a pencil. He replays in his mind the message sent from his contact at MI-6. *'Imminent attack on US soil.'* Such a plot would have to be Bin Laden. His contact insisted it is an Egyptian plan and believes the organizer to be Egyptian. Alistair looks out at the morning light spreading across Cairo. How can something so big be planned without the lines of information being ablaze? Someone somewhere will have leaked the information, unless. His mind runs the possibilities and a name comes to him like a bolt between the eyes.

"Of course, he would know!" The Commander says out loud rising to his feet. Alistair pauses as a new thought comes to him. It touches a nerve of caution. *'If he does know, then why hasn't that greedy bastard been knocking down my door trying to profit by it? Unless!'* The cold reality of the situation hits him and he stands frozen on the edge of a decision. 'I have to know, if not for myself, for the Americans.' The thought of the Americans brings his mind back to Cody. He desperately needs to hear from him, know he is all right, and find out what he knows.

218

Alistair finds his phone lying on a stack of papers. Picking up the phone, he punches in Cody's number. A message plays back to him down the invisible line.

*"It's not possible to contact the owner of this mobile device. The phone may be switched off or out of signal range. Please leave a message or try back later."* The Commander closes his phone and sets it in the drawer. He has sent a text message and has left several voice messages. Cody is too good an agent to have his phone switched off. He must be out of signal range.

"Damn, we just don't get the equipment we need out here." The Commander says out loud. He walks around the desk and studies the map of Egypt hanging on the wall. He last contacted Cody just before he left Asyut. Jason is traveling downstream, which puts him. "Damn, right in the middle of nowhere, there is nothing but desert for miles."

McAllen sighs, his mind made up. He has to know what is going on. *'I'd better be sure about this.'* Alistair thinks. He picks up the phone on his desk but is assaulted by the inherent crackle of the Egyptian infrastructure. Fifty-year-old phone wires do not make for clear conversations but they do make excellent cover for surveillance. There is too much chance of the latter. He replaces the receiver in its cradle. Going to the door, he announces, "I'll be going out for a little while." Tarra comes out in time to see the office door close as he goes.


## The SS Karim, somewhere in Fundamentalist territory
## 09:42 September 8, 2001

Abu peers down the dark paneled corridor after the man he has followed all day. He wants desperately to see what he is up to but he can be too easily spotted. Abu has no reason for being here since Cody's room is one level below. He sits and waits, hiding behind the potted palm in a recess of the wall. Abu is waiting for the man to emerge from the room. A room no worker from the lower decks would have any business in. The man is either stealing from the passengers or meeting someone.


Abu is about to leave and inform Cody when the door to the cabin cracks open. A head pokes out and the man steps into the corridor. Abu shrinks back behind the urn as the mysterious man walks towards the stairs. He reaches Abu's hiding place and stops, considering the palm. The sound of the lift catches his attention and he hurries down the steps.

Abu breathes a sigh of relief. He slides out from behind the plant and down the hall to the cabin door. He turns the handle and finds the door is unlocked. A veil has been hung at the entrance to the cabin. He can only see blurred images beyond.

He pushes aside the veil and his heart catches in his throat. In the chair next to the bed sits a man in a fine gray suit reading. Abu's mouth works over words and excuses while his mind focuses on reality. He comprehends what his eyes have already noticed. The man is not real. The cabin crew of the SS Karim creates towel art for passengers. . In this cabin, they've made a life-size dummy using the occupant's clothes and a book. The effect is so convincing Abu nearly called out.

With the shock over, Abu makes a thorough search of the cabin to discover who the occupant is. He knows the cabin has been absent of its occupant since he and Mister Cody arrived. Thinking about it, Abu finds it strange. The moment he and Cody arrive, the occupant should decide not to return. The Karim's director received a message saying he was called back to Cairo and would rejoin them later. Abu looks through the drawers and closet but something is missing. He enters the bathroom and his suspicions are confirmed. There are no personal items in the room. In the bathroom, a lone toothbrush stands in a glass. Abu slips out of the cabin and makes his way back to inform Mister Cody.

## Old Cairo 09:49 September 8, 2001

Commander McAllen exits the taxi in front of a spice shop. He makes his way to an alley running back from the El-Sharaf road. He sidesteps a pile of old spice boxes and comes to a familiar bright blue door. He knocks once and is greeted by an elderly woman who welcomes him into her house. She takes his hat and escorts him to the third floor, where the roof is open and the breeze from the Nile blows cool air. An elderly man in white robes rises to greet McAllen. Alistair looks over the old furnishings of the dwelling as he seats himself on a low chair.

Abydos is not the type who shows off his wealth or hides jewels and gold about his house. Many a burglar has tried to find his hoard but has come away empty-handed. The last of these it is rumored, was a cousin of his, who Abydos helped to search. It is said he did this to silence once and for all the rumor of piles of gold. The cousin had gone away just as empty-handed as the others. The reality is Abydos has invested his wealth in his children. Even his daughters have gone to the best schools and his youngest has graduated from St Andrews with Prince William. The association has set him up nicely in English society. Abydos proudly shows McAllen a photo of his son and his new girlfriend.

"She is the daughter of an Earl no less." He says proudly and examines the photo again.

"Not bad looking either. My son has the good taste of his father." He muses and smiles at his wife, who lays the tea before the men. She smiles and returns to the lower floors to allow the men to talk.

"It is thanks to you my children's future are assured. So ask me what you will, Commander. If it is in my power, I will grant it." McAllen speaks low and spells out his request. All the while, Abydos becomes more and more agitated.

"Please Commander. You are my friend. I beg of you to ask anything of me but not this. This, my friend, will only bring death." He sits back, attempting to close the subject but the Commander is not so easily put off. McAllen sits forward and speaks pointedly.

"Abydos my friend, I assure you that I have no intention of getting myself or anyone else killed. I've been in this game for a long time. I have stayed alive by knowing how and when to move. All I am asking for is to talk to this man. Just tell me and I will leave you a richer man than when I arrived."

"No!" Abydos waves his hands in front of himself, blocking the words. "I will not take money for this. That would be taking payment for your death. Please trust me Commander, you and I have been friends for many years. We have worked together and profited on many things. Always I have given you facts, not the fiction some sell. Please listen to this fact. If you pursue this, you will die as surely as the sun will set." He sits back, crossing his arms and holding himself tightly.

For the next hour, the two men go back and forth arguing. Finally, Abydos relents and gives the Commander the information.

"I beg of you please do not divulge this to anyone. These people have ears in the highest places. Even old Samule, the man who told your people at MI-6, received a knife in the back for his trouble. No Commander, you must not tell anyone."

"Surely I can visit this man at the El-Kahir and ask him what he knows." Argues McAllen.

"No, that is sure death. The place is watched at all times. This man Darius only goes out when he must. His business is in a shambles and no one dares to visit his shop." McAllen creases his brow and sits back, considering the situation.

"Abydos, do you know of an assassin who uses large black crossbow bolts?"

"Commander, first you ask about that which will get you killed and now about death herself. Ahh! I will give you the information about the assassin but tell no one. Please you must keep death from my door." Abydos leans forward a whispers something in the Commander's ear. Commander McAllen looks at Abydos for a moment, then says.

"Good, and now." He places his hands on the table in front of him, his eyes intent. "If I cannot visit Darius at his home or shop, then tell me, when does he go out?"

### Cairo's Business District 15:49 September 9, 2001

Taara Sefi goes through the motions, looking the part of a tourist, picking up one then another small replica of the sphinx and examining them. She has been in the shop for over fifteen minutes and it's time to move to the next, or

225

she might arouse suspicions. The shopkeeper has left her to her browsing for the past five minutes. This is the fifth time she has been in this shop. Taara steps away from the statues and walks to the entrance where she can better see the street. On the corner opposite is The Bank of Egypt. Sources informed Abydos, Darius is deep in debt. Abydos had refused to help the Commander in approaching Darius at his business. So the Commander has come up with this plan and Taara has been drafted in as lookout.

Taara is tired and her feet hurt from standing all day. She steps out into the street and puts her hand to her mouth, speaking low.

"No luck, and it's ten minutes to closing. I think it's time we give up on this McAllen. His life is obviously more important to him than the money." She drops her hand and glances up the road to where the McAllen sits hidden in a small white delivery van. His voice speaks to her in the earpiece.

"Let's give it ten minutes. Darius has to do something, or his creditors will close him down."

"Why aren't you out here?" There is silence at the other end of the line. "I'm talking to you McAllen." She shouts in the direction of the van, drawing curious looks from passersby.

"We have gone over that Agent Sefi. My face is too recognizable in Cairo and if we are not careful, we will miss Darius." Taara replies.

"How could we miss him? He's probably hold up in some hole or dead already."

"Or, he is entering the bank you are supposed to be watching."

Taara twists her head around in time to see a small balding man in a white linen suit step from a car. He looks furtively up and down the street, then bolts for the bank's entrance.

"Now cross the road and see what you can find out." Taara stares bullets at the van.

"Don't tell me how to do my job!" Taara mutters, crossing the road. She enters the bank in time to see Darius being shown into the manager's office. She makes a pretense of examining the displays of literature. Taara notices near the manager's office, there is a large display of artifacts. Making her way to the display case, she reads the tags on the shards of pottery and jewelry.

"Can I help you, madam?" The question comes from a young bank clerk. Taara puts on her best American accent and smiles.

"Oh I hope it's okay I'm here. I work at the Bank of Virginia and I promised my friends I would visit at least one bank while I am in Cairo. Bank of Cairo, what could be better?" The clerk smiles and says the Bank would be closing soon. He asks if she has any business to transact.

"Oh, of course, I wouldn't want to keep you. What I do need is to change some American Dollars for Egyptian money. Can I do that here?" The clerk smiles and says.

"Yes, of course, Madam." He allows her to stay and examine the artifacts. While he checks the exchange rate and changes fifty dollars for her. As he is counting out the Egyptian Dollars, the manager's door opens and Darius steps out with the manager.

"I assure you, Mister Darius the bank will be only too happy to help you. We will see you tomorrow at this time to finalize the paperwork." Darius thanks the manager, glancing at Taara before he leaves. The young clerk has finished counting out Taara's money. She picks it up, taking her time to place it in her purse.

She strolls from the building, making sure Darius has ample time to get away. Out on the street, she speaks into her hand.

"Did you get that McAllen?"

"Yes, perfect! Let's get back. We have a few arrangements to make before closing tomorrow."

"No, McAllen, you can make them. I'm going home to a bath and dinner. My part in this is done." The Commander sighs and says.

"Yes, perhaps that's for the best."

## The SS Karim 18:03 September 9, 2001

Cody listens to Abu's story about the mysterious man. He followed Cody to the informant's house in Asuyt and Abu saw him enter the cabin of the missing passenger. Jason remembers the words of Mister Kohlemete. 'He is our most loyal passenger. Every year he makes the journey from Aswan to Cairo. This year for the first time, he has been called away on business.' Jason thought it odd the passenger left when they arrived. With Abu's information, it seems more than coincidence.

Cody goes to the reception and speaks with Mister Habid. "So is there an empty cabin on an upper deck?" He inquires.

"Not really Mister Cody. You see the occupant of the cabin has been called back to Cairo on business and may return at any time." Cody presses.

"Or he may not return." Habid smiles his most endearing smile and says.

"I am very sorry Mister Cody but the cabin has been paid for and if a passenger wants to pay us to transport his suitcase to Cairo..." He lets his words hang as he shrugs. Cody smiles and turns to go leaving one hand on the counter.

"Oh, one more thing Habid," Jason turns back.

"Yes sir?"

"I was wondering the name of this passenger."

"I am sorry sir but we cannot give out names of other passengers without their consent and I know this gentleman is most conscious of his privacy." Cody rubs his chin and moves in close whispering.

"Uh', I don't suppose you could bend that just a bit this time. You see, my publisher is looking for a particular type of individual for a special in the Cairo Times. They want an interview but I've checked the other passengers and they don't match the profile. The Cairo Times wants a successful businessman but they don't want the usual office based interview. They're looking for a new angle, successful man on holiday. Your man sounds like he's perfect. So what do you say can we bend the rules this time?"

Cody holds up three Twenty-Dollar notes spreading them evenly in his hand. Habid glances left and right, then at the notes making a face.

"Mister Cody you must realize, such an act would put my position in jeopardy. It would be most difficult you understand..." Cody cuts Habid short by adding another twenty to the stack. Habid looks around again. Cody adds another twenty and fans them back and forth as if cooling himself. Habid clears his throat, looking at the money.

"Last chance Habid. We make a deal, or I simply put these away." Cody starts to fold away the money but Habid puts out a hand.

"Wait." He whispers. "I know a way." He takes a deep breath. "If I were to say leave the registrations file out where someone could accidentally see it." He leaves the thought hanging. Cody picks up the thread.

"I have been known to be careless with money, leaving it places where others might pick it up."


Habid smiles nervously. He dips into a drawer pulling out a large file. He looks meaningfully at Cody and steps into the back room. When he returns, he announces.

"Yes, Mister Cody you can access your safe deposit box. They are in the back room." Habid whispers as he raises the counter.

"Please be quick!" Cody smiles reassuringly as he passes, pulling the door closed behind him.


Jason opens the file and glances at the name on the registration form for the current voyage. He flips through and finds another for the previous year. There is too much information to remember. He pulls out his camera and photographs each page. As he shoots his way through the pages, he picks up one or two items. The man's name is Mohamed Hotep Djoser and his address is listed in Cairo but it is not an area Cody is familiar with.

After Jason photographs the last page, Cody finds himself staring at the back of the manila folder. There is a penciled notation with a phone number Cody recognizes as a Cairo number. He looks closely, trying to read the words but is unable. Jason hears someone asking to see their safe deposit box. He snaps a shot of the back cover and pushes the papers back in place with the cash. Jason opens the door and thanks Habid for his help. Habid escorts Missus Covington into the safe deposit room and helps her remove her box. As he leaves, he scoops up the file and pulls the door closed. Outside, Habid fishes out the notes slipping them neatly into his pocket.

Back in his cabin Jason sits at his laptop busy preparing the photos and report. He studies the consecutive check-in sheets. The passenger, Mister Djoser has given the same address and phone number each year except for the third year he boarded the Karim. He flips to the photo of the back cover of the file and finds it to be the same number. It's a Cairo number which is obviously important enough to note. Cody picks up his phone for the third time looking for a signal, nothing. He is finishing his report when there is a knock on the cabin door.

Jason opens the door expecting to find Abu. Instead, his eyes find a more pleasing sight.

"Well, Mister Cody I've not seen you all day. So I thought to myself. If he isn't going to come up to the bar and talk me into going back to his room, there's only one thing a girl can do." Sara pulls from behind her an open bottle of wine and two glasses. Jason smiles and reaches to take them but she pulls them back at the last moment. "Oh, sorry but you see it's a package deal." She holds her arms back, so the glasses and wine are just out of reach. Jason steps forward, admiring her slender form under the black evening gown.

Jason places his arm around her waist and pulls her to him. His lips meet hers and Sara comes alive under the silk gown. The sound of a glass bouncing off the carpet brings the two out of their embrace. They look around embarrassed by their loss of control. Sara retrieves the glass from the floor and Jason pulls her inside, closing the door.

"Sara, I have an assignment in El Minya, so..." Sara raises a finger to Jason's lips and produces a wicked smile.

"Didn't you hear Kedesh at diner? We don't dock in El Minya for thirty-six hours. Thirty-six hours, Mister Cody."

She says, pulling at Jason's collar. "What do you suppose we should do with all of that time?"

# *Nine*

## Cairo Business District 12:32 September 10, 2001

The heat of the day is at its worst, which allows no cool place on the street. Commander McAllen has parked in view of the Bank's front door. A second van is parked at the opposite side of the bank's entrance. The number of pedestrians walking along the road has diminished to only a few. Only tourists are willing to endure the heat as they hunt for bargains. The Bank of Egypt, being a large institution, takes up the entire corner with its doors facing the intersection. Two tall bronze doors make up the entrance. In the days of the Kings, the bank employed doormen to assist the customer's comings and goings but no more. The Commander sits thinking how much Egypt has changed over the years. The days of Egypt's innocence are gone, hattered by the gunfire of Fundamentalist youth.


McAllen pokes his head up to look out the window. He can see the front of the second van but not its passengers. He returns to the back and speaks into a microphone.

"Are we ready?" The reply comes back quickly.

"Yes, say when." McAllen focuses his attention on the video screen as sweat runs down his face. He checks the time.

"The Bank will not close until five in the evening but you never know. The time they set may have been a diversion." He says to no one.


Alistair sees the same make car as the day before round the corner.

"We have movement." He is right. The car door opens and the same small balding man in the same white suit pokes his head out. He hesitates for a moment.

"It's him, on my mark." The man rises from the car and takes the first step towards the bank's door.

"Go! Go! Go!" The commander barks down the microphone.


The doors of the second van bang open and three large Egyptians rush the small man, bodily picking him up. He starts to cry out but one man holds a rag to his face. The men are retreating to the van when there is a loud noise. From overhead McAllen hears the unmistakable sound of a rifle shot. It echoes down to where he sits watching. The small balding man in the white suite goes limp. Two more shots ring out and the men on either side of the mark are dead. The last man realizing what is happening holds up the body of Darius, using him as a shield. He makes it to the van and jumps in. The Van makes a jump forward as another shot ricochets off the roof.

The van is picking up speed and McAllen pokes his head up to follow the action. He watches the van lurch into second gear. From a crowd of tourists, a teenage boy breaks off at a run. Reaching the van, he passes something through the open window. The boy runs off, melting into the crowd. A Moment later, an explosion blows out the windows and ignites the interior of the van. McAllen watches horrified, as the van continues to roll across the intersection, flames leaping from its windows. He sits back down and holds his head in his hands. The flaming image of his failed attempt taunts him from the screen.

What to do now? Darius was his best and only lead. How he wishes the FBI had provided them with satellite phones. He feels a deep need to talk with Jason but has no way of contacting him. McAllen pokes his head up, deciding it is time to go. He pulls himself into the driver's seat and makes a U-turn. As he finishes his turn, a very unconvincing tourist pulls out an old Nikon camera shooting several photos as he drives off.

## SS Karim, 04:32 September 11, 2001

The azure sky is accented by the stars and the last quarter of the moon. The last mountain slowly slides back revealing the lights of El-Minya. They glow brightly against the night's sky chasing away the lesser stars. The boat makes the final bend around the mountain and the Karim comes into range of the first mobile tower.

A low buzzing sound breaks the regular churning sound of the great wheel and pulls Jason from a deep sleep. The buzzing sound returns more insistent this time. It persists a moment longer and Cody's eyes open to the blackness of his cabin. Half asleep, his mind lazily searches his dreams for what the buzzing could be. The buzzing returns, louder this time. Jason wakes to his mobile phone vibrating on the surface of the bedside table. He tries to sit up but a stray arm falls across his face. Cody panics for a moment and then remembers the arm belongs to Sara. Slowly he untangles himself from her arms and legs, covers her with a blanket, then picks up his phone.

He puts on trousers and steps into the hallway. The phone screen shows two voice messages, both from McAllen. Cody listens to the messages, the first a request to call the office and the second, McAllen explaining the MI-6 memo. Cody checks the time, 04:44, and no one is in the office at this time. He checks the signal strength and decides to send off his report.

Jason slips back into the cabin and switches on his laptop. He clicks on the email icon and watches the screen as the computer negotiates with the mobile. Cody knows it will take some time and returns to bed, pulling Sara close. He pushes his face next to hers enjoying the scent of her perfumed skin. Jason kisses her and she snuggles into his shoulder. He closes his eyes in peace. He dreams of palaces in the sand and of his mother's face as his father protects her from the stones.

### SS Karim, El-Minya 06:43 September 11, 2001

Cody awakes from his dream with a start sitting up in bed. He stands, seeing the morning light slipping around the heavy blackout curtains. The light allows him to see his guest has left. He turns on the lights and checks the laptop. His files have gone off and he has received a more detailed report from Washington about the MI-6 memo. He reads it through but it says little more than what McAllen told him. He turns back to the bed and finds a note from Sara on the pillow. It promises a repeat visit if he can join her and her father for drinks. Cody smiles and thinks. *The conditions have begun but why not? He finds Clive Peters an easy and interesting person to talk to.'*

Cody takes his time cleaning up knowing breakfast will be late today. He emerges from his cabin at 8:20 am and walks to the dining room deck. There he takes up his usual seat opposite the Covington's. As the waiter is pouring his coffee, Sara enters with her father. Her eyes smile at him as they take their places at the other end of the table.

Mister Kedesh enters and says.

"Ladies and gentlemen, we are now in the heart of Fundamentalist Egypt. Please, ladies you must keep your shoulders and head covered at all times when you are out. Also do not wear clothing which might be seen through in the light. We must be respectful of the beliefs of the people of the region. You will also note the crew is erecting a temporary blind on the port side of the boat. This is so the ladies can continue to sunbathe without upsetting the religious views of the residents. Thank you!"

"Is this where the shootings were a few years ago." Mister Forester inquires. Kedesh is ready for the question and says.

"There were some reports but these were never confirmed." Forester smiles and says.

"So, you are putting up the blind as a precaution then?"

"Yes, exactly," Kedesh says, relieved the guests are being understanding and misses the irony of the statement. "Oh yes and please do not enter the Mosques. The locals are very sensitive to outsiders going near their holy sites. If any of you would like to visit a Mosque, I will be happy to arrange a visit when we reach Cairo." Kedesh smiles his goodbyes and moves to the next table. Forester smirks and adds just audibly.

"For a small fee, I'm sure." The group chuckles at the comment.

Cody stands and stretches at his place, stepping away from the table. He finds Sara and Mister Peters waiting for him outside.

"We were hoping you would join us for drinks tonight Mister Cody." She smiles with expectation.

Cody returns the smile.

"Please, it's Jason and I would be happy to." Sara beams her approval and Mister Peters smiles but it is part joy and part concern. The three continue to talk as they walk up the stairs to the lobby area.

Jason excuses himself, returning to his cabin. He enters but as he attempts to close the door, it pushes back. Abu enters, closes the door and leans hard against it. Cody can see he is out of breath. Between gasps he manages to get a few words out.

"Mister Cody,,, we must go now." He pants.

"What, why," Cody asks.

"Now! Mister Cody,, must go now,, the man,, the man with no name. We must follow him."

"The mystery man, he has left the ship?" Cody asks as he reaches for his bag and hat.

"Yes, he has gone. We must go now, or we will lose him." Abu pulls the door open and grabs at Cody's arm to pull him out of the cabin. As the two hurry through the lobby, they see the Covingtons waiting for the others. Cody calls out to them.

"Would you tell Sara I received a call and have to do an interview. I'll talk to her when I return." Mister Covington attempts to respond but Cody is already out the door and halfway down the gangplank.

Abu sprints ahead on quick legs up the stairs to the street level. He stops, searching up and down the road. Nothing. Wait, a glimpse of a shirt and a dark head of hair but maybe. He runs across the road between two donkey carts.

Cody makes the top of the stairs in time to see Abu shoot between two donkey carts and receive a string of curses. Cody runs along the street, paralleling the boy's movements. Jason dodges around a parked car. Abu spots who he is after and shoots into an alleyway.

Cody has to backtrack to get around a sweets vendor and his cart. When he does round the obstruction, he crosses the road and enters the alley at a dead run. Cody looks ahead but sees no sign of either man or Abu. He hopes he has not lost them. The alley turns and opens out onto a market road.

Jason jogs along the market road as the shop owners set up for the day. Cody ignores them looking for signs of Abu or the mystery man. Craning to see over the shoppers, he works his way down the road. A small hand grabs his and pulls. He absently shakes it away and continues but the hand persists and grabs again pulling harder.

"Mister Cody," Abu whispers. "This way." Cody follows the boy off to the side of the road. Jason allows Abu to pull him down to a crouching position.

Cody's eyes have not stopped scanning the road for any signs of the man when Abu speaks.

"He went into the tailor shop over there." He says, pointing across the road to a small shack. After a few moments, a man enters and then another. The shop is too small for so many people. He is about to mention of this fact when the door opens and three men exit the shop. Something is wrong.

Jason stands and walks to the shack. Abu sprints ahead and pulls the old door aside. The interior of the shack is empty, as it sits in the opening of an alley.

"Damn it!" Abu jumps at the curse.

"I am Sorry Mister Cody." Abu shrugs his shoulders and holds up his hands. Cody sighs.

"It's not your fault Abu. You couldn't have known. Let's see if we can find this guy." Abu leads the way into the alley.

As they are rounding a corner, Abu flattens himself against the wall. Cody stops. Abu raises a finger and waits. After a moment, he waves Cody forward and the two hurry around the corner and down a path. This pattern repeats as the two pick their way through a maze of alleys and narrow roads. The sun blazes overhead and sweat drips from Cody's back. Abu is intent on his task. He will not let the man get away from him twice.

They have stopped for a long time and Cody asks what is going on. Abu steps back allowing him to see. In front of them lay a long road. It passes a newly built complex of houses set back on the left. Cody asks.

"Do you know where he went?"

"Into the new houses," replies Abu.

"Who lives there?"

"My Uncle told me of new houses built for the Imam, the holy men of Islam. My Uncle says many of those connected with al-Gammaa al-Islamiyya also live there."

"The Muslim Brotherhood?"

"Yes." Cody steps out in plain view. There is no helping it. He has to follow.


Cody and Abu cross the open road feeling exposed. They walk near the enclave and walk in the shade of the outer wall. The wall is ten feet high and wraps around the houses like castle defenses. Jason and Abu walk down a dirt road, which circles to the left of the enclave. Cody hopes it will lead to a back door. At the back, there is a large gated entry. In the brightly painted wooden gate, they discover a smaller door set in it. The door is closed but not latched. Jason carefully pushes it open.


Inside the road turns to tarmac with stone walkways. The houses look like the mud-brick buildings of the city but modern two-car garages are attached to each one. Some have new cars parked in front of them, Japanese and German models mostly. Cody searches the area for signs of trouble. Nothing. He signals Abu to stay and walks up the road.

The main road of the complex makes a sweeping left turn. The road opens onto a large circular central park. In the center of the park is an impressive Mosque, newly whitewashed. It stands out in comparison to the mud color of the houses. Jason senses someone behind him and turns Beretta ready. It's Abu looking startled.

"I thought I told you to stay!" Jason whispers sharply.

"I can help Mister Cody. I am small and can get into places you cannot."

"If I tell you to get down, do it."

"I will!"

The park looks like an oasis with towering palms. Low ferns and other shrubs fill the spaces. As they circle, two gardeners are packing up. Abu pulls at Jason's sleeve and points to a low building behind the Mosque. Crouching near one corner is the man they have been following. As they watch, he rises and walks behind the building. They cross the road and jog past the Mosque. The mystery man is nowhere to be seen. They pass under an archway between the Mosque and the building. Cody is about to try the door but he hears a car pulling up. He and Abu slip around the back of the building and conceal themselves in the shrubbery.

Cody can hear multiple cars arriving and the sound of footsteps on the gravel path. One set of footsteps is getting closer. Cody can see a guard in a light colored suit and sunglasses through the bushes, a rifle slung over his shoulder. The guard walks halfway down the path, looks around then returns to the corner. He pulls a chair from behind the bushes and opens a pack of cigarettes and lights up.

Jason can hear more cars arriving and people entering the building. He settles his back against the wall and waits. Someone pulls open the window above them. Cody can hear the conversation as it echoes off the marble floor inside. Two men stand at the window and talk in low voices. Cody can hear what is being said but does not understand. From his left, a small hand cups his ear. Abu whispers barely audible.

"They are members of the al-Gammaa al-Islamiyya, what you call the Muslim Brotherhood. I will translate what I hear for you."

# *Ten*

The preliminary speeches have been made and Abu has diligently translated all. It confirms they have stumbled onto a meeting of the Muslim Brotherhood. The elder representative of the El-Minya area is introducing the man who is the reason for the meeting. Rather than give his name, he says.

"Please welcome our leader, whom you all know." Cody squirms in the frustration of not being able to see. The leader takes the stand. Cody concentrates on Abu's translation.

"My friends, I have asked each of you here today to announce our days of living in the shadows are over." The assembled members make astonished noises. "Yes my friends, each of you has known the small part you will play in the rebirth of Egypt. Each of you knows some of the changes which will occur with the rebirth. However, none of you know the full extent of Egypt's return to the true practices of Islam. Or its place in the coming war." At this, voices call out. "Be patient, my friends. All will be revealed. Soon there will be such a flood of rumors and lies from the west. I feel you must know the truth, or you could

250

be misled." He pauses. Cody pulls out his phone and switches it to audio recording. He holds it up to the open window.

The murmurs subside and he resumes his speech.

"In three days, we will re-establish the true practices of Islam in Egypt. Not the corruption brought in by the New Constitution. In three days my friends, we will take control of the Government and our great land. We will join with our Islamic brothers and drive out all western influences from the lands of Mohamed." A general cheer rises but is stifled by the speaker. "In three days, my friends. The might of the Egyptian Army will join our Palestinian brothers and drive the Jewish invaders from the holy lands. We will seize their weapons and cleanse our lands of the American infidels." This time the room erupts in cheers and Cody hears chairs banging on the floor.

"My friends, this is not talk or idle boasting as some of you may think. Thirty years ago, on this day, the misguided Egyptian Government separated Egypt from the rest of Islam by passing the New Constitution. On September eleventh, 1971, we the true followers of Islam became outcasts, rebels in our lands. In pursuit of the western ideas and western money, those traitors to Islam spat on the teachings of the Holy Koran and embraced the blasphemy of the West." The room becomes quiet.

"As I speak, the first wave of attacks on American soil is being carried out. Using their own planes as bombs, we will hit three targets. The first will be the center of capitalism. The second will be the center of their military and the third target will be the center of their government." The room is hushed in disbelief. "My friends, I have not brought you here for idle boasting. We will see this miracle so all will know the might of Mohamed and the power of his faithful!" Cody feels his mind and body go numb. Abu continues to whisper in his ear but he does not hear. 'Three targets on US soil' is all he can think. The words thunder in his brain. 'This man must be the architect to have such intimate knowledge of the plan. He must know who the perpetrators are.' He has to get a good look at the man.

At the corner, the guard is halfway through his pack of cigarettes and bored. He is idly glancing around the back of the building. As he lights another cigarette, he sees something odd. Under the window, a small metallic object protrudes from the bushes. He puts away his lighter and rises to have a look. He holds his rifle loosely at his side as he walks. He approaches and sees a hand Attached to the

252

object. The guard stops, realizing what he is seeing. He lifts his rifle as the cigarette drops from his mouth.

Cody watched the smoking guard approach. He was alerted by the sound of the man's shoes on the gravel. He sees him staring at the phone. The guard's face changes and the cigarette begins to drop from his mouth. Cody responds smooth and precise. He leaps at the man, his right hand balled into a fist. As the guard raises his rifle, Jason strikes him just under the chin. The force of the blow lifts the man from the ground. He lands on his back, his gun clattering to the ground.

Inside, the speaker has instructed his bodyguards to open a cabinet which holds a large screen television. As they pull open the doors, they find not only the television but the mystery man who Cody and Abu have been following. The bodyguard is the first to react and the first to die. A single shot rings out and the bodyguard falls. Panic erupts in the room. Those seated jump to their feet and bolt. The few guards inside pull their guns. They attempt to shoot the mystery man through the escaping crowd while the mystery man is trying to get a look at the speaker. The guards outside run to the windows opposite Cody and open

fire. The fleeing participants are cut down by the spray of
bullets. The shooting ends as the guards exhaust their clips.

The mystery man leaps from his hiding place in the TV
alcove. He rolls, picking up a discarded gun while shots fly
overhead. He finishes his role and leaps out of the window.
At the same time, Cody seeing a break in the gunfire grabs
the rifle and shoots the guards in the opposite window.
Several of the participants in the room turn and pull guns.
Jason swings around and empties the remains of the clip
into those who stand. The mystery man leaps through the
window landing, behind Cody.

Cody swings around, aiming at the mystery man as he
rises. The man also aims his weapon at Cody. The two men
stare at each other for a moment before the man speaks.

"You're empty." Says Jason

"So are you." The man raises his other hand and fires
over Cody's shoulder. Jason turns and sees a guard go
down behind him. The mystery man roughly pulls Cody
down. He speaks rapidly as he looks for threats.

"I am Mohamed Kahlid Aslamid, Egyptian Central
Intelligence."

"Jason Cody, FBI. I've never heard of Egyptian Central Intelligence." Kahlid looks at Jason.

"In 1967, I helped to protect President Anwar Sadat from an assassination attempt. Since that time, the Egyptian Central Intelligence Agency has been in existence. We answer only to the President and are known only by him."

"How many of you are there in this Egyptian Secret Service?" Cody asks. Kahlid says.

"Myself and a few other trusted friends. Our sole mission is to protect our President and our Country. Now Agent Jason Cody, if we are through with the questions? I believe it is time for us to leave."


Another gunman steps around the corner with his gun blazing. Cody drops as Kahlid fires once in a gunman's direction. The gunman is hit in the chest and falls. Kahlid rushes forward and drags the man's body behind the building. He searches him for weapons and ammunition. When he stands, he has the man's AK47 and a 45-caliber revolver. He turns to see Cody has done the same with the still unconscious guard by the window. Abu stands next to Jason with his knife drawn and ready.

"So you are the keeper of the little rat. Hello, again little one." Abu holds his tongue. Kahlid smiles seeing the mistrust in the boy's eyes, "good, this one learns quickly."

Kahlid grabs the guard's chair from the corner.

"It's no good going that way. They're watching for us." He indicates the gravel walk. "Better to go over the top, more of a surprise. I'll go first. You hand up the boy. When you get up there, stay low." Placing the chair under the roof edge, Kahlid jumps and pulls himself up with the strength of a gymnast. He pulls up Abu and helps Cody. The three stay low against the roof as Kahlid crawls to the far side. He signals Cody and Abu to remain behind.

"Stay down little rat. Your knife will be of no use up here." Kahlid raises his head enough to see the street. He waves Cody forward.

The street before them holds a few cars, a Porsche 928 and two Mercedes. A Mercedes limo is parked outside the building. Cody and Kahlid crawl forward on the roof, looking for the gunmen. Nothing.

"Quick, we jump." Kahlid launches himself from the roof, lands and rolls.

"Abu let's go." The boy scurries to Cody and is lowered down to Kahlid. Cody jumps and rolls to his feet.

"They have rushed the back to surprise us," Kahlid says. "We will cut them down as they return." Kahlid plants himself in front of the path. Cody takes a position at the Egyptian's side, his rifle at the ready. Suddenly Jason feels a tingling on the back of his neck.

"Limo!" Cody shouts. Both men spin in unison, their rifles fire as one. The driver convulses with each bullet, his gun falling to the ground. Cody drops the empty rifle. Pulling out his Beretta, he drops to his knee to cover their backs. Jason scans the line of green shrubs over his handgun. A shrub twitches a leaf. It twitches again, Cody's shot goes straight through it into the shoulder of the man hidden there. The man falls on the path holding his shoulder with his gun hand. An empty clip bounces at Cody's side telling him, Kahlid cannot help.

Three men rise from the shrubs with guns aimed at Cody. They've timed their attack with the changing of the clip. Three shots leave the Beretta, two strike home hitting the head, then heart but the third man moves and Cody misses. The wounded guard and the other aim their guns at Cody. He can get one but not both. He fires hoping the second man will miss. From his left, Kahlid fires at the same time, dropping the nearer man. A hot iron creases Cody's side and pulls at his bag. The nearer man got off a shot before Kahlid's bullet hit him.

Cody makes a quick assessment of his side as Kahlid kills two more guards. Cody sees Abu lying flat on the ground.

"Abu." Cody whisperers sharply. Abu's head pops up and Cody breaths a sigh of relief.

"The rat knows when to keep his head down," Kahlid says without emotion. "We need to get away from here." He drops the rifle and pulls out the 45. Cody and Abu stand ready as Kahlid searches the area for the best way out.

"Let's get to the houses. Maybe we can borrow one of the cars." The three jog from the cover of the park. Cody catches up and passes Kahlid, who is slowing down. Cody pulls up, looking back at Kahlid who is walking slowly and holding his side.

"Kahlid are you alright?" The Porsche starts and lurches forward aiming, straight at Kahlid, who stands still. The Porsche driver is intent on hitting his prey but a second from impact. Kahlid jumps and rolls to the right. He stands as the car passes firing. The car swerves and strikes the curb, bounces and rolls to a stop.

Kahlid runs for the Porsche and catches it as it comes to rest. Cody and Abu pull up the rear. They see the driver's window shattered and the driver lying sprawled across the wheel. Glass is spread over the body and most of his face is gone. Kahlid pulls the body from the seat and gets in the car. Cody pulls open the passenger door but stops seeing the blood and tissue splattered across the seat. Man and boy stand in shock.

Kahlid Looks at the two and says.

"Yes. I was hoping for the Mercedes as well." He smiles. Cody cracks a smile. He pulls forward the seat for Abu. The boy nimbly jumps into the back and Jason follows into the passenger seat. The engine revs and Kahlid puts it in first as Cody pulls the door closed. The car screeches around the wide bend.

They speed from the complex as Kahild shifts into fifth gear. Jason reaches into his bag for his phone but pulls out shattered plastic and metal. Inspecting the bag, he finds a bullet has passed through it and the phone.

"You need to phone home FBI?" Kahlid hands his mobile to Cody. Jason checks his watch, 12:24.

"They are six hours behind Egypt. You may still have a chance." Kahlid says. Cody dials the secure number.

# *Eleven*

**Washington DC 06:31 September 11, 2001**

Neal Roberts listens to Agent Cody on the phone as he picks his way through traffic. He hits the lights and siren on his unmarked ford, pulling out of traffic. He runs the light, a gray Buick nearly hitting him. As Jason finishes his report, Roberts is hitting 60 mph in town. He rifles past FBI parking security, grazing one of the barriers. He swerves through the maze of pylons in the underground car park and skids to a halt at the door.

Security guards step out from their posts, rifles raised. Neal flashes his ID. When one guard protests, he quiets the man's words with orders, saying.

"You stay here and park my car." He tosses the guard his keys. "You're with me." They run into the building past the metal detectors, picking up another guard along the way. At the elevator, Neal keys in a priority code and seconds later, the doors open. They ride to the eighteenth floor, the situation room. Inside, one of the guards hits the intercom calling for any secretary or clerical personnel. He finds a

261

typist from the second floor. She is escorted up while Neal calls Nathan McDonald and the FBI team of tactical advisers.

### Boston Logan International Airport, Boston, USA

### 07:29 September 11, 2001

*'Last call for American Airlines Flight 11 for Los Angeles. All passengers, please proceed to gate E7.'* The announcement is repeated as Mohamed Atta presents his ticket to the attendant. He looks back at the departure lounge and notes two of his fellow hijackers in line behind him. He passes onto the plane and takes his seat in business class as his confederates pass him on their way to economy.

### Washington DC, FBI Headquarters 08:22 September 11, 2001

Nathan is the last to arrive. He sits down as Roberts finishes reporting the details of Agent Cody's report.

"...from what we know at this time, the attacks will be using our own planes. Our agent believes the targets will be here on the East coast, the White House, Pentagon and possibly the Twin Towers."

"White House air defenses are on high alert. Any planes small or large will be blasted from the sky." Nathan Replies.

"We need to know where they are and how we are going to repel them," Neal concludes.

"Repel, what are we talking about here? Are you talking about escorting them away from targets, or what may I ask?" General Riker speaks as he shifts in his chair.

"That will depend entirely on what they are threatening, General," Roberts replies.

"Threats! I know I'm old school but I don't recall terrorists playing by any rules of engagement. For all we know, they could be in the air right now, a couple of Cessnas loaded with explosives flying straight for the White House." The General says.

"That gentlemen brings up another unpleasant subject." Says Martin Gray, the military analyst assigned to the Pentagon. "I think it's unlikely they would bother to stuff explosives into a small plane when they could use a standard commercial jet." Roberts stops and glances around the table at the assembled experts. He looks back at Gray.

"You mean a private jet, don't you?"

"Why not a commuter jet? Think of the explosive power of even half full tanks on a 747 for example. The devastation from the explosion would only be the start. The fire from that much jet fuel could double or even triple the destruction of the initial blast."

"What brings you to that conclusion?" Nathan asks.

"Your information coupled with an FBI report. It details suspected terrorists engaged in piloting classes. That information alone would indicate a hijacking. With this new information, it would make sense to use a commercial aircraft, as a, a flying bomb!"

"I didn't want to believe it but our man on the ground said the same thing," Neal says as he sits, his hand going to his temple.

Silence covers the room as each man sits with the possibility of an attack using a commuter plane full of hostages, a built-in human shield. What do you do in that case? What could you do? Who would give the order to shoot innocent people out of the sky? A rattling coffee cup pulls the men back to the present. The secretary drafted in to make coffee is visibly shaken. She steps forward a half filled cup in hand, coffee pot still held over it.

"Would they do that? I mean, would they just kill hundreds of innocent people like that? I mean, I don't know, I'm not supposed to be here. My mother is flying back to California this morning. Shouldn't we stop them from taking off or something? My mother might be on that plane. Shouldn't we stop them?"

She looks at the experts, her eyes pleading as Neal's secretary Jean steps forward and takes the cup from her hand.

"Why don't you and I go outside and call the airport. We can make sure your mother doesn't get on that plane. Okay?" The girl nods repeatedly. "What's your name?"

"Shelly."

"Okay Shelly, we can find the number for Dulles and stop her getting on the plane. She is flying from Dulles, isn't she?" Shelly nods again as the two walk from the room.

## World Trade center, North Tower, New York 08:39 September 11, 2001

Jennifer Cody steps into the elevator with her briefcase and lunch balanced in one hand, her new blue dress suit chaffing a little as she walks.

"What floor Miss," asks a young man in his late twenties, brown hair, blue suit and tie. He smiles as she balances her things in one hand.

"Ninety-sixth please," Jen says.

"Sorry, this is a local elevator. You might try taking one of the express elevators next time. I'll push seventy-eight for you. You can change there."

"Oh. I didn't know." Jen says, blushing slightly.

"First day." He enquirers.

"Yes, I just started at MMC."

"Nice. I'm with Hadley and Smith on the sixty-eighth. Hopefully, I'll see you around." He smiles and Jennifer's blush deepens.


"Fifty-fourth floor please." Says an older gentleman who enters and stands between Jen and the young man. The elevator accelerates up and Jen is caught off guard, catching her lunch before it falls. She recovers as her phone rings in her pocket. She turns to the corner and answers.

"Jason? Hey big brother, how are you?"

"Jen, where are you?"

"I'm on my way to work. Why?"

"Jen, don't go! Don't go near the tower!"

"What? Why? I'm here in the elevator. It's my first day. I have to go."

The elevator stops and the elderly gentleman steps out.

"Jen, you have to trust me! Please just get out of the elevator." The doors close and Jennifer has an empty feeling in the pit of her stomach as the elevator accelerates up.

# *Twelve*

### Over New York City, American Airlines Flight 11,

### 08:42 September 11, 2001

Mohamed Atta is seated at the controls of the Boeing
767. The Radio is alive with calls for him to answer. Atta
ignores the demands as well as the pounding and yelling at
the cockpit door. He grips the controls and points the plane
directly at the North Tower, chanting Allahu Akbar!
Allahu Akbar! Allahu Akbar! Allahu Akbar!


### World Trade Center, North Tower, New York 08:43
### September 11, 2001

"Jason! Tell me what's going on."

"Jen, remember when we were young. When I had those
dreams and they came true."

"When mom and dad were killed. Oh my god, Jason!"

"Jen, I've been having them again. Now please get out!"
The doors open and the young man exits, looking back at
Jennifer. She looks at him, her eyes going wide.

"Miss, are you alright?" The young man asks, reaching back and catching the doors before they close. Jennifer steps out of the elevator, still holding the phone to her ear. He lets the doors close as Jason pleads. Jennifer pulls the phone from her ear and asks.

"Why did you do that?"

"I don't know. I thought you might need help." There is an explosion overhead. Jen screams as she's knocked down.

"Jason, what's happening? Help me!" Jen's phone shatters as her hand strikes the floor.


**Washington DC, FBI Headquarters 08:52 September 11, 2001**

"Do we close the airports and search for the terrorists among the passengers." The General asks and thought goes round the room. "What do you think, Neal. Do we shut down the nation's airports?"

"Nathan."

"Yes, sir."

"These people were picked up. Tell me we have photos."

"Yes sir, we do. I'll get them out to every airport and local PD."

"And get Jean back in here pronto!" Neal says.

Nathan McDonald runs from the room, summoning Neal's secretary as he goes. Jean only gets to the door when Neal starts firing off instructions.

"Get the FAA on the line. Not some desk-jockey either I need the director on the phone now!"

"Yes, sir."

"Will you close the airports?" The General asks again.

"I've got no choice, General."


General Riker shifts in his chair and shakes his head.

"Well, we have a plan but I have to ask you Roberts, how reliable is your information?" Neal looks at the General and says.

"It's solid. One of our best men got it from the horse's mouth." The phone rings as Jean's hand touches it. She puts it on speaker.

"Neal, it's Nathan. You better contact the director and get down here! The wire services are on fire."

"What is it? What's going on?"

270

"An explosion at the Twin Towers. They say a plane struck the North Tower." Silence and shocked expressions pass around the room. Martin Gray looks at his watch. 08:56.

## Cairo FBI Offices 16:05 September 11, 2001

Taara walks the long hallway from the elevator to the office, paper in hand. Approaching the office, she notices the door ajar. Her hand drops into her purse, pulling out her HK 9mm. She lets the paper fall, the image of the collapsing South Tower on the front page.

Taara advances to the partly open door. A kick sends the door flying back, bouncing against the stop so hard she puts out a hand to prevent it from closing again. A large brown stain fills the center of the hall carpet. McAllen's glasses lay on the floor next to it. Taara fears the worst.

"Commander?" The office is silent in response.

Taara moves down the hall, looking for McAllen. Stepping around the stain, she checks the rooms. All have been turned inside out. Desks and chairs are turned over, files and papers are everywhere. The display cases in

Roberts's old office smashed. Her heart is pounding. She fears for McAllen. She picks up the phone but the cord had been pulled from the wall. Confused and afraid, she backs out of the offices, her hand shaking. 'Get out now!' Her mind screams. She backs into the hallway and runs. Her heart is pumping and she can barely think. She retreats to the elevators, hiding around the corner.

Closing her eyes, she hides her face behind her hands as she slides down the wall to sit on the floor. 'What am I doing?' She thinks to herself. 'Cody's gone off chasing leads to nowhere. The Commander is wounded, dead most likely.' She shakes herself, putting her hands down.

"I'm not doing that!" She says out loud to no one.

Closing her eyes, she hides her face behind her hands as she slides down the wall to sit on the floor. 'What am I doing?' She thinks to herself. 'Cody's gone off chasing leads to nowhere. The Commander is wounded, dead most likely.' She shakes herself, putting her hands down.

"I'm not doing that!" She says out loud to no one.

Taara stands and charges down the hall, gun in hand. She enters the office, taking one room at a time, all clear. She enters McAllen's room, looking for his notes. Searching his office, she finds nothing. In Alistair's office, the phone is still working. Taara picks it up and dials Washington. As she waits for the phone to connect, she says out loud.

"Everything has gone bad since I got here. I am not going to let this get the better of me. Now answer the fucking phone!" The phone clicks, an Egyptian voice cuts in the line, saying.

'I am sorry but all international lines are engaged at this time. Please try back later.'

"Shit!"

# *Thirteen*

**The SS Karim, 06:22 September 12, 2001. On the Nile South of El Minya.**

*Jason Cody stands on the observation deck of the World Trade Center. He steps down to the bottom set of seats and leans out over the railing looking down along the smooth sides of the building. He sees at the metal edging running down the building. They appear to merge further and further away. His eyes are drawn down, pulled down the building. His mind reels as vertigo grips him. Shifting his eyes to the horizon, he grips the railings.*

*In the distance, an object catches his eye. A jet banking against the cloud streaked sky. It appears motionless as if suspended by strings. He can see the vapor trails off the tips of the wings and the tail section with the AA symbol. The sun glints off the wing as it turns. He can see the line of windows and the passengers in their seats.*

*Before the wing, a movement grabs his attention. In one of the windows, someone is waving. He can see a little blond girl smiling and waving. He lifts his hand to return*

*the wave as the plane turns and accelerates directly*
*towards the tower under him.*


*The shock wave rockets up the structure knocking him off*
*his feet. Cody is thrown to the floor. The elevator bell*
*sounds and the doors open. An elderly gentleman and his*
*dog step out as the crowd fights to get in. The jet fuel*
*bellow ignites. A ball of flame bursts from the open doors.*
*It blows the man and his dog off the observation deck,*
*burning as they fall.*


*Cody makes it to the edge. He looks down the side of the*
*building. He sees people leaning out screaming, praying*
*for help. Then it begins. The fire forcing them to flee the*
*building. They leap from the windows only to find they*
*have escaped a burning death for a sudden one. One man*
*turns in mid-air and tries to regain the flaming floor but he*
*drops away, bouncing down the side. One couple kiss and*
*fall hand in hand.*

*"Noooooooooooooo," Jason screams.*


*Another shock runs through the building, throwing Cody*
*to the floor. The glass barriers explode and a figure*

*appears before him, on fire. It's his little sister Jen. She runs towards him, imploring him to put out the fire.*

*"Help me, Jason! Please help me!" Flames leave her lips as she speaks. She begins to blacken before his eyes. She screams and melts to the floor, a pool of flaming ash.*

*The floor is moving again. The screaming of the people below is deafening and the agony of the building palpable. A groan from the metal under him is hear as the structure gives up its long fight against gravity. The floor under Cody drops away and he falls. A cloud of dust rising up to engulf him.*

Blackness surrounds Jason as he sits up. The sound of Jen's voice rings in his ears. It took three attempts to reach her. When he did get through, she argued with him. Then he heard the blast and Jen scream. *'Jason, what's happening? Help me!'*

'Get out Jen, get out of the Tower!' was all he could say before the line dropped. The not knowing has raised every demon, past and present. His mind projects images onto the blackness in his cabin.

Cody puts his hand out and finds the light switch. The light chases away the waking terrors. Jason's brain hurts from being drowned in brandy last night. Sara tried to help but in the end, he had been inconsolable. Now, he sits in his own sweat, the night terrors having done their worst. Jason stands and thinks of Sara. He was cruel and pushed her away when she only wanted to help. He held the information the US needed to prevent the attacks. If only he had picked up the phone earlier, he might have saved thousands. He might have saved Jen. If only he had phoned earlier, he berates himself.

The previous day replays in his mind the desperate call to Washington, the more desperate call to Jennifer. He tried for hours after but the phone lines to the States were overloaded. He tries again only to find he has no signal. He remembers the Karim left El-Minya the moment everyone returned.

Jason looks at the empty brandy bottle by the side of his bed and wishes he had more to pour on his guilt. He has to keep busy. He grabs a towel deciding to shower. As he finishes dressing, there is a knock at the door.

"Please Mister Cody, the Captain would like to see you right away." It's one of the ship's crew.

"Tell the captain I will be up in a minute."

"Yes sir, I will wait." Cody pulls the door shut long enough to check his Beretta. He pulls out the shoulder holster and slips it on under his vest. Jason checks his spare clips. After yesterday, he isn't taking any chances. Stepping from his cabin, he follows the crewman to the front of the boat. They step into the wheelhouse, where he finds an Egyptian boy standing at the wheel.

"Captain, I believe you wanted to speak to me."

"Yes, I do Mister Cody." The voice comes from behind Jason. He turns to find an Egyptian man, five-foot-eight with deeply tanned skin. He is a thin man in the face, about fifty years of age. His arms show the strength of years of hard work. His eyes are lighter than most Egyptians and reminiscent of a sea captain Jason once knew. The captain looks Cody over, taking the full measure of him. He is silent while he lights a long thin pipe. He puffs it hard a few times, bringing the heat of the match to bear on the tobacco.

"A vice I picked up from you tourists many years ago." He says in explanation. "I am Kopi, Captain of the Karim." Jason nods. "My friend Kahlid says you are good in a fight." He squints at Cody through the smoke of his pipe.

"I thought the same of him," Jason says, seeing no reason to hide behind his cover story any longer. "Where is Kahlid."

"He has left us, always like the wind Kahlid. He shows up when you least expect it and always brings trouble. Do you always bring trouble, Mister Cody?" Cody attempts a smile.

"Don't really know. I've haven't had too many complaints."

"Then this must be bad luck." Cody is taken aback.

"What do you mean?" Cody asks, facing the captain.

"The trouble, it has come to us today."

"Trouble, what trouble?"

"That trouble." Kopi points with the stem of his pipe out the far window of the wheelhouse.


Cody looks across the water to the far shore. He sees the captain's meaning. While he has been self-absorbed in guilt and pity, the world has continued to turn. Highlighted by the orange morning light, groups of armed men line the water's edge. Some of the men are stationery but some are running to keep pace with the boat. A white car with men and rifles sticking out the windows is racing along the shore, moving ahead downstream. Cody looks forward and sees an unending line of men with guns stretched out along the shore. In places, they are spread out, in others, they are five or six men grouped together. Cars are racing along or stopping to collect zealots upstream as the boat passes and deploying them downstream.

"Someone has let slip we have an American Agent on board. An American Agent who single handedly killed five of our religious leaders." The captain gives Cody a piercing stare.

"I wouldn't say single handed." Cody returns.

"Don't worry Agent Cody, I know it was Kahlid. Where Kahlid goes, there is always death. Death follows him like a trained dog, always ready, always loyal." The captain looks down at the deck and spits out a piece of tobacco saying. "We are okay in this part of the river. They can only get to us from that side. Later on, it changes to the other side and again we will be okay. These things I can manage without your help. However, tomorrow we come to a part of the river where it is narrow and accessible from both sides," Kopi pauses. "There is a lock. Once we are in the lock, we are at their mercy." Kopi looks at the far shore. I will do my job. I will protect my Karim and her passengers. My crew will do the same." He fixes Cody with piercing eyes. "What will you do, Agent Cody?"

## Cairo FBI Offices 06:53 September 12, 2001

Taara slams down the phone and picks up her mobile for the seventh time, dialing the Washington number. She hears a recorded message in Egyptian, telling her that the International lines are busy. Please try later. She disconnects her phone and lets her head fall forward to the desk with her arm outstretched. She lies there for a few moments closing her eyes. They burn and she shuts them tight against the tears. Her mind races for a solution but ends back where it began. 'No word on the Commander from either police or Egyptian Security. No word from Washington, though she believes, it is to be expected. They must be working twenty-four-seven trying to co-ordinate a tactical response.' Taara wants to talk to her parents. She needs to talk to someone just to know the whole world hasn't gone mad.

All of yesterday she has felt so conspicuous, so transparent to the locals. Her Egyptian singles her out to

281

everyone. The shopkeepers and clerks immediately switch to English. Her clothing, she was so sure concealed her origins, calls out to the world saying, I am a tourist, an alien in your land. In her search for the Commander, she has phoned and visited numerous hospitals and military bases. In each location, she found the continual reminder of the tragedy. Televisions and radios at every office at every street corner reminding her of the attacks. People gathered four and six deep, trying to see the destruction of one of man's great monuments.

By afternoon, the news turned to the Islamic reaction in the Middle East. Then the street demonstrations began with men in turbans firing their guns in the air while teenagers on their knees pledg their lives to Islam. The scenes are repeated throughout the day and evening. She has spoken with official after official, each one saying the same words in their best English.

"I am so sorry for your loss." The words have been repeated so many times she thinks it must be the official government response. In the end, she returned to the FBI offices and split her time between cleaning and trying to contact Washington. Near exhaustion, Tarra lays on the edge of sleep, wishing someone would tell her what is going on, what to do.

The phone she holds at arm's length buzzes against the rings on her right hand. The chime joins the vibration of the phone with an incessant beep, beep, beep. She looks up at it in surprise, sits up and answers.

"Hello. Agent Cody! Jason, thank God you're okay. What? No, I haven't been in touch with Washington. The lines are completely jammed. What? Jason listen, the Commander is, well I think he may be dead." Taara squeezes out the words not wanting to say what she already knows. "No, Jason, we have to assume he is dead. No, Jason listen, you don't understand." A switch flips in Taara's head. As tired and helpless as she feels, the man at the other end needs guidance. "Jason." Her voice cracks. "Agent Cody, I need you to report! Where are you and why aren't you back in Cairo."

The lines burn between the Cairo FBI offices and the satellite phone onboard the SS Karim for the better part of thirty minutes. When the conversation is finished, Taara marches out of the FBI offices and corners the morning receptionist at the elevators.

"Our offices were broken into last night and I have to go out. You are to watch our door and make sure that no one enters except for myself and the locksmith who you will call right now. I will be back in one or two hours and I expect the door to be repaired and secure locks in place when I return. Do you understand?" The young man at reception presses back in his chair, trying to distance himself from the force of the young woman before him.

"Yes, Yes right away!"

Twenty minutes later, Taara steps out of a taxi and up the steps of the Egyptian Presidential Palace.

# *Fourteen*

Taara stands in the outer offices waiting to be seen. A string of officials run in and out of the carved doors of the reception hall. Some eye her, some look past her but most avoid her altogether. It's apparent they're not ready for her visit. She has been waiting for twenty minutes and the number of people in the reception hall is diminishing fast. She attempts to stop a secretary with an arm full of files. On seeing Taara, she stops and flees in the opposite direction.

'This is not looking good,' she thinks.


A lower secretary steps out of the security door with his eyes down, avoiding catching Taara's gaze.

"I don't have time for this," She says. Stepping forward, Taara catches the door before it closes. Inside she pulls her scarf over her face and slips past the guard. She spots the signs for the President's office and strides forward. She passes officials in tight circles, arguing points of protocol and politics. Halfway down the carpeted hallway, a short stocky official sees her and blocks her path. Gesticulating

285

wildly, he bars her progress. She steps to the right but he matches her maneuver.

"Our President will see you when he has the time. We cannot change his schedule at the drop of a hat. Would you please leave so we can properly prepare to receive you." She moves to the left and again but he matches her move. His words become louder and the room of officials has taken notice of the intrusion. More officials move to block her view of the President, denying her access until they are ready. The official in front of her becomes more insistent, pushing her back and out of the room yelling.

"We are not ready for you. You will leave now!"

"Mister President, Mister President." Taara tries to yell above the verbal onslaught but his voice outshouts her.

A second official who Taara recognizes as Mister Ahmes, the representative of the El Minya, stands between her and the President.

"You, American, you are not welcome here." He spits out her nationality like a curse. "You have meddled in Egypt's affairs for the last time. Get out!" It is apparent they will refuse to see her. She will be barred from entry to the grounds and official complaints will be sent to Washington.

Her next move is not out of desperation. No. It's the pain she feels from the loss of thousands of American lives and the loss of the Commander. The short official physically pushes her. Taara stumbles. His words are insulting and vile. Her hand dips into her handbag. The Heckler and Koch 9mm appears and she jams it into his protesting mouth. He squeals as he bites down on cold steal. She can't believe what she has done but there is no helping it now. She presses her advantage, pushing the gun into the back of his throat. He makes gagging noises as he stumbles back, his arms flailing outwards for balance, files scatted to the carpet. The response is quick. Guards at the door raise rifles on either side. She knows she has only one chance to make her plea.

"Mister President," She yells. "This is not an official government visit and it is not directly related to the attacks on America." The President peers out of the office around the officials attempting to shield him.

"Bring her!" The doors at either side of the hall bang open and a stream of soldiers enter, rifles raised and ready. She tries to move forward but the solders press in, with the sound of safeties being released. Taara stops eyeing the circle of trained marksmen. She has run out of space and time. "Mister President, My visit is not an official visit but my presence is as a representative of the United States of America. Any aggression against me will be seen as aggression against America and her allies. I need only a moment of your time to avert further attacks on foreign nationals."

"It is you who are the aggressor here. We want none of you or your threats." Ahmes blurts out.

"Your views are well known Mister Ahmes. Are your words to be the ones I take back to my President." Taara retorts.

From behind the wall of cowering officials, one man stands straight and addresses Taara. He is a tall man, thick through the chest with square features. His olive skin deeply tanned compliments his dark hair and eyes. His suit is a charcoal gray three-piece of the finest Egyptian cotton and Italian tailoring. His voice is deep and soft but rises from depths of power. On his first word, though barely audible, the clamor of the room turns to silence.

"What, foreign nationals?" The President walks through the collected officials approaching Taara.

"Twenty-six British and one American."

"Where?"

"About eight miles South of El-Minya on board the SS Karim."

"King Faruk's boat!" He pauses in thought. "And is this the reason for your unofficial visit?" He eyes Taara's gun still pressed into the back of the official's throat. Seeing his look, she is embarrassed. Her hand drops to her side and casts the weapon under the feet of the soldiers. There is a palpable relief as the soldiers set their safeties.

"Yes, that is the reason for my visit and to speak to you privately."

"No Mister President, it is a trick she seeks to assassinate you. She must not be allowed." Ahmes protests fiercely. "Let me lock this assassin away from your sight. Guards, take her."

"Stay where you are! Need I remind you, it is I who command the military of Egypt Mister Ahmes. Young lady, I thank you for the information but I have no time for this." He waves to the guards and dismisses her.


Two guards move forward in well-rehearsed actions and restrain Taara.

"There is a plot against your life Mister President."

"Yes, and we have diffused that plot by catching you haven't we, assassin."

"Ahmes be silent! What plot?"

"I must speak with you alone, Mister President."

"To give you a perfect opportunity to kill the..."

"SILENT!" The President runs his eye over Taara deciding what to do.

"You know me Mister President and you know who I represent."

"You, bring me her handgun. You stand over there and keep your rifle trained on her. If she makes a move, shoot her. Come with me." He walks to the corner of the room and points to a spot five feet in front of him. "Stand there and make no move."

Taara stands absolutely still head down and recites the information she had learned from Cody. While she speaks the President examines her handgun. Taara finishes and raises her eyes to meet the President's. He does not look at her. Instead, he continues to examine the gun.

"This is a good weapon, very reliable in a fight. I have never had one of these fail and I have never heard of one misfiring. If only people were as reliable as this gun, life would be so much simpler." He sighs and looks at the assembled officials. "Do you see those men?" The President indicates the officials at the door. "They should represent the hopes and needs of the people of Egypt. Instead, they represent only themselves. You have taken a great chance coming here like this. In any other country, you would be dead or in prison by now." The President pauses and says. "This is a good weapon I hope you are as reliable as your weapon."

The President removes the clip and checks the chamber then places them in his pocket.

"In the future please comply with our security protocols and check your weapon with the guard. Captains hold Mister Ahmes and his assistant. I may want to question them further." The color runs from Ahmes's face as he complains.

"Mister President, I assure you I am only acting in the interest of Egypt."

"I am sure you are Mister Ahmes but some of us have different ideas of what is best for Egypt. Either way, we will soon find out the truth. Captain, contact the owners of the SS Karim and find out why they have not reported the trouble themselves. You two, escort Miss Safi to my private office. See she has everything she needs. I will talk with her later." The President eyes her meaningfully as he hands her pistol to one of the soldiers.

## The SS Karim 08:35 September 12, 2001

Cody makes his way to the dining room, trying to put together a story for the passengers. His first job is to keep them calm. *'I can't have a lot of panicked people running about demanding to speak to the consulate.'* He thinks and then turns to Mister Kohlemete.

"Are they all here?"

"Yes Mister Cody, I have done as you asked."

"Good, thank you."

"Don't thank me. I think they are more ready for you than you are for them." He says as he returns to his office. Cody watches him go, wondering what he means. Jason approaches the dining room and takes a breath. He pushes through the doors and finds the passengers talking quietly among themselves. As Jason steps forward, they go silent. The awkwardness of the moment throws his concentration, he pauses.

"I believe it was you who asked us here Mister Cody, may we know why." It is Gerald Forester who speaks, breaking the silence.

"Yes, I did. Ladies and gentlemen, I do not wish to alarm you but the recent events in both America and here in Egypt have made travel on this section of the Nile." He pauses, looking for the right word. "Hazardous. The militant factions of the region are planning to board the Karim in an act of terrorism. Some of you may have noticed men with arms lining the banks of the river. The captain and I..."

"How many are they?" Forester asks.

"What?"

"How large are their numbers, one hundred, two hundred, a thousand." Cody hadn't thought about it.

"I don't know. It's hard to estimate with them moving downriver as we pass. I would guess about one or two hundred."

"You say they are moving them downriver, so we see them as we pass. That's an old trick. They want us to believe the whole country is up in arms. It's probably more like the numbers you mentioned. With the captain keeping us well away, we should be safe for the moment. Now, what arms do we have?"

"Excuse me Mister Forester but I think you should leave the defenses to the crew and police. They are trained to handle..."

"Nonsense! I know these men, good at their jobs, yes but they will not be heroes on our account. Not if it means getting themselves killed. I have a plan I think might do the trick if you would like to have a look."

"Mister Forester this is not a civilian matter. We should wait for military escort which..."

"May, or may not, be on its way. I think you will find our Mister Covington has a thing or two to say about the matter. Andrew?"

"Well Mister Cody, we've been monitoring the political situation in Egypt for the past fifteen years or so and..."

"We! Who are we?"

"Oh my apologies, Andrew Covington, MI-6, retired." He steps forward and shakes Jason's hand. Forester also steps forward and salutes, saying.

"Lieutenant Colonel Gerald Forester RAF retired.

Cody nods in recognition and returns the introduction.

"Agent Jason Cody FBI. I am glad to have you both onboard."

"Oh, and I thought you were CIA." Missus Forester says.

"Oh no dear, our Mister Cody is far too nice to be CIA." Missus Covington says, smiling. The three men look at Missus Covington for a moment and then return to business.

"There are only the two machine guns of the Tourist Police assigned to the Karim. Aside from ourselves, no one among the passengers has any experience with firearms," Mister Covington says.

"Mister Covington," Abu steps around Jason. "There is the armory, sir."

"What armory Abu?" Cody asks.

"Below deck Mister Cody, I have seen the Military Police going in to clean their weapons."

"Abu, could you ask Mister Habid to step in here," Cody says. Abu runs from the dining hall and returns with Habid in tow. "Mister Habid, are there weapons below deck?"

"Yes, Mister Cody but they are the property of the Military."

"Is it not the duty of the Military to ensure the safety of the passengers Mister Habid?" Colonel Forester asks.

"Yes, but I cannot tell them to hand over weapons. You must ask them." Habid shrugs, "I have no authority in this matter."

The two Military Police are sent for and join them in the dining room. After a short discussion, it is agreed they will distribute the four rifles and ammunition when needed. The ladies not to be outdone discover two amongst them have medical training. Fran Goodwood and Emma Forester go to reception to make an inventory of the available medical supplies. By the time the three men have a working plan, a makeshift infirmary is set up at one end of the dining room. The other passengers move tables and bring mattresses from the cabins and dormitory life is established.

Mister Kohlemete enters furious with the disruption to his boat.

"Mister Cody I said you could gather the passengers. I did not in any way indicate that you could dismantle this vessel." Covington smiles good naturedly and retorts.

"Don't worry Mister Kohlemete. This is only a temporary situation, until we get over this little rough patch. All will be set right once the military arrives. It's just the ladies' worry at times like this. They feel better when they are together, for support you see." Covington puts his hand on Kohlemete's shoulder and lowers his voice to a conspiratorial whisper. "It will only be for a few days and we will put everything back in its place, you'll see." He gives the director a dismissive slap on the back and turns back to the planning.

Cody inquires.

"Mister Kohlemete, you put in distress calls to your head office this morning?"

"Oh yes and last night as well."

"Are there no military bases in this area that could assist us?"

"Oh yes there are excellent forces in all areas of Egypt."

"Isn't it strange none have arrived to help? Perhaps you should contact the military directly." Kohlemete pauses seeing Cody's point and says.

"Yes, yes, I see what you mean. I will contact them at once."

"It's as I feared I'm afraid," Covington says, watching the man run back up the stairs. "The political factions supporting the militant fundamentalists are not just hot-headed youth, as the authorities would like us to believe. Many of the sympathizers are spread through the military and government. We may be in for a long stand-off if he can't get through." He looks meaningfully at Cody.

"My superiors are working on it as we speak Mister Covington. I wouldn't worry too much if I were you." Cody replies but thinks. 'Come on Taara don't let us down.'

Midday passes and a light lunch is served from the kitchen. While the passengers busy themselves in the makeshift dormitory. The two self-appointed leaders sit discussing strategies for getting through the Lock at Beni Suef.

"I've spoken to Habid." Forester says. "The lock at Beni Suef will take five minutes for the boat to enter, approximately ten minutes to lower and another five to make our escape. If you add in the time we are within rifle range of the connecting damn and walkways. I can't see how we could make it without support. They don't have to shoot us, Once we are inside they can swarm the boat. Two machine guns may stop one side but they can't protect a vessel of this size. Not with so many."

Cody walks the upper sun deck, his Beretta loose in its holster. He feels weary already though he has done little. He thinks of Missus Covington organizing the passengers like battle-ready troops. He tried to intervene when she led the passengers to inspecting the crew's fire preparations. She looked him in the eye and told him without the slightest hesitation.

"Young man as a girl I helped rebuild London after German bombs made a mess of it. We all did. You will find when there is a crisis Mister Cody. We English accept it and get on with what must be done." Jason stepped aside at that point, as the crew had when she made her assignments, every passenger given a task.

Cody enters the dining room as the passengers are finishing their dinners. Some have pulled out the tables and continue to make the most of the holiday while others looking defeated, sat in groups, eating their evening meals. He pulls together a sandwich from the assorted meats and cheeses. Jason is making his way out, stepping around dining passengers, when Abu enters with four crew members carrying a wooden crate.

"Abu, what's this?"

"Dynamite Mister Cody. We have Dynamite!"

"Well done young man Gerald forester says."

"I've been going through the lower deck looking for things to help and this is what I found," Abu says proudly.

"Mister Cody," Fran Goodwood says.

"Yes."

"Have you seen Sara?" Cody's brow creases.

"No, I haven't." The truth is, he's been avoiding her. He thinks back on the previous night and how he treated her so badly. Fran pauses a moment then says.

"Well I saw her earlier but no one has seen her for the past hour. Her father thinks she has gone up to look for you but he says she isn't anywhere on the sun decks. I think we should keep track of everyone, don't you?"

"Your right. I'll look for her." Cody puts his coffee down.

"We'll help," Emma says. "Yes, we should help look for her." Missus Covington chimes in.

"Okay, fine but no one goes outside. Start with the lower decks and then move up." Cody orders.

"Why don't we spread out? Emma and I can take the top deck. Andrew take the middle deck and you can take the bottom deck," says Missus Forester.

300

"I'll look around down here, the kitchens and all," adds Fran. Cody reminds them not to turn on any lights, making them easy targets for sharpshooters. Even though the shore is too far away, they may paddle out and shoot from mid-river.

Cody works his way down the aft cabin section of the boat, knocking and checking each cabin as he goes. Finding nothing he moves to the forward section noticing the door to his cabin is ajar. Jason quietly pushes the door inward, one hand on the door one on the Beretta. In his cabin, he finds Sara sitting in front of his laptop. He tenses, not knowing what she may be looking at. As he approaches, he can see the screen.

The screen glows with the CNN news page he downloaded. He must have left the laptop switched on before he drank himself into a stupor. She is scrolling down the pages to a picture of American Airlines flight 11 crashing into the South Tower. Cody's stomach tightens, the screams from his dreams ringing in his ears. Not thinking, he places a hand on Sara's shoulder.

"Oh! Oh Jason, I'm so sorry. I don't know what I was thinking. I'm never like this. I wanted to see you but you weren't here then I saw your computer on." Sara stops for a breath and races on. "I opened it to see how it's turned off and there was the news. I don't know I started reading. I couldn't help myself. Oh, you must think I'm a horrible person to look into your private things but the photos. I couldn't take my eyes off of them." Cody puts up a kind hand to still the rush of explanation. "Those poor, poor people, how could anyone do such a thing. I am sorry I forgot how badly it affected you. Are you all right you don't look all that well. Perhaps you should lie down."

"I'm fine thanks. I didn't get much sleep last night."

"Then you should lie down." She concludes and stands up as if action is needed.

With Jason standing so close, she collides with him. Slightly embarrassed by their closeness, she stammers.

"I, I mean you should take care of yourself we're depending on you. I don't mean you alone of course there will be help coming from the military, we just don't know when. I'm sure it will come soon," Sara says. There is a pop sound and the paneling behind them splinters. Cody grabs Sara, pulling her onto the bed. She lets out a little scream as they roll off the bed onto the floor. He rolls the two of them over, so he is pinning her down. He listens.

"Jason, please. Yes, fine but not so rough!" looking at Sara, Cody is confused by her comments. Another pop and the window glass explodes inward. Another and the flower vase on the side table explodes showering the two with water and ceramic shards. Sara screams as Cody jumps up, slamming closed the laptop screen, shutting off the light source. He returns to the floor next to Sara.

"We go out the door together. You first turn left and go straight to the dining room."

"What about you?"

"I have to get to the wheelhouse and find out why we have moved so close shore. When I say go, we run."

"Okay." Sara's eyes have the look of a frightened child. Her heart pounds in her ears. Following Cody's instructions, they get to their knees.

"Go!" They run low into the passage, Cody pulling the door closed after them. A fourth shot blows a hole in the door panel as they escape.

Sara runs to alert the passengers while Cody is taking the stairs two at a time. He enters the pilot house to find it dark and empty.

"Down, get down before you get your head blown off." Cody sits on the floor and lets his eyes adjust to the dark. He recognizes Captain Kopi seated in front of the wheel, driving by poking his head up from time to time.

"What happened?"

"I think he must have dozed off," Kopi says, indicating with his head the back of the wheelhouse. Straining his eyes, Cody makes out what Kopi is speaking of. Against the back wall lay the young assistant Jason saw the other day, a dark pool of blood under his head.

"They picked him off with only the reading light we use to check the gauges. It must have been a lucky shot, eh."

"I don't think so. They have at least one marksman in their ranks." Cody says, turning back to the captain. "Are you okay?"

"Oh, yes. I had some sleep. In fact, I was on my way to relieve him."

Looking at the body Kopi's face became soft. His mouth works without speaking. Silent words sent off to a dead boy who would never see his own children grow or taste the sweet wine of love. Feeling he is intruding on a private moment, Cody shifts. The noise pulls Kopi out of his melancholy and he pops his head up quickly checking his position in the river.

"We should be okay but I would keep everyone down in the lower decks. We don't want any more of this sort of thing." Kopi says, gesturing with his head to the back of the wheelhouse.

"Are you sure you're all right?" Jason asks.

"Go on, don't worry about me. I don't need as much sleep as young people do. I'm fine." He stops and looks straight ahead downriver.

"When you've got everything settled down there, send up some of my boys to take care of Gamal." Looking back to the body again, Kopi continues. "But not too quickly, I may have a few things to say to him before he goes." Cody nods and slips backwards out the door.

Jason makes his way across the dining room and finds Emma Forester supervising the treatment of Amy Henderson's arm.

"Is everyone okay?" Cody inquires.

Emma pulls him away as she speaks.

"Yes, she's fine. She caught some glass from a window upstairs. Poor thing, all of this is just too much for her." Mary stops and faces Cody. "It's their honeymoon you see, the Henderson's."

"I didn't know." Cody glances back to the girl in her twenties and the young man who hovers over her.

"Mister Cody how could you miss it. Every evening she has been wearing a new gown and they always sit by themselves. They are obviously newly in love. I would think they would have taught you common sense in the FBI."

"I guess I missed that lesson." He replies.

"Well, do try to be more observant in the future." She returns and moves about the room making sure everyone is comfortable.

As much as Cody tries to prevent it, the news of the boy's death spreads. Though no one knew the boy, the fact someone so young could be killed dampens the passengers' spirits. The dining room begins to feel like a prison with the doors being watched by the crew. Only Cody and a few others are allowed to leave. The passengers sit on mattresses and play cards but no one has their hearts in it.

Very quickly, the confinement becomes too much. Amy Henderson paces between the tables and beds spread around the floor. She has made a path and will not be calmed by her husband or any of the ladies. The other passengers sit or lie listlessly around the room, lost in private thoughts. Clive Peters has rescued his radio from his cabin. He slowly turns the dial looking for news updates.

*"Wheeeeeewheyw,,,, static."* a faint signal turns out to be an English broadcast of the news. *".....and the Bush administration has pledged, the perpetrators of these crimes will not go unpunished. He has declared Osama Bin Laden the enemy of the American people. 'We will not rest until those who are responsible for these atrocities are brought to justice.' In other news..."*

"Please Mister Peters, there must be something better on your radio. Please may I." Clive sees the anguish of a young lady's face, denied her honeymoon.

"I would be very pleased if you would try." He says with a smile, handing her the wireless. Amy spins the dial mercilessly, jumping from one station to the next finding only static and Egyptian. She is about to give up when a faint sound is heard at the far end of the dial. She concentrates and slowly tunes the radio to the signal. The music blares out with Cher singing. *"....Do you believe in life after love! I feel so good inside myself..."* Amy smiles and she reaches out for Clive's hand.

"Come on Mister Peters, help me make my husband jealous. Dance with me." She insists and pulls him up from the floor, moving her hips and shoulders in time to the music. Clive smiles and joins in, making the best of the moment. He manages a few moves in the tight spaces between the tables and mattresses. The other passengers are clapping in time to the music and getting up to dance. Quickly the need for a dance floor outweighs the need for sleeping and eating. Mattresses are cleared to the sides and the passengers are up dancing. All thoughts of terrorists and gun play become things of fiction. Mister Covington has a word with the chief steward and the crew enters the room with a cart of drinks and snacks. Mister Peters has disengaged himself from Amy by returning her to her husband. He is making his way back to his chair when Jan Harris grabs him and dances him back out onto the floor.

The lights come up and the whole of the passengers and crew forget about their troubles. A few of the crew stand on the sides clapping and dancing in place. Peters gets his radio back. He makes a few adjustments clearing the signal. The music comes in strong, the DJ announcing five hours of non-stop dance music. The boat cheers. Cody rushes into the room, taking in the scene. His jaw drops, not believing his eyes. Missus Covington pulls him out into the middle of the floor.

"You see Mister Cody, I told you. We English don't let adversity get us down."


The SS Karim glides on the waters of the Nile, making its way downstream. The music and dancing continue through the night, the tension of the past day forgotten. The music and light coming from the lower deck cut through the quiet of the Egyptian night. On the far shore, four figures watch the ship. They huddle around a fire speaking in whispers, the youngest runs to a motorcycle. He starts it on the second kick. The sound of the two-stroke engine cuts through the silence of the desert. He races ahead, determined to deliver the message he carries, a message for the forces stationed downriver at the lock of Beni Suef.

# *Fifteen*

After several hours, Abu convinces Cody to rest. Returning to his cabin, Jason pulls the blackout curtains. He lies down for the first time in thirty-six hours. Kopi too finds time for sleep but he makes his bed in the back of the wheelhouse where he can keep one eye on his new apprentice.

With the help of the waiters, the passengers have converted the dining room back to an eating area. The passengers are finishing their breakfasts when Mark Harris and Chris Goodwood approach Mister Covington.

"Mister Covington." Clive begins. "Mark and I have been thinking. We overheard you and Mister Forester saying to get through the lock at Ben Suef we would need cover fire." Covington looks up at the two men. Clive continues. "We think we might have an idea."

"Well speak up. What is it you two have in mind," Covington asks.

"Well, Chris, I mean Mister Goodwood and I are engineers and young Marcus Henderson works in a metal shop. The three of us noticed a large air compressor the Karim is transporting to Cairo. We thought given the circumstances, they wouldn't mind if we were to borrow it and make,,, Oh perhaps we should show you."

The three men make their way to the lower deck. They find Marcus Henderson in a welding mask and gloves, putting the finishing touches on the first of their creations.

"What is it?" Covington inquires.

"Well, with a compressor of this size." Mark Harris points to a machine the size of a small car. "We can run at least four of these and a launcher," Henderson says.

"A what," Covington demands.

"I think it's best if we show you," Marcus says. He connects the high-pressure hoses to the compressor. He then adds a small amount of petrol to the tank and signals a crewman to fire up the compressor. The diesel engine thumps into life and the air hoses go stiff. Marcus lifts the pipe onto the railing while Chris holds the welding torch in front. Marcus yells.

"Ready? Fire!" A bright yellow flame shoots from the pipe out the side of the boat. It reaches over one hundred feet before it dies back.

Covington stands in awe of the sight. He turns to see the three men beaming with pride.

"Good god," Covington says, then turns to Harris and asks. "How many of these can you make?"

"We have plenty of materials for six or seven flame throwers but we are short on high-pressure line. We can manage two at the front and two at the back but I'm afraid we only have enough line for one launcher." Mark says, his face showing disappointment.

"Launcher, what do you mean launcher?" Covington asks.

"Well, Marcus came up with the idea and we slapped together this." Clive pulls a burlap covering off of a tube mounted on a platform with an adjustable bracket. Covington recognizes it immediately.

"That's a mortar. What on earth can we fire from that? We've got no shells."

"Well, we hoped we could use some of the dynamite," Harris says. Covington eyes the Mortar and the three men. A wicked smile slowly creeps over his face.

"What sort of range would it have?"

The Karim becomes a hive of activity. Goodwood and Harris are assigned the task of arranging the boats stationary defenses while Forester works with the mortar. They spend the morning launching empty wine bottles and marking off the range. Covington comes up with a light bulletproof shield using burlap and cotton batting from the hold. He presses them between sheets of ply-board. Saying they should stop most small rounds. The crew gets into the act and produces two stout bows and a cache of arrows they use for sport.

Covington has the crew stack crates around the flame-thrower positions. The sound of the preparations wakes Jason Cody. He pokes his head out the door as Sara runs by with an arm full of sheets.

"Well hello, sleepyhead." She says, smiling at him.

"What's going on? What is all of this?"

"Well if you're going to sleep all day, you will miss a thing or two you know." She smiles. He catches her arm and pulls her back to him the pile of sheets between them.

"Sara I'm sorry I."

"Don't you worry, I understand. You're not the first man I've seen in pain. You should have seen my dad after mum died. That was a full week session with the bottle. I finally had to put my foot down before he drank himself ill." She smiles slightly embarrassed. "Anyway, I do understand." She pulls away from him but he pulls her back and kisses her soundly on the mouth.

"Now, don't you start. I've got a job to do."

"What are you doing?"

"Mister Covington and Mister Forester have everyone on the march. We're preparing the boat's defenses."

"What? Do you know where they are?"

"On the sun deck last time I saw them. Oh but watch out for that Mister Kohlemete. He was looking for them as well. He's gone absolutely ballistic." She says as she pulls away. Cody runs up the stairs to the sun deck and the midday heat. He finds Forester and Covington arguing over what looks like a squashed mattress between sheets of wood.

"It won't work, I tell you." Forester yells.

"And I tell you it will." Covington fires back, only slightly calmer.

"How can I ask anyone to shelter behind that thing when I know it won't work." Forester repeats.

"What won't work," Cody asks.

"This ridiculous thing Andrew is trying to tell me this flimsy wood and cotton will stop a bullet. I cannot accept it would stop even arrows." Forester answers in a huff.

"Well, let's find out. High powered 9mm at twenty-five feet should do the trick." Before Covington can get out from behind the shield, Cody steps back and fires. The bullet hits directly in front of Covington, the impact rattling the shield in Andrew's hands. Forester's mouth drops open. Covington looks down at his trousers then at Cody. He braces himself up facing Forester.

"You see safe as steel."

Forester and Cody examine the shield there is a clean entry hole in the front and no sign of the slug in the back.

"Buried deep in there, I should think." Forester says. He looks at Covington saying.

"Excellent job Andrew. I should never have doubted you. As you say strong as steel." He salutes and turns to go muttering under his breath. "Bloody reckless Americans."


"Are you alright? Cody asks.

"Yes. Yes, as you guessed I would be," Covington smiles. "Certainly shut up old windbag. Not that I blame him, he's old school military. Likes his Armor big and heavy, doesn't believe anything this light could stop a bullet."

"You've done a nice job. Will there be more than one?"

"Oh yes, we should have three or four of these by this afternoon. Mark Harris and Marcus Henderson have designed a system of defense including a mortar launcher." Cody raises his eyebrows at the comment and Andrew spends the next few minutes bringing him up to speed.


"You're not thinking of trying to run the lock at Ben Suef are you?" Cody's face shows his misgivings. Covington wrinkles his forehead and replies.

"No, I'm hoping we won't have to but to tell you the truth, I'm more than a little worried. It has been a day and there has been no word from the charter company or the government. All we get are promises to look into it and static. Poor Kohlemete has been on the phone every five minutes for the past day and look what it has brought us. Nothing. I'm sorry Jason but I think we've only ourselves to depend on."

Marcus Henderson and one deck crew drag high-pressure hoses up the stairs to connect to the launcher. Hot on their heels is Kohlemete bristling and sputtering with furry.

"What is the meaning of this Mister Covington? What do you think you are doing tearing up my boat, using fine cotton we are transporting to Cairo. Do you have any idea, the cost of these things and using the compressor? It's our first delivery to the Alexandria shipping yard. This is inexcusable. I demand you cease at once and return everything to its proper place. At once," Kohlemete screams the last words and his eyes nearly popping out of his head. He stands with fists clenched breathing hard. The Karim begins to shudder under them as the boiler room puts on more steam. The two big wheels at the stern pull deeply into the Nile and the whole of the boat creaks with the strain. "Now what, now what," Kohlemete yells.

Cody looks up and sees captain Kopi hurrying back to them with an easy lope.

"What is it," Jason calls out.

"There." Kopi points upstream and the three men turn. They see a small cruise boat coming up behind them about a quarter-mile back.

"That's the Pharaoh's Head. She's one of the fastest boats on the Nile. She may not look like much but she's got two Rolls Royce engines in her belly. Her captain is a rich kid who bought her to use as a party boat. He's been following the Muslim Brotherhood, trying to impress the leaders. You see the smoke coming from her. They're pushing her hard." Cody looks upriver studying the boat.

"Are you sure? Maybe he is just out for a joy ride." Kohlemete offers. Kopi looks Kohlemete in the eye and says.

"Not a chance. He hopes to get in with the Brotherhood by chasing us down."

"But his boat is so small. How can he hope to stop us." Kohlemete asks.

"That thing is made of steel. The Karim she is wood. He only needs to damage the wheels and we are helpless."

"Can you outrun her," Cody asks.

"No. My Karim is many things but fast she is not." Kopi looks upriver, judging the distance between the boats. "I can give you an hour before she is on top of us." Cody looks at Covington.

"How many of those bulletproof panels do you have."

"Just the one but in an hour I can have another for you.

"Two will do just fine. Marcus tell me about the mortar. Do you think we could use it as a bazooka?" A smile spreads across the young man's face and he nods.

"Give me fifteen minutes and I'll set you up with a crude sight."


Covington drafts the ladies to help make the panels. Marcus and Mark Harris put together a working sight for the bazooka. With Forester's help, they test it marking the distances off with a grease pencil. Kohlemete refuses to allow any of them to move until Andrew Covington sits him down, explaining the situation. When Andrew is finished, he rushes downstairs, determined to contact the head office.

The passengers and crew are working flat out but the twin engines of the Pharaoh's Head are faster. After thirty minutes the steel ship comes within rifle range.

Jason watches as the Pharaoh's Head gains on them. Armed men onboard take potshots at the Karim. Covington, Mark Harris and Marcus Henderson join him behind two bulletproof panels.

"Are you running out of material Mister Covington? The new panel looks thinner than the first." Cody asks.

"It was a bit of a rush job. What with that speed demon gaining on us but she should be plenty thick. Yes, plenty thick." He stands his panel upright with himself behind it. Cody notes they've added rope handles to the back and cut out a hole for the Bazooka.

"What do you think," Harris asks.

"I don't think I could ask for a safer firing position," Cody replies. Marcus moves up with the converted mortar staying low.

"I thought Forester was right behind me bringing the dynamite?" As he speaks, Gerald appears at the far end of the sun deck, running low. He arrives sweating and sets a case of dynamite down behind the men.

"You didn't have to bring a whole case, man. If one of those shots were to hit it would blow the boat in half." Covington complains.

"I only brought what we need." Forester says, opening the box to reveal two sticks of TNT and a coil of fuse.

"You have two shots to disable that steel menace, Mister Cody."

"That's generous of you Mister Forester but one should do the trick," Cody replies and waves at the front of the Karim. Abu waves back and runs to the wheelhouse.

"What was that all about," Forester asks as Cody sits back down.

"A little diversion to bring our unwelcome guest a bit closer," Jason replies. The four men look at each other in confusion. In the wheelhouse, Abu gives Kopi the thumbs up. Kopi nods and spins the wheel putting the Karim's bow towards the starboard shore. He looks at the approaching shore and curses.

"That damned American better not miss."

Onboard the Pharaoh's Head, a young captain Ismear slouches over the wheel. He wears a white silk shirt and tailored linen trousers covering the tops of alligator shoes. His shirt is open down to his navel, showing off three heavy gold chains. A heavy Rolex hangs loose on his wrist. His attention is on his cigarette rather than the boat he is chasing. A shout from the deck brings his attention back to the river and the Karim.

"What is that ignorant pig Kopi doing." He swings the nose of the Pharaoh's Head around to match the new course. "He doesn't think he can out maneuver me in that piece of shit." The change in direction brings the Pharaoh's Head another fifty yards closer to the Karim. Sensing a kill Ismear pushes the twin throttles all the way forward. The Rolls Royce engines roar and Ismear smiles wickedly as the Pharaoh's Head surges ahead.

"Let's see you get away now you pig." He sneers and spits. One of the men on the gangway leans in and comments.

"We will catch them for sure captain." Ismear does not acknowledge him but kicks the door closed on the man's fingers.

Kopi spins the wheel to the left and the Karim's direction changes again.

"He's not very smart that one. If he was on the ball, he could have had me that time." Kopi thinks. On the sun deck, the rifle shots are ricocheting around the bulletproof shields and across the deck. The high-pressure hose is fitted and the first load of dynamite is placed in the tube.

"How much time do we need on the fuse," Forester asks.

"How long will it take to load this thing and fire," Cody asks back.

"Once I light the fuse you tip the barrel up to set the charge in the back of the weapon. Then it's aim and fire."

Cody looks at the big pipe, feeling the weight. He tips up the business end of the bazooka up and the dynamite slides inside. Jason tips out the dynamite and runs through a practice simulation. He allows for a one-second delay between his call and Marcus, releasing the air pressure.

"I call it Three-seconds. Better add a couple more for safety." Forester nods and cuts the fuse adding a third second for his own peace of mind, pushing it into the stick of dynamite.

"That should do it." He says wiping the sweat from his brow.

Cody looks at the big pipe, feeling the weight. He tips up the business end of the bazooka up and the dynamite slides inside. Jason tips out the dynamite and runs through a practice simulation. He allows for a one-second delay between his call and Marcus, releasing the air pressure.

"I call it Three-seconds. Better add a couple more for safety." Forester nods and cuts the fuse adding a third second for his own peace of mind, pushing it into the stick of dynamite.

"That should do it." He says, wiping the sweat from his brow.

Cody nods to Forester who places the charge in the end of the barrel. His hand shakes as he sparks the lighter and holds it to the fuse. The fuse sparks and Cody snaps back the barrel of the weapon, waiting to feel it drop to the bottom. Nothing.

"Shit!" He exclaims. The dynamite lands five feet behind Jason and rolls towards the edge of the deck. Harris reacts first, leaping towards it. He snatches it up, tossing it to Cody. Cody catches and drops it in. He feels the solid *'thunk'* of the dynamite hitting bottom. He pushes the tube through the notch in the panel, taking aim.

On the Pharaoh's Head Ismear leans over the wheel. He is two hundred feet off of the Karim's stern ready to plow into the old ship.

"Get ready for collision." A cheer goes up from the riflemen onboard. On the Karim, a man jumps out from behind some boards and runs across the deck. The men of the Pharaoh's Head stop cheering and shoot. Their first clear shot at any of the passengers. The man dances back behind the boards and the gunmen continue to fire at his hiding place. The Pharaoh's Head closes the distance to the Karim another fifty feet, the wheel of the Karim moments from destruction. Ismear smiles wickedly as he notices a pipe sticking out between the boards on the Karim.

"What is that?"

"Mister Cody we have no time." Forester yells over the gunfire.

"Fire!" Marcus has been mentally counting down the seconds and is already throwing open the valve.

"Mister Cody we have no time." Forester yells over the gunfire.

"Fire!" Marcus has been mentally counting down the seconds and is already throwing open the valve.

There is a "Thump!" and a roar of air escaping. The projectile flies across the short distance straight into Ismear's chest. It knocks him against the back wall of the wheelhouse. His eyes search for the insult to his body as he struggles for air. The dynamite rolls to him and he screams, watching the burning fuse disappear inside.

The explosion rips the front of the ship to pieces flaming metal and wood fly in all directions. The men lining the gangways on either side are blown into the river. The front decking of the ship becomes a flaming gash, the interior decks exposed. Flames leap through the boat and the crew left alive abandon ship. The twin Rolls Royce engines continue to race on, pushing the bow of the Pharaoh's Head ever closer to the great wheel.

Kopi has seen the explosion and the closeness of the pursuing ship. He pulls the wheel slowly to the right, willing the Karim to move from harm's way. The boat slowly turns out of the path of the flaming battering ram.

Several of the Karim's crew pull out long poles to try and push the Pharaoh's Head away. The poles prove too short. The crew can only watch as the bow of the Pharaoh's Head moves closer and closer. Cody and the others put down the equipment and run to the back of the ship and watch.

"Is there nothing we can do." Asks Peters.

"There's no time." Cody returns. "Only Kopi can save us now."

The bow of the Pharaoh's Head is feet from the Karim bobbing in her wake. Only moments from disaster the Karim finds extra speed. Kopi sees the mad gesturing of his crew and increases his pull on the wheel. The angle between the ships increases as the Karim turns, the bow of the Pharaoh's Head surges forward to take its revenge. For a moment it pauses resting its nose against the rotating boards of the wheel. 'Clunk, clunk, clunk, clunk.' The sound reverberates through the ship. The passengers in the dining area hold their breath. The sound stops. The bow of the Pharaoh's Head is pushed away by the thrust of the great wheel. The two boats separate, going in different directions. The Pharaoh's Head makes its last journey to the bank of the Nile and the Karim to the lock at Beni Suef.

The ship makes a collective sigh of relief. Kopi runs back to the stern of the boat and orders the engines shut down.

"I have to inspect the wheel to see how much damage that thing did to her." He turns on Cody. "Next time don't leave it so damn late." He storms off. The four men look at Cody and laugh.

"Oh my," Marcus exclaims. "Andrew, are you all right?"

"Yes, of course, why do you ask," Andrew Covington replies.

"Uhm well." Marcus points to the panel Andrew holds. Covington looks down and sees the end of a bullet sticking out of the panel. Cody reaches over and pulls the bullet from the board.

"That was lucky." He comments and hands it to Covington.

"More cotton batting." He exclaims. "It needs more cotton batting." He repeats the phrase as he carries the panel downstairs.

Kopi finds Cody on deck watching the burning boat hit the shore.

"I'm afraid that will be the Pharaohs Head's last voyage." Cody acknowledges the captain. He stretches, feeling the fatigue of the past few days.

"How is the ship," Cody asks.

"Not bad. She will need some repair when we get to Cairo but we should be okay for now." Cody nods his understanding. "There is something you should know. Before we started those maneuvers, I overheard Ismear talking on the radio. He was talking to several other boats upriver from our position." Cody's head comes up.

"How many boats?"

"At least six and big boats not like the Pharaoh's Head. The boats he was talking to are at least twice the size of the Karim some bigger, each able to carry two or three hundred men."

"Are they fast?"

"Not as fast as that burning hulk but faster than we are."

"How much time until they reach us?"

"If we keep at this speed, hours."

"Any chance we can get around them and head back upstream," Cody asks. Kopi shakes his head.

"They will reach us the same time we arrive at the Lock." Says Kopi. Cody examines the man's face looking for a sign of hope.

"So, no place to run," Jason says.

Kopi looks Jason in the eye and says.

"No place to run."

# *Sixteen*

The light of the day plays across the shuttered room where Taara has been confined the past twenty-four hours. The opulent Presidential rooms, which feels more like a prison to her. The two guards stand, weapons at the ready, one directly in front of her and one behind. These are the third or fourth set of guards. She doesn't know for sure as she slept for seven hours overnight.

She has received no food or water. As far as she knows, she is a prisoner waiting for death. A death announced by a note on a silver tray saying. 'We, the officials of Egypt, find you guilty of the attempted assassination of our President.'

She pushes the thought from her mind and shifts her weight on the seat keeping her legs from going to sleep. The guard in front of her moves, blocking her view of the painting behind him. 'Must be a state secret.' She thinks. She stretches her neck. The door opens and a secretary

331

enters. She is carrying a tray of food. She speaks to the guard in front of Taara and the two guards leave the room.

The secretary says.

"The President sends word the guards are no longer needed. He has sent some refreshment." She places the tray to the side of the settee. Taara snacks on dates and cheese but notices the lack of a knife to cut the bread. She tears off a chunk and eats.

With nothing else to occupy her, she wanders around the room. Standing in front of the painting the guard had blocked, Taara enjoys the freedom to examine the large portrait of the President.

"It's my wife's favorite." The President says as he enters the room.

"Your wife must have a keen eye for art, Mister President." She says, turning as he walks to his desk.

"I want to apologize for my behavior Mister..."

"Your behavior is inexcusable Miss Sefi. A formal complaint is being written to your government requesting your removal and appropriate disciplinary action be taken against you." He sees his words are sharp enough to bring the young lady up. He turns to the girl who has been watching Taara and bids her to leave. He waits until she has shut the door. In lowered tones he says.

"Of course, that letter will never be sent. The letter I am about to write will be sent by myself following our conversation. In this letter, I will thank your President for his continued friendship and pledge our support as I had in my telephone call to him yesterday. What else the letter says will depend on what I find out in the next few minutes." He sits in his chair and motions her to a chair opposite.

"I want you to know you have placed me in a challenging position. I must show my cabinet. I do not tolerate interference from foreign governments. Their President cannot be seen as weak. Such display cannot go unpunished." His eyes narrow as he looks at Taara. He sits back and resumes. "To complicate matters more, you have brought vital information which may save my political career, perhaps my life." He smiles. "The problem remains, what do I do with you? Have you any suggestions." He stops and fixes Taara under his gaze.

"Mister President I cannot apologize for my actions enough. My only concern was you should learn of the attacks on innocent foreign nationals and the threat to yourself." Taara looks to the ceiling for a solution. She brings her head down and says. "I know the information we bring to you is not concrete but Agent Cody heard the head of the Muslim Brotherhood tell his followers. The fact Commander McAllen has been killed, I believe confirms it. And then there is the situation with the boat."

"Yes, the boat." He interrupts. "I sent my soldiers to the offices of Nile Tours Ltd. Unfortunately, they were unable to find them until this morning. They assure me the vessel is safely in port in El-Minya. I have been in touch with the military in the area and they say there is no uprising. I have difficulty accepting your story without some proof." He holds her under his gaze.

"Mister President may I ask, did you, yourself speak with any of these people?" He smiles.

"No, I did not."

"Then Mister President, may I suggest the best way to find out what is happening on the Karim, is to contact her. All boats sailing the Nile for tourism carry satellite phones. The phone on the Karim should be listed." She says. He holds her under his gaze a moment longer, then reaches for the phone.

## SS Karim South of El-Minya Egypt 13:47 September 13, 2001

Mister Habid hears the phone slam down and Mister Kohlemete pounding the desk in frustration.

"Mister Kohlemete, what is it?"

"I have been trying to reach someone in government for two days, someone who will help us out of this mess and finally, that instrument from hell rings." He drops his head into his hands and pushes back his hair.

"Who was it?"

"I could not believe it. After two days of calls, some idiot calls and claims to be the President of Egypt." Habid's eyes widen and he asks.

"What did he say." Kohlemete looks up at the reaction of his second in command. His voice becomes unsure.

"He asked if we were in port at El-Minya," Kohlemete repeats woodenly.

"What did you say?"

"I told him no. A bunch of crazy extremists is chasing us. We will fight our way through the lock at Beni Suef and then have tea with Cleopatra. Then he asked how many foreign nationals we had on board. I told him we had fifteen Winston Churchill's, sixteen Margaret Thatchers and one President Kennedy."

Habid's mouth drops open and he turns an unhealthy shade of green. Kohlemete seeing his reaction continues unable to stop himself. "Then I called him a stupid pig and told him to go have dinner in hades." Habid's hand goes to his mouth. Kholemete looks at the desk and pounds it again. He stands shakily and holds a finger before Habid.

"Tell no one." He threatens and storms off.

"No. No one will I tell that you have insulted our President and condemned us to certain death. No one." He says sitting heavily at his desk.

"A ship. A ship!" Cody and Covington run down the sun deck to the rear of the boat to where Forester is. They take turns looking through his field glasses. They can see the bow of a large white ship approaching fast. As they watch, two more boats come into view. Kopi joins them as the ships round the last bend in the river.

"I count at least six." He says. "We have no choice. We have to try for the lock." The men nod and Forester asks.

"How long until they get to us."

"Maybe an hour but that is not the problem. We must get inside the lock before they can jam the doors open with one of their boats. I'll order full steam and hope we can make it in time."


Marcus Henderson and Mark Harris join the men at the back railing. Mark speaks first.

"Marcus and I have been thinking. If we shorten the pressure hoses to the flame throwers, we could add two hose lengths to the mortar. It would give us additional portability." Cody looks at the two and asks.

"How far could we stretch it?" Marcus speaks up.

"Well it wouldn't do us much good upfront, the hose isn't that long but we should be able to reach the rear railing."

"How long would it take," Covington asks.

"A few minutes," Mark replies.

"Do it," Covington says.

They hurry off to reroute the lengths of hose. The ladies make themselves useful, providing sandwiches for the passengers and crew, though no one is hungry. Tables and chairs are stacked along the rear railings to provide cover. Mister Covington joins the work on deck dragging with him two bulletproof panels. The flotilla of boats is gaining on them and Kopi calls down to the boiler room for more steam. The preparations are complete the crew and passengers take their positions and wait.

The Karim's wheel is churning at full speed propelling the old ship towards the lock. As the ship moves closer to the lock, Kopi calls out to Cody. Jason climbs up to the wheelhouse and stands next to the captain as he peers through field glasses. He hands the glasses to Cody and says.

"Take a look. I think we may be in luck."

Cody looks over the length of the lock dam, trying to find the 'luck' Kopi spoke of. Jason sees the dam across the river, which keeps the water level of the Nile from dropping too low. For boats to get past the dam, there is a lock set in it. The lock is a channel built into the dam with sets of watertight doors at both ends. A boat enters via the upstream doors. The water level in the lock is lowered to the level of the river below the dam. The doors open, and the boat continues on its way. In essence, the lock is a boat elevator.

Cody spots the 'luck'. The upstream doors of the lock stand open. This means they can go straight in. He focuses on the lock house and sees movement at the windows. Someone is hiding inside, watching them through the windows.

Jason lowers the glasses and says.

"I think we may have a problem. There's a man in the lock house watching us. They may try to lure us closer and shut the doors before we enter." Cody says. Kopi looks back at the flotilla behind and says.

"They will try to trap us between the lock and those boats. Once they have us pressed against the dam, they can swarm the boat." Kopi spits out tobacco as he finishes.

"Then we will have to make sure their man doesn't get a chance to close those doors," Cody says.

"How do we do that, may I ask," Kopi says, looking at Jason to see what magic he will produce.

"The rifles in the Armory, I believe one of them has a decent long-range sight on it. If they wait until the last minute, we might have a chance." Kopi looks at Cody with new eyes.

"You could do that. Kill a man just like that."

"If I don't, he and his friends will kill you, me and everyone on this boat. Which would you rather." Cody's eyes harden. Kopi looks at Jason and sighs.

"Don't worry, I'm with you, or rather, I should say I will be when I'm in the lock house pushing levers." Cody nods.

"Captain, captain the boats they are gaining on us." Abu shouts from the sun deck.

Cody and the captain step out to see the boats spreading out across the river. They have indeed gained on the Karim. Sensing the time is right, they are closing in for the kill. Along the railings are armed fighters ready to fire.

"We don't have time for a better plan. Which of the men is carrying the long-range rifle?"

"I'll get it. You make the shot." Kopi says and runs off along the gangway while Cody climbs down to the sun deck. He finds a good spot to take the shot from.

"Mister Cody, Mister Cody!" It is Mister Kedesh who runs across the deck yelling. Cody signals for him to stay down and the man crouches as he runs.

"Mister Cody there is a problem with the two men who will be shooting the arrows." He says.

"Problem? What problem, I thought they were excellent shots?" He asks.

"Oh yes they are Nubian and excellent hunters but they are also devout Muslims. They will not raise their bows against their fellow man." Cody looks at Kedesh.

"I am sorry but they asked me to tell you they cannot kill. The teachings of the Koran forbid it." Kedesh smiles apologetically. Cody's expression hardens in response. "They asked me to tell you. I am sorry." Kedesh repeats quickly.

"Get them up here now with their bows. Tell them I won't ask them to hurt anyone but we need them to help us defend this ship. Hurry" Kedesh goes running.

Jason Cody runs across the sundeck of the Karim, keeping low. He stops at the circular sundeck-bar and finds Forester coaching Abu on ammunition supply. A voice cuts across the noise of the preparations.

"Jason! Jason!" Cody turns as Sara Peters runs to him. "Jason, I'm sorry!"

"Sorry? About what," Jason asks.

"Jason, I'm sorry. I saw your sister's number on your phone and I asked Mister Kohlemete to call but the lines are all jammed. He hasn't been able to get through. Are you sure she was in the North Tower?" Jason pauses, hearing his sister's screams in his head. He sighs and looks down, saying.

"Yes, thank you! But you shouldn't have done that. Kohlemete should be calling for Military support. We need them to get through this."

"Jason, Kohlemete says they're not coming. As soon as he mentions the Karim, they hang up. Jason, we're on our own." Jason looks into Sara's eyes and seeing the fear there he cups her head in his hands and says.

"Sara, I promise you we will get through this, all of us. I won't let anything happen to you or the others." Tears fall from Sara's cheeks as she mouths, *'I love you.'*

"Sara, you need to get to safety. Please." Sara steps back but stays silent amid the tangible fear infecting the Karim. She holds Jason with the pain in her eyes and the tears that fall from them. A stray bullet strikes the deck next to Jason's foot and brings the two out of their trance.

"Jason!"

"Sara, get below. Go now!"

"Please be safe!"

"I will," Jason promises and runs the short distance towards the forward position he'd picked out earlier. As he approaches, he cannot see Kopi or the rifle he asked for. Jason looks across the sundeck. All eyes are on him, waiting to see what magic he will produce in their hour of need.

Kopi runs up the same time as the two Nubians. Cody speaks to the Nubian's quickly, explaining his plan. When he has finished, they take their positions wearing mischievous grins. Kopi grips Cody's arm and says.

"To close the lock doors, he has to hold down the lever. Once you see the doors moving, you have to take the shot. He presses the long rifle into his hands and a canvass bag of ammunition. Cody sits on the deck with the gun and checks the action. Unloading and reloading, making sure it works smoothly. It's an old Russian weapon but well cared for. Forester, Covington and Peters run up with Marcus not far behind.

"They're fencing us in." Forester says, pointing to the boats behind.

"I know," Cody says.

"We'll only get one chance at this." Forester returns.

"I know that too," Jason says as he stands and slaps Forester on the shoulder. "Good luck to us all."

"I second that," Clive adds. The men spread out, taking their positions. Jason notes there is no hesitation.

Jason turns to take his position as a roar is heard from the dam. Looking for the source, what he sees chills his soul. From both banks of the river, hundreds of fighters are running across the dam Shouting and shaking their guns in the air. A louder cry rises from the men on the boats. The noise is deafening. Men climb over each other to see their quarry. They raise their weapons and scream for blood. The men on the dam return the cry. The dam is crowded with men screaming and chanting. The chanting unifies. The sound of so many voices echoes and reverberates from the canyon walls, repeated over and over. The crew of the Karim stands silent. Each man knowing the words but not daring to speak them allowed.

Kedesh in the lower bar breaks out in a sweat despite the air-conditioning. His face takes on the look of a doomed animal. Habid cannot move from his chair as he grips the arms, his knuckles turning white. Kohlemete sits, his eyes wide, his forehead covered in sweat. His mouth is moving with the words.

"Death, death, death to the infidels! Death, death, death to the infidels!" The passengers do not understand the words but they know the message. The high spirits they enjoyed preparing vanishes and is replaced by a sense of impending doom. Cody is the first to shake free of the spell and he runs forward to his position. Andrew Covington yells to Clive through the chanting.

"I should have thought of this."

"What do you mean?" The other man shouts back over the din.

"You know, psychological warfare. Defeat your enemy's spirit and you've already won. What we need is something to rally around. Something to raise our spirits in the face of adversity. I wish we had *'God save the Queen.'* That would put the fight back in us." Clive brightens and says.

"I haven't got that but I might have something," he races below deck. Cody sets out the bag of shells to his side and slides several rounds into the weapon. He pulls up the sight adjusting it.

The chanting echoes across the canyon is amplified by the cliffs, as the Karim races towards to the Lock. The pursuing boats make their move, closing in on the old steamer. The chanting increases. Rather than tiring the fighters grow bolder, their victims moving closer to the trap. The lock and following boats are within range. Bullets ricochet across the sun deck, glancing off of railings. Cody takes aim at the lock house as bullets strike the deck around him. The old paddle steamer surges forward, her boilers at maximum and the great wheels showing no sign of slowing.

The thunderous chanting melts the resolve of the strongest passengers and crew. Several of the ladies shake as they cling to one another, the crew slump down, hiding. Even Covington and Forester have given up trying to outshout the noise with words of encouragement. They submit to whatever fate may await them as bullets fly. One man holds out hope. He runs down the hallway towards the reception desk.

"Mister Habid." Clive shouts over the noise. "Mister Habid, you told me this boat is equipped with a state of the art sound system. Is that right?" Habid looks at the man as if he is mad. His life is about to end and this fool wants to play music.

"Yes, yes, it is brand new and state of the art but that will not change anything, Mister Peters."

"Yes, it will." Clive nearly screams. "It will. It will make a difference. You have to trust me on this Mister Habid. I need you to play this CD at full volume." Clive yells as he shoves the disc across the counter to him. "I want to blast it across the river."

"Believe me, Mister Peters, if I play this at full volume, we will blast it all the way to Cairo."

"Perfect!" Clive exclaims and runs upstairs. Habid looks at the CD with dismay but obeys, hoping for a miracle.

"Maybe it will help," Habid says as he turns the amplifier to ten. Clive ducks from the bullets as he runs across the deck. He takes up his station, giving Covington the thumbs up. Andrew can only manage a half smile.


Under the echoing reverberations of the chanting, a new sound is heard. The sound of an electric guitar being plugged in and a few notes being played through a stack of twenty Marshal amplifiers. The guitar is played by a man standing on stage at the Monterey Pop Festival. As the Karim's state of the art sound system reproduces the first

347

track of the CD to perfection. A screaming electric guitar peels off the first notes as Jimi Hendrix plays his rendition of the *Star Spangled Banner*.

The electric guitar screams across the waters of the Nile, breaking the spell of fear. The chanting is replaced by the sounds of the Stratocaster played by the master guitarist. The Militants of Egypt stand in awe at the display of courage from the Karim. The crew and passengers are again themselves. Covington finds his courage and stands amidships in the diminishing crossfire.

"Archers to the front, Bazooka to the rear!" He shouts at the top of his lungs. "On my command." Cody lays quiet adjustmenting his sight while men scramble across the decks. Bullets fly and ricochet around him as he quietly mouths the words to Francis Scott Key's poem "...by the dawns early light, what so proudly we hailed..". The massive doors of the lock begin to close. Jason can see the man in the lock house leaning on the control lever. He takes aim. "whose broad stripes and bright stars, through the perilous fight,..."

Cody squeezes off the round. The man convulses over the control panel and drops. Cody chambers another round as the lock doors go still.

At the rear of the sun deck, Covington and Peters are bracing the portable bullet-proof panels against the force of the bullets. Forester holds the bazooka, taking aim on his target. Forward the two archers crouch behind crates with sticks of dynamite tied to arrows notched and ready. Small oil lamps are burning at their feet, to spark the fuses. Covington picks up the words as though a single train of thought runs through the boat. "...the ramparts we watched were so gallantly streaming and the rockets' red glare..."

"Fire!" He shouts. The two archers light, stand and release their sparkling arrows skyward as one. The two projectiles arch up and over the crowds, finding stacks of crates on the dam. Jimi flies into a guitar solo which feeds back through the Marshal amplifiers, imitating the sound of missiles as the two arrows arch and explode. The blasting reverberations and the electric guitar add to the confusion. Screams of terror run through the fighters on the dam. Those with less conviction break and run but the range of the archers is greater than they realize.

Aft Forester gives the command.

"Ready, light and release!" Thump, roar. The air pressure sounds in the barrel. The TNT shoots straight for the wheelhouse of the largest Cruise ship. It smashes the window and drops to the back of the room. A moment later, the wheelhouse explodes out and flames engulf the front of the boat. Men scream and run for safety while debris litters the water. The explosion rocks the boat and from somewhere inside the craft, the call goes out to turn. Slowly the big boat makes a turn to the right while its engines reverse. The result is mass confusion. The other boat captains see the destruction and pull back to a safe distance.

At the front of the Karim, archers have fired off several volleys each, scattering the charges amongst the fighters. Debris and fighters fly from the top of the dam. Several fighters on fire throw themselves into the river. The mob of armed zealots breaks in earnest and run back along towards the shores. Having dispensed with the boat at the rear, the four men reposition their mortar amidships and begin lobbing charges after the fleeing attackers on the dam. Cody has held his position at the front of the boat. He's picked off several fighters who tried to climb the stairs to the elevated lock house. Jason's aim has held true as he stops another. He digs into the bag of ammunition and finds six rounds left.

The Karim approaches the open lock at full speed, her great wheel only now showing signs of slowing. The order goes down to the boiler room for a full stop. A maneuver Kopi knows may cause the paddles to splinter. As the ship enters the lock, the flame throwers go into action. Bright orange flames shoot out clearing the docking area of any who thought to attack. The flame throwers are backed by the Tourist Police and their machine guns. They lay down a spray of fire clearing the last of the zealots from the edges of the lock. The Karim appears a great flaming dragon protected at her four corners by flames. The wheel engages full reverse as the boat speeds into the lock far too fast. The boat begins to shudder and creak from the reversing wheel, shaking the decks.

The Karim groans as Kopi runs along her top deck, shouting orders to his crew. Three crewmen swing out the gangway normally used to disembark passengers. They guide the long metal walkway with skill, placing it on top of the lock house landing. Below two men jump for the lock while others feed them lines. They wrap the lines around the large bollards at the top of the lock. They throw them around three times then pull with all their weight against the forward momentum of the Karim. The battle seems lost. The boat will surely crash into the downstream doors but the combined effort of the reversing wheel and the actions of the men slows the charging vessel. The noise of the mooring lines and the cavitation of the great wheel

351

sound a painful groan as the Karim comes to rest inches from impact.

Kopi runs up the gangway to the lock house. He pushes open the door against the weight of the dead man whispering a prayer for his soul. He completes the dead man's job of closing the upstream doors of the lock and throws the switch starting the lock cycle. The men at the side of the Karim change their positions, managing the Karim as the water level drops. The Karim sinks below the edges of the landing as the *'Star Spangled Banner'* strikes it last note. The CD changes and the song, *All Along The Watchtower* sounds its first chords.

As the Karim lowers in the lock, her upper decks become level with the top of the dam. The combined efforts of the explosives and firepower have driven the crowds of fighters back but as the Karim lowers, it looks more easily reachable. A refreshed flurry of gunfire is heard as men rise up, looking for targets. The intensity of fire forces the defenders to take cover. One of the hands manning the ropes on the lock is hit. He is lucky and falls hard onto the lower deck of the Karim. The flurry of bullets chews away at the defenses like ravenous insects.

Staying low and avoiding the onslaught. Covington spots a cluster of crates on the left landing with ten or twelve men firing on the Karim. He signals to Forester, yelling the coordinates. Nodding Forester sets the angle, lights a charge and drops it. Marcus throws the valve and the dynamite holds its position above them, and then drops amongst the crates. The explosion is so close debris is blown back onto the decks of the Karim. With the nest of gunmen taken care of, the archers lob charges into other hiding places, sending fighters running. The water in the lock is lowering but too slowly.

Cody drops the empty rifle running back to check on the others.

"How are we doing for ammunition?" He asks.

"I don't know about the other weapons but we only have one bundle of dynamite left." Replies Covington. Cody looks concerned and yells to the two archers. They indicate they are running out as well. He thinks for a moment.

"Do you have any fuse left?"

"Yes, plenty. Wait a minute, I can hear the water drain from the lock. The shooting, it's stopped." Forester says. Cody sticks his head up and looks around. The guns have indeed gone silent. During the firefight, the boats had pulled back. Cody spots one boat moving forward to the upstream doors. On its foredeck, there is a sandbag position set up with a high powered machine gun. It's a matter of minutes before they are under heavy fire.

"Untie the dynamite and separate it. I need one stick forward and one stick for Kopi to disable the lock controls." Covington works fast, shoving a fuse into the three sticks as Forester cuts away the cord binding them together. "That leaves you one stick and one shot to take out that gun emplacement." Cody indicates with his head and Forester wheels around to see the boat moving up fast, the gunner making ready. Forester grabs one stick and cuts the fuse short. Cody takes the others, running forward. Gerald Forester raises the mortar pipe to his shoulder bazooka style. Marcus balances the dynamite in the end of the tube while Clive makes ready his lighter.

"Ready Marcus, I need a full blast this time." The gunner sees Forester standing. The machine gun fires, the weapon tearing up the deck of the Karim.

"Fire!" The lighter goes to the fuse and Forester leans the pipe back, dropping the charge to the bottom. He takes aim as two bullets from the machine gun hit. One tears up the panel, the second grazes Forester's leg. He winces but never loses his concentration. "Aim and,, release!" The TNT shoots true. The gunner has to duck or be caught in the head. The stick hits behind him and bounces. He rises to run but before he takes a step, the fuse burns in. The explosion catapults him and the machine-gun from the front of the boat in a low arch. They splash down between the boat and the lock doors.

The damage to the boat infuriates its owner. He orders the men that line her railings to fire on the infidels. A new shower of bullets sprays the deck. Covington and Peters have a difficult time holding the panels against the onslaught. One of the Karim's tourist police armed with his machine-gun fires at the boat's captain. The captain has a change of heart, frantically pulling the bow of the vessel out of harm's way. Cody sprints to the middle of the sundeck and surveys the attack. On the left, the flame throwers and two machine guns are holding them back. In the river at least twelve boats all faster than the Karim lay waiting to rejoin the pursuit should they get past the lock. To the right.

"What are they doing?"

A large column of men is marching across the dam towards the Karim. At the head strides a large man dressed in white leading a new chant. His followers raise their weapons. He is organizing the attackers. The man is too far for his Beretta to reach. Jason calls down to a crewman with a rifle. The crewman looks at the crowd and backs against the bulkhead, unwilling to act.

"They will not fire Mister Cody." It is Abu who appears at his side speaking.

"Why not?"

"He is an Iman. To harm him means eternal damnation." Abu says.

"Do you have any good news?"

"We are out of dynamite and there are no more bullets." Cody looks at the boy.

"Sorry." Abu shrugs his apology.

"What is he saying?"

"He says that Allah will shield them from the oppressors of the faith. He says that no bullets or flame will harm them if their faith is pure. He says..."

"I get the picture. Abu run forward and have one of the Nubian's tie this dynamite to an arrow. Don't let him fire it. I'll take care of the holy man. It seems I'm already scheduled for eternal damnation."

Cody runs to the gangway placed against the lock house and calls.

"Kopi, Kopi!" The captain looks out the window, ever cautious. Cody tosses him the last stick of dynamite which he catches. "For when you finish." Kopi looks at the dynamite and nods. Cody runs low to the front of the sun deck, where Abu crouches with one of the Nubians. The man's nimble fingers are making the last knot tight. He cuts the string with his teeth and hands the arrow and bow to Cody. The Nubian turns away and begins to mumble words that Cody cannot make out.

"He prays for his soul and yours Mister Cody." Cody looks at the man huddled in prayer.

"Tell him thanks. I'll try not to kill anyone."


Cody notches the arrow and stands while bullets ricochet around him. The fighters are rallying and preparing for another attack. Cody knows they will not survive another push from so many. He bends the bow and Abu holds up the flame below the fuse. Cody dips the fuse in the flame, and it sparks to life. Jason angles the arrow up and releases. The shaft leaps from the bow. He means it to drop directly in front of the crowd but a gust of wind catches it and carries it farther. It strikes the Holy man in the center of his chest and drives him back into his flock. The explosion

357

throws men in all directions. The crowd falls about in shock. The man they looked to for strength is in pieces.

"Shit!"

"You said you wouldn't kill him?"

"I just wanted to scare him off."

"He is dead."

"I know that Abu." The crowd comes to its senses and in one voice calls for revenge.

"This is very bad. You should stop killing people Mister Cody it only gets us in more trouble."

"Thanks, I'll make a note of that." He turns from the angry mob that is now working themselves into a frenzy and yells to Abu. "Go below and tell everyone to arm themselves. Get those crewmen off the landing and back on board. Tell them to push us into the middle of the lock. We'll have a better chance there. Go!" Abu runs off at top speed, disappearing below deck. Cody sprints towards the stern and yells to Kopi over the increasing gunfire.

"Kopi, we need to leave now!" Kopi looks out the window at the water level in the lock. The level has dropped but is still too high.

"I will do what I can." He calls back. "You protect my Karim!"

"I'll do what I can." Cody returns. Kopi grabs the lever for the downstream doors. The machinery engages but the doors are held back by the weight of the water in the lock. He manages to open the doors a crack allowing the water to empty faster. The movement of the doors alerts the fighters and bullets pepper the lock house. The windows shatter, glass flying over Kopi he drops below the window level but one bullet finds a gap in the steel enclosure and ricochets into his right leg. He convulses with pain, his upper body falling out the door of the lock house.


On deck, Mark Harris and Emma Forester are tending Mister Forester's leg. Mark hears the bullets pelting the lock house and the captain's painful curse. He turns to Emma.

"Are you all right here?"

"Yes, fine." She answers.

"I'll be right back." He says, running across the deck and up the gangway to the lock house. An explosion of bullets follows him every step as he sprints into the protection of the steel building. He collapses in a heap opposite Kopi, out of breath. The bullets spraying the lock house where

Kopi lay. He holds out a hand to Mark. Mark pulls him back into the protection of the building.

Kopi screams from the movement and clutches at his leg. Still breathing hard, Mark begins to cut away the captain's trousers to expose the wound. He reaches in the bag he has brought, producing gauze and sterile wrappings.

"The bone is shattered. I can tell. It won't take my weight." Mark looks concerned but continues. He thinks. *'Do what Emma Forester instructed. Stop the bleeding first. Worry about broken bones later.'*

"I think you're lucky. There doesn't seem to be any arteries damaged," Mark says.

"I think you're lucky. You are not lying on that gangway dead." Kopi smiles at the man. "I don't suppose you have a plan to get us out of here."

"I honestly wasn't thinking that far ahead." Mark smiles as he cinches down the last knot on the bandage. The gangway slips and falls away, hanging useless at the side of the boat. Mark sees it fall and turns to the captain. "You weren't planning on going anywhere, I hope."

Kopi grimaces and asks.

"Can you reach the lever at the far right and pull it down."

"I can try," Mark replies. He shifts position and grabs the lever. The great doors move, slowly opening. A new barrage of bullets rattles the lock house. Mark pulls his hand in and the doors stop. The bullets abate, he tries it again. The doors move further as he holds out longer. A third try and the doors open halfway. A lucky shot strikes his hand. He pulls it down and holds it close.

"Ah, just a flesh wound." He says and smiles. "You know? I've always wanted to say that." He winces as he reaches for the lever again, the machinery whines and the doors move, then silence. Mark tries the lever again but there is no movement.

"Forget it I was wondering how long it would take them to figure out the power could be cut at the junction box on the damn."

"How do we reach that?"

"We don't. We can't, it's too far. They would cut you down in seconds." Kopi fishes in his vest pocket and pulls out his pipe. "Do you smoke." He asks and smiles.

Below, Cody has emptied the last clip of his Beretta. The last of the arrows are spent. The Tourist police are down to a few rounds. The only thing keeping the attackers away is the flame throwers and those positions are being hammered by bullets. Forward one of the crew operating the flame thrower catches a round in his head. He falls back dead. Other crewmen pull him away but no one thinks to replace him. There is a surge of attackers running at the Karim yelling as they approach. They jump from the landing towards the boat. Some missing and dropping into the waters of the lock, others claim purchase on the railings. The crew responds, beating them away and Clive Peters jumps into the hot seat of the flame thrower, showering the attackers in orange death.

Marcus has checked the flame throwers and approaches Cody with petrol can in his hand.

"There is only a few minutes of petrol left. Sorry, we weren't supposed to be here this long." Cody looks at the man, in that moment the attackers start lobbing fire of their own. He and Marcus grab up the torches and throw them into the water but they are covered with pitch. The pitch sticks to the deck and begins to spread. The fire crews move about the deck, one of the passengers is struck by a bullet. The call for a medic goes out and Emma runs to the scene. Cody crouches by the injured woman. She grits her teeth as Emma treats the wound.

"We're okay here Mister Cody but you have work to do. More flaming projectiles strike the deck and they have their hands full throwing them into the water.

One of the flame throwers starts to sputter and the mob swarms the landing throwing themselves against the Karim's sides. The crew do what they can but the fighting soon spills onto the decks. Cody flies from one attacker to the next. A flying kick into one sends him over the side. A blur of punches and a big attacker crumbles under the assault. Cody is hit on the side of the head and staggers. He regains his balance, throwing the attacker over the side. Jason becomes a machine making quick work of the assailants.

Cody grapples with a man who carries a bayonet mounted rifle. A quick kick puts the attacker over the side and the rifle in Cody's hands. Covington is being beaten down by two attackers. Cody runs at the men and impales them both. He pulls Covington up and they stand together, Covington with a long knife and Jason the rifle. A new group attacks and the two men are separated by the force of the onrush. Cody makes quick work of two, only to be replaced by three others. He is beginning to tire. The mob is dragging the Karim closer to the landing. Soon they will swarm the boat. He kills two more attackers as a shadow passes over him. He looks up and sees three Military Helicopters flying overhead.

# *Seventeen*

The two smaller assault helicopters split off and open fire on the crowds of Fundamentalists on the dam. The third, a large troop carrier fires a line of bullets in front of the boats. The two smaller copters take either side of the lock, firing at the armed fighters. The three choppers hover protectively over the Karim, killing any who dare to stand and fight. The fighters on the dam are in a full retreat. Some scream curses while others drag the wounded.

The smaller assault helicopters protect the Karim's flanks while the larger troop carrier drops ropes. Cody stands over Covington, fighting for their lives. Behind him, a rope appears from the sky. Covington lying on the deck, sees it but dares not believe. Four Egyptian soldiers appear on deck as if by magic. They waste no time. Short blasts from their machine guns clear the remaining fanatics. The man Cody is struggling with drops out of his hands. Jason looks up and sees a dark-skinned soldier in full combat gear, holding a bloody knife. Cody raises a hand saying thank you. The man nods and moves off to help his comrades. Jason pulls Covington to his feet. Looking around, they see the cruise boats are making a fast retreat upriver. The Egyptian soldiers have secured the landing and two men are patrolling the top deck.

A scream comes from the deck below. Cody and Covington race down the stairs. On the lower deck, the fighting continues to rage. Passengers armed with Pots and pans are beating nine zealots and the small crowd of attackers has become the victims. Cody and Covington join the melee helping where they can.

A big man with a short sword bursts from a side hall and runs at the center of the crowd. Cody catches his sword arm and pulls him down hard. Jason spins the attacker around and turns him over in one move. The attacker finds himself face down, his arm pinned behind his back. He tries to flail at Cody with the sword but Jason is not having it. He jerks the man's arm up cleanly, dislocating it at the shoulder. The assailant screams as Cody takes his sword and clubs him over the head.

Most of the attackers have been neutralized but Sara continues to work on one. He is lying on the floor, trying to protect himself from her blows. She is expertly wielding a long-handled omelet pan.

"How dare you touch me, you ugly bastard!" She strikes his elbow and he pulls the arm down in pain.

"I'll see you in hell!" She screams. Her next blow lands squarely on his head and the fighter goes limp. Not being satisfied, she continues striking him.

"Don't you ever, ever touch me again!" As she raises the omelet pan for another strike but a large hand catches her arm. She tries to pull away but the man holds it firm.

"Thank you, young lady. I think it best if you allow us to do our job." A tall, muscular soldier with an angular face holds back her blow. He nods to his companions, who pick up the unconscious man and drag him to the door, dumping him in the lock. The soldier releases her while his men clear the deck.


"Who is Kohlemete." He asks. Mister Kholemete steps forward, dragging a cricket bat. The passengers and soldiers notice it is streaked with blood.

"I am Mister Kohlemete." He responds.

"I am Captain Muhammad Nefer. I need you to point out to me the..." He pauses and pulls a paper from his top pocket. "The thirteen Winston Churchill's, fourteen Margaret Thatchers and one President Kennedy." He quotes. Kohlemete gulps audibly as sweat beads on his brow. The Captain watches his discomfort looking stern but saying nothing.

"Captain, there are wounded among the passengers and crew. Some need medical attention." Emma Forester says. The Captain turns to one of his men and speaks in Egyptian. The man runs up the stairs and returns with a Medic.

"You will show this man to the wounded. He will tend to them." The Captain says.

"Thank you. There are also some of our people in the lock house. I think one of them may be wounded." She reports and moves off with the Medic. The Captain relays the information to a soldier who salutes and goes to help.

"Mister Kohlemete if you could gather all of your passengers into the dining area, my men will make the boat secure." The passengers move slowly into the dining room but few discard their weapons. Cody turns to the Captain.

"You must be President Kennedy." The Captain says, looking over the man in front of him. He is tall and strong. His arms are cut and bleeding and his shirt nearly ripped off. The Captain notices his hands and knuckles are red and bleeding from the fight, his body sweating. *'A good man in a fight,'* he thinks and offers his hand. As they shake hands, they hear a voice say.

"His proper name is FBI Agent Jason Cody." It's a voice Cody has only heard on the telephone but recognizes instantly. He turns towards the stairs and greets Agent Taara Sefi, as his superior and savior.

On a low hill, the Man-in-Black stands and observes the battle. He sees the helicopters approach and curses the gods that work against him. A second man stands next to him, an officer of some distinction. The officer puts down his field glasses and addresses the Man-in-Black.

"Things don't seem to be working out the way you planned."

"This is only temporary. I will catch up with Mister Cody. He has not escaped me yet. The Man-in-Black says.

"He may not have escaped you but he has made powerful friends. Only the President could order those men into battle."

"What do you mean?"

"Look at the insignia on the helicopters. That is the presidential guard. No one has authority over them except the President. I think your plan may be in jeopardy."

The Man-in-Black turns on the officer.

"The plan is set to go no matter what. Even if I were to be killed, the plan would go ahead. No man, no power can stop what is coming. You and your troops had better be ready."

"We will be ready and we will move when we see the thing is done. Not before! Your ability to show results is not filling me with confidence." The officer scowls at the Man-in-Black as he speaks.

"You will see your results, Abasi. You see a military approach is not always the best option."

"What do you mean." General Abasi inquires.

"The snake is more deadly than the wolf. A lesson you should learn and I think, so should Mister Cody." He pulls a small radio from beneath his robes and speaks quietly into it. Looking into his field glasses, he focuses on the aft section of the boat. There he sees a man in a white coat step out onto a balcony from one of the cabins. The man holds one hand high for a moment.

"You see, Abasi. Snakes are rarely noticed, even on the water."

The Medic works quickly and confidently, treating and dressing the wounds. Two crewmen have been killed during the assault. One who drowned when he was pulled into the lock by an attacker. The rest have been more fortunate and only Kopi needs hospitalization for the shattered leg. As one of the helicopters lifts off, taking him to a nearby military hospital. The passengers and crew are receiving a well deserved rest.

The dining room, crowded with the injured and well wishers, again becomes the center of activity. However, signs of victory and self congratulation are few.

"Of all the foolish and stupid things to do. You just decide to go running off through the crossfire. Do you think because someone gives you a bit of gauze and tape you're suddenly a trained Medic? My God!" The lecture has been going on for the past few minutes and shows no sign of slowing. Mary Covington has had enough. She steps forward and puts her hands on Jan's shoulders quieting her for a moment.

"Mark I would like to tell you that Kopi, our Captain is being flown to a local hospital for treatment. I spoke with the Medic and he said, you did an excellent job for someone with no training. Moreover, I would like to thank you, Mark. It was a courageous thing you did. To run up and open the lock doors. All the time, knowing there was no escape. Kopi told me you never hesitated. I don't know about Jan here but I want to say thank you for your willingness to sacrifice yourself for your wife and the rest of us." The others in attendance raise their voices in a mighty "Here, here!" a small round of applause goes up. Mary feels the girl under her hand begin to shake and the sobs begin. She releases Jan to her husband. It is time for tears, time to release the grief and pain. Sara looks around the room for Jason but he is not there.

The power cut on the dam is fixed. Soon the lock doors are open and the Karim is ready to continue. Cody announces he will not be going on as he must get back to Cairo. He says a private goodbye to Sara with promises to see her in Cairo when she arrives. Taara and Cody make their way across the sun deck and find the passengers and crew assembled.

"Agent Sefi, if you will permit us, we would like to thank Agent Cody for all he has done. If it is all right, we would like you both to join us in a toast." Champagne and sparkling water appear poured and ready. The trays of the bubbling liquids are passed around between the staff and guests. All stand, glasses at the ready, as Andrew Covington raises his glass.

"I would like to propose a toast to our Mister Cody." One of the white-coated waiters moves into position behind Jason. He holds a single glass on a large tray. Taara glances at the man, her eyes registering something her mind does not. Covington continues.

"To Agent Cody, for his courage under fire and his willingness to lay down his life for his fellow passengers. We salute you, Agent Cody." Glasses are raised high. "To Cody," Taara raises her glass along with the others but her eyes stray to the waiter behind Jason. The man starts to move but not for his glass. He is reaching for something under his tray. The glass on his tray overturns as he readies his knife.

"Knife!" Taara yells and reacts without thinking. Her hand drops to her side, pulling her gun so fast, it collides with her glass on its way to the deck. The man's arm flashes back in a serpent-like motion. Sefi's aim and the firing of her weapon occur in the same moment. The first bullet hits the man's head and explodes out the back. The second and third strike shots his chest and he is thrown back on the deck. Sefi finds herself standing over him, kicking the knife away. She sees herself holding the gun and the blood running red across the deck. The back of the man's head is missing. She starts to shake and the shake becomes a convulsion. She steps away from the blood pool, moving to the railings as the soldiers move in to examine the corpse.

Taara looks around wildly, searching the sky for air but cannot find any. Cody is there taking the gun from her hand. She can't breathe and she doesn't know why. She knows something is wrong and feels she is dying. Cody forces her to bend in the middle. Her head is over the railing. She might fall but he is holding her. Taara looks around wildly, searching the sky for air but cannot find any. Cody is there taking the gun from her hand. She can't breathe and she doesn't know why. She knows something is wrong and feels she is dying. Cody forces her to bend in the middle. Her head is over the railing. She might fall but he is holding her. She is sick, her emotional pain, making her body ill. She sobs for her life and the life she has been forced to take. The crying continues for several minutes as the passengers and crew look on. When she rises, her eyes are red and she is confused. Someone hands her a tissue and helps her as she walks to the ladies' room.

374

She sobs for her life and the life she has been forced to take. The crying continues for several minutes as the passengers and crew look on. When she rises, her eyes are red and she is confused. Someone hands her a tissue and helps her as she walks to the ladies' room.

Sara was standing in front of Cody, smiling with pride for the man she cares for. She froze when she saw the woman pointing a gun at him, then the shot and the confusion. Her heart leapt to her throat, thinking she is killing him but the bullet was not meant for Jason. She stands confused and shocked at the violence.

Sara watches the way Jason handles himself, automatic, no sign of grief or remorse. He does what is necessary and stands ready for what may come next. *'What may come next? Could I be happy with this man?'* Sara wonders. She turns and finds Emma Forester at her side.

"It's okay," Emma says. "I know what you're thinking. Would I be happy with him? Am I strong enough to love him? Can I accept the fact his job may kill him at any time? A job you will never be able to share in." Emma looks down for a moment. "I've lived with those question most of my life. Unfortunately, it's not something anyone can answer for you." Emma squeezes Sara's hand and smiles kindly. "It's best to decide soon. I've seen the way you look at him and later, may be too late." Sara looks at Jason as he turns towards her, their eyes meet. Sara feels a pang in her heart and looks away.

Abu slips into the back of the helicopter, where he saw the soldiers put Mister Cody's bag. He pulls a dark green tarp over himself. Peeking out one last time, he shifts deeper inside.

# *Eighteen*

**Cairo, Egypt 06:14 September 14, 2001**

Jason walks down Sudan Street opposite the National
Research center. The taxi driver could have dropped him at
the office but the sky is too blue and the sun too bright. He
unconsciously touches his side and the bandage there. A
bullet grazed him during the fighting. The thought of it
causes him to flex his fists, easing his still swollen
knuckles. Jason thinks himself lucky to come away with
only scrapes and bruises. He makes his way past the
hawkers and trinket sellers, stopping to buy a bottle of
water. As he pays the seller, he notices a yellow taxi
pulling up across the street. Taara Sefi steps out into the
morning light.


Jason can see the dark cloud over her. Since shooting the
assassin, she has been a closed book. Taara talks of only
work. She pursued the subject the entire return journey.
Only when Jason's eye began to close in the taxi did she let
the subject drop. Watching her now, he sees she holds tight
to the puzzle the Commander left them. No one will take it
from her until it is solved. Unfortunately, they have little
time. Not only are the three days running out but
Washington is sending replacements. When they arrive,

Taara and Jason will fly back for debriefing. With the attacks on the US, Congress has opened the defense budget. There will be changes and Jason does not know where he will end up.

Jason arrives at the seventeenth floor as Taara is opening the new office door. He goes to follow her but an armed soldier steps forward, holding out his hand.

"It's okay. This is Agent Cody." She tells the man. He steps back to his post with a military salute.

"How did you manage that?"

"What? Oh the guard, the Egyptian Government is anxious no harm comes to any foreign nationals. Especially FBI agents! We are to be protected until our people arrive and can provide for our own security." She flashes him a half-smile and goes to her office.

Cody decides it is time to say something.

"I didn't get a chance to thank you yesterday for saving my life."

"It's okay I, I just,,," Taara squeezes her eyes shut. Her head drops and her whole body convulses for a moment. She holds back the sobs that might have been. Both hands

378

go blindly to the desktop. She leans forward as a single tear splashes down. She rights herself, stepping back to her chair and sits heavily. Her hands go to her face, grief for the dead man and for her own soul. She breathes deeply as she wipes away a few stray tears.

"I never expected to have to do anything like that." She speaks softly, looking at her lap. "When I was recruited into the FBI, I told them I could never harm another person. My faith would not allow it. And now,,," She breaks off. Jason stands silent and listens, not wanting to say anything to stop the flow. He knows she needs to talk and he needs to be a good listener for her.


"When they recruited me,,," Taara begins again, then pauses. "Recruited, I, I volunteered, I don't know if it was money, the chance to see the lands my family come from and he business opportunities for my family. I don't know why I did it. My father was all for it. He still is. With the contacts I've made, he has opened up branches to his import business. He has a shop on the edge of Georgetown but most of the business is done with the retail outlets. You know Persian carpets and all of that." She lowers her voice. "Did you know when I pulled that trigger, it was the first legitimate action I've taken for the FBI? My life is a lie. I churn out reports for Washington but the reality is every contact I've made. All the information I gathered was fed to me by the people I'm supposed to be keeping an eye on." She looks around the room, ignoring Cody's presence. "My mother warned me this would happen. She tells me about the boys from the Mosque who ask after me. How many of my girlfriends are married with babies. She says I should stay home and raise babies too." Her eyes swell with tears but this time, she does nothing to stop them. She takes a long time playing with the material of her blouse and letting the tears run down her face. She raises her tear streaked face to Jason for the first time and says. "I don't know what to do. Everything I've done is against what I believe in. How can I go on like this? How can I do anything, anything that might cause the death of more people? I can't. I couldn't."

Jason looks at her face and sees not the hardened shell of an agent but the troubled young lady who hides beneath. Her eyes implored him for answers. He crouches down in front of Taara. Her eyes locked onto his, hoping he might have an answer, a way to release her from her torment. He doesn't and he knows it.

"Most people,,," Jason pauses. "Most people go through life, never knowing how they may or may not affect others. They might do something heroic, give blood or volunteer as the local softball coach. They never know if what they have done will have any effect on others. Will the kids on the softball team learn from what they are taught. Take those lessons through life to be better people, or will the example be the very thing that drives them to drugs. They don't know if the blood they give will save a life or if it contains some unknown deadly consequence." Cody looks down at Taara's hands folded in her lap. You have a luxury those people do not.

"What do you mean?" Jason looks Taara in the eye.

"I mean, you know what your actions have done, at the moment when you took a life. You saved another. You gave another a chance to go on living and hopefully help to solve this puzzle. Stop this coup. And by the way, this consequence is extremely grateful."


For the first time since she pulled the trigger, a light shines from Taara's eyes and a tiny smile comes through the tears.

"You are very welcome, Agent Cody. I suppose I can at least say I have never lost an agent under my command. So that is something."

"I would say it is something quite admirable," Cody says. "Sorry, it's just I'm..."

"No your right. Jason, there is little time for feeling sorry for myself. We need to make sense of these clues and do it quickly."

Cody looks again and finds the toughened exterior of Agent Sefi brushing away the last tears.

"So we need to know who and how," Jason says.

"Exactly, but we are short on information. We don't know the answers and I believe it's because we don't have the Commander's notes. I have looked everywhere for them but..." She holds up her hands in frustration. Cody creases his forehead in thought.

"They must be here somewhere. I know the Commander will have hidden them or left a clue."

"No, they are nowhere. I searched the Commander's office. The compartment in the false bottom of his desk drawer was open. If they found it, they may have taken the notes. I have looked in all the secret hiding places and there is nothing." Taara insists.

"You searched this office as well?"

"Yes, I searched but I found nothing."

"Well you obviously didn't search everywhere, or you would have found them." Cody and Taara spin around to find the Commander standing in the doorway of Taara's office.

"As I said, if you had looked everywhere, you would have found them but you did not." The Commander steps into the office looking like he never left, except for his arm being in a sling. Taara, astonished at Alistair's appearance, meets him halfway.

"Where have you been you pompous old,,," She throws her arms around him and plants a kiss firmly on his cheek. "You had me worried you old fool. You could have at least sent word you were alive."

"I did try but you were engaged at the presidential palace. Something about a small-arms incident?" McAllen arches one eyebrow at her. Taara looks away in response hiding her face.

"As I was saying, if you had looked everywhere, you would have found my notes. Allow me to show you." He walks to his office with both agents in tow.

"As you may have guessed, I was working when the intruders paid me a visit. I only had moments to conceal the tape and my notes and there wasn't time to get to Mark's office, so I hid them in plain sight."

"In plain sight but when I got here, your desk was turned over and I could see nothing of your notes. The compartment at the bottom of your drawer had been cleared out and,,,"

"Exactly!" McAllen interrupts. "You saw the hidden compartment was empty, so you assumed my notes were taken."

"Yes, there was no,,," Taara pulls in her breath, realizing what the Commander is saying.

"You must know, people who go around forcing doors haven't the faintest idea what they're looking for. If they find a secret compartment in the bottom of a drawer, they assume they've struck gold and look no further. So I put some fascinating archaeological notes in the drawer and my notes in their place."


Alistair turns to a bookcase behind his desk, once enclosed by glass doors, now smashed.

"Oh, bother! Why do bullies always feel the need to smash everything in sight." He pulls a file from between two large volumes on Egyptology and lays it on his desk.

"You see the best place to hide something is in plain sight."

"And the tape?" Cody asks.

"Ah! Just as apparent." The Commander pops open the top of the answering machine sitting at the corner of his desk and pulls out the tape.

"Everything in plain sight." He turns to Taara and says.

"I am sorry for not letting you know I was all right but the messenger I sent arrived after you left for the palace." Taara smiles.

"I'm just happy that you are okay. How is your shoulder." She inquires, looking at his arm.

"It will be fine. Not the first time I've taken a bullet." He eases his arm in the sling as he speaks.

"More importantly, I believe You have the original garments with you. Is that right.?" Cody smiles and produces the two garments he's been carrying in his bag since leaving the Karim.

"Excellent. Your photos were very good but it's always best to work with the original." The Commander and Taara quickly become involved with the symbols on the garments and Jason just as quickly feels useless. Jason goes to his office, setting out his computer and begins cleaning his Beretta.

After a few minutes, he hears his name being called. Jason sticks his head into the Commander's office in time to hear him say.

"Could you run down to the National Research center and get me a couple of books. I'll give you a note for the librarian. He knows me and should not be any trouble." The Commander scribbles out his note while Cody mumbles.

"Why don't I just go for pizza and beer while I'm out."

"Good Idea! But I think it's a little early for beer and too hot for pizza. Why not ask one of the boys to bring up tea and snacks for everyone on your way out." Cody takes the note, mumbling about being an errand boy.

Abu sees Jason leaving and hides in a copy and print shop across the road. He watches as Cody walks away from the office building. Abu runs across the road and into the building. A few minutes later, he has found the kitchen and is making fast friends with the boy there.

Cody takes his time as the heat of the day is at its peak. He makes his way back along the road with two large volumes in hand. Arriving at his floor, Jason sees the tea boy entering the office with a tray held high. He comes up behind him and holds the door open. Jason directs him to the Commander's office, where Alistair indicates a side table. The boy begins laying out the tea. The guard who has followed them in yells in Egyptian and draws down on the boy.

"What on earth!" The Commander shouts. The boy backs against the filing cabinets at the far side of the office, hands held high.

"Jason isn't that your little friend from the boat?"

"Abu? Abu, what are you doing here." Cody asks.

"This is not the tea boy on duty today." The guard says. "Commander, your life may be in danger."

"Perhaps but I don't,,,"

"Commander? You are Commander McAllen. I have been instructed to give this to you." Abu drops his hands but the guard steps forward and cocks back the hammer of his side-arm. Abu freezes.

"Please, Commander, my father asked me to give this to you," Abu says, looking the guard in the eye.

"Who is your father boy?"

"You knew my father. He was Mohammad Abu Nassar Horemeti."

"Yes, I did know your father. We've worked together many times. I heard of his death, and I'm sorry for your loss. What is your name?"

"I am Mohammad Abu Nassar Horemeti the third," Abu says with pride and attempts a small bow while still watching the guard.

"That won't be necessary." The Commander waves the guard back but he stands with his gun drawn and ready.


"What is it you have for me." Abu eyes the guard for a moment then turns to the Commander.

"My father told us he had some information for you and it would be worth a great deal of money. He says if anything should happen, one of us must take this to you and you would pay a king's ransom." Abu smiles as he repeats his father's words.

"We will see. Show me what you have." Abu nods, slipping off his waistcoat. Taking his knife, he undoes the needlework along the bottom edge. He pulls out a long piece of fine Egyptian cotton with symbols on it.

"I see." The Commander says and he and Taara compare the names and titles with the second cloth Cody recovered.

"Yes, very good! This will put us one step closer to finding who is responsible for the plot."

The Commander consults one of his reference texts, translating the Egyptian symbols from the cloth Abu has provided. He translates the top three names on the list. Abu says.

"This cloth is very valuable, I think. I think you should pay me five thousand US dollars for it. Okay?" Abu says.

"Not Okay." McAllen retorts. "This cloth isn't worth the time it took to sew. These translations are meaningless."

"They must say something," Taara says.

"The one-eyed pig, old fox in the desert, man with staff, these things say nothing about who these people are." McAllen stares at the cloth in frustration.

"It's a code. It must be." Taara offers."

"Yes but what kind of code. For all we know, these are names assigned at random, known only to the designer of this plan. It could take us weeks or months to work it out."

"I don't understand. You mean the three clues we have mean nothing? We are going to hand all of this over to our replacements and just leave. What about the plot it is supposed to be happening as we sit here. What about the takeover of the Egyptian Government and the impending attack."

"Jason!" McAllen shouts in a warning tone. Cody glances around the room, realizing he may have said too much in front of the guard but continues. "It must mean something. We are missing a piece of the puzzle, or we do not see it. There must be something you are not taking into consideration." He holds his hands out in frustration.

"Well let me enlighten you to the hard reality of the game Agent Cody. You can't always have the answers fall in your lap. The bad guy doesn't always get it in the end and 'X' never marks the spot. This is reality, not James Bond fiction. Even when you are one hundred percent certain, there's always a chance you may be wrong." McAllen looks at Cody and softens his tone a little. "It's like this. The first piece you brought us shows a pictorial representation of what we assume is a plan for the government after a military coup." McAllen spreads out the robe on his desk.

"The second garment you recovered is a list of the Egyptian characters, each with a Cartouche associated with it. Each Cartouche is the name of a Pharaoh or prominent figure in Egyptian history. I had hoped the last garment would give us the actual names of the individuals who are involved in the plot but as you can see, it does not. Unless one of us knows who the 'One-eyed Pig' might be." He searches the faces of those present but gets no response. Taara notices the guard's face changed when he saw the third garment.

"Do you recognize any of these?" She asks him.

"Yes and no, I'm not sure." He replies.

"What are you not sure about," McAllen asks.

"This design the boy has brought." He reaches down and grasps the edge. "The work here depicts a very famous scene from the Palace."

"Where in the Palace? I don't remember anything like this." The Commander returns.

"Oh, most people do not see it. It is on the far left wall at the entry. Past the first set of columns." He says.

"How do you know it then," Taara asks.

"My Uncle was one of the artists who designed and made it. My family is very proud of him. Every time I go to the Palace, I stop to look at it."

"If you look at it every time you go, why are you unsure," McAllen asks.

"This is excellent work but I am afraid it is wrong." The guard says apologetically.

"What is wrong or different." McAllen presses.

"This symbol at the top is not the President. The symbol of Horace should be down on the right, not at the top." The guard points out. As he does, he lifts the robe from the bottom so he can see it better. "Here is the symbol for the President but,,, but this is bad." The Commander rises and steps around his desk to get a better look. At the bottom of the robe is a small depiction of a Pharaoh, face down.

"No, that is not good." The commander comments.

"What is so bad," Cody asks.

"It depicts the fall of the Pharaoh, the crown of upper and lower Egypt struck from his head," Taara replies.

"Yes and here, this symbol is the leader of the Shoura Party and he holds the crown." The guard says, looking at the sleeve.

"Wouldn't that be normal if the President were killed," Cody asks.

"Yes, it would." The Commander stops, his own words hitting home. "Yes, of course, it would. It would be perfectly natural for the leader of the Shoura Party to take over. So natural no one would even think to question it." He exclaims and grabs the garment Abu has brought. "Taara do you have the Cartouche for these two symbols."

"Yes, here they are. The symbol with the broken crown you said was Menkaure 2532-2504BC, and the symbol holding the crown." She pauses, searching the notes. "Here it is Psamtik 664-610AD. There is no pattern in the dates." She says.

"Perhaps it isn't the dates that are significant." The Commander returns as he pours through one of the reference volumes Cody had returned with. "Ah, here it is, Menkaure. 'It was said the Pharaoh Menkaure or Mycerinus moved Egypt away from the old gods and religion. His reign became an affront to the gods. It was said he brought one hundred and fifty years of suffering to the people of Egypt for following him." McAllen reads.

" Mycerinus! The informant in El-Minya told me the same story." Cody says. "Psamtik, he returned the old religion to Egypt. That's what the informant told me." Cody says.

"At the time, it meant the return to the worship of the first gods. The gods from the old kingdom. In today's times, it would mean the return to a more fundamentalist form of Islam." The Commander says.

"The return to the old laws before the new constitution. Where the will of Islam ruled this country, not the will of the people." The guard chimes in. Cody looks at the man and says.

"The same constitution enacted thirty years ago."

"Yes, on September eleventh, nineteen seventy-one. How did you know?"

"The informant told me." Cody looks over the hieroglyphics on Abu's robe.

"So in this,,," Jason pauses to collect his thoughts. "scene, we have the old Pharaoh knocked down and his crown stolen by the leader of the Shoura Party."

"Not stolen but given to him. Look here on the right sleeve. It depicts Horace presenting the crown of Egypt to the figure of the leader of the Shoura Party. McAllen says as he shows Cody the sleeve.

"Okay, but do we know who takes the crown from the President," Cody asks.

"Yes. Look at the bottom hem of the first garment." Taara says as she steps forward, lifting the bottom of the robe.

"You see it is sewn into the bottom border. You can see the figure of Horace striking down the figure of the President."

"So Horace will strike down the President and deliver the crown of Egypt to the leader of the Shoura Party. Making himself indispensable and sitting at his right hand. Is that what we're talking about here?" Cody asks.

"It would seem so." The Commander responds.

"So who is Horace," Cody asks, looking at the guard. The guard is held mesmerized by the border Taara holds between her hands. Cody prods the guard to break his trance, asking again.

"Who is Horace?" The guard pulls his eyes from the border, saying.

"In the depiction at the Palace, the figure of Horace is the Commander of Egyptian Military, General Asra Seif Nader." He says without emotion.

"But he was assassinated only days ago," Jason says.

"Who would take his place?" Asks Commander McAllen.

"Major Haraddi, of course, he..." The guard stops mid sentience and looks at the Commander, then says. "He would temporarily act as the head of the Military."

"Where would we find Haraddi now?" Cody presses.

"You cannot. I mean, the Major is unavailable."

"Where is he unavailable." The Commander demands. The guard stops himself and looks at the border still held by Taara.

"If there is a threat to the President, he is placed in a secure bomb-proof bunker somewhere in the city."

"What threat," Jason asks.

"Early this morning, a black crossbow bolt was fired into the President's private quarters, killing his valet. Security forces transferred the President to the secure bunker shortly after." The guard replies.

"Yes, but where is Haraddi?" McAllen asks, leaning over the desk.

"It is required by law the Commander of the Military accompany the president at these times." The guard recites.

"Where is the bunker?" The commander repeats.

"Only the heads of security and a few top-ranking officials know its location."


"So there is no way of contacting the President when he is in this bunker," Cody asks.

"No. None. The President can call out but as I said, only a few know the number to the bunker." The guard looks stricken.

"What about the other Presidential guards? Would any of them know how to reach the bunker." Taara asks.

"All of the guards having security clearance of that level will be with the President."

"I suppose Haraddi is the one who hand picks the men to accompany the President." The Commander says as he sits.

"Yes, he is the most trusted by our President."

"As was Brutus by Caesar." The Commander says. The guard looks confused at the comment.

"So we need someone with a high enough security clearance to get us in to see the President," Taara says almost to herself. Cody looks up at her comment.

"I might know someone."

"Who?" Taara asks as Cody turns to the guard.

"Can you get word to Mohamed Kahlid Aslamid and ask him to contact me." The guard looks shocked.

"How do you know this name." He demands.

"He's an acquaintance of mine. I met him in EL-Minya. You know him?" The guard hesitates.

"I know of him yes." He says cautiously.

"Good, then you can get a message to him and he can inform your President." Taara encourages.

"I might be able to get a message to him, yes." Again the guard speaks cautiously.

They hear the door to the office open and someone approaching. The guard makes no effort to intercept the intruder. He knows who is approaching.

"I believe you are looking for me," Kahlid says as he pulls an earpiece from his right ear. The guard looks down

398

caught spying. Kahlid slaps the man on the shoulder in a friendly manner.

"Don't blame Hamid here, he is a good soldier who does as he is told. I am afraid it is I who am responsible for eavesdropping. Please don't look at me like that, Mister Cody. You have all of the clues. I thought by returning to Cairo, I could find out from my contacts but the information channels have gone quiet. No one is saying anything. They don't want trouble with the wrong side and since no one knows which side that is." He shrugs, spreading his hands.

"No one is willing to say anything." Taara finishes.

"Exactly! Since you have been able to gather the pieces, I thought perhaps you who would solve the puzzle."

"So you decided to spy on us to learn who is responsible for the plot against your President." Cody accuses.

"Yes, I am afraid so but I think you would have done the same if the situation were reversed."

"Who are you," Taara asks.

"Oh, sorry! This is Mohamed Kahlid Aslamid. He is..."

"I am very close to the President and it is the President who needs our help."

"What about your men," McAllen asks.

"I have only Hamid here who I can trust. The others are engaged in tasks in other areas of Egypt. I fear they would not get here in time."

"Why would you trust us. We have no loyalty to your President." Cody asks.

"No, that is true but you do not desire his death either. I am faced with a choice. Put the life of my President in the hands of soldiers who may turn on him or the soldiers of friendly nations. Nations who would not benefit from the destabilization of the region." Kahlid replies.

"I think he has a point. We cannot stand by and watch forces hostile to both our countries take over Egypt. With the might of the Egyptian army, Bin Laden could ignite the region. The end result would be, Israel would no longer exist. Bin Laden would be heralded as the hero of Islam. It could force the West to recognize him as a leader. The leader of the largest oil producing area in the world. Oil, he could cut off anytime he'd chose. The Russians would be quick to form an alliance. The Chinese, North Koreans and all of Africa would move to ally themselves with the Islamic State." McAllen says.

"It would be a truly global war, with Russia and China playing both sides." Kahlid says.

"No, it would be an apocalyptic war. The US targeting The Middle East." McAllen adds.

"You mean nuclear weapons? Wouldn't it be madness to use 'nukes' in today's world?" Taara asks.

"Not if we took them out first. A preemptive strike could shock China and Russia into breaking allegiance." Cody says.

"If they strike Bin Laden they could shorten a war by years. After all, no one cares if their gasoline is radioactive, so long as they can fill up any time they like." McAllen says with disgust. "I am afraid Kahlid is right. We have no choice."

"I'm glad you see it my way." Kahlid smiles. "We must make plans as we travel. We've been too long talking." Kahlid says. Cody turns to Taara.

"Perhaps someone should stay and..."

"This building can watch itself, Agent Cody. Our job is to stop the assassination of the Egyptian President. I suggest you focus on that and that alone." She gives him a tight smile and says. "I think it's time to make a difference, don't you, Agent Cody?" Cody returns her smile.

"Hamid get the car." Kahlid orders.

"Abu, stay and guard the office until we return," Jason says.

"But Mister Cody..."

"Do as he says, boy. If we are right, you will not only have your five-thousand dollars but the undying gratitude of your President," McAllen says.

# *Nineteen*

Racing along the Salah Salem road, Cody notes the number of churches next to synagogues next to mosques. Even in religion, there have been multiple coups, each set of beliefs bringing its army of followers. Salah El-Din Citadel with its Alabaster Mosque looms up fast on the left.

Kahlid folds away his phone and remarks.

"Still busy, we will try to contact the President from the gate." Hamid makes a sharp left. The black Mercedes shoots across opposing traffic, drawing the horns of drivers. It bounces up a low curb and stops before a large iron gate. Armed guards step out from shaded booths on either side of the gate, leveling their polished machine guns at the car.

Kahlid speaks rapidly, waving his credentials in their direction. One of the guards approaches and snatches them out of his hand. He walks back to his hut and picks up the phone, dialing slowly. He stands for several moments as if waiting for the other end to answer while his partner keeps

403

the car in his sights. It is Hamid who sees it, slipping into reverse. The guard drops the phone stepping out of the booth. Hamid hits the gas and an emergency switch near his seat. Kahlid's window shoots up, nearly taking his arm off. The window puts a layer of bulletproof glass between him and the machine guns, the black Mercedes squeals backward into the flow of traffic. An oncoming car is unable to swerve in time.

Crunch! The right front of the Mercedes is smashed and the five passengers are thrown about. Hamid doesn't stop. He presses the accelerator to the floor. The big Mercedes picks up speed, shooting backward through traffic. The oncoming cars are swerving out of the way, the Mercedes races backward, weaving through oncoming traffic. Hamid spots a side street and they screech around the corner.

The guards had sprayed the Mercedes with bullets as it crossed the road but now it is out of sight. The guard who took Kahlids identity papers runs back to his post and picks up the phone. This time he dials the number and does not leave his finger on the hook. The communications officer picks up the phone.

"Yes, I will get him." A young officer runs from the Communications and Security room and returns with the Man-in-Black. The Man-in-Black takes the call listening to the guard as the security screens light the room. He creases his brow as the guard reads the name on the identity papers. The guard insists they appear genuine. The guard says.

"Sir, if it weren't for your orders, we would never have suspected." The Man-in-Black reassures him.

"If he is an agent as he claims, then why have I never heard of him. No, this is a clever deception. You and your fellow soldier have done well and you will be rewarded. Keep a close watch. They may try again." The Man-in-Black says and hangs up. He turns back and notices the communications officer with one hand on his earphone listening. The officer quietly pushes a switch then turns to the Man-in-Black.

"Are you finished, Sir?"

"Yes, I am finished. Tell me, do all communications pass through this room?"

"Yes Sir."

"Even the calls the President makes from his private rooms." The Man-in-Black asks.

405

"Yes Sir. You see the panel at the back of the room here. Each time a light comes on, the panel shows one of the outside lines from the President's office is being used. This panel controls the lines from the Cabinet." The soldier points to the panel next to the President's.

"So if I throw these large handles, what would happen." The Man-in-Black asks what he already knows.

"You would not want to do that Sir. That would isolate the complex from the outside. No communications would be able to get in or out except the gate. Of course, you know this as you also know that only the President can order the cutting of communications. That is why these switches are locked. Only the President holds the key."


"As you say, these things I know." The Man-in-Black smiles his words. "I wanted to be sure you know your job. This is no drill. The Presidents life is at stake here and we must do all that we can to protect him." His words became hard and the soldier snaps to attention.

"Yes Sir. I understand. I am sure you also know no one can enter this room without a key. This room is bombproof, bulletproof and soundproof. They would have to kill me before they could take over communications." The man salutes and places one hand on his sidearm in a gesture of readiness.

406

"Very good solder, I see all is as it should be here, at ease." The man relaxes a little dropping his hand away from his weapon.

"I did not know this room was soundproof as well." The Man-in-Black says in mock surprise.

"Oh, yes, Sir. The engineers tested it while I was training. Not many people know it but they fired a handgun in here and you could not hear the shot outside." The solder reports proudly.

"I did not know that. We should test it, I think." The Man-in-Black says as if in thought.

"Yes Sir." The man responds automatically but he creases his brow as if trying to think of how they could do such a thing.

"Yes, I think we should test it." The Man-in-Black repeats.

"Yes Sir but I don't know how we can at this time." The man returns.

"Oh I think it is easily done. Like this." The Man-in-Black slips a handgun from a hidden pocket. He presses it against the man's chest and fires. The surprise on the man's face turns to pain as his life is ripped from him. The Man-in-Black winces at the sound of the shot as it reverberates around the small room. He leans hard against the consul, dropping the handgun. Clutching the side of his head, he opens the door and lets in the guard waiting there.

"Get the bolt cutters." He half shouts, while the pain in his head beginning to subside.

Another soldier enters the room and moves the body of the communications officer. At the direction of The Man-in-Black, he places the body slumped over his workstation, his forehead resting on his hands. The first soldier returns with bolt cutters. The Man-in-Black directs him to the padlocks on the large switches. After a few moments, the soldier has the locks off. The Man-in-Black inspects the panel and noting no lines are lit. He throws the switches and places locks of his own on, preventing anyone from reconnecting the outside lines. The panel controlling the Presidents lines has one light lit. The light goes out and the Man-in-Black throws the switch, isolating the complex.

The black Mercedes 500 speeds around the corner and up a narrow street. Khalid folds away his phone.

"It's busy." He says. "We must get to the Blue Mosque before it is too late," Kahlid says.

"Another entrance." McAllen inquires.

"Yes, a back door. No one but the President and one of the Clerics knows of this. I must ask all of you to forget it as soon as we finish this business." He says as Hamid makes a sudden stop and turns the big car around in the narrow street. They race down the narrow side roads, passing under the Salah Salem highway, into the lower levels of the Blue Mosque.

Kahlid walks around to the trunk where Hamid is opening the latches to a false bottom. He lifts the panel to reveal a small arsenal. Kahlid picks up a Mac 10 machine pistol and hands it to Taara and passes a large Mauser pistol to McAllen. Alistair takes it and removes his sling, flexing his arm, while Kahlid takes a Mac 10 for himself. Hamid arms himself with an AK47 with a laser sight and Cody is handed an Uzi machine pistol. Kahlid leads the group to a loading area at the right of the little square.

"We are at the back entrance of the Blue Mosque of Aqsunkur. We will not be bothered until we reach the lower levels and enter the common of the security complex." Kahlid says as Hamid slings his weapon over his shoulder and leans into a stack of crates on the landing.

409

Habid pushes the crates aside, revealing a modern steel door. Kahlid reaches into his coat and produces a code card. At the right of the door, Kahlid slides his card through the reader. They hear the sound of a heavy bolt being thrown and the door pops open a few inches. The five enter a wide passage, which four men could easily walk abreast in.

"Commander McAllen, if you will watch our backs, Hamid and I will take point. Miss Sefi and Mister Cody will watch our flanks. With any luck, we will get through this in one piece." He smiles and leads the small group down a spiraling walkway lit only by the occasional lamp at foot level.

The walkway makes a wide turning as it slops down in a spiral. They move in a tight group hugging the center wall. The path comes to an abrupt end at a double steel door. Kahlid turns to the group saying.

"When I release this door, an indicator light will show in the communication center. With any luck, it will go unnoticed but we must be ready to move quickly. On the other side is a large parking area. It is not normally guarded but be ready. On my mark," Kahlid says as he slides his card through the reader and the door pops open. In the communications center, a single red light shines illuminating the soldier's face, his dead eyes the only witness.

Hamid pushes the door shut as McAllen passes through. They find themselves in a large underground garage. Cody looks around, inquiring in a whisper.

"Is someone expecting an invasion?" Across the vast garage lie row upon row of tanks, half-tracks and armored personnel carriers. Stacks of ammunition crates lie against the walls. Hamid and Kahlid go over to these.

"Here!" Hamid whispers. He expertly pries the lid off of one crate. Inside under layers of straw, he pulls out Russian made hand grenades and passes two to each of them, taking several for himself.

"American tanks, small Russian arms, what else," Cody asks.

"We like the American tanks but they are expensive. The Russian tanks are not as good but they make very reliable firearms. Most of our soldiers carry them and they are cheaper than the Americans." Kahlid replies.

"I guess it pays to be friendly to both powers," Taara adds.

The small assault team weaves its way through the heavy machines to the far side of the garage. As they pass Cody notes some, of the equipment still has the wrappings on.

"Kahlid!" He whispers. "When did you order this equipment?"

"I didn't know that we had. Why?"

"Most of the vehicles we've passed are new. They haven't had their first service."

"How do you know this?"

"The protective wrappings are still on them, look." Cody points to the armored personnel carrier they are passing, factory covers still on the seats.

"These are factory fresh. A purchase of this size would have been reported. I haven't heard of any major arms sales to Egypt for years," Commander McAllen says.

"Nor have I." Kahlid wonders. A clank is heard echoing across the expansive garage. They take cover. Voices echo across the distance but they are too far away to make out. Hamid signals he will investigate and disappears around a tank. Moments later, he returns. Kahlid and Hamid speak for a few minutes, Kahlid reports.

"Maintenance crews are preparing the vehicles. We must move quietly. They are near the exit and should not get in our way but be alert."

The group moves quickly, staying low. They come to a large space between rows of jeeps. Hamid checks all is clear, then signals them forward. Cody notes these vehicles are stripped of their wrappings. Empty ammunition crates are strewn around each. As they reach the far side, Cody sees what they have passed is only a small portion. He makes a quick calculation. There are enough vehicles parked around him to supply two full battalions. With no reports of arms sales, this was arranged in secret over the years. Kahlid reads Cody's mind commenting.

"I am sorry to say you are right. If we don't stop this mad man, the entire region could fall to the control of Bin Laden."

"You had doubts." Cody returns.

"Only small ones." He says, looking over the rows of ready assault vehicles.

"Quickly! We must stop this before it starts." Kahlid says, leading them through a set of doors. Inside, the walls take on the pale green color of a military building. Hamid goes

413

into a low stance signaling they should do the same. They move along a wide corridor with multiple steel doors lining both sides. Kahlid signals a stop.

"This is storage but just ahead are the sleeping quarters and a recreation area for the Presidential guard. We must remove the threat before we can proceed. If we have to use grenades, it will draw the remainder of the guard."

"Can't we slip around them," Taara asks. "It would make more sense than bringing more guards down on us. They could be loyal to the President."

"We can't take the chance. As far as we know, all of these men are traitors. They are hand-picked by Haraddi. What else could they be? We have to assume they are part of the plan. Don't worry. No one will hear the explosions. The Presidential rooms are on the other side of the complex. It should be okay." Kahlid says as he steels himself. Hamid moved ahead to reconnoiter the area returns but his face drawn in an expression of disbelief.

"What is it."

"Something is wrong. I, I don't know. They do not move."

"Show me." Kahlid pushes forward to the doors of the soldier's sleeping areas. He cracks open the door of room

414

and sees men sleeping in rows of beds but something is wrong. It strikes him. They are lying in awkward positions. They have been thrown on the cots and their boots and they are all wearing their boots.

They carefully push the door open ready for a trap. Kahlid prods the nearest man and finds rigor is setting in. The group enters the room as Hamid keeps watch. McAllen goes to the closest man and examines him. He turns the body over to find the face of the man gray and contorted.

"Gas, they've used gas to poison the lot," McAllen says in disgust. "What a waste." Taara steps back from the horror, whispering a silent prayer for their souls. They check the other rooms and find all the men dead.

"Is this area cut off from the rest of the complex," McAllen asks. Kahlid thinks for a moment.

"Yes. I remember it as completely separate from the rooms of the officials. To prevent any contaminate released here from reaching the President."

"So they could safely gas all of the soldiers here and the rest of the complex would have no idea." McAllen states.

"This is true," Kahlid agrees.

"This may be a blessing in disguise." Remarks McAllen.

"What do you mean," Cody asks.

"If Haraddi was forced to kill these men, it reasons the forces loyal to him will be much smaller," McAllen says.

"Yes. he is right. These men are here to repel a direct assault on the complex. There is only a hand full of guards needed to protect the President." Kahlid says.

"How many?" Asks Jason.

"Twenty, no more." Kahlid says.

"Then it's time to stop playing defense," says Cody.


They return to the corridor and find another double door. Kahlid pauses and looks at the others.

"Once we are through these doors, we will be in a large lobby. Guards will be posted, protecting the elevator to the surface. There will also be guards posted at doors to the right and the left. These doors lead to the cabinet and Presidential quarters. There may be other soldiers in the area. If we start shooting, others will join in." He says.

"What about alarms and cameras," Cody asks.

"There is an alarm switch near the two guards to the left," Kahlid says.

"What's the plan," McAllen asks.

416

"Hamid and I will enter and approach the guards in the center. It should take us no more than ten seconds to cross the area around the fountain."

"Fountain? They have a fountain down here. Where is it?" McAllen asks.

"It's in the center of the room about four feet high but it should not get in the way." Kahlid answers.

"Any other surprises," Cody asks.

"Only if they manage to hit the alarm. Then the room will be sealed and filled with knock-out gas."

"Great! So what do we do." Asks Cody.

"You three must take the other guards and we cannot fire our weapons." Cody, Taara and McAllen give each other doubtful looks.

"Remember ten seconds after we enter." Kahlid slides his card through the reader and the door clicks open.

Hamid enters first, talking back over his shoulder to Kahlid. Kahlid follows, staying close and hiding his Mac-10 behind his back. They walk quickly across the intricate mosaic floor, which slopes down in the center. A small pool of water forms in the depression and a stream of water dances four feet in the air. The sound of the water dropping to the floor covers the conversation between Kahlid and Hamid. The guards watch as the two move confidently across the room. As they pass the fountain, Kahlid recognizes one of the guards in front of the elevator. He greets him with a gesture and asks if he has a smoke for him and his friend.

Cody, Taara and McAllen stand tense behind the metal door counting.

"Three one-thousand, four one-thousand,," Taara whispers.

"I'll go first and stop the two at the alarm. You two cover the guards to the right." Cody directs as Taara nods and looks to McAllen. She continues the count.

", six one-thousand, seven one-thousand,,"

Kahlid steps up to the guard on the right while Hamid faces the other. They greet them as old friends and comrades. The two guards relax and fish in their pockets for cigarettes. The other guards around the room, seeing the four men being friendly, relax lowering their weapons.

", nine one-thousand, ten one-thousand go!" Cody shoulders the door knocking it wide and he sprints to his left. The Commander and Taara follow going to the right. Kahlid and Hamid jump back two paces and level their guns on the men's noses. Cody runs while yelling for the men to drop their weapons. Kahlid and Hamid echo his words in Egyptian. The guards near the alarm stand motionless, taken unawares. The guard on Cody's right reaches for the alarm button. Cody's foot moves twice as fast pining the guard's hand to the wall. The second guard seeing this raises his weapon. Cody backhands the man hard across his jaw with the Uzi, dropping him in a heap. The guard with his hand under Cody's foot makes another push to free himself but finds the barrel of the Uzi, pressing his head against the wall.

Cody grabs the first guard by the collar and pushes him far from the alarm button. The Uzi comes down again, dropping him to the floor. Jason turns and finds Hamid and Kahlid have made quick work of the soldiers by the elevator. Hamid not being so forgiving to the traitors, is cleaning his knife on one. Khalid walks towards the Commander and Taara. They have also taken their targets by surprise and hold them at gunpoint.

Kahlid steps up to the first man and relieves him of his weapons. A quick blow to the back of the head and he crumples. The second man seeing this, drops his weapons freely and raises his arms high.

"That's what we need around here, a bit more co-operation," Kahlid says. He directs the man to drag the unconscious and dead soldiers into the communications room. Hamid follows him in on the last trip. As Hamid returns, he sheaths his knife and closes the door.

"We must move quickly. Kahlid says as he hurries to the door of the President's private rooms. He stops and speaks to Hamid. Hamid pulls a hat and puts it on. He slips his knife out of its sheath holding it behind his right hand. Hamid pokes his head through the door, looking down the long corridor to the guard standing there. He raises a hand holding a packet of cigarettes, offering the man a break as he walks forward. The guard looks confused and does not see Hamid's right hand flash up, sending the knife straight into his chest. He wheezes, falling forward to the floor. His rifle clatters on the marble before Hamid can reach him. He grabs the man and drags him back along the corridor to where Kahlid waits.

"Quickly!" Kahlid whispers. Cody closes the door. They wait for a moment. When no one appears, they enter the hallway.

"Cody starts down the hallway towards the double doors but Kahlid holds him back. He pulls back one of the heavy tapestries on the wall to reveal a door hidden behind. Using his card, they enter to find an opulent bedroom with a four-poster bed in the center of it.

"We will slip in from here. It will provide more of a surprise." Kahlid says as he goes to the far door in the room. He cracks it open and peers in. After a moment, Kahlid quietly closes it and whispers.

"There is a screen directly in front of the door. They may not notice us. Major Haraddi is standing in front of the President, wearing black robes and a turban. He is the man we saw in El Minya." Jason looks surprised and says.

"You mean Haraddi is the Man-in-Black?"

"If that's what you call him, yes."

"How could he be if he was in Cairo while we were in El Minya?" Kahlid stops and says.

"Whoever he is, he is standing in front of the President and we need to neutralize him." Three soldiers are also in the room, one behind this man and one on either side of the President's desk. Hamid, you will take my card and enter from behind the Man-in-Black, taking the soldier on the far side of the President. Mister Cody and I will take the other two soldiers as we enter. Miss Sefi and Commander McAllen will take the near corners. We must act as one." He instructs.


  Kahlid hands Hamid his card, who disappears into the hallway. Khalid pulls the door slowly open. The four crowd the narrow doorway. Kahlid concentrates on the room. Under the threatening words from Man-in-Black, he hears the sound of plastic rubbing against metal then, Click! The door pops open. The attention of the soldiers goes to the door. At the same moment, Kahlid kicks down the screen and the four pour into the office. One shot and the guard near the door drops. Kahlid and Hamid press their weapons into Man-in-Black's head while Cody, Taara and McAllen hold their targets at gunpoint. Cody steps up and relieves them of their rifles and sidearms. He piles the weapons in the center of the room. Hamid follows suit while Kahlid holds his Mac-10 at the base of Man-in-Black's skull ready, to pull the trigger.

The room is cleared and the remaining two soldiers are held in the corner. Kahlid searches the Man-in-Black's robes for weapons, who has been silent since they entered. Kahlid spins him around. He stops, pulling the turban from the Man-in-Black and says.

"General Asra Seif Nader! I thought you were dead!"

"So the man killed at the Palace was a double! Am I right General Nader," McAllen says, as General Nader glares at the Commander. "If you need to be dead for a while, why not create a double? Is that not so General?" General Nader ignores the Commander, facing Khalid he says.

"What is the meaning of this? Who are you?"

"I am Mohamed Kahlid Aslamid. Egyptian Secret Intelligence assigned to protect the President."

"I have never heard of you."

"If you had, it would not be a secret." Says Kahlid.

"He is who he says he is." The President says. "He serves me now, as in the past." Kahlid bows his head to the President, who sits unmoved by all that has transpired.

General Nader looks at the assembled agents and says.

"I don't understand. What do you want with me?"

"I believe you know very well what we want with you, General. You are the architect of the attack on America. However, you didn't stop there. The attack only shows your allegiance to Bin Laden. Your true goal is to restore fundamentalist Islam to all of Egypt. The only way to do that is to eliminate the President. He is the one man who stands in the way of uniting Egypt and all of the Middle East under one flag, the flag of Islamic State," Commander McAllen says.

"You have no proof of this!"

"On the contrary, our Agent Cody has witnessed you addressing the Muslim Brotherhood immediately before the attack on the twin towers."

"As did I." Says Khalid.


General Nader turns to the President.

"Mister President, you must know that I am loyal to you. I would never do anything to put you in harm's way. There has been a mistake. You must know what I said before was only to protect you and Egypt from an insurgence. Yes, a plot to kill you and overthrow your government. Mister President please you must believe me..." Kahlid sees a man who knows he has lost and relaxes his hold on the machine pistol. Cody and McAllen equally relax as the man pleads for his life. Taara turns from her captives and observes the scene but something is wrong.

*'This is wrong,'* Taara thinks. *'Something is very wrong.'* She lowers her weapon. The death it holds, interferes with her seeing the truth. The General's words speak of an innocent man deceived and pleading for his life. Taara turns towards the sobbing man, making a step in his direction. It feels right. Something tells Taara she needs to be closer but why?

"Please Mister President, my President is kind and forgiving,,," Taara closes her eyes to block out the words. When she opens them, the scene is distorted.

General Nader is crystal clear but all else is blurred. What is he doing? His actions do not match his words. His back is arched, his shoulders are up. His words say *'I Give up,'* but not his posture. Taara steps forward. Her eyes locked on his hands.

*'What are his hands doing free?'* She thinks. *'They should be cuffed.'* She has halved the distance to the President. Her feet moving on their own, *'his hands, what is it about his hands. Why don't I like his hands? His sleeve, there is something up his sleeve. He could hurt the President. No!*

*Kill the President. A gun, he has a gun up his sleeve!'* At
that moment, Kahlid lowers his pistol to speak.

"Mister President, I think we have heard enough of..."
General Nader's right hand stretches towards the President,
a small automatic pistol appears.

Taara is moving before she sees it. She takes one step and
springs. Her body arching forward and rolling to her left as
she flies. General Nader pulls the trigger as Taara flies
between the General and the President. It is a small caliber
weapon but no less lethal. The bullet enters Taara's body
and fragments wildly, ripping through her heart and lungs.
She lands across the President who catches her. General
Nader leaps backward tripping through the open door.
Cody's Uzi peppers the space where he once stood.

Kahlid jumps to the door in pursuit but a shower of
bullets from the small gun pushes him back. Hamid knocks
Kahlid aside and runs down the hall in pursuit. Kahlid
turns back to his President, who holds Taara's body in his
arms. He places her on his desk. She coughs, blood passing
between her lips. Cody and McAllen move in. The room
full of men transfixed by one helpless, dying girl. She
coughs again.

"Why? Why didn't you shoot." Cody asks.


"You know why..." Taara struggles to speak.

"You know why Jason. I couldn't. Not again, my heart could not take the pain. Its better this way." She coughs violently, spraying blood. Her body convulses for a moment. The President uses his handkerchief to wipe the blood from her face. She grimaces, slows her breathing and continues.

"One life for another. I have taken one and I give one back." She gasps through the pain.

"One for another. I hope it will be enough, I hope,,," As the words leave Taara's lips, her eyes become dull, her body limp. Confusion and pain leave her face. Death granting her peace at last, never again to be troubled with life.


The men gather around Taara's body, each with his own thoughts. A noise comes from the center of the room and the Presidents hand is up. He fires off one round at the floor. They turn to see the two guards creeping up on the pile of weapons.

"You two will carry the body of this girl. She will be honored as a patriot of Egypt." The President says, his eyes never leaving Taara's face. The closer man spits a curse in Egyptian. Before he can finish it, the President fires his weapon, striking the man in his forehead. He dies with the curse on his lips.

"You will carry the body of this girl with care." The President says, the pistol aimed at the second soldier. The soldier visibly flinches.

"Yes, Mister President."

"Why are you all standing around here? I want that traitor's head in a box by midnight. Go!"

Hamid returns.

"I pursued him to the other side. He picked up more soldiers and they made it through a door. Your card would not work. I ran back to report." He says between breaths.

"The passageway leads to the Council's private apartments. Only the Council's cards are coded for it." The President says. "There is a passage from those quarters to the garage. You must hurry, or he will escape."

Four men start for the door but the President calls out.

"Commander!" McAllen stops and turns.

"Let the younger men do this. I would like you to bring me up to date."

"How can I be of assistance Mister President?"

"I think we must plan for contingencies," The President says.

The three men race through the complex towards the garage. Hamid is through the door as rifle shots ring out Kahlid and Cody duck to avoid being hit. Hamid keeps running and returning fire. The attacking soldier goes down with his second shot.

The sound of a diesel engine starting up reverberates through the concrete structure. A Russian T-84 tank makes the jerking first movements of a novice driver. Hamid jumps into a Bradley Armored Transport. A moment later, he has the engine fired up and is moving at speed. The tracks of the Bradley spark and squeal against the concrete floor as Hamid puts it through a tight turn.

"What's he up to," Cody asks.

"He will try to block the exit to the desert. If The General gets into the desert, we could lose him.

Cody and Kahlid watch as the Russian tank and the Bradley race for the desert exit. Hamid is closer but must go around rows of parked vehicles. The T-84 has a straight shot for the passage and is racing ahead. Hamid squeals around the last turn with the exit is in sight. He leans on the throttle of the transport, the front lifting as it accelerates. The sound of the two armored vehicles reverberating through the garage is deafening.

Kahlid leans to Cody's ear and says.

"There are two exits. If Hamid succeeds in blocking this one, the other is for you and me. With any luck, Hamid will stop him altogether." The two armored vehicles close on each other. The Russian is clearly faster but the Bradley has the advantage. Cody covers his ears in anticipation. Their combined speed is well over sixty miles per hour. They reach the exit at the same time but the Russian tank goes wide to make the turn. Hamid in the Bradley sees an inexperienced driver's mistake. He turns the Bradley side on as the T-84 makes the turn.

The T-84 hits the transport broadside. There is the sound of ripping metal as the tank plows into the Bradley, the force of the collision breaking the transport. Metal flies from the Bradley as the Russian beast claws at its armor. Squeals echo across the garage as the tank attempts to climb over the transport but the ceiling is too low and the track snaps on the T-84 and the diesel revs.

Hamid scrambles over the Bradley onto the back of the T-84. He opens the top hatch and drops a grenade inside. The tank heaves from within, shrapnel and smoke erupting from the tank. The blast echoes loudly through the garage.

Kahlid is saying something to Cody. Jason has to strain to hear.

"I think that should do it..." Khalid's victory announcement is cut short by the distant sound of another diesel engine starting up. From the far side of the garage, they can see one of the tanks moving out of formation. They see General Nader driving the T-84. Shots ring out and the two men dive for cover. They look up when they hear return fire and see Hamid shooting from the wreckage of the T-84. Hamid provides cover fire as Cody and Kahlid wind their way through the maze of armored vehicles.

"Quickly! I need your help." Kahlid is dragging a large green crate. Cody helps get the box into a Stingray II tank. Inside Kahlid takes the driver's seat and fires up the diesel. Cody braces himself as the tank makes a high-speed swivel. The tank races up a long passage, the sound of steel tracks against the concrete and the roar of the diesel preceding it.

Cody manages to secure the top hatch and find a seat before the Stingray leaps out of the passage at speed. The brightness of the morning sun blinds him momentarily. Jason belts himself in examining the controls.

"Never mind those," Kahlid yells over the noise. "Uncrate the live rounds. You will have to load them while we are moving. Be careful with them. One dropped shell and this will be our final sunrise." Kahlid takes his eyes from the road long enough to fix Cody's. "You understand?" Cody nods. He straddles the box, trying to pry off the top but it is screwed down. Looking around for a pry bar, he finds an old screwdriver. It fits and he goes to work.

The Stingray flies from the passageway at full speed, landing in a dirt courtyard. It is not difficult to follow General Nader's path. At the far end of the courtyard is a flattened gate. Kahlid opens the Stingray's throttle as soldiers, surprised by the tank, jump from its path. The Stingray accelerates into a paved parking area. At the far end, Kahlid spots soldiers struggling with the remains of a barricade.

He drives the Stingray down a road designed for two cars. A red Mercedes pulls out backward, its occupant's ear glued to his phone. Kahlid ignores it and the tank's left track catches the rear of the car, crushing it to the ground, the tires exploding. The bewildered driver gets out of his car in time to see a tank passing the guard hut. Kahlid hangs a sharp right and enters the flow of traffic.

The Stingray skids across the tarmac, tearing up the road's surface. They follow tracks cut into the Highway by the T-84, towards the City of the Dead. Ahead, Khalid can see traffic piling up. He swings out onto the shoulder and accelerates another hundred yards. A wide load blocks his progress. Kahlid pushes out further, taking down a lamp post in the process. He makes it to a junction and exits into the City of the Dead.

# *Twenty*

The narrow streets of Cairo's oldest section are barely wide enough for the Stingray to pass. In some areas, the tank scrapes the mud-brick walls as they pass. They travel deep into the ancient city then pivot left at an intersection. The big gun of the Stingray knocks down the top of a wall. He has to find the T-84. He opens the driver's hatch to get a better look as he navigates the tight roads.

Cody has been thrown around for several minutes in the back while he struggles with the screws holding down the lid. With the tank slowing, he removes most of the screws. He forces the lid off, ripping the wood and exposing the contents inside lay three 105mm shells. He turns to the auto-loader and finds the loading port. Dragging the crate towards him, he cradles one of the rounds and eases it in.

Kahlid spots a wide road ahead and makes for it. He enters the crossing, the big gun preceding him. As they enter the road, movement catches his eye. Kahlid spots the T-84 turning to fire and slams the Stingray into reverse. He pulls himself into the tank as the T-84 fires. The shell hits the building behind, showering him with dirt.

"Ouch! What the hell are you doing up there." Cody yells, having struck his head on the body of the tank."

"Sorry, my friend but I seem to have made a wrong turn," Kahlid yells back. "Be careful with those shells and hurry. I think we will need them sooner than I thought. In fact, I think we need them now!"

Kahlid has the Stingray in full reverse but is only halfway to the intersection where he turned. He can see the T-84 pulling across the road in front of him. It stops and the turret rotates bringing the gun in line with the Stingray. Kahlid slams the control sticks in opposite directions pivoting the tank on the spot. He reverses as the T-84 fires. The shell strikes where they sat the moment before, destroying the tarmac.

"Ouch! You are really not helping, you know." Cody yells.

"Hurry my friend. We are running out of time." The Stingray speeds backward down a narrow path, shaving dirt from the mud-brick walls. Cody struggles with the last of the shells and slams closed the breach of the auto-loader. Jason opens the top hatch and looks around. He sees the T-

84 racing along a parallel road matching their speed. The road they are on narrows and comes to a stop in fifty yards.

"Why are you going backwards?" He yells down into the tank.

"It seemed a good idea at the time," Kahlid yells back.

"You're about to run out of road." Cody returns.

"I'll change direction. Let me know when." Cody looks between the buildings and spots the T-84 slightly behind them. They move behind a house blocking his view of the T-84. Cody yells.

"Now!" Kahlid slams the controls forward and the Stingray makes a nasty metal on metal grinding complaint. The tank jumps forward, throwing Cody and Kahlid hard against the steel hatches.

"What now?" Cody yells down.

"We have to get out of this alley. We need room to move the turret so you can blast that Russian beast."


Jason drops into the turret and switches on the controls. He makes a few moves right and left to get a feel for them. He locates the targeting controls.

"Okay, when you are ready." He yells to Kahlid.

"Hold on!" Kahlid slams the sticks over and the Stingray spins on the spot ninety degrees to the right. He pushes the throttle to full and the tank leaps down a wide road with low buildings. Cody is able to swing the big gun around ready to fire. The end of the road holds two tall buildings. Jason elevates the gun, avoiding them. As they enter the crossroads, Kahlid slows to give Cody a better shot. The General is looking for them on the parallel road and does not see the Stingray in front of him. The T-84 stops, giving Cody the perfect firing solution. The tank rocks back as the shell leaves the barrel. The T-84 takes the hit dead center.

"What the?" Cody yells. Instead of the tank being ripped to shreds, the shell explodes on the outside leaving, a red maker dye.

"Damn It," Kahlid exclaims. He was watching the shot and punches the Stingray into high gear as the T-84 fires off a round, tearing up the street where they stood.

"What happened," Cody yells.

"Practice rounds. You didn't clear the autoloader and we only have practice rounds in the breach."

"How do I get the live rounds to feed?"

"You have to fire off the practice rounds and work your way down to the live shells."

"Fine. Do these things have any effect on that Russian beast." Cody asks as the T-84 turns onto the road they are racing down.

"Well, if you get hit with one of those, it will give you a nasty headache."

"More than one?"

"A migraine at least, I would think," Kahled responds.

Cody takes quick aim and fires a second practice round. It glances off the tank's side and sprays the wall with red marker. The T-84 lowers its gun to bear on the Stingray. Cody looking backward, sees it is about to fire.

"Kahlid we need to turn. Now!"

Kahlid turns right knocking down a wall and sending livestock running. The T-84 unleashes another round, as Kahlid picks his way through stock pens.

"Kahlid, he's following us. We need to make better time."

"I don't want to hurt the animals."

"He doesn't care about the animals. He's trying to kill us."

"Right," Kahlid says as he breaks through the far wall. He slows down, making a sharp turn behind a building.

Cody drops into the turret and studies the display. He finds the autoloader readout. It shows six shells in the loader, the last three live rounds.

"Kahlid, I need to fire off more shells before we get to the live rounds," Cody yells over the noise of the tank's diesel.

"Okay. I think I have a target for you."

"Where?"

"How about that tank chasing us." Cody looks around and spots the T-84 pacing them on a parallel road. As he watches, it turns into a small empty field between houses, taking down fences and the occupants washing in the process. It bounces onto the road and pulls up behind them. Cody swings the gun around taking aim but the T-84 moves left. Cody fires. It glances off the tank's tracks. Cody hears the whirring noise of the autoloader as it loads the next shell.

"We need to get off this road. He's faster than we are."

"Oh, you only noticed that," Kahlid says.

The T-84 turns right, avoiding Cody's aim, as Kahlid turns the Stingray hard to the left. The tank skids on the asphalt street, tearing it up as they turn into a narrow lane, knocking down a wall. Kahlid leans on the throttle. The Stingray flies down the lane. A donkey cart standing in the way splinters under its tracks. The T-84 is too wide for the

439

alley. Cody sees it's gun turning. He fires hitting it dead center, painting it bright red. The autoloader clears the breach and prepares the next shell. The Stingray makes a hard right turn following the road. The right side of the tank is lifted high off of the ground as it rolls over a low wall. The tank comes down with a bang. The autoloader stops.

Red lights and warning bells sound, Cody reads the display. *'Loader Malfunction.'*

"Kahlid, the loader is jammed!" He shouts.

"It must be a shell caught in the mechanism. See if you can knock it free but be careful. You don't want it to explode."

"No shit," Cody yells as he climbs down, clearing the empty shell casings. He sees the problem. The shell is caught against the breach. He can see it through holes smaller than his fist along the side. He tries to push it but the steel casing is firmly jammed on something. He starts kicking it repeatedly, each time harder, his effort proportionally to his frustration.

Cody hears a shell explode close by, his ears ringing from the explosion. The tank swerves wildly. He climbs back up to the turret.

Jason pulls himself into the seat and looks at the screen. The City of the Dead has disappeared and there is only desert around them.

"Where are we." He yells, trying to clear his ears.

"The Eastern Desert." Kahlid returns.

"Why are we here."

"We ran out of road. That bastard was waiting for us. Before I could get back into the city, he fired on us. I had no choice but to run." Kahlid pulls the Stingray to the left and the tank jumps from the edge of a sand dune. They drop onto the far side as a shell explodes the dune in front of them. Kahlid pulls the stingray right as sand showers them. He drives into the cloud of sand, hoping it will hide them long enough to gain some advantage.


As the Stingray exits the sand cloud, the T-84 pivots and fires, the shell catches them a glancing blow on the near track, lifting the sand beneath them. The stingray continues for a few feet then stops, its track broken. A new sand cloud envelops them. Jason coughs, trying to find air. His head is swimming, and his vision is blurred. He holds his ears, trying to ease the pain. The blast was too close. He can feel his brain pressing against the inside of his skull

The sand cloud around the Stingray clears. Cody looks forward and sees Kahlid's body slumped over the hatch. Jason tries to move but his body it will not respond. He slides down to the turret control seat, holding his head in pain. He opens his eyes willing his brain to work. They need to get away. He is about to climb out but something catches his eye. The firing panel shows green. The blast knocked free the shell in the autoloader.

He pulls himself up enough to see the T-84 on the ridge of the sand dune turning to leave. Cody pulls the turret controls and the gun responds. Using the laser sight, he targets T-84. The gun makes a last adjustment on its own *'Ready to Fire.'* He hits the button and the back of the T-84 explodes in red. On his screen, he can see the T-84 hesitate. It slowly pivots around and starts down the face of the dune. Cody follows it with his laser sight as it moves.

"The T-84 is moving in for the kill. Cody keeps the laser sight on it. The red *'Loading'* message flashes. His heart leaps into his mouth. *'Loading'* is replaced by *'Malfunction.'* He keeps the laser on the T-84 but the display jumps from 'Loading' to *'Malfunction'* and back again. Sweat breaks out on Cody's brow as he watches the T-84 stop, its turret turning towards him. The display goes green showing the shell in the breach. *'Firing solution complete.'* The T-84's gun points directly at him. Cody hits the button.

The big gun of the Stingray recoils and she rocks back on her one good track as the armor-piercing shell leaves the barrel. It strikes the T-84 dead center where the turret meets the body, the effect is instant and devastating. The shell slams through the armor of the Russian beast. It explodes nearly removing the turret in the process. The whole tank jumps to one side as white light from the explosion blasts out of every opening, the unexploded shells in the T-84, adding to the ball of flame and destruction. Cody covers his head as pieces of metal clatter across the skin of the Stingray. His screen shows the T-84 sitting off its tracks, blackened and burning.

Jason pokes his head up, wanting to see with his own eyes. The dead mass of metal sends up black smoke and flames. Cody watches for a moment rubbing his head, then looks forward. Kahlid is up watching the T-84 burn. He pushes himself up, sitting on the Stingray. He turns to Cody and gives him the thumbs up. Cody smiles and returns the gesture.

# *Twenty-One*

## Old Cairo, Egypt, 19:32 September 14, 2001

Cody exits the taxi, making his way through the narrow alleys. He puzzles over the note he's received. Why would Kahlid want to meet at the safe-house Mark Rider was killed in? He and McAllen have been over the place. Jason's thoughts are clouded with the events of the morning and returning to the safe-house is an unpleasant reminder of how it all began. Thoughts of Mark and the guilt of the investigation going wrong cloud Cody's vision. Before he knows it, he is standing outside the door.

Jason has been so preoccupied and he's not been paying attention. He looks around to see if he was followed. Seeing no one, he enters. Cody pulls out his Beretta, allowing his eyes to adjust. One small lamp burns in the room. Not much has changed from that night. The corners remain strewn with broken furniture, remnants of happier times.

Cody holds his pistol at his side and walks across the room. It feels like he is retracing his steps from the night of Mark's murder. He walks through the inner door leading to the hallway and back rooms. Jason stops. Standing at the other end with his pistol trained on Jason is Kahlid. Kahlid cracks a thin smile.

"You should know better than to have your weapon down. I could have killed you easily." Kahlid says as he holsters his weapon.

"Thanks. I guess I wasn't paying attention. How is your head?" Cody asks, tucking his pistol away.

"Better. Yours?"

"The pain killers have helped." Cody walks to Kahlid's end of the hall.


The carpet that once concealed the opening to the small room lays in a heap. Jason can see the bloodstains still on the dirt floor. Kahlid sees Jason's gaze and comments.

"I never meet your friend, Mister Rider but I have heard he was a man to be trusted. That is a rare thing in this business, trust." Cody looks at Kahlid. He tries to see past the surface of the man he knows so little about. Kahlid has been playing the game too long and his face gives nothing away. He looks into the room where the gunmen came from and notes the large sideboard has been moved away. He remembers McAllen saying the Police moved it in front of the hole. Jason makes a mental note to ask the Commander.

"So why did you want to meet here of all places," Kahlid asks. Cody turns to Kahlid, caution in his voice.

"It was you who wanted to meet me."

"No, It was I who wanted to meet you both."

The two men turn and see Major Haraddi holding a Mac-10 machine pistol on them. He stands aiming at them through the hole in the wall. Cody's hand twitches towards his gun but Haraddi lets off a spray of 9mm rounds at his feet.

"Teflon coated." Major Haraddi says. "Body armor is useless." He steps carefully through the hole keeping his eyes on both men.

"Mohamed Aslamid Kahlid and Agent Jason Cody, you two have a habit of playing havoc with my plans. Yes, you heard right my plans. It was I who planned the coup and the assassination of the President. I was to be the next ruler of Egypt and the Holy Land. I was going to bring the holy city back into the fold of Islam. I would control the oil flowing from these lands." He smiles. "You didn't expect me to capture Israel, the Middle-East and hand it over to Bin Laden, did you? He is an old fool. He is surrounded by people who take his money and use him for their own purposes. Do you know why he has kidney treatments? The drugs they've been controlling him with ate through them a long time ago. He is a dying old man."

"Al-Qaeda would never let you walk off with a prize like that," Kahlid says and shifts his weight as he speaks. Haraddi lays down blast at his feet.


Haraddi continues.

"They are fools. They think one or two bombs, a few dead Americans and all of Islam will rise up and follow them. What nonsense! They know nothing of how the world works. They think the leaders of whole countries will follow them for attacking America. Idiots! Those countries need America to protect the flow of oil. I have trusted people around the leaders of the oil-rich countries, ready to take control. Oh yes! Removing the leaders would have been child's play."

"It was you who assassinated General Nader's double." Says Jason.

"No Mister Cody, not I. I have a specialist for those jobs, a very odd sort of man, if you can call it that. You would probably like it, you Americans go in for those types of perversions. You see it is only half a man. The other half is,,," Haraddi freezes mid sentence. Cody hears a hissing sound from behind Haraddi. He sees Haraddi straining to keep an eye on them and look behind. Haraddi breaks into a sweat and from his lips comes a single word. "NO!"

Cody hears the Twang of a crossbow. Haraddi's chest heaves forward. He is lifted from the ground, carried forward into Jason and Kahlid's arms. The force of the man flying at them sends all three to the floor. Cody catches a glimpse through the hole of black robes running from the room. He makes to get up but Haraddi clutches at his coat.

Kahlid springs through the hole in pursuit. Cody pulls away and stands. Haraddi raises the Mac-10 in one last attempt to kill Jason Cody. Jason kicks the gun from his hand, his final effort thwarted. Haraddi dies only inches from where Mark Rider was murdered. Kahlid returns jumping through the hole in the wall, his gun drawn.

"No sign of him. Vanished into thin air," Kahlid says and looks down at Haraddi's dead body. "At least we have our man." Cody looks at the dead man nodding slowly. He looks at Kahlid and says without emotion.

"Yes. At least we have this man."

# Twenty-Two

Cody slowly makes his way through the crowds across the Cairo airport concourse to the rows of check-in desks. He presents his passport to the American Airlines agent. As she is arranging his seat, a familiar figure approaches. Jason turns and finds Kahlid standing to his right speaking into his sleeve. The attendant hands him his ticket and passport, glancing at the security agent. Jason thanks her and walks away with Kahlid at his side.

"Are Egyptian security forces giving tourists personal escorts to their planes, or do you want to be sure I leave?" Kahlid smiles sideways at Cody as he listens to a conversation in his earpiece.

"We are watching the airport and train terminals. The assassin who killed Harradi has struck again. We pulled one of those oversized crossbow bolts out of a man in Cairo yesterday."

"Who was he," Cody asks as they wander across the concourse.

"Another information broker. A seller of secrets and arranger of death. We think he may have been the assassin's contact here in Cairo. The killing of his contact

449

means the assassin is covering his tracks. Possibly making his escape." Kahlid says as his eyes scan the people they walk past.

"I made inquiries about the crossbow bolts and discovered they are hunting bolts. They have not been used since the days of the Roman Empire. It must take an incredibly powerful crossbow to propel a bolt that can lift a man, the way it did Haraddi." Kahlid says.

"With modern materials, a powerful crossbow could also be light." Kahlid nods and considers the fact and says.

"So it could be a woman. Is that what you are saying?"

"I hadn't thought about it. Why?" Cody asks.

"In our investigations into the crossbow, we ran across an antiquities dealer from a small village near El-Arish. It's a town out on the coast near the border with Israel. This antiquities dealer was known for working reproductions of ancient war machines. We went out to look him up but found the entire village had been murdered five years ago. It's not unusual. They found a few dead Israelis and assumed it was a cross-border raid. It's one of the risks the trading villages take, being so close to the border."

"So you think the weapon came from this village?"

"Yes and possibly more." Cody looks at Kahlid, his eyebrow raised in question. "The same Antiquities dealer had a son." Kahlid pauses. "At least we think it was a son. We only have sketchy reports from neighboring villages. The child was born with both male and female characteristics. It was not discovered until he or she, reached puberty and started to develop breasts. The village saw the child as a demon and expelled it. Since then, no one has seen the child."

"Until?" Cody says. Kahlid stops and faces Cody.

"Two years ago, Bin Laden was reported to have trained a specialist assassin. Someone who could pass through any security net. This person was reported to be feared by other trainees. It was said Sadi had the strength of two men and killed a fellow recruit for making a joke about him. His neck was broken as he slept in a tent with five other people. No one heard a thing."

"Drugged?" Jason asks.

"Perhaps but the stories say no."

"So who, or what are you looking for."

"We don't really know. We have an idea of the man but we have no idea what he might look like as a woman."

"So this is surveillance for its own sake."

451

"No, training. I have twenty-three new recruits to my section and very little time to get them ready. So,,," Kahlid says and shrugs.

"On the job training?" Asks Cody.

"Exactly."

"Well good luck with your new recruits and thanks for all of your help."

"It is I who should be thanking you for saving my life."

"All in a days work." Says Cody as Kahlid runs a trained eye over two men who walk by.

"Oh! I almost forgot." Kahlid pulls an envelope from his coat pocket. "The Capitan of the Presidential Guard passed this to me. He said a lovely young lady on the Karim was very anxious you should receive it before you left." Kahlid hands the letter to Cody smiling. "I didn't know people still wrote love letters."

"Love letters?"

"What would you call it?" Jason turns it over and sees Sara has sealed the envelope with a kiss. Her red lipstick leaving a perfect impression of her lips. Jason smiles.

"I think I'll open this later," Jason says as he pockets the letter.

"I'm happy for you my friend, to find love in the middle of so many deaths. That is a rare thing." Jason smiles and says.

"Take care of yourself Kahlid."

"And you my friend. You will always have a home in Egypt. So don't be away too long." Kahlid smiles and the two men shake hands.


Jason Cody passes through passport control, then wanders around the duty-free shops and newsagents. He finds a New York Times and looks for a comfortable place to sit. As he passes out of the shop, he spots a familiar figure and walks to the benches along the back wall. There sat behind a London paper sits Commander McAllen.

"Hello, Agent Cody." Alistair says without looking up.

"Please Commander, after all this time I'd hoped you would call me Jason."

"Of course, Jason. So you are off to America. I hope things are not as bad as the papers are making out.

"So do I," Cody replies and loses his smile. "Why are you here?"

"Unfortunately, things have become a little too hot for me here. I've decided to take up the retirement I am supposed to be already enjoying." McAllen says folding his paper into his lap.

"Where will you go?"

"Europe, I suppose. There are plenty of places in Spain or Greece where a man can comfortably disappear."

"Sounds nice." Cody remarks as he sits down next to McAllen.

"Yes, and what about you, what's next for the young agent."

"Back for debriefing and reassignment, I imagine."

"Off to South America do you think?"

"I hope so. It's what I trained for but with the current situation, things may change."

McAllen folds back his newspaper and indicates the front page story.

"It looks like your President has declared war on Afghanistan."

"Yeah, I wouldn't mind being involved in that if I'm not assigned elsewhere."


McAllen studies the face of the young next to him.

"You mean that don't you?" He says.

"Yes, I do," Cody replies, unsure of why the Commander is looking at him in disbelief.

"Here all of this time I thought it was our job to make sure this sort of thing didn't happen." The Commander rustles his paper in Cody's face and sits back in exasperation. "All the times I could have sat back and let a war break out, even encouraged one. Maybe it's I who have been playing the game wrong these past twenty years." He says looking at Jason.

Jason leans forward and says.

"Maybe you don't understand. The American people need a victory now. We need to see justice done, to see these terrorists brought before a court of law and punished." Cody says with more anger in his voice than he intended.

"I don't understand. I don't understand!" McAllen says leaning forward in his seat. "My country has been attacked by both foreign powers and terrorists for decades. In London, there was a time when you couldn't go a month without a bomb going off or an assassination. We have been living with terrorism for years and I can tell you this. A direct military strike will only send the terrorists underground, leaving your people exposed. How many women and children will have to be murdered in order to satisfy your American blood lust? How many governments must topple before the all powerful United States is satisfied that justice has been done? I tell you now, you may go in and attack Afghanistan, you may even succeed. Your tanks and armies may roll over the countryside like the Russians but you will not win. While you're attacking one place, the terrorists will simply move to another or even join you. Terrorists don't care how many innocent people get killed. They will end up being your best friends over there. Pointing you to their enemies, while they sit back and laugh. No, you won't have your victory. In the end, you will have an impoverished country in need of international aid. A political system in tatters and an army of Taliban fighters, waiting for America to pull out. Then they step up and take back the country you cleaned up for them. You haven't a clue what you are in for."


McAllen sits back in disgust and shakes out his newspaper. Jason can only stare open mouthed at the man he thought he knew.

"It won't be like that. America won't let its obligations go like that. We will,,,"

"Oh, really? You mean like in Vietnam. You're going to stay and fight down to the last man, are you? You may fool

456

yourself Agent Cody but you do not fool me. This war is like every other war in history, its politics. It's an opportunity for your President, to be seen as a defender of democracy, a protector of America but you don't get it. None of you do. This time there is no country to defeat. No power-hungry mad man to annihilate. There are only people, not one person, people!" Cody blinks.

"I don't know what you mean."

"Think Jason. Think! Think about what Taara did. She made a choice between life and death. Why, because she was more afraid of blackening her soul. Her fear of going against her beliefs was stronger than her fear of death. Now, look around you. Go on, look!" McAllen indicates the airport and the people walking past.

"Look at the people around you. How many of them have that same strength of belief? How many of those consider you, an American, their enemy? Think of these people multiplied by tens of thousands scattered all across the planet. They are normal individuals who work hard, sell you newspapers. Their children go to school with yours. They are perfectly behaved, upstanding citizens. Then one day they get a call, not all of them but some, those trained for the work. Suddenly, there is a small army of terrorists ready to take on America. Why, because their beliefs tell them to do so. Their beliefs tell them, they must defend Islam against those who would see her destroyed. In defending Islam, they are ready to die for their religion. Who are they? How can you tell who among this crowd is willing to do that? There are no metal detectors or bomb sniffers. No anti-terrorist squads who can predict who those people are. They are invisible! And, they are in every city, in every country, all over the world!"

Cody looks at McAllen still unable to believe what he is hearing.

"You are talking as if America has declared war on Islam."

"Yes, and to the devout, you have. You've declared war on Bin Laden. To some, that's enough to make you attackers of the faith." Cody struggles with the idea.

"But that's not what we're doing."

"Well then, you tell me what is America doing."

"We are defending our borders against attack." Cody recites.

"attack from where, from a country?"

"Not exactly."

"His followers see him as a religious leader, not a politician. If you hunt down and kill a leader of a religion, are you not attacking the religion?" Cody goes to speak but it hits him.

He can see the trap America has walked straight into. The trap the President has committed them to. Jason's brow furrows with the possibilities.

"Now you see it. Now you see the trap. Take that knowledge back to America with you. Make them see how damaging this war will be. Not to the terrorists, to America." The Commander sits back grim faced, watching the young man grapple with the problem.

McAllen studies Jason for a moment and says. "You see Jason, taking out one terrorist only incites three others. Eliminating those incites another nine and so on. Trust me in this. We have been making those mistakes for years. I hope you can learn from our past and find a way to circumvent a disaster. I truly do." Cody looks at his watch. He has time but he wants to get away and think.

"I better be going. Thanks." Jason says flatly.

Commander McAllen appraises Cody as the young man collects his paper and says. "Jason. It's not all bad, you know."

"Sorry?"

"We did stop a major coup." Jason looks away and without conviction says.

"Yeah, I know."

"But you don't know!" The Commander counters. "You, Agent Cody, handled yourself with honor, bravery and distinction! If it wasn't for you, we would be fighting on two fronts. One in Afghanistan and one in Egypt herself."

Jason takes a breath and raises both palms to the Commander.

"Stop! Commander, please stop. You know, I had no idea what I was doing out there. I'm lucky more people weren't killed because of me." Jason looks to the ground as the Commander steps in front of him and says.

"Luck, had nothing to do with it! I've spoken with both Kahlid and your young man Abu. You, sir, handled yourself as if you have been playing the Game all your life. Kahlid told me, if he could have five agents with your instincts, he could secure Egypt against any threat. No

Agent Cody, you are worth more than you know." The commander adds. "Besides, when we're out there, no one knows what they're doing. We follow the bread crumbs until the crumbs run out, then we improvise. I would say, you get top marks on both counts and that is precisely what I put in my report to Washington." Alistair smiles at Jason who glances at him then looks away shaking his head.

"Oh, I nearly forgot, Abu asked me to give you this, if I saw you." Alistair produces the carved club Abu used in Aswan. "He says you cannot leave Egypt without a souvenir, or people may think you are a spy." Jason manages a small smile and says.

"Does he now?"

"Yes and more importantly, Washington says they've located your sister and she is shaken but unhurt. She is staying with a friend in Manhattan." Jason catches his breath and looks Commander McAllen in the eyes.

"Thank you, Alistair. Really thank you! My only wish is, I could have found out about the attacks sooner."

"So do I dear boy, so do I. But, in this game, there are always things we cannot change. All we can do is keep on moving forward, making the best of what we have. Good Luck, Jason! Perhaps we will meet again in better circumstances." The Commander says and the two men shake hands. Jason manages a smile and says.

"Thank you, Alistair, for everything."

"The pleasure has been all mine, Agent Cody." The two men part as friends and the Commander sits again on the bench.


McAllen watches as Jason makes his way to his gate, passing into the secure holding area to await his plane. He shifts his small suitcase from the floor to the bench space beside him. A moment later a young woman in a scarlet head scarf, red hip-huggers and a low cut white top sits down next to him, placing one arm casually over the suitcase.

"I thought you would never get rid of the American." She comments.

"You should watch yourself Sadi. That American is now your enemy." She smiles at the comment.

"I have no enemies McAllen. Only eager young men like that one. They all want the same thing you know. My legs wrapped tightly around them. All smiles and promises but they die so easily." Sadi snaps her fingers making her point.

"My love can be very dangerous, don't you think Commander."

"I think you are playing a very dangerous game Sadi. You now have more enemies than friends. I have to say I was surprised when you took the job and killed Haraddi. He must have been a gold mine for you with all of his enemies." McAllen says turning the page of his paper.

"He was a gold mine. Yes, but not the way you think. He had many enemies. Several of them have paid nearly as much as you are about to."

"I had no issue with Harradi." Says McAllen, "I knew the architect of a plan that ambitious had to be in a position of influence and able to move without question. I wasn't sure it was Haraddi until your phone call. All I wanted was to stop whoever it was before they struck again."

"That is exactly what I have done, saving your young Agent and the Head of Egyptian intelligence in the process. It's all worked out for the best don't you think Commander?"

"I think your luck may run out very soon Sadi."

"Why, do you know something I don't?" Sadi asks, looking around.

"No, but I do know you don't walk away from an organization like Al-Qaeda." Sadi turns and looks at McAllen.

"Alistair, when I shot that bolt, I resigned from Al-Qaeda. They pay me peanuts to do their dirty work while they make millions selling death, my skills. My days of being their puppet are over. I am what you call a free agent and I work for the highest bidder."

"I would be careful if I were you. Death comes quickly to those who deal it on a daily basis. Your day may be coming sooner than you think."

"Before that day comes, I think you may find yourself in the cross hairs of my bow McAllen."

"So we both have something to think about," Alistair says looking down at his newspaper. He chances a glance at Sadi then back at his paper while she looks straight ahead at nothing.

*Last call for Turkish Airlines flight 104 to Istanbul, at gate number four.* Comes across the loud speaker.

"Well, that's my plane McAllen. It has been very nice doing business with you and a real pleasure killing that pig Haraddi but I have to go." She grasps the case about to get up but McAllen puts a hand on hers' and looks her in the eye.

"I expect I will never to see you again Sadi. I think for both of us that would be best."

"Have it your way McAllen. After all, you are the man and men do like to get their way." She smiles at him as she pulls the case from his grasp.

Sadi weaves her way through the seats finding her gate. She presents her passport, as a soldier looks past her. McAllen sits for a while longer reading his paper. He watches as Sadi and then Cody pass through security gates, each of them flying off in opposite directions and opposite purposes. When he is sure both are out of sight he folds his paper under his arm and steps around his seat to the wall behind. Standing with his back to a door he leans back and passes through. He will be just as careful as he leaves Cairo. There will be no record of his movements, no trace he has ever been. Only a trail of secrets uncovered and bodies counted.

Jason Cody finds his seat in the aisle next to an elderly Egyptian man in a gray suit as the plane begins moving towards the runway. The Egyptian man is having difficulty locating something in his briefcase.

"I am sorry." He remarks as he rifles through the case. Jason stands to give the man some room as the fasten seatbelt sign comes on with the announcement.

465

*"Ladies and gentlemen, the captain has turned on the fasten seatbelt sign. Will all passengers please return to their seats now. The plane will be taking off in just a few minutes."*

"Ahh, I found it. Thank you for understanding." Cody smiles and notes there are beads of perspiration on the man's forehead.

"That's alright." Jason says.

"Please I do not mean to intrude but you are American, yes?" The man asks.

"Yes, that's right," Jason says as he sits.

"Please, let me say, I am so sorry for these horrible attacks on your country."

"Thank you, yes they were horrible." Cody stops and thinks of The Commander's words. Knowing his sister is safe makes all the difference. He cannot wait to get back and see her. The gentleman searches his coat pockets for something and then asks.

"Please, I am sorry for the inconvenience but I cannot find my earphones. Would you mind if I play my music? I will put the speaker to my ear, so it is not loud. It helps me relax when we take off and land." The gentleman smiles apologetically.

"No, that's alright. I don't mind. It might help me relax as well." Jason says with a smile. The gentleman thanks him and places his briefcase under the seat.

An attractive blond stewardess approaches and says.

"Sir you will have to fasten your seatbelt we are about to take off." She smiles.

"Oh sorry, of course," Jason says, straightening his coat and reaches for the seatbelt. The stewardess glances back, seeing something fall out of Cody's pocket. She returns and picks it up from the floor, handing it to him.

"I believe you dropped this sir." She smiles.

*"Attendants to your seats,"* The captain says over the intercom.

"Thank you," Cody responds taking the piece of paper. He wrinkles his forehead as he unfolds the piece of paper. Inside is a note in Commander McAllen's hand writing, which reads.

*'I'm certain I'll be seeing you when the game again turns my way.*

*Because, you know, it's never really over.'*

Jason smiles and thinks. *'So that's retirement, huh?'* The Egyptian man next to him starts his tape player and the music reaches Jason's ears.

*There's a man who leads a life of danger…* Jason smiles at the irony. *To everyone he meets, he stays a stranger.* As the jet engines accelerate, the music becomes louder. *Secret agent man, secret agent man. They've given you a number and taken away your name.*

The plane lifts away from the runway as McAllen flags down a taxi. The Commander looks up and watches Jason's plane as it climbs into the sky. The Commander smiles and says.

"See you around Agent Cody."

# Epilogue

Arriving at JFK airport, agents met me and escorted me to FBI Headquarters Washington DC. There I was debriefed by a team of specialists. The debriefing lasted three or four days. They don't let you sleep much when they are questioning you so it's difficult to judge time.

A couple of days later, a new face appeared, Chris Daniels. He asked how I knew the third target would be the Twin Towers. After intense interrogation, I told him about the dreams I had the weeks before September 11th. His interest peaked and he inquired whether I'd had similar experiences in the past. I made the mistake of saying yes and telling him about dreams I had weeks before my parents' deaths. At that point they restrained me and put me on a military flight out of DC. When we landed, I was hooded and bundled into a Jeep. It was hours on bumpy roads before the hood was removed.

I found myself in a compound with barbed wire, guard towers, the works. It looks like a prison, so I asked, *'what have I done?'* Chris Daniels was there, he said.

"It's not what you've done. It's what you're going to do."
That's how I got to 'The Camp.' They say this place is a
research center for the study of extrasensory abilities. I
don't understand what they want with me but they've
scheduled me for treatment tomorrow.

I don't feel I can trust anyone in the FBI, so I'm taking a
real chance of reaching out to you. Please, don't let me
down. I have to get back before they catch me out of my
cell. I'll try to get access to this terminal in two days' time.
Wish me luck!"

JC

*The Story Continues In*

*Book 2*

*Jason Cody*

*In The 9/11 Series*


*Standing On A Landmine*

*To Be Released In 2022*

If You Have Enjoyed Reading

Wheel on the Nile,

Please Leave J Cruz

A Review On His Amazon Page.


Thank you.

Poseidon Publishing

**J Cruz**

Born and raised in California, J moved to the UK in 1996, where he studied and worked. On the day of the attacks of September 11th J, like many Americans, was struck by the destruction and disregard for life. The pain of seeing his fellow Americans dying pushed J to write 'Jason Cody' into existence. For months J wrote, often into the small hours of the morning. A year later he put aside his writing. J believed the scars from the attack were too new, the emotions too raw for it to be published. It's been twenty years since that terrible day and J feels it is now time for Jason Cody to be born into the literary world.

Note:

*The dreams Jason experiences in **'Wheel on the Nile'** are the same nightmares that plagued J Cruz in the months that followed 9/11.*

**You can follow J Cruz through the Poseidon Publishing Facebook Page.**
**@Poseidon.Promedia**

Printed in Great Britain
by Amazon